# Great Sky Woman

*One World*
*Ballantine Books*
*New York*

# Great Sky Woman
## Steven Barnes

*a novel*

Copyright © 2006 by Steven Barnes

Published in the United States by One World Books,
an imprint of The Random House Publishing Group,
a division of Random House, Inc., New York.

ONE WORLD is a registered trademark and the One World colophon
is a trademark of Random House, Inc.

Map and illustration by David Lindroth, based on a design by Toni Young.

Library of Congress Cataloging-in-Publication Data
Barnes, Steven.
Great Sky Woman : a novel / Steven Barnes.
p. cm.
Novel.
ISBN 0-345-45900-8
I. Title.

PS3552.A6954G74 2006
813'.54—dc22        2006040039

Printed in the United States of America

www.oneworldbooks.net

2  4  6  8  9  7  5  3  1

First Edition

*Text design by Laurie Jewell*

For my own Great Circle:

Joyce, who taught me to read.

Nicki, who taught me to love.

Jason, my living example of how life
and learning begins.

Tananarive, a daily reminder
that miracles exist.

Bless you all.

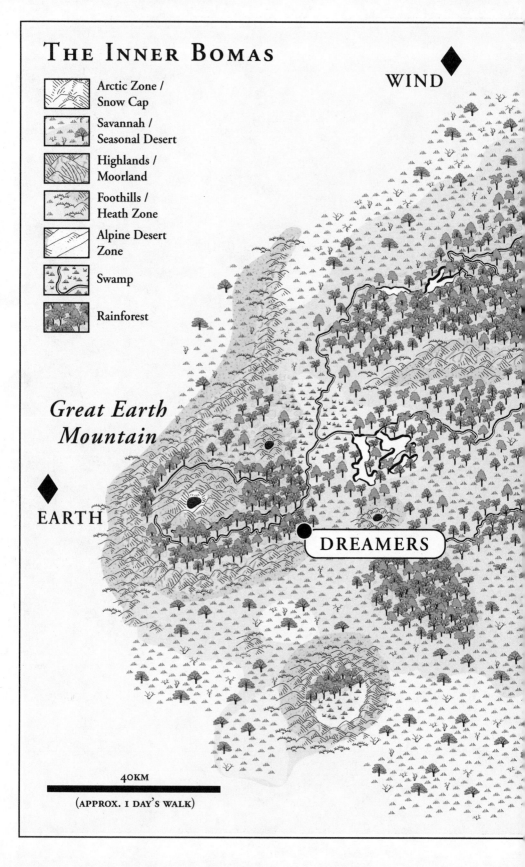

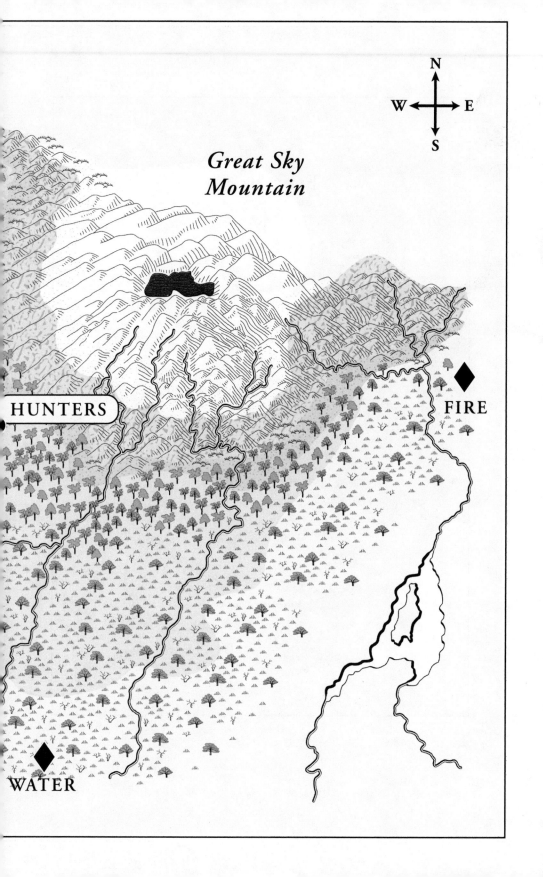

# Fire Boma

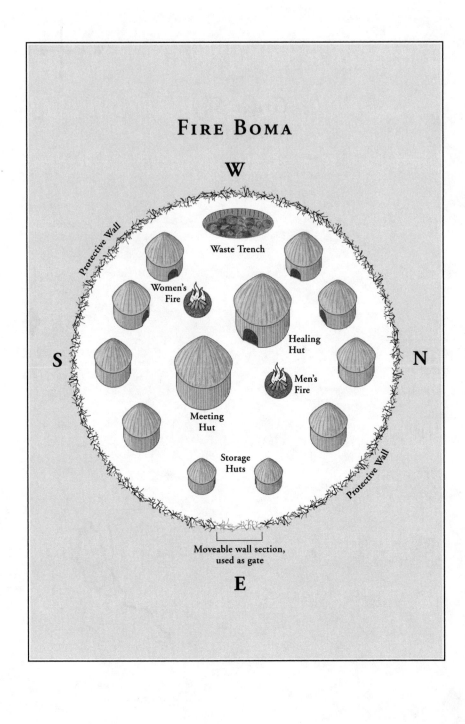

W

Protective Wall

Waste Trench

Women's
Fire

Healing
Hut

S · N

Men's
Fire

Meeting
Hut

Storage
Huts

Protective Wall

Moveable wall section,
used as gate

E

# Dramatis Personae

**THE INNER BOMAS**

Frog Hopping

Fire Ant (*Frog's brother*)

Hawk Shadow (*Frog's eldest brother*)

Scorpion (*Frog's stepbrother*)

Uncle Snake

Lizard Tongue (*an older friend*)

Break Spear (*boma father*)

Little Brook (*Frog's sister*)

Gazelle Tears (*Frog's mother*)

Wasp (*little brother*)

Hot Tree (*boma mother*)

Zebra Moon (*T'Cori's mother*)

Water Chant (*T'Cori's father*)

Lion Tooth

**THE DREAM DANCERS**

Stillshadow (*chief dream dancer*)

T'Cori

Small Raven (*Stillshadow's daughter*)

Blossom (*Raven's older sister*)

Dove

Fawn Blossom (*Dove's twin sister*)

Sister Quiet Water

**THE HUNT CHIEFS**

Cloud Stalker (*grand hunt chief*)

Owl Hooting (*son of Cloud Stalker*)

**THE MK*TK**

Flat-Nose

Notch-Ear

# In the beginning …

*A hundred and seventy-five million years before the first men raised their faces to the sun, the lands of Earth were grouped together in a titanic sprawl now referred to as* Pangaea. *Africa, mother to all mankind, lay nestled in its midst. When Pangaea began to fragment, the first to break away were Antarctica and Australia.*

*Three gigantic cracks appeared on the eastern side of this fractured supercontinent. Arabia broke free, creating the Gulf of Aden and the Red Sea. The two other cracks created rift valleys, straight-sided trenches averaging thirty miles across, running south from the Gulf of Aden thirty-five hundred miles to Mozambique.*

*A hundred and seventy million years later, a desert wasteland that would one day be called the Sahara expanded, creating a barrier virtually impassable to land animals. South of it, the once endless forests contracted, spawning vast grasslands: the savannahs.*

*One class of monkeys and one of apes moved into these lush green fields. The monkeys were the baboons.*

*The apes were the earliest ancestors of men.*

*Here in this new environment, the baboons descended onto all fours, but our ancestors discovered the art of walking erect. In doing so, they freed their hands to create artifacts of wood and stone and shell, to craft tools and weapons.*

*Biologists and anthropologists have debated for centuries, asking what unique quality separates human beings from other animals. It is possible that only one observable, incontrovertible behavior separates human beings from any other creature: humans are the animals that create and use fire as a tool.*

*How humans discovered fire, whether through volcanic activity or perhaps lightning strike, no one knows. That we learned to duplicate it with our own tools is a major miracle, dwarfing any other discovery in human history. However it happened, fire changed everything. With the conquest of flame, spear tips could be hardened, animals frightened away from campsites or driven into killing grounds. But not only was meat more readily obtained, cooking also made complex animal proteins more digestible, leading to taller, stronger humans with larger brains, brains that in turn devised more complex and efficient hunting strategies.*

*This positive spiral was one of the forces driving human evolution.*

*There was another, less tangible benefit.*

*For the first time in the history of life on Earth, a creature could create and control shadows. In observing the relationships between living things and their two-dimensional representations, these fire users quite possibly began the process of abstract thought itself, as demonstrated in cave paintings dating to thirty thousand years before the birth of Christ. It is very nearly as if the ego awoke and said, "I am." In addition, as firelight pushed back the night, human beings, poorly adapted for the darkness, had more time in which to interact, to communicate, to dance and speak of the day's events. These early pantomimes allowed the old hunters to teach young ones the methods of avoiding predators and obtaining prey. Storytelling allowed human beings to create their identities, to ask questions about their world only later generations could answer.*

*Humans created story, but in another, perhaps deeper sense, story created humanity.*

*Seven hundred thousand years earlier, the ancestors of these first modern humans witnessed the birth of the mountains called Kilimanjaro and Meru.*

*By far the larger of the two, Kilimanjaro was born when an ocean of magma burned its way through the earth and broke free to the surface. Liquid rock gushed and then cooled. Every few years or centuries this blazing, viscous fluid deposited layer upon smoldering layer. Eventually the volcanic spire would dominate the equatorial horizon, a beacon to the adventurous long before the first Arab ship logs described it in 200 AD.*

*Scaling Kilimanjaro is like walking from the equator to the Arctic in a single week. For the first six thousand to nine thousand feet, its vegetation is a virtually impassible tropical rain forest, an eternal dank green canopy thick enough to blot out the sun. From nine thousand to thirteen thousand feet this transforms into equally dense heath and moorland. From thirteen thousand to seventeen thousand feet, all of this changes: vegetation recedes and alpine desert dominates. It is a world of cactus and harsh gravel, of piercing sun and thinning air, a change often disorienting in its abruptness.*

*Above seventeen thousand feet exists an alien winter world, the only snow to be found in equatorial Africa. Here, where the air pressure is less than half that at sea level, no animals can live. No plant life is to be found save lichens. Europeans say the mountain went unclimbed until 1887, when a German named Hans Meyer found a way through the rock and ice.*

*If one believes the old stories, the Europeans are wrong.*

*The Chagga, folk who have lived at Kilimanjaro's feet for thousands of years, have ancient legends of princes whose courtiers died carrying them to the top, that they might see the sunrise before any of their subjects. The detail in these legends is consistent with the reality of the climb.*

*This is the story of the first courageous souls to scale this, the tallest freestanding mountain in all the world, folk who lived in the shadow of Kilimanjaro and its nearby, smaller mate, Mt. Meru. It tells of our distant ancestors, the first animals with more information in their brains than in their genes.*

*This is the tale of the first to look down from this great peak's impossible heights: a boy who discovered a new world, and a girl who ended the old one.*

# Nameless

# Chapter One

Stillshadow was ancient now, what her people called a "woman of dust." Four tens of warm rains had moistened her deeply weathered face. Daily walking on plains and hills, hot tea brewed from the poison-grub plant's spiky leaves and milky roots, and the grace of Great Mother Herself kept the old medicine woman's back straight and her tread light. Stillshadow was thought tall, standing a handsbreadth higher than the average Ibandi woman, the height of a typical male. Her skin was the color of dark clay, her black hair tightly coiled, her wise old eyes black and flecked with gray. Like other medicine women, other dream dancers, she covered her breasts and genitals with beaten and softened deerskin flaps, partially for protection from the cooler air atop Great Earth, but also in recognition that her seventh eye belonged to Father Mountain and His sons the hunt chiefs.

She clicked and clucked to herself, and slipped a wrinkled hand into the speckled brown deerhide pouch dangling at her waist. From it she extracted a fibrous pellet of crushed insects, ground leaves and herbs, bound with fresh moist fungus from sacred caves on Great Earth's western face, the powerful hallucinogenic mixture medicine women called godweed. The crone tucked it between her gum and lip, savoring the chewy texture with anticipation. Her cheek tingled as the extracts of nettle-berry, thistleroot and poison-grub leaves filtered their way into her blood.

Her eyes rolled back in their sockets, exposing the whites. Stillshadow surrendered to the divine connection, sinking back against the broad flat rock she and the mothers before her had called their sitting stone. From there, she gazed down from Great Earth's heights to the valley floor, the rock-tumbled, bamboo- and grass-filled plain, familiar slopes she had walked and climbed since childhood. Two days' walk to the north, filling the horizon, stood Great Sky, the tallest mountain in all the world, in whose misty heights the Creators themselves lived their fierce, jealous, eternal love.

Squatting, eyes tilted to the clouds, Stillshadow hummed a trance song to herself, idly scraping lines and curves in the loose black soil with the tip of her walking stick. Her eyelids slid closed, newborn stars scintillating in the pulsing blackness. Once immersed in this state of waking dream, the old woman's scrawling intensified. After a time she opened her eyes to examine what she had created. Most days, little met her eyes save an overlapping tangle of meaningless doodles. From time to time her mystical state produced something of unusual symmetry, truth or beauty. Those few drawings she etched again upon her sitting stone, carved into a tree trunk or painted upon one of the countless rock walls and shelves jutting from Great Earth herself.

Four hands of small huts were arranged like mushroom rings on the slope behind her. Constructed of wood and patched with mud, most were lashed firmly together with vines and green branches, but one central hut was sturdier, a wasp's nest of sticks and clay. Come rainy season, the unfired clay would dissolve, the sticks separate, the roof and walls collapse upon themselves. The drawings sheltered beneath it would fade like last moon's dreams. This, however, was considered no tragedy. Indeed, this was the way it had always been. Come the dry season Stillshadow would begin anew, as had the grandmothers before her. In hands of pictographs she would recount the previous year's events, adding memories of the deeper past, as well as inscribing visions from the future. Until, of course, the rains erased those as well.

But that was good, as appropriate as spring's sky-spanning butterfly swarms, the golden clouds heralding the return of the vast and vital herds: gazelle, giraffe, deer, eland and countless others of Great Mother's four-legged children in mouthwatering profusion. Ultimately the rains, however harsh, were merely another part of the cycle. They destroyed nothing.

A short, slight girl with a deer's wide-eyed grace approached from behind her. The child paused a respectful moment, then softly asked: "Mother? What do you see?"

This was Stillshadow's youngest daughter, Small Raven. Raven had lived just eight rains, but her exquisite shadow-dancing had already earned a place at the Spring Gathering's central fire. Raven spent too much time twisting her hair into patterns, cared too much for the bits of shells she laced onto her necklaces, and for inventing meaningless little snatches of song she would caw in the voice of her namesake. But the girl had an undeniable talent for medicine as well. If she proved as powerful a dancer as Stillshadow hoped, and she stayed the course, her future held great promise.

"Many things," Stillshadow murmured. "Not for you. Not yet."

"When?" Raven asked.

"One day. Or not." She rose, walked two hands of paces and stooped to enter the central hut. Its entrance was low enough to force entrants to crawl humbly, a reminder of their status before the great mountains. Through strategically placed holes in the roof streamed yellowish light, illuminating the glyphs and grooves scrawled in the dirt below. The symbols represented moon and sun, birth and death, rain and wind. This was the history of the Ibandi, Great Mother's first and favorite two-legged. The mural was recreated every year, beginning at the first full moon after the butterflies returned, to be completed before the orb melted and was reborn.

Raven followed her mother at a respectful distance, again waiting as Stillshadow squatted, peering at the designs. "How can I help?" The child's wide eyes sparkled.

Stillshadow raised her palm in a clear message: *By remaining silent.* She scrawled in the dirt, muttering to herself in singsong. "Wolf's woman Twilight bore two children. See how the line grows!" She pointed at an extension scratched in the dust a mere hand of days before. "More and more are born. Something new comes. Something new . . ."

"New?" Small Raven asked.

Too late: once again, Stillshadow had vanished into her waking dreams.

"You scare me, Mother," Raven whispered.

When the crone finally emerged from her trance and regarded Raven, her dark, ancient eyes were webbed with blood, the pupils contracted tightly. The girl shrank back.

"I am sorry," the medicine woman said, her voice still thickly furred with godweed. "But Great Mother takes me to far places, and where she leads, I must follow."

Raven nodded, confusion sharpening her narrow little face. "What do you see?"

Stillshadow paused before answering. "For lives beyond counting our people have ringed the mountains. Soon it may be time to go."

"Go?" Raven asked. "Leave Great Earth? Great Sky? What would we do? Where would we go?"

"I can see it," Stillshadow said. "But I know not when, or where. The world changes."

Through narrowed eyes Stillshadow watched the horror dim her daughter's fire, knew the strength required to control it, and felt great pride. She took her daughter's hands. So smooth, where hers were rough and wrinkled with age. For a moment she remembered when Night Bird, her mother and mentor, had held her own small hands. How impossibly wise and beautiful and ancient Bird had seemed. How wondrous to know that Raven doubtless saw her the same way. "I hope one day my seat at the spring fire will be yours. But it may not be here, in this place."

"You hope?" Raven said, young voice plaintive. "You do not *know*?"

"I do not know," the old woman confessed.

"Where do we go?" the child asked again.

Raven's *num*-fire wavered with confusion, and Stillshadow regretted her inability to assuage it. She shrugged. "I do not know. And I may not live to see it. But I feel one truth: a child will be born. She comes, and in her seven eyes lives our new home. We must search for her."

Raven peered more closely at Stillshadow's symbols. Some resembled monkeys, or elephants, or sunrises. Stillshadow suspected that Raven thought some to be mere meaningless scrawls. That would be understandable: Small Raven's training was far from complete. Stillshadow felt that the eyes of Raven's face and hands and feet were wider and clearer than those of any child she had ever trained. When at last Raven's seventh eye opened, she might be the greatest dreamer of all.

Sometimes Stillshadow wondered if those were merely the hopes of an old woman with more sunrises behind than before her. She could not serve her people forever, and hoped it would be one of her fleshly daughters who carried on. Certainly, she had not kept all of her children. Those unsuited to this severe life were raised in the bomas below. One of Raven's brothers as well as two older sisters had been raised in Water and Wind bomas, the villages to the south and north. But one sister, Blossom, lived the dream, and one brother ran with the hunt chiefs, so the flesh continued.

But was Raven destined to lead the dream dancers? To lead their people in concert with a boy, perhaps already a man, who would one day join the hunt chiefs on Father Mountain?

Stillshadow did not know. In time, Great Mother shared all knowledge. That time was yet to come.

·    ·    ·

Raven lowered her eyes, steadied her breathing so that her mother could not read her fire. It would not do to have Stillshadow see her fear, know how terrified she was that another girl might come to the mountain, a girl wise enough to save them from some unimaginable future horror, mighty enough to destroy Small Raven's destiny. She peered down at the images Stillshadow had scrawled. *Future. Birth.*

*A child will be born.* . . .

The hope of their people? The thief of Raven's rightful heritage? There was another prophecy as well, one Stillshadow had not mentioned in several moons. This one claimed that one day, a nameless girl-child would herald the fall of gods, of their land and way of life, would bring death to all within the shadow.

Her mother should have mentioned it. Why hadn't she? Could Stillshadow herself be afraid of one so low as to be unworthy of a name?

Raven did not know, and shuddered to learn. She had never seen the child, and already both loved and hated her.

# Chapter Two

The girl was born to Zebra Moon and her husband, Water Chant, in Water boma, the cluster of huts a day's walk south of Great Earth. There, hands of hands of folk lived in the shadow of a single thorn ring-wall higher than any man or lion could leap. Most within were blood kin—brothers, sisters, aunts, uncles, cousins—or married into the clan. They hunted eland and warthog and ostrich, and gathered berries and tubers, melons and beans. The dusty-skinned, gray old hunters crouched around the men's fire sharpening their spears and pit stakes and arrows, laughing and joking and recounting tales of their youth as they worked. The young hunters spent half their days in this fashion, singing and learning wisdom from the old ones. The gray-hairs smoked their pipes and leaf-rolls, sang of tracking and trapping and killing leopards in the manner taught by the hunt chiefs. Several paces away was the women's fire, always protected by a semicircle of stones, not an intact ring like that protecting the men's fire. Here the old women prepared skins: curing, chewing hides, scraping fat, pounding and softening the deer and giraffe skins with ground plant gums, then stitching them into pouches and loincloths. With brittle bones they danced last night's dreams, sharing their own secret knowings.

The boma's women and their daughters were primarily responsible for child care, remembrance of family songs, and the interpretation of dream memories. What had occurred in the dream world? Who could show a dance step learned in that shadowy realm? The best steps were repeated for the dream dancers when they visited. Sometimes a visiting wise woman marveled, agreeing that boma folk had joined them in the dream dance. On such happy occasions, their songs warmed the clouds above.

Men rarely visited the women's fire, and women rarely sat beside the men's. Only the youngest children moved easily between the fires as they teased and raced and made games, dancing and singing their days. Men and women alike tolerated them with great good humor and little harsh discipline, knowing that the years ahead would be challenging enough to provide all the rigor a child could ever need.

The older children traversed the worlds of male and female with greater difficulty, and as they neared the age for marriage, the nudges and disapproving comments toward those who strayed across the invisible line intensified, until there was little communication between the two genders.

There was currently one exception in Water boma, the man called Thorn Summer. Thorn lived in Fire boma, to the northeast, but was visiting Water because it was his sister whom the gods had blessed with child.

Thorn was thick-bodied and slow of temperament, soft-muscled but of good spirits, one of those rare men with but a single scar on each cheek. He had chosen not to complete his manhood ceremony, not to become a hunter. Thorn would never be offered a worthy bride. No father would give a beautiful, strong daughter to such a man. Thorn Summer was considered not male, and not female either. He was a "Between," of low status, but still of the Circle.

Thorn ran toward Zebra's hut, one water-filled ostrich shell in each hand. A small girl trotted at his side carrying water in a stitched eland skin. As they did, a woman's shrill, anguished screams rent the air. Hunters squatting nearby glanced toward the hut and then pointedly turned away, trusting in their wives and sisters to deal with this strange and rather magical challenge. One small, dusty male child watched Summer and the girl as they ducked down into Zebra's straw-roofed hut. When he took a halting, curious step in their direction, his father took his arm and gently but firmly pulled him back.

Childbirthing was a thing only for women, and for those males who would never be men.


The largest of the hunters at the fireside was Water Chant, boma father. The coarse knotted hair above his narrow face was chopped low to the scalp. His scarred hands were strong enough to break the strongest vines or tear a tortoise shell apart without a leverage stick. His hard black eyes could track a warthog across rocks on a moonless night, and his broad nose could smell zebra scat half a day distant. He squatted at the men's fire, chipping away at a new blade, occasionally offering a knife prayer to Great Earth, the colossus of rock and forest swelling just north of the boma.

*Let the blade be strong. Let my arm be strong. Let the leopard tremble, and the gazelle offer her throat to my spear.*

As boma father, responsibility for the poor hunting might well be laid at his feet. So far, despite their occasional grumbling, he was still much honored by his fellows. That, of course, could change in a single moon or moment. Nervousness made his hands slip, tearing his own fingernail.

"Father Mountain!" he growled, and thrust the injured finger into his mouth. The world of women was a mystery to him. Touching a woman in her moon-blood could drain a man's strength. A hunter who witnessed a woman's ceremony without permission might offend Great Mother Herself. Any self-respecting zebra or eland would be ashamed to die for such a weakling.

Five rains ago Water Chant's first wife had perished giving birth to a son who, in turn, ceased drawing breath before his second moon. Water did not want to lose another: his people might think him a man whose seed killed his own children. With such a reputation, fathers would be less likely to offer his sons their daughters . . . if sons he ever had.

His gray-bearded cousin Leopard Paw crouched next to him, sensing his unease. "She screams," Leopard said, scratching in the dirt with the blunt end of his spear. In a year, perhaps two, Leopard would no longer run with the hunters. "Big voice, that woman."

"Makes for a strong son." Water Chant's face was set strongly, revealing no concern. Father Mountain thought excessive emotion unseemly in a man. Who cared what the hunter next to you felt? When the lion charged, all that mattered was a strong arm, sure aim, a cool heart, and nimble feet. Any fool knew that much.

The sun was dying when the midwife finally emerged, a big, dusty, bloodstained woman whose moon face was tired but satisfied. "The child is born," she said.

Water Chant's lips pursed and he made a sound like a burbling brook, a way of asking fortune from the earth spirits for whom he was named. He stood, then crouched to pass the flaps of striped, gut-stitched zebra skin, chosen to complement his wife's totem. Their hut, floored with packed earth and lined with sweet grasses, was just large enough for a family of four to sleep side by side. The walls were of lashed sticks, the gaps between them packed with mud. The ceiling was multilayered, interwoven with sticks and vines in the Ibandi fashion, and covered with straw in such a way as to repel rain while admitting a cooling breeze.

That ventilation was important: the air reeked of blood and sweat and woman fluids. There in the shadows Zebra Moon lay exhausted. Blood stained the woven reeds beneath her. A glistening wet child lay panting on her swollen breasts, emptied by the effort of clawing its way from the dream world. The umbilical cord had been cut and tied, but still dangled, as long as Water Chant's thumb. In time it would wither to a nub.

Zebra's sister Meadow held the child out to him. The hunt chief gazed at it, studied the space between its legs. "Not a son," he grunted.

"A strong child," Meadow insisted.

He spread the girl's legs more fully, checking to see if perhaps a penis might be concealed within the moist folds. With a resigned shrug he handed her back. The child thrashed and wailed now, her cries of distress filling the hut.

Chant wished to wail his own disappointment. He needed a son, a boy to whom he could pass on his knowledge of the hunt, a son who might bring him meat in his old age, a new dancer for the men's fire.

"Let her mother take her," he said, then turned his back and left.


Night's mantle settled about Water boma's thorn walls, shrouding Great Earth's misty peak. The family was settling into its nighttime routine: roasting meat around the hearths, singing, nursing sleepy children, laughing in a rapid succession of clicks. Throughout the day, each adult in the boma approached Water Chant with congratulations, many of them giving small gifts for the girl's health.

"A strong girl-child is good," said Thorn, handing Chant a melon. "She will work hard. Her husband will be your son."

Chant grunted, respecting the Between, but not his opinion on such matters. Thorn had made an honorable choice: better for a man to admit he was no hunter than lie to himself and his brothers, only to fail in the tall grass. "For a few rains," he said. "No. Sons are better. Three daughters she gives me. No sons." He pushed past the well-wishers and entered his hut.

There in the darkness he watched the infant as she nursed blindly. Zebra Moon smiled, still deeply drained.

Chant's thin, weathered face was impassive and observant. After a few breaths, he left again.

. . . .

As days passed the moon swelled, birthed stars, then swelled again.

In the fashion of Ibandi women, Zebra kept her baby with her at all times, either held in her strong arms or suspended in a sling of brown eland skin. Most Ibandi mothers carried their children slung at back or hip, dangling low to the ground so that older children could entertain their younger siblings. These they stroked and taught and regaled with song, offering morsels of fruit and berries and urging them to speak.

Today Zebra knelt by the streambed, pounding caked sweat and dirt from old hides on the smooth stones among the rushes, shoulder by shoulder with her sisters, singing as they hammered with rocks, softening the hides' stiffness. She liked the work and had returned to it two days after her birthing, enjoying the sense of reclaiming her body after pregnancy.

This was Zebra's third child, and as with the others, the warmth of a sleeping infant, the sweet sensation of her nursing, even her occasional cries seemed to make the day and all about it a brighter, happier time.

Then . . . Water Chant pushed his way through the reeds, and her belly soured. She glanced away, fearing to meet his eyes.

"Give me the child," he said.

"She nurses," Zebra protested.

"Give me the child," he said again.

Zebra searched her sisters' and cousins' faces, seeking support and finding none. Reluctantly, she waved a swarm of little blue-black flies away from her daughter's face and handed her up to her father.

The baby's eyes were dark brown with odd greenish tints. They stared sightlessly, lacking focus. Something like a spark of pale light swam within them, a glimmerance that tingled Water Chant's skin.

The child was staring *through* him, seeming to concentrate on Great Earth herself, instead of the fleshly father who held her.

By this age, most children had begun to respond to light and shadow. True, their eyes followed only with difficulty, but follow they did, perhaps after a short lag. This girl saw nothing, reacted to nothing, save her mother's nipple.

Chant's lips and tongue fluttered in a succession of pops and clicks. When she spoke, Zebra Moon responded in the same fashion. "Why can't she see?" he asked.

"Give her time," the mother said. She continued rapidly, "Her inner eye will open. I thought to call her—"

Water Chant threw up his hands in horror. "No!" he said. "No name. Not until she sees. No name."

Zebra continued in a coaxing voice. "Without a name, she has no totem. Great Mother will not know her. Father Mountain will not protect her."

He waved his hand in front of the girl's face. No reaction at all.

"If she cannot see the mountain," he said, "the mountain cannot see her."

Zebra Moon seized her daughter from her husband, squeezing the child to her breast.

"The girl is blind!" Water Chant said. "How can we feed her? Protect her? I have watched for days. Thought much, and listened to the wise men. You know what they say."

"She is my child!" Zebra Moon made a low, keening sound. Her grief sound. As a girl she had danced that sound before the tribe, telling a story of a lost zebra colt wandering beneath a full moon, terrified of lions. The dance had ended in triumph when the colt rejoined its mother and herd. She suspected that this, her new story, would not end so blissfully.

"No man will want her," Water said. "For all her miserable life, she will be a burden."

"She is my child."

"Yes," Water conceded. Then his face hardened. "But is she *mine*?"

Zebra forced her voice to soften. "Yes," she said. "*Your* child. See her eyes. Ask your sisters if they are not like yours."

"Those eyes do not see me," he said, unmoved. He leaned closer. "Let me take her, leave her out for the mountain to see. Let the mountain decide whether or not she is Ibandi."

"She is our child," the mother insisted, desperation souring her voice. "*Your* child." She dropped her eyes. "Do not shame me."

Water Chant stepped back, suddenly seeming to grasp the seriousness of his accusation. He had no reason to think her false. His own mother and aunts had watched Zebra carefully, and if she had crept into the brush with other hunters, trading her honor for a chunk of meat, their tongues would have wagged at once.

"You have been true," he conceded. "But the spirits are not to be trusted. Perhaps I made wrong sacrifice."

"Listen to me," she said. "She will grow strong. See her legs! She will be able to carry, and work. . . ."

"And stumble, and walk into trees," said her husband. "Do not anger me, woman. Three daughters have crawled through your body, but no sons. Some whisper that witchery is at work here."

She dropped her head at this ultimate if implied threat. She held her tongue, perhaps praying that Great Mother or Father Mountain might warm her husband's heart.

*The child was not blind. Indeed, she saw far too much, so much that she did not, could not react to light or shadow, to human hands and faces and tongues.*

*She drifted like a bubble in a lake of sun-bleached whiteness. A fantasia of stars and moons hovered in that swirling cosmic shroud.*

*She reached out to touch one of the glowing orbs. It popped like a bubble, exploded into light. The girl cooed, both startled and delighted.*

*The barest outline of nose, a chin, and eyes appeared in the midst of the field, a face vague enough that it could have been almost anyone or anything. Gradually, wrinkled lines congealed, followed by wise, tired eyes, and an old woman's braided gray hair. The sight of this woman gave the child the same feeling that she found from fumbling her lips around her mother's nipple.*

*Warmth. Comfort. Nourishment.*

*The stars devolved into lightning, followed swiftly by a downpour. The sounds of thunder fractured into human voices.*

*Angry voices echoing in her ears, the girl-child began to cry.*

# Chapter Three

A day's run northeast of Water stood the thorn-ringed clutch of huts called Fire boma.

A pair of healthy young boys, brothers of five and six rains, ran and played in the scorched-grass clearing around the camp, the area burned each moon to deny cover to the lions or leopards who might slink close enough to fang the unwary.

While it was risky for them to play beyond the walls, Fire's future welfare depended on its hunters' ability to recognize and avoid danger. If they could not learn those skills now, in the shadow of safety, of what use would they be later, alone on the savannah? Not six months before, their own father, the great hunter Baobab, had been taken by lions. On that same bloody night their uncle Snake had lost his left eye and ear and his status as hunt chief. Life went on, but such disfiguring lessons were not easily forgotten.

Their mother, Gazelle, had been renowned for her beauty, admired by young hunters at Spring Gathering for years before Baobab won her by climbing the sacred Life Tree for which he had been named. Father had been so great and powerful! Some said that he might have challenged Break Spear for boma father. Such a position might have set his own sons on the road to leadership. That was no more than last moon's dream now, a barely remembered ache.

The boys' names were Fire Ant and Hawk Shadow. Hawk Shadow was a rain older, a finger's width taller, but no stronger or faster than Ant. Both were thick of body but moved with formidable ease and lightness, so strong and coordinated it was almost as if they were half their true weight. Back to back atop a tree limb or rock, they could slap off a horde of other boys, but if there were no other ears to box Ant and Hawk competed with each other: wrestling, running, jumping, playing some game of hide-and-seek that sent their bodies flipping and plunging, raising dust clouds and scraping knees and elbows, testing the limits of their physical agility and appetite for pain. They loved play-fighting with stripped branches, jabbing each other as if the dull tips were spear points.

"I will win!" yelled Fire Ant, loud enough to be heard across Fire River, an easy walk to the east.

"Never!" panted Hawk. "You will never win. Everyone knows I win every time!"

Shorter, leaner Fire Ant mocked him. "You are stronger, but *I* am faster."

"Anyone can run away," Hawk Shadow retorted. "But which of us can stand and fight like a hunter?"

The footrace ended in a chortling victory for Fire Ant. Hawk shrugged, dunked his brother and immediately suggested that they try climbing one of the dreaded thorn trees: any truly good day was crowned with a glorious new array of scrapes and bruises.

This day held special possibilities. On this day, their mother, Gazelle Tears, was giving birth to their beloved father's final child. All wanted to know: would it be a boy, who might grow to be a mighty hunter? Or a girl, to bind them more tightly with another boma and bring new life to the great Circle?

Either possibility made their hearts proud.

A few breaths later their younger sister, Little Brook, ran through the gap in the boma's thorn wall, fat tummy wobbling, stubby legs pumping, her small round face aglow with excitement. "Hawk! Ant!" she called. "Baby come!" Instantly, the two boys abandoned their games and chased her back through the gap.

Eight huts were clustered within the thorn circle, each sheltering a family of five to ten. Another two huts were for storage of meat and vegetables, another for healing, and yet another for honored guests or special meetings. To the west, at the extreme opposite of the boma wall's gap, was a trench reserved for nighttime relief of bowels and bladder. Although Thorn Summer shoveled dirt over the waste every morning, a strong sour odor drifted up from the site, wrinkling Fire Ant's nose. Most chose to hold their waste and water until morning, using a trench a swift eastern walk away from camp. There, the inevitable swarms of dung beetles burrowed beneath the shoveled soil, packing and rolling and carrying away what the Ibandi left as waste.

From time to time, when the stink grew too strong or the fleas and mites too bothersome, the entire boma moved to another nearby campsite, perhaps one they had occupied a few years earlier. At such a location the waste pits would have dried, the pests crawling off in search of other nourishment.

A new sibling! Brother or sister, it made little difference, as long as there were two hands for holding, two feet for walking and a pair of keen eyes for tracking or foraging.

Fire Ant's ears prickled as the shrill cries brought him up short. The boma's mother, Hot Tree, was a medicine woman almost as wise as her birth sister, Stillshadow herself. Hot Tree knew the name of every plant and insect for a day's walk in all directions. If greater magic was needed, help was five days away: two days to Great Earth and three for the return trip, for medicine women could not travel as quickly as hunters.

Hot Tree crawled out of the hut's low mouth. She was a bulky woman, thick through the hips but a whirlwind in dancing, shorter than her powerful sibling but twice her width. She had squatted beside the birthing woman since before dawn, and her back was stiff. Tree pushed against her hip with one strong flat hand and winced with pain.

"Fetch your uncle," she said. "The family has a new hunter."

Hawk Shadow whooped and leapt into the air, somersaulting before he touched back down, grabbing wrists with Fire Ant. The two brothers capered in a circle, lips split wide in smiles. The other children danced with them, even Lizard Tongue, the tall, thin orphan boy with the hollow eyes, who belonged to everyone and no one.

Fire Ant first beheld his new brother that day, in the waxing of monkey moon. He thought the new arrival was just splendid, a healthy, squalling brat who would one day make Uncle Snake proud. Surely their father, Baobab, danced with joy atop Great Sky.


The infant's first days were uneventful. As with all newborns, Fire Ant's brother was oblivious to anything except the need to cling to his mother, to suckle and to sleep.

After the first hands of days the boy began to awaken, although his eyes were still groggy and wandering. He cried less frequently during the night, and slept longer. When he did awaken, he avidly sought his mother's breasts, and gurgled with a child's contentment as he nursed.

"He sucks all the time," Fire Ant said to his mother, Gazelle.

She nodded, eyes deep-rimmed with fatigue. "When awake. But he sleeps more than you did." She traced a loving hand along her middle son's cheek. "You slept less and suckled harder," she said. Then her eyes closed as if echoing the newborn's own expression, mother and child in nurturing embrace, his tiny, soft fingers gripping at her skin as if it was all that held him in this world.

# Chapter Four

Stillshadow and her two hunt chief escorts had been walking single file since before dawn, and now the new sun danced just above the eastern horizon.

The morning heat reflected from the sand, challenging calluses as thick as rhino hide. This sun was like most others: sung to life each morning, dying every night. It was notable only for being more piercing than most, and Stillshadow wondered if the morning's sun song had been displeasing to Great Mother's ears.

Her old calves ached. Once a year she made this circuit of the four inner bomas, starting with Fire in the east and working around to end north with Wind boma. As a girl, she had eagerly anticipated the annual pilgrimage. As age transmuted her bones to rock, some of the pleasure had drained away. Inevitably, on some not too distant day she would come to dread it, and on that day she would pass the responsibility to another—her daughter Raven, she hoped.

She crunched across the blackened gap surrounding Fire boma, relishing the sight of her evening's resting place. Running at full speed, the orphan boy Lizard passed through the hole in the thorn walls. Despite the sadness she always sensed about him, he was quick and inquisitive, and at the moment also excited. "Stillshadow is here!" Lizard called. He was a good boy, of five rains, whose parents had been bhan, the folk who lived among the outer bomas. By family custom Lizard had been adopted into Fire boma.

When and if he eventually passed his manhood ceremony, Lizard might one day be considered full Ibandi.

Lizard's mother and father had been slain by unknown raiders, perhaps the mysterious beast-men, hulking half-apes some hunters claimed to have seen lurking out on the savannah.

Did they truly exist? She did not know, could only say that her love, Cloud Stalker, leader of the hunt chiefs, believed them real. For this and other reasons she never left Great Earth's slopes without an armed companion.

The entire boma ceased their patching and wrestling and basket weaving as the old woman passed through the thorn wall's gap. Five paces behind her, the two young hunt chiefs squared their shoulders, aware that every eye—especially every female eye—was upon them. Although hunt chiefs did not marry, they had their pick of widows and unmarried girls. Ibandi nights were always warm, but some were more humid than others.

The crone straightened her back and sharpened her gaze as she walked, aware that all eyes were upon her. She was glad that none of the young ones could read her fire. A spine could be straightened at a thought, but she was certain that fatigue dimmed her fire, so the least of her students could count her years.

Ah well. One mouth could not simultaneously praise wisdom and curse old age.

Other than this yearly circuit, or times of emergency, most Ibandi saw Stillshadow and her sisters only at Spring Gathering, in the shadow of Great Earth. Spring was a chance to see cousins and sisters who had married away, an opportunity to learn new dances and hear new stories to mold their dreams. There she gave names to new babies, something that ordinarily didn't happen until their second full moon.

Dream dancers and their guardians were offered lodging immediately upon arrival at the boma gate. Stillshadow waited, hunching in the shadowed recess of the thorn wall's gap, leaning on her knobby walking stick. Her two young male escorts, hunt chiefs from Great Sky, maintained their usual distance. "I will eat before I sleep, but I can still bless before I eat. Bring the children to me," she said, and smacked her withered lips together. The thought of newborns, so fresh from Great Mother's bosom, warmed her heart.

Thorn Summer, not a man or a woman, with the rights of neither but with some strengths of both, greeted her with an embrace and a gift of water. His eyes widened joyfully as she accepted his offering and sipped from his ostrich shell. Thorn had studied his name for many years and come to the conclusion that it was his place in life to offer cooling drink and shade to pierce the heat. "Have you walked long?" he asked.

"A day and a night," she said, returning the shell.

The boma began to awaken to her presence, its folk coming to her, stamping the ground and spitting toward Great Sky in greeting.

"Please," said a small, dusty woman. "Bless my child before you sleep." This request was repeated again and again as one and yet another mother brought her young ones forward. All had been born since Stillshadow's last annual visit. Most had been named already. Two had not.

Fire boma's father, Break Spear, was a man of broad shoulders, with a vast belly that had once been flat and muscular. Now it was hard and round, as if he had swallowed a muskmelon whole. It shook as he roared in pleasure and held up his hands. "Not so many! The wise one is tired!"

Stillshadow laughed, accepting the playful challenge. "No! I am not too old to bless our fruit. Bring me more babies!"

She weaved a bit, intoxicated both by her people's nearness and by the herbs and leaves that she ate, drank or smoked to keep herself moving through the long night's grueling walk. Much of her time was spent combining various roots for effect, teetering on the edge of dream for days at a time.

It was her place to offer blessings, but she would stay no more than a day or two. During that time she would dance stories, sing songs, answer questions, grind and compound leaves and roots into precious medicines. Then, with her guards, she would travel on to the next major boma. The entire circuit might take her more than a moon. True, she would be exhausted by the time she and her escorts returned to Great Earth, but that was the Ibandi Way, the Way she had inherited from her own mother and teacher, Night Bird. The Way she taught to her own students and daughters.

"Ah! I know this one!" she said, eyes bright, as another mother offered her naked, squalling babe for blessing. This baby's face was shiny and wet from crying, his eyes reddened, little lips stretched tight, dark gums shiny. "I knew your father. Threw your father's name! This one will be strong, but a rascal. And this one . . ."

A fourth naked bundle of squirming arms and legs was offered. Stillshadow pressed her lips against the girl's smooth, warm forehead. She looked slantwise at the child, fuzzing her vision until she could see the life-glow. "This one's fire is clear," Stillshadow said. "She will be a great beauty, and men will break bones wrestling for her hand. Watch her carefully—she is sweet enough to draw leopards from beyond the horizon."

Break Spear's broad brown face split in a smile. "Bring Stillshadow water and meat. Welcome her to the boma."

So she ate baboon with relish, and pretended to enjoy the zorilla meat, nibbling until she could tuck the rest into the fire pit. Then the villagers displayed dances learned in their recent dreams, and she devised songs and shadow-play to accompany them. As the day wore on the tribe gathered around Stillshadow, all other work and play coming to an end. Finally, the newest baby was brought before her, displayed on the ground upon a yellow eland skin.

The old woman paused as the infant sprawled before her. The long walk and profligate sharing of *num* had taken its toll at last. Her eyes watered as she peered at the newborn. The hairs at the back of her neck began to itch. Just fatigue? Or was there something different about this one?

She closed her eyes.

*In her waking dream she saw his future. He was slender, strong but not tall. His running and jumping were not particularly good, but there was something odd about his* num . . . *the fire about his head was brighter, clearer than she had ever seen.*

*He jumps with his thoughts, not his body.*

*What?*

Her mind spun. Such images, such thoughts, were unknown to her.

*Now he was running. Leaping. Over . . . what?* Dead water. *He was being chased by a man with a spear. A man he knew and loved. Then he stood still, the heaviness in his limbs saying that he was prepared to accept death. There was steam and fire and . . .*

*And terrible, terrible cold.*

She blinked her eyes open. What was that vision? Great Mother, she was tired. Strange. Such vivid sights usually came to her when a girl was destined to be a dream dancer, a sign to convince her mother to let the child journey to Great Earth. Boys competed fiercely to catch Break Spear's eye, that he might nominate them for hunt chief. Only rarely did she have insights into their future status.

But this one . . . there was something strange about him.

This, she knew, was a great moment, a moment that would shape the boy-child's life, the Circle's life. Either now, in this ritual, or at the Spring Gathering, every Ibandi child came before her to be judged. She needed to peer into his *num*-fire, the glow that flickered around the edge of his body when she slanted her eyes just *so*. It was important for her to inspect the hands and feet to see if those eyes had yet winked open. Reading these signs would tell her things she needed to know, but for the life of her she found it difficult to read this boy. His seven eyes were dim, nothing special. . . .

But his head. The crown of his head. Such fire!

So *bright*.

A devastating wave of fatigue clawed at her suddenly, rooting all the way to her marrow. Was that natural? Or a demon seeking to cloud her inner eyes when she needed them most?

"This one is strong," she said. "Very powerful . . ."

She peered into his tiny brown eyes. She saw something, felt her own questions and uncertainty, but made a momentous decision. "He will be a skilled hunter," she said. "A jumper," she continued, remembering the vision. "I call him Frog Hopping." Her eyelids were too heavy to prop open any longer.

Break Spear discerned what she tried to conceal. "Mother is tired," the boma father said. "No more. More when the sun rises. Now she must sleep. Come! Show Stillshadow to shelter!"

As they led her to the meeting hut, she glanced back at the newly named Frog Hopping, wondering if she should have spoken more bluntly about what she saw. But at her age flesh was sometimes stronger than will, and the crone allowed herself to be led away to a place of rest.


Curled on her side against the matted grass, Stillshadow drowsed, staring up at the darkness, her mind wandering in that odd place between the dreaming and waking worlds. In that place just before sleep, where the worlds of day and night melded, Great Mother sometimes whispered to her.

Something was amiss, but what, she could not say. A mild, cool wind filtered through the boma's thorn wall, and then into her hut. She shivered.

Was that shudder from the cold? Or something else?

Had she made a mistake? Had she . . .

Then fatigue overwhelmed her, and she fell asleep again, trusting that the night's walk in the world of dreams might resolve the mystery, if mystery there truly was.

## Chapter Five

Water Chant crouched in the dry streambed, rubbing crumbly gnu droppings between thumb and forefinger. Spit on his fingertips made the flakes gummy. Chant sniffed deeply, then touched them with the tip of his tongue. Judging by texture, the droppings were at least seven days old. The acid taste suggested that the gnu had been sick and tired. The streams feeding Water boma had dried, forcing the shaggy, horned beasts to begin their yearly migration unseasonably early. Their local water holes were now little more than mud.

Water boma's folk had taken to eating fill-cactus to still their stomach rumblings, and this was bad. Fill-cactus pulp quieted the belly but did not feed the flesh.

Discouraged, he trudged back to Water boma's high, familiar thorn walls. If things did not improve, they might have to move farther south. The bhan sometimes moved several times a year. In all the world, perhaps only the Ibandi knew where their children would sleep next year. Was that about to change?

"Chant!" called his cousin Leopard Paw. "We have meat!"

"Your hunt has been good?" Chant called hopefully.

Leopard shook his head. "No. Great Father smiled on Earth boma's hunters. A giraffe welcomed their arrows. They followed until the poison made it sleepy. Then they sent it to Great Sky with their spears. There was meat to share."

Water Chant nodded, too ashamed to speak. Ibandi rarely went hungry.

By tradition and inclination, the bomas shared. Still, it was not right. Was he not a man, and therefore capable of feeding a family?

But an even greater shame gnawed like a snake in Chant's gut as he approached his hut and bowed to crawl through the door. The roof flap was open, and dusty yellow daylight eased the darkness. He would have preferred not to see what it revealed.

Zebra nursed her daughter with a desperate intensity, flinching as he entered. Even after four moons, his newborn still gazed blankly out at the world, still registered nothing at all.

Chant felt his breath stop within him, heating until he thought he would burst. Then the words flew from his mouth like angry birds. "We cannot feed such a child!"

"She is my flesh," Zebra Moon insisted, as she had every day since their daughter's birth.

Water Chant fought to keep his temper. "Every day the pigs and deer are harder to find. My body aches, but I hunt. I bring you whatever meat I find. The fruit of my body is given to the fruit of yours, and it is wrong!" Chant slammed his fist against the ground.

She flinched away, raising a protective arm over her child. "She is mine!" Zebra Moon held the baby close, and her lips curled away from bared teeth. Chant backed away toward the entrance, already seeing that there would be no easy or happy resolution for this.


In night's first quarter, Zebra had backed herself against Water Chant, rubbing her ample buttocks against his groin even before he had fully emerged from antelope dreams. His root awakening before his mind, Chant had taken her roughly but not painfully. Zebra had eagerly accepted him into her body, responding to his thrusts with joyful cries, fevered skin and an enthusiastically arched spine.

The heat had flared and receded like some ancient body tide. Afterward, they pressed against each other, the hut perfumed with their scent and sweat. After passion came the time for sleep.

No. That was not truth.

For Water Chant merely *pretended* to sleep. He counted the slow rise and fall of Zebra's inhalations to five over and over again, until certain that his woman was deep in the place where Father Mountain and Great Mother opened the endless caverns of dream.

Then, being very careful not to awaken her, he slipped the sleeping girl-child from beside his wife's pendulous breasts.

Her arms and legs were so tiny, her foot smaller than Chant's thumb, her skin as smooth as a new blade of grass. Water Chant hardened his heart. As boma father, it was his responsibility to lead the way.

From childhood he had dreamed of being a hunt chief, as had his father before him. The chiefs could and did have children, but could not raise their families without living in the great Circle . . . thereby abandoning the path of hunt chief. But there were other rewards in life, such as being chosen boma father. That had been honor and joy enough for Water Chant. He would hold that office as long as he could make the yearly hunt run at Spring Gathering—in other words, as long as the younger hunters wanted him to lead. But never had he imagined he would have to make decisions such as this.

How could he? How could anyone imagine such a choice?

Every soul sheltered within the boma's walls had to contribute, or all would suffer. He loved the lives of *all* children within the thorn ring. If the other bomas knew his wife had produced a blindling, it might even cheapen the value of his other daughters.

"Forgive me," he said to the snoring Zebra, and crept from the hut.

His cousins' sleeping sighs wound through the huts, borne by a night wind almost as warm as the day's. The gate was tied shut so that hyenas and leopards would not sneak in to steal food or babies. If anyone awoke in the night, they might look to the gate, and he did not wish to answer questions tonight. Chant went to the back wall, near the store hut, and unraveled the vine there.

Thorns tore his hands, but such pains were trivial and distant. All seven eyes remained fixed on the task before him. Water Chant slipped the skin from around his shoulders and laid it on the ground, setting the girl-child upon it. Her eyes seemed to hold his, so that for a moment he thought the infant could see him. For a handful of breaths a brief, hollow flash of guilt was more intense than a leopard's bite.

When he realized the infant's empty, green-flecked brown eyes were merely staring *through* him, his heart hardened again.

Water Chant pulled the bush aside and, on his belly, crawled out through the hole. The spines tore his back. The pain, joined with the agony in his heart, distracted him from what he was about to do to his helpless third daughter.

Once on the barrier's far side Chant reached back and grasped the zebra skin, pulling it through with the nameless child stretched upon it.

The baby looked up at him, through him, blindly. Her pouty wet lips curled in a smile.

Chant felt sickened. He could not do this.

No. As boma father, he *must* do it.

This was what it meant to be a man in the world.


Spear in his right hand, blind daughter cradled in the crook of his left arm, Water Chant ran. A *huh* sound accompanied every exhalation, Chant not consciously sucking air in but forcing his body to breathe for itself using the very motion of running. The hunt chiefs atop Great Sky had taught him this hyena running. So long as Chant sang in such a fashion, he would never tire. He ran, the tiny child's fingers clutching at his chest hair.

He could not understand why she did not cry.

He ran until half-night, starlight guiding him, heart too sick to find pleasure in the familiar *slap-slap-slap* rhythms of heel striking ground.

Descending into a cactus-spotted gully, he lay the baby down. She gazed up at him, blind eyes wide. Suddenly they seemed to focus, for the first time to mark him out from the surrounding web of light and shadow.

*Too late. Too late . . .*

No. Not too late. Did awareness live behind that empty gaze? Did she know he was there? Did she know anything at all?

Now, at last, his tears came. Now, at last, Chant gave voice to thoughts he would never have shared with Zebra.

"My daughter." He knelt beside the child. "If you see, show me now. Please. This is a bad thing I do." The wind rustled the trees. Their moon-shadows stretched like souls climbing Great Sky.

She looked directly at his chest, and the sense of connection swelled within Water Chant's gut. On a hunch, he stepped to his left.

The infant continued to stare straight ahead, fixed on Great Earth's misty, horizon-filling expanse. Chant felt dizzy, but the sickness was a quiet thing, a thing he could survive. For a while Zebra would hate him, but then eventually she would forgive. Life would go on.

Water Chant peered northward. Invisible from here, a day's run beyond Great Earth, stood her titanic mate, Great Sky. The two mountains were the twin hearts of their people.

Great Mother had lived beneath Great Earth until courted by Father Mountain, who had impregnated Her. She had birthed all life, then gone to live with Him atop Great Sky.

When mortal life ended, the flesh went into the ground, and the spirits climbed Great Sky, there to be gifted with new sacred bones crafted by Great Mother's mate Himself. Some said the stars were their hearth fires. There atop Great Sky—unclimbed by living men save the great hunt chiefs who lived on its slopes—their ancestors lived again in a vast, eternally cloud-shrouded boma, dancing in dead water. And dwelling at the very top were He who had created the world and She who had filled it with life and love.

Hunt chief Cloud Stalker's magic was unfathomably powerful. From this awesome one, Water had heard the stories of the death demons that haunted Great Sky's heights, of the dead water that rotted the flesh from bone and made strong hunters too sleepy to walk, then stole their *num* and turned them to stone. What manner of men could resist such evil he did not know, did not *want* to know. They were the hunt chiefs. They kept the bomas safe. They held council with the ancestors. That was enough.

Only hunt chief magic had enabled men to reach the top, to speak to the dead or even the Creators themselves. He, Water Chant, had spent moons training on Great Sky's slopes but had never been invited to join the climb to speak to the ancestors or sit at the feet of the gods. He hadn't sufficient *num* to survive such an experience.

"Father Mountain," he whispered, "Great Mother, if this is your child, come take her. If not . . ."

He spat. The specks produced by his dry mouth never reached the ground, whipped away by the wind. In the distance, a hyena chuckled.

"If not, forgive me."

Jaw trembling, he pressed his lips against her forehead, trying not to inhale her scent for fear he would lose his purpose. Chant folded the skin over her naked body and ran back toward Fire boma. *Fast. Faster. Fastest.* Swiftly enough for the wind to dry his eyes before the tears ripened and fell.

# Chapter Six

Morning mists pooled in the east, paling the night sky even before the mountain women sang the new sun to life. At times the blazing infant orb rose as swiftly as a hawk in flight. On this morning, dawn blossomed with terrible slowness, and Water Chant was awake long before those first rays wormed their way through the hut's interlaced straw wall.

Zebra Moon was still asleep. Chant merely pretended to be. He often was out and about his tasks by now, making arrows or sharpening spears, preparing poisons or setting snares: the hunter's eternal chores. This day, he could not. His heart would burn if he let Zebra discover her tragedy alone. That was a coward's way. Many bad names Chant could be called, but *coward* was not among them.

His woman awoke slowly, as if pulling herself from some deep quagmire of fatigue. On previous nights the infant had disturbed her sleep frequently, draining her of both milk and *num*. An unbroken night's slumber had dragged her effortlessly down into its depths.

His two other daughters were still unmoving, curled against each other for comfort, not warmth. The nights were always warm, even when the night sky wept with joy and the clouds flashed with Great Mother and Father Mountain's love-play. When Zebra awakened, she stretched her arm out and found . . . nothing. Her eyes snapped open.

Her fingers scattered the straw. "Where is she?" Zebra searched the hut quickly, and then shook her man's shoulder. "Wake up! The baby is gone." She stared at him accusingly. "Where is my baby?"

He pretended not to hear her, yawning and scratching as if not entirely awake.

"Where is my baby?" She struck at Chant with her flat palms, scratched at him with her nails.

He hunched away from her, then turned cobra-swift and grabbed her wrists. Water Chant snarled, his eyes but a thumb's length from hers. "I don't know where the baby is," he said. "Perhaps Great Mother took her home."

Rage and defiance and guilt sizzled like the air after a summer storm. Finally Zebra turned away, raspy hiccoughing sobs stirring their daughters from sleep.

Outside, some of their neighbors had heard the sounds of distress, but pretended to pay their argument little notice. In private, of course, tongues would wag.

He passed the village women, busy with their morning tasks, using round stones to pound sunfruit and yams into breakfast mush. A quick trot took him to the muddy, trickling brook, where he washed himself, singing to the water in accordance with his name. When the boma women learned the baby was gone, they would wail with his wife and try to comfort her with delicacies such as ostrich egg and tortoise meat. They would groom her and sing with her and rub her wrinkled belly with stone-pressed nut oil.

Distantly, out across the veldt, a leopard coughed. Water Chant shuddered, remembering the terrible, necessary thing that he had done, and then wrapped thorns around those feelings. They served nothing. He could allow himself to *feel* nothing.

His mate was a woman and therefore straddled the realms of dust and dream, not living in the hunter's world of flesh and fire. She did not understand the things that men must do, just as he did not comprehend women's ways. Water Chant straightened his back, disowning all softness.

But still, later, when he returned to the boma, he brought Zebra special fleshy pieces of yellow sunfruit. As he anticipated, she threw them to the dust at his feet. The next day he would do the same, and so would she. And the day after that. But eventually, he knew, she would take the fruit and eat its peppery-sweet, pulpy flesh. And eventually, she would join bodies with him again.

And they would make another child. A healthy child.

A child who would not force him to kill his heart.

# Chapter Seven

Stillshadow had always loved the mornings. She rose to begin her walks before the new sun was sung to life, just to treasure every moment. Morning shadows were the darkest, the crispest. She could almost hear the morning dew as it dried, smell the first wisps of perfume from the morning glories as they opened, feel the cool sand crunching beneath her naked feet as she walked.

Two guardians following respectfully behind her, Stillshadow sought the herbs, barks and six-legged creatures she smoked or ate or drank to elevate her mind. Some might be dangerous, but it was her place to lead the way in all things. These plants she dug herself, or were dug by her students, scraped from the walls of the sacred caves or bartered for at Spring Gathering when the bhan entered their circle and danced the dream alive for another year.

Eventually, Stillshadow would dance with her ancestors atop Great Sky, and in that mighty time the clouds would part and all would be known. On that day, she hoped to tell those wise and mighty grandmothers that she, too, had faced the mystery with courage.

Suddenly, at the very edge of her vision a small, soft shape appeared, forcing her to stop and look again.

Laid out beneath the red flowers and spiky branches of a fever-bush was the scraped reverse of a zebra skin. And in the precise middle of the skin, an infant lay on its back. The soothing eddies of its bluish *num*-fire proclaimed the infant a girl, but there was something oddly intense about that first impression that took Stillshadow aback. The child's little body was wrapped in a soft, beaten antelope skin, the small dark head poking out. The face was of extraordinary sweetness, displaying an uncommon calm. The unblinking eyes stared up at Stillshadow almost as if the old woman had been expected.

The crone crept closer, holding her breath. Was this a bhan child, an infant from the outer bomas, parents slain or impoverished? Could this possibly be a trap of some kind? A snare, perhaps a disguised hunting pit?

But who might want to hurt her? And what demon or witch would bait a trap with a *child*?

Even more strangely, why did the infant make so little fuss? She couldn't imagine it. The girl should be howling.

Whoever had left the child here, southeast of Great Earth's foothills, had abandoned her within the shadows of a fever-bush. Stillshadow came closer, less afraid now, more fascinated. The old woman lifted the child to her eye level. The infant's lips were dry, but there were no other signs of dehydration such as sunken eyes or rapid breathing; she checked the soft spot at the top of the skull and was relieved to find it unsunken. Good, but when the sun blazed at its full power the precious remaining shadow would disappear. By night, the little one would be dead.

The infant's lips curled up. That smile was like the birth of a second sun, pure and broad enough to rock the old woman back on her heels. When the baby's eyes slid past her, Stillshadow realized that the foundling wasn't really looking directly at her. More . . . *through* her. What in Great Mother's shadow was this?

She unwrapped the antelope hide, confirming her intuition that the child was female. Well . . .

She waved her fingers before the infant's face, watching to see if the face-eyes would focus. They did not. But they did *follow*. The attention was directed not on the fleshly fingers but rather the *num*-fire surrounding Stillshadow's body. Never had the old woman seen the like.

Stillshadow examined the infant's stubby feet. She gazed at them with her eyes wide and focused tightly, and then rolled her eyes up in her head until all went dim, except a glowing after-image.

The girl's foot-eyes were bright: this one would walk far. Stillshadow went through the same process with the infant's hands. Not surprisingly, her hand-eyes glowed even more brightly.

*Who was this child?*

Stillshadow's hunt chief escorts stood respectfully away from her, shifting uneasily.

Nothing . . . then, after a moment, the girl gurgled. Stillshadow squinted and sat, *whuffing* down next to the scraped zebra skin. The old woman reached into the deerhide pouch at her waist. Extracting the leaf-wrapped medicines, humming a recipe song, she mixed and rolled them together into a ball, then crushed the pellet beneath the infant's nose, releasing a strong minty aroma.

A moment later, the baby blinked hard. Her eyes wandered away . . . and then back. And then away . . . and then back. And remained on the crone. Not exactly focused, but . . .

Stillshadow moved to the side, and this time the infant's eyes followed more closely. Back the other way. *They followed.*

Strange. She had initially assumed the foundling was blind. With this new development, it seemed almost as if the girl had been waiting for Still-shadow before deigning to focus on things of this world.

The medicine woman gazed up at Great Earth's misty expanse. "Who is this baby?" she asked.

There was no response. She raised her voice. "Do you know this girl-child?"

If the wind was the mountain's voice, Great Mother chose to whisper her reply, and Stillshadow's old ears could not hear. She held the infant up higher. "Who are you?" she asked. "Can you see me? What do you see?"

The child thrashed her arms and legs. The little round brown face wrin-kled up tightly. With a faint liquid sound, greenish curd flowed out of her behind and plopped onto the ground. Stillshadow squinted.

"You shit like a man-child," she said.

The baby smiled at her with infinite satisfaction.

Stillshadow's blood bubbled like water running over rocks. Not two moons ago her waking dreams had whispered of a coming. Could this child be the crucial One she and the other dream dancers had anticipated? But . . . there were other stories, tales that Stillshadow had heard from her teacher, who had heard them from hers.

*We change,* the old stories said. *We are not as strong as once we were. But there will be more. There will be new people. And the old people will die. In time even the gods themselves will die.*

*There will be two, and one will be a girl with no name.*

Sighing with a strange contentment, the crone enfolded the infant in her arms and rose to carry her home.

.    .    .

Originally, Stillshadow had planned to travel farther south to Water boma, but now decided to return to Great Earth. While her guards maintained a respectful distance, she walked with spine erect, carrying her new charge in arms suddenly as strong as they had ever been. "My girls! My girls! I am back, and I have brought a new sister with me. Come out, lazybones!"

Although it was a two-day trek up Great Earth to the ash cone hidden behind her summit, the dream dancer encampment was only a half day above the plain, a steep and beautiful walk between honeysuckle and weeping fig trees, tall blue-green grasses and countless berry vines.

Like other bomas, their camp was ringed with thorn walls. Unlike the camps around Great Earth and Great Sky, the dream dancer camp had been in the same place for a generation, the dancers using their magic and knowledge to keep it clean and free from pests. In all her journeys, Stillshadow had never found another permanent boma.

The waters flowing from Great Sky nurtured a constant source of game and fruit, such that the Ibandi had remained in its shadow for all their history. They traded with other tribes from the north and the east, their people migrants, following the herds and the seasons. Only the Ibandi were rooted, all the proof she needed that they, and no others, were Father Mountain's first and best-loved children.

Dream dancers, chosen at birth, were selected and trained for the clarity of their seven eyes. Although they did not take mates or raise families as the boma folk did, they lay with hunt chiefs and had children, that both flesh and spirit might live on after breath had ceased. But their hearts were trothed to Father Mountain, and their bodies belonged to the people themselves, rather than any mere mortal men.

The wooden lean-tos and huts rustled, and one at a time her students emerged: some small, some of them tall and strong, some as young as five springs, others women old enough to be her sisters. All were curious and powerful, all learning and growing under Stillshadow's protection.

Several of the younger girls approached, accompanied by their teacher, a toothless dreamer named Far Eye. In her youth, Far Eye had been a great walker. Now she rarely roamed far from her hut, and soon, Stillshadow suspected, she would return to the mountain.

Eight-rained Raven grinned as if she had received a present. "Back so soon? We did not expect you until full moon!" She peered more closely at her mother's bundle. "A new dancer? From Fire boma?" Stillshadow watched the girl carefully, knowing that beneath her good spirits, Raven was doubtless of two hearts concerning any new addition to their boma.

Stillshadow shook her head, and Raven's smooth forehead wrinkled. "Then, where does she come from?"

Far Eye spat to the north. "The dream world. Her mother's body. The place all babies come from, silly thing. We need to make room. Bring soft skins, and call your sister. Her milk came down hard, so one more child will be no great burden. Blossom!"

Blossom was Stillshadow's eldest, a broad-hipped, sharp-eyed girl of ten and ten rains. Blossom emerged from her hut. In her strong right arm she carried a drowsy baby nursing from one enormous breast. Her left hand toyed with a half-finished braid. "Far Eye? Mother? You called me?"

"I have another baby for you," Stillshadow said.

"Another baby?" Blossom cut her eyes at the medicine woman slyly. "If I take this baby, someone else will have to take some of my cooking and gathering."

Stillshadow laughed. This one was loyal but lazy, and not half as bright as Raven. Despite her potential, the girl had never fasted and prayed to Great Mother as she should, and her hand and foot eyes had winked closed once again. Now she managed best simply letting her body function in its most basic fashion: eating, sleeping, loving, making and feeding babies. "Yes, and I suppose you will need extra food."

"Yes." Blossom bobbed her head. The loose braid fanned in front of her eyes. "Good. Well, let me see her." She began to inspect the foundling. "All fingers and toes." Blossom peered more closely still, moving her hand before the child's eyes. At first there was no response, but then the small moist lips curled in a smile. The baby gurgled merrily, eyes fixed on the moving fingers.

"Is she the One?" Raven asked, voice a bit nervous.

Stillshadow fished in her deerskin pouch, then crouched and threw the bones, staring at the broken white pieces quizzically. She threw again, and then again. Each time her expression grew more discouraged.

Finally she looked up. "I cannot see her nature," she said.

Raven licked her lips nervously. "Then . . . she cannot be given a name."

Stillshadow scowled and stood, listening to her knees crackle. "So. Until we know her nature, we will call her T'Cori, meaning 'nameless one.' In another moon, perhaps, a totem will come to me. One day she will have her name."

Her students murmured. All of them remembered the story. *A nameless child will come. She heralds the death of gods. . . .*

The child's eyes had gone a bit vacant again, wandering, and the girls were puzzled. "Her face-eyes are strange," Raven said, and kneaded the tiny hands. "I think she sees."

"More than most," the old woman said. "She is new from the dream, closer to Great Mother." She peered into those eyes again, and then smiled.

So tiny. So helpless. With such wide-open eyes in face and hands and feet. Without aid, the child would have been dead within a quarter. But why and how had she survived the night, if someone had left her the previous day? Was she bhan? Had her people been killed, as poor Lizard's had been? Had she been left to perish, or could someone have known that Stillshadow would come along?

Or . . . if not some*one,* then what?

Stillshadow sent her apprentices to their tasks. She needed to make certain the child would be properly nurtured. Only then could the old woman continue her circuit of the inner bomas. At the moment, she noticed that her bones did not feel the usual fatigue, and despite lingering fears about the nameless child's future, that was as good a sign as any that Stillshadow had done the appropriate thing.

# Butterfly Spring

# Chapter Eight

At ten and two springs, Frog Hopping was considered neither a child nor an adult. He considered this a perfect age, with greater freedoms and few responsibilities. Neither disease nor leopards had taken him. Frog had survived an intense fever in his fifth spring. A plague of tiny red mites that had killed two other boma children in his seventh had not crawled in his ear to devour his *num*. He was a fine, knobby, gap-toothed boy the color of spearwood bark, with busy fingers and questing eyes.

Spring Gathering was Frog's favorite time, a time when fortunes were told and dreams were danced by Great Earth's wise and mysterious women. Such frenzied movement seemed to open a door to the sleeping world, the world in which all men spent half their time, a world as rich and varied as that viewed through open, waking eyes.

Some among them even believed that the dream world was the more genuine world, a world in which the four-legged still spoke to men, in which Great Mother and Father Mountain revealed Their faces. Who could truly say which world was more real?

At Spring Gathering, Stalker and the hunt chiefs came down from Great Sky to predict where water and hunting and herbs might best be found. If that lay many days' run from the current locations, then some of the clans might move, or join boma walls as they did in the lean years. Frog knew of no Ibandi who had died from hunger, because the Circle was spread over a large enough area that none of the prey were hunted to death, and the foraging was always good *somewhere*.

At the foot of the eastern edge of Great Earth stood the Life Tree, the largest baobab that any Ibandi had ever seen. Its branches were as wide as the horizon. Its top leaves supported the clouds.

Inscribed in the trunk were tens of symbols dreamed by dream dancers over the years: gnu and elephants and giraffes and clouds and women birthing children, as well as symbols no man could name.

This was the first year that Frog had been allowed to climb the Life Tree. Always in previous years he had been told he was too young, had been forced to watch as the other boys earned their bruises.

Now it was different. Now he waited with others of his age, untried boys hoping to prove their fitness to become hunters, perhaps even hunt chiefs.

Numbering hands of hands, the boys waited in eager rows. Beside Frog, his stepbrother Scorpion, no older but half a head taller, bent and whispered in his ear: "I will push you from the tree," he said. "Today you die."

That was just Scorpion's attempt to make Frog so afraid that he might lose his balance and fall. Scorpion didn't really mean it. Or so Frog hoped.

Then the starting drum began to beat. With a roar, the boys leapt eagerly out toward the great tree.

As a swarm, youngsters jostled and elbowed each other out of the way in a blur of thin, dark limbs, clambering up to the prize: a deerskin tied to one of the highest branches.

With despairing cries, one boy after another tumbled to earth. Most caught branches on the way down, but some few fell twisting onto the heaps of grass and soft branches clustered around the trunk. The grass below the Life Tree grew tall, but mothers sometimes crept out at night to push even more leaves beneath the tree, that their sons not cripple themselves in pursuit of glory. In truth, few were ever badly hurt, although lumps and bumps and sprains were commonplace, and baobab scars the source of mirth and merriment for moons to come.

And here, at last, was an arena in which Frog might outperform his brothers Hawk Shadow and Fire Ant. They were stronger and faster than he, but there was more to the climbing of trees than mere muscle. As one climbed higher and higher, the branches grew thinner, so that a small, skinny tadpole such as Frog actually gained advantage.

"I will catch you!" Fire Ant panted, snarling at him from a branch just an arm's length below. He was making his anger face, a sure sign that Ant was laughing inside. Frog scrambled to another branch, fighting for position with River Song from Water boma. The two boys jostled for the same position, wrestling in midair, and Fire Ant pushed River with his foot. The boy lost his grip, lost his balance and fell, hitting another branch on the way down, which tore skin but broke his fall.

Father *Mountain,* that must have hurt!

Branch by clambered branch, Frog approached the elusive skin, only his stepbrother Scorpion and a smaller boy whom he did not know still even with him.

Scorpion howled as his grip failed, and he slid back down along a branch, scraping a strip of skin from his thigh as he did.

Suddenly Fire Ant was surprisingly close below him, clutching at his leg. Frog broke free and eeled along a narrow branch. Fire Ant followed. In trying to clamber ahead of Frog, he made a mistake: the branch would not hold his weight. Frog had seen this before. Neither of his brothers understood how large and heavy they were. They were so strong that what to another might have seemed clumsy weight was like an ape scampering effortlessly through the forest.

The branch cracked. The Ibandi gathered below screamed with mirth as Fire Ant plunged, scrambling to catch this or that branch to slow himself before smashing into the heaped grass, leaves and branches at the tree's foot.

To much laughter, Fire Ant staggered to his feet and danced a few painful steps to show that he remained unslain.

Rejoicing at his fortune, Frog climbed and climbed, feeling that this time at long last he was in his glory. There remained only one rival to rob him of his victory.

This one was even smaller than young Frog, almost as small as some of the tiny folk who sometimes came in from the outer bomas. He raced among the slender branches like a monkey, with eye-baffling agility and a complete disregard for risk to skull or bones.

His competitor grabbed the deerhide token and scrambled back down the tree. Frog pursued him: if he could catch the boy, snatch the skin and push him from the Life Tree, victory might still belong to Frog. But with breathtaking balance and agility this one leapt from branch to branch, heedless of the risk. Frog scrambled after his rival, but no matter what he tried the boy remained ahead of him, finally jumping down from the lowest branch to land upon the heaped leaves as lightly as a grass mouse.

Only then did Frog hear the hooting from those on the ground, and as the rest of the boys reluctantly returned to ground, he saw what had caused the mirth.

The winner slipped on a headband, and then a shell necklace. He doffed the gazelle skin waistlet and donned a dream dancer's short leather skirt. The boy was a *girl.*

Frog Hopping's cheeks burned.

The crowd cheered for the embarrassment of the groaning boys, even as they simultaneously made wet burring sounds at the girl for doing such a thing. The women were more upset at her than the men, who seemed to find it delicious that their sons had been shown up in such a fashion.

"It serves you right! Climb harder next time!" Uncle Snake called at him, laughing. Even Scorpion and Fire Ant chortled, which confused him. After all, he had beaten them both! What in the name of Great Sky did *they* have to laugh about?

T'Cori was still breathless, but exultant. Never had she climbed so! Surely now she would be given a name: Sunshine Treeclimber, perhaps. She could explore that name, would have no trouble living up to it. A name like that she could be proud of, and maybe her sisters would stop teasing or twisting her hair about a prophecy made generations before she was born.

Most of the dream dancers chided her for her climbing performance. Some frowned, but a few girls stood back, eyes aglow with admiration.

Two, a pair of twin sisters named Dove and Fawn Blossom, made hard faces. "She thinks she can do anything," Dove said.

Her larger sister, Fawn, spat toward Father Mountain. "Stillshadow thinks your eyes are so wide. But look at the old woman's face now! Did you see *this* trouble, Nameless?"

She hushed her voice as Stillshadow shuffled forward to face the girl. T'Cori gazed up at the old medicine woman. Despite Fawn's words, T'Cori's face gleamed with perspiration and joy. Would today be her naming day? Perhaps Stillshadow would even call her daughter! The thought thrilled her, for T'Cori loved Stillshadow with her whole heart.

The dream dancer extended her hand, palm up. "This is not a thing for women," she said, voice thin with fury.

"But—"

"No!" The single word was very nearly a scream. "Look at me, girl! Feel my fire. What do you see?"

The happy expression on T'Cori's face flattened, died. Never had T'Cori felt such anger from her mentor, and she fought the urge to turn, to run away. Instead, she crossed her eyes slightly, blurring her visual field. Instantly, Stillshadow's *num*-fire appeared, spiked and burning red, the solid masses churning within proclaiming both age and anger. "I—I am sorry," she began, but Stillshadow cut her off.

"Everything under the sky has its place, and that place is good. Do not seek to change what you do not understand. You have entertained your sisters and shamed the young hunters. Do you think that you make them stronger, braver, wiser by doing such things?"

"But, Mother—" she said, and then stopped herself. Only the medicine woman's actual daughters were allowed to address her so.

The flat of Stillshadow's palm cracked across the nameless girl's cheek. Pain, bright and sharp, flared suddenly. Worse by far than the pain were the shame and humiliation, coming so soon after a moment of victory.

The crone's face was set in stone. "Now I see why Great Mother denies you a name. There is none so low that you would not shame it."

Tears started from T'Cori's worshipful eyes. The crone's hand reached out again, and the girl flinched. But instead of striking her, the wrinkled palm turned upward, and Stillshadow merely said: "The skin."

The girl handed her the deerhide that she had taken from the top of the baobab tree, by rights the mark of her victory.

Stillshadow handed the skin to Raven. "Burn it," she said. The old woman's daughter, tall and graceful, her hair more beautifully braided than any other Ibandi woman's, took the striped prize in her hands, bowed slightly, and without a backward glance walked toward the fire.

T'Cori tried to turn away, but Stillshadow's hand fell on her shoulder. "And, girl," the dream dancer said, voice flat and cold, "don't call me mother."

The nameless one sobbed as the crowd dispersed. Their initial amusement had transformed into shame, embarrassment and anger at the entire business. Even the young dream dancers who had cheered now echoed Stillshadow's mood, sneering, unwilling or unable to remember that just moments ago their delight had been as great as hers.

Of all the mockery that Frog endured, beyond a doubt his sister Little Brook's was the worst. "You beat your brothers but lose to a *girl*?" she asked, her voice like a sharp stone. "Just wait for the next time Uncle tells you to obey me. You won't finish your chores until the moon sets." Anger and shame sat in his belly like a stone, like a bad nut that he could not pass. His head knew that the emotions would eventually fade, but his heart said, *This is always. They will never let you forget.*

.    .    .

That night, Stillshadow tossed and turned, struggling to find her way to the world of dreams. She regretted humiliating the nameless one. The girl was usually meek and obedient, but spirited when it came to running and climbing games. This was fine when she confined such competitive urges to her sisters, but it was not right to shame the young men. Such doings would bring nothing but grief. If she had not struck the girl, Raven and Blossom would have taken it upon themselves to punish her later, in secret. So such things were best done publicly.

But then . . . T'Cori was different. Stillshadow's own teacher, Night Bird, had said that people in the old days could speak to animals in the world of flesh as well as dream. T'Cori, the nameless one, was like that. She saw the fire, read the *num*-flames without tricks or teaching, more easily than anyone Stillshadow had ever known.

But that did not change one important fact: there was a line between women's things and men's things, a line to be crossed only at peril. Why were the men willing to risk their lives hunting? One thing and one thing only kept them on guard between the lions and the boma: the fact that such dangerous tasks were matters of masculine honor and pride. Women were born to the mysteries of childbirth, and no man, however worthy, could step into that circle. When women began to do men's things it caused confusion, fear and pain, upsetting the balance that had kept the world as it was since the first Ibandi walked from Great Mother's womb.

If Stillshadow did not control her dream dancers, Cloud Stalker would have to do it, and that she could not allow. Hunt chiefs provided meat, protection, companionship. Any of these might be withdrawn if Stalker was angry. And what might that do to their relationship? Her love for Cloud Stalker no longer burned with the sexual heat of their youth, but his touch still soothed. What if he declined to sleep with her? True, he would be punishing himself, but he would find young women eager to sleep with him more easily than she would find worthy young men. However much she might hate that truth, truth it remained.

Stillshadow rolled up to sitting and then crawled out of her little temporary lean-to at the edge of the Gathering. Beneath her, the rows of huts stretched as far as the eye could see, faded to paleness by the night and the full moon.

She found her way to the hut where the girls slept. Stillshadow studied them carefully, confident that she would swiftly spy T'Cori's sleeping form.

The girl was so small, even now at ten and two rains, that when she curled into a ball, her thumb thrust into her mouth, she resembled a baby still.

No, she was not there.

Stillshadow felt no alarm. She knew where she would find the girl, and backed out of the hut without making a sound. She walked through the camp, hearing the occasional snore and murmur, a few low grunts and slapping wet sex sounds, some whispered conversations.

The camp was at rest, or at play, save for two. Herself, and . . .

*Yes, there.*

The Life Tree tossed in a gentle midnight wind, the topmost branches swaying in a peaceful rhythm deceptive enough to lull one almost to sleep. There at the top, barely visible to Stillshadow's tired old eyes, clung T'Cori, the nameless one. She had climbed so high that perhaps no one else in all the tribe could have surpassed her. The girl was as light as a child, but as strong as a young man.

In times past Stillshadow had wondered why the girl spent so much of her time in solitude, climbing among the cliffs and trees.

Now, watching the baobab's branches swaying in the night wind, she understood. There, careening at the very height of the tree, T'Cori raised her arms up to Great Sky. There, at the top of the tree, the foundling called out wordlessly to the mother of all to be the mother of one, to pluck her up and take her to a world where she might find greater peace and acceptance.

Stillshadow found a place to sit, and watched as the Life Tree's branches bent back and forth, the girl held her arms out to the misty mountain, and the moon looked down on all.

She understood. The climbing was a kind of prayer. Great Sky's white-shrouded summit must seem so close to the girl, close enough almost to reach out and touch. And that must be very nearly more than T'Cori's aching heart could bear.

Stillshadow did not sleep that night, watching the girl and the tree with heavy, anxious eyes. At last she heard the old dream dancers singing their sun song, and the first pink flush of dawn painted the eastern horizon. T'Cori climbed back down. She saw Stillshadow, perhaps, but did not speak to her, and crawled into a lean-to of sticks and hide for whatever sleep she might manage before the new day's songs and struggles began.

# Chapter Nine

Two days later, Stillshadow found T'Cori weaving a basket streamside with Far Eye and Blossom. All greeted the old woman, but T'Cori still could not meet her gaze.

With a sigh, Stillshadow sat next to her and plucked up a reed from the side of the stream, her fingers automatically beginning to weave.

"I was thinking of dancing a story tonight at the fire, T'Cori," she said.

"What story is that, honored one?"

"I think you have heard it before, when you were younger. It is the story of Medicine Mouse," she said.

Blossom laughed. "That is a good one," she said. "A good one."

"I don't think I know it," T'Cori said.

"Ah, then you would be a perfect judge for me." Stillshadow stood, inhaled slowly, and began to dance.

Her hands, her hips, her face and eyes, her song all told the story, and the nameless girl was swiftly pulled into its spell:

*Once upon a time there was a hyrax named Medicine Mouse. She was a great healer, and all of the creatures of the forest depended upon her for the herbs and knowledge that kept them well. But she gave more than that. She also taught them the wisdom of life, which she had learned from her mother, who had learned it from hers, and on back until the beginning of time.*

*One day, Medicine Mouse was walking through the forest and happened upon a black crake. Crake lay exhausted between the trees, a sack tied to her feet. From the tracks, she had dragged it a long long way, and could carry it no farther.*

"*What are you doing here?*" Medicine Mouse said. "*You should fly away. A snake will find you and have a fine supper.*"

"*I cannot move, I am too tired,*" Crake said. Her black feathers were crusted with salt sweat, her white bill flecked with dried spittle.

"*What happened to you?*" asked Medicine Mouse, thinking that perhaps some terrible disease had cursed her friend.

"*Oh, it is a sad story,*" Crake said. "*I was flying through the forest and struck my head upon a branch. It hurt so much that I promised myself I would never do that again. And the best way I could think of to make certain that would never happen is to break the branch off and carry it with me, so I did.*

"*I flew away, carrying the branch, and although I wasn't able to fly quite so quickly, my heart was gladdened, knowing I would never strike that branch again. But it made me clumsy, so that I struck a tree trunk. Angered, I swore I would never strike that trunk again, and tore the chunk of bark away, placing it in my sack for protection.*

"*The sack was heavy by this time, and I could not fly, but that is all right, because I run very well! I ran and ran, carrying my sack, until I tripped over a rock. I put the rock in my sack, which was by now very very heavy, and dragged it behind me. By now, I seemed to hit my head and stub my feet on everything, and even though I put everything that hurt me in the sack, there were more and more mistakes. And then I was exhausted, and the sack was too heavy to carry, so I wait here. I will catch my strength,*" Crake said. "*And then I will go on.*"

Medicine Mouse thought about all that she had heard, and finally said, "*I have an answer to your problem. I have here a sacred knife, and with it I can cut away the bag, and bless the contents, so that none of them will ever bother you again.*"

"*Oh, would you?*" Crake said, and lay quietly as Medicine Mouse did her magic. She cut and cut, and then blessed. Her friend Crake thanked her, and then shook out her wings and flew away.

Medicine Mouse buried the sack, as Crake should have done from the beginning. Then, singing a healing song, she continued on her way.

"What do you think of the story?" Stillshadow asked, breathing hard as her dance ended.

T'Cori stirred her finger in the water and then met her eyes squarely for the first time in days. "I think it is a very good one," she said. Tears flowed from her eyes, and she threw her arms around her teacher's neck, giving her a hug.

Then Stillshadow went away, leaving Blossom and Far Eye and T'Cori at the riverside. And as she did, she heard laughter behind her, and knew that it was good.

Two days later, Uncle Snake and a few of the men took Frog and other boys out from the Gathering to teach them the ways of hunting and surviving in Great Sky's shadow. This was a tradition, another sign that Frog was traversing the invisible meridian between child and man. The plan was to stay out for several nights, traveling southwest.

He struggled to match his own small stride to Uncle Snake's long, easy steps. Scorpion stayed even with them, perhaps jealous of any time Frog and Snake spent together. Snake's own wife had died the year before the lions had killed Baobab, and after his wounds healed, he had married Frog's mother and hunted for his nephews and nieces, folding his own son and daughter into the extended family.

Scorpion, Frog believed, had always resented them.

For the last quarter of the second day, Snake had seemed unusually alert as they walked through a patch of shrub-spotted sand. "What are we looking for, Father?" Scorpion asked.

"Earlier this year I made friends," Snake said, turning his blind left eye to them. "We hunted together, and all ate well. I promised to return."

The sun was near the western horizon, where a tiny dot appeared on the plain before them, slowly swelling into the aged walls of a small, dirty boma, a disorganized web of mismatched branches and uprooted thornbushes. "Ho!" Snake called, repeating his cry again and again until three short, knobby folk appeared in the gateway.

By Frog's reckoning, these bahn could not have been good hunters. To his young eyes they looked hungry and not well. Their skin was too tight around their skulls, their eyes huge but cloudy, their skin pocked with boils and disease scars. It felt strange to be near them, almost as if they were not even bhan, not quite people at all. As if they were smaller than but similar to the hulking beast-men Frog had occasionally glimpsed at the edges of a festival, crouched and hairy and ugly, gathering the Ibandi leavings and then scampering away rather than challenging or interacting.

Through a series of postures and hand signs, Uncle Snake communicated his desire for parley. The bhan children seemed fascinated by the deep, beautiful scarring on the left side of Snake's face and were too simple-minded to pretend otherwise.

Scorpion shied away from them, his shoulder brushing Frog's. "They stink," his stepbrother said.

"Shhh," said Frog. "They have ears."

"But do they have noses? They stink!"

And it was true. The boma smelled bad, as if they were too ignorant to shovel dirt over their scat. Their bones jutted beneath the skin, and their teeth didn't seem to fit in their jaws properly, and the bones in their fingers were twisted. Tiny blue flies crawled on the whites of their babies' eyes.

The village leader's name was Silent Warthog, a twisted man barely Frog's height. Warthog was hospitable enough but had little to share save lizards and rats that any child or beast-man might have caught. Frog noticed that Uncle Snake managed to actually leave more food than he took. A good trick, he thought. Snake's single good eye saw more than most men's pair.

They were offered space within the rude thorn walls, but Snake declined.

"I thank you," he said. "But these boys need to sleep beneath the sky, learn to build fires and shelters. I will return to enjoy your hospitality another moon."

After additional polite conversation, their little group moved out into the gathering darkness. Frog was grateful. The stench would have made sleep impossible.

They walked until the boma was out of sight, and then Snake stopped them and they cut thornbushes, built fire and prepared for sleep. Beneath the open sky Frog tossed uneasily.

With the unconscious cruelty so common among children, he chuckled to himself at the poverty and weak-mindedness of the hapless bhan. Why had Uncle taken them there? His people had no need for their food or shelter. Why? And then he thought he understood. It was so he might thank Father Mountain for creating the Ibandi with such power and beauty. Feeling deep shame for his prior thoughts, Frog rolled over onto his back, staring up into the clouds, promising himself that he would give extra thanks to Father Mountain come next ceremony.

And then he slept, his last fuzzy thoughts of the boma's stink.

If he'd known then that he would never see most of those bahn alive again, dreams might not have come so easily.


The next morning, Uncle Snake gathered them into a circle after their wrestling and breakfast. "Our bows are strong," he said. "But when we climbed Great Sky, Father Mountain taught us to make our arrows stronger still."

He lowered his voice. His empty eye socket and the web of scars over the stump of his left ear gave his words an eerie authority. "You must be careful with what we will teach you. One touch, and you can die."

Uncle Snake's lion-scarred eye was a knot of dead tissue, but his keen right eye missed nothing. He seemed a flowing fountain of knowledge, constantly pointing out plants and spiders that could be used to make death medicine, reminding them over and over that everything they saw, everything they touched, was alive. Still, none of the plant or animal death-spirits in this place was quite strong enough; none was the kind used by the Ibandi.

He sang endlessly of grubs and toads but only became truly excited when they came upon a dry river wash. There, growing at a lean, was a bush as high as Frog's chest with straggly black branches festooned with little green berries. "The poison-grub plant." Smiling, he crouched to scratch at its roots.

Swiftly, Uncle Snake found several brown cylinders resembling curled dried leaves. "Poison cocoon," he whispered. "Don't wake them. If they die sleeping, they go directly to Father Mountain and bless His arrows." The boys all gathered closely around. Very carefully, he plucked up a cocoon, squeezing it between thumb and forefinger. The pinkish pulp oozed over the arrow's tip.

"This is the weakest poison, but still better than nothing," he said.

"How do we make it stronger?" Frog asked.

Uncle Snake scrubbed Frog's head. "We learn that soon. Now, put the pulp just behind the arrow's point."

"Why?" Frog asked.

The other boys laughed.

"So that if you nick yourself, you will not die!" Snake answered.

So all of them did this, and Snake squeezed sap from the poison-grub plant and mixed it with the insect pulp. He taught them different ways to do it, and how to add certain red-jawed beetles to increase the effectiveness. As he ground them together with the gray, sour-smelling bark of what Snake called a stinger bush, he told them what he knew of its effects. "If you are struck by your own arrow, you will get fever but feel cold. You will have thirst no water can quench. Your piss will turn brown."

Frog felt as if he could sense the poison in his blood even then.

"Your head hurts, and you will grow hungry for air," Snake concluded. "And then you die."

"Is there a cure?" Frog asked.

"The dream dancers have cures, if you can reach them. Better not to be stuck," he said, and then rolled the tips of his arrows in a brownish paste.

Snake led them on a hunt, and within a quarter day hushed them and pointed through the bamboo at a large spotted deer. In absolute silence, he notched an arrow, drew his bowstring, and fired. The deer bucked as it felt the strike, turned, and ran so quickly that Frog hadn't time to blink.

To Frog's surprise, it did not die at once. Was not the poison strong? He had been warned so many times not to touch it, and the things his uncle had taught chilled his blood. Always, he had imagined that a single touch would bring death at the gallop. But the deer was disappearing into the brush.

Disappointed but game, the boys began to sprint after it. "There is no need to run," Uncle Snake said. "Save your wind."

So they tracked it, slowly and steadily, and before the sun touched the horizon came upon the numbed and dying deer. Its sides heaved as they approached, gazing at them with eyes that, even as they watched, grew more glazed and distant, duller and less reflective of light. It was too weak, frightened, or resigned even to resist as Snake sliced its throat with his sliver of black stone.

"Thank you, my brother," he whispered in its ear. "May your spirit fly to the mountain. May you have green grass and look down on your rutting grandchildren with pride. Thank you."

Its flanks grew still.


There was time for the boys to explore, always with at least one partner, more often in threes. Frog found himself partnered with Scorpion, who led them back to the poison-grub plant.

"See what I can do," he said, and as Frog watched, Scorpion sharpened a stick and ground several of the poison grubs into a mass, tarring the tip with their guts.

"What are you going to do?" Frog asked. At times, his stepbrother seemed cruel merely for the sake of cruelty. He had seen Scorpion burn beetles with a flaming stick, just to watch them struggle.

"Just watch," Scorpion said, pointing at a small green lizard. Fast as his namesake's striking stinger he was on the hapless creature, stabbing it through the tail. Frog had seen lizards shed their hindquarters and run away, and he hoped that this would be one of that variety. It was not.

Scorpion left it pinned there in the sun, watching carefully as it shivered and shook. Frog felt sickened. It was an affront to Father Mountain to kill a living creature except for protection or food. This was disgusting.

"I will not watch this," he said.

"You are soft," Scorpion said. "It will be the death of you."

Frog left Scorpion there toying with the dying reptile, a small, cold, satisfied smile on his stepbrother's face.

That night they built a fire, and its flare attracted two other hunters who had been far to the east and were traveling to Spring Gathering. They shared their kills and, together with Uncle Snake, danced stories of the hunt.

Frog did not know them, although he had seen them at prior gatherings. They were lean and honorably scarred on both cheeks. The way they postured, mimed and contorted themselves so that their shadows flew like arrows, seeming to capture the very spirits of the animals they had stalked, told Frog that these were men of formidable skill.

Uncle Snake seemed to know these men well, and let them share knowledge of gutting kills, of smoking meat, of songs from distant peoples. The shorter man taught them knots by firelight, saying, "Your elders will teach you many good knots, but each of you will devise your own. They will be your mark, and when you make traps, tie them with your knots and other hunters will know who the meat belongs to."

Frog found himself watching not the dance but the play of light and darkness. While the other boys were lost in the facts and fantasies, Frog etched images on the ground, thinking of shadows.

Shadows. Men. Shadow-images of men. What were they? Fire was alive, he knew. It ate, it breathed, it died if drowned or neglected. It roared with anger through the brush, it drove game and was given a portion of the food in reward.

But what were shadows? They might be the soul-force, some form of *num* . . . he wasn't certain, and had never heard a story that really helped him understand. But when he stared at them, he thought of sacred drawings on Great Earth's rocks and trees and wanted to make such images himself.

Frog shook himself from his reverie. The two visiting hunters had retired for the evening, and Uncle Snake had stopped dancing. His muscular torso gleamed in the firelight. "Men are weaker than beasts," he said, panting. "But we have fire! And we have spears! And by the shadow of Great Sky, we choose what will live—" His right hand opened. Within it lodged a black pebble. The boys groaned in appreciation. "And what will die!" He opened his left, revealing a white pebble.

"My father is a great magician!" Scorpion whispered to Frog. Frog said nothing, irritated that Scorpion would say "my" instead of "our."

Even distracted by thought, it seemed he had been the only one to see Uncle Snake take the pebbles from his waist pouch as he danced. Had no one else glimpsed that furtive motion? The other boys remained entranced. No, they had seen nothing. Then Snake sank to the ground in ritual conclusion. The boys drummed their feet on the ground in appreciation.

Snake's single eye peered up, locked with Frog's.

Uncle Snake knew that Frog knew.

And Frog knew that if he said nothing about it, neither would Uncle Snake.

At night they lay back against their skins, and Frog pointed up at the clouds. "It looks like a baobab," he said.

Scorpion squinted. "How do you see that?"

"You cannot see it?" Frog asked. He pointed up at one foamy edge. "The trunk, there. And the edges are branches. And the stars are like shrikes, perched on the branches."

For a moment Frog thought that Scorpion understood, might answer with his own discovery. That would be good, to have at least one brother, or stepbrother, who could see what he saw.

Instead, Scorpion said: "If you are trying to fool me, I will beat you." Genuine anger made his voice brittle.

"Perhaps I was mistaken," Frog said, and stretched upon his hide and tried to sleep.

In the morning, his stepfather let the visiting hunters lead the boys through a variety of rolls and movements designed to stretch and strengthen their bodies, to prepare them for wrestling. "Watch the monkeys when they awaken!" Uncle Snake said as they suffered. "They do not just get up and spring for a sunfruit. They bend and twist and yawn and stretch. Look at the great cats. They stretch before they hunt, and before they lay down, and they are greater killers than men. We must learn from them." His ravaged face made it impossible to dispute his hard-won knowledge. Some of the other boys thought the wounds were terrifying. Frog found them beautiful.

So, thought Frog, these were the lessons of the hunt chiefs and the boma fathers. It was good to hear these secrets, the things that men knew. Perhaps when he knew more of them he would no longer be afraid of Scorpion and the larger boys.

One at a time, Snake wrestled with the newcomers, and they demonstrated how hunters grew strong in the northern bomas. Then they taught the boys. Frog lost more than he won, of course, but he lost "pretty," which was considered better than winning "ugly," or without grace, as Scorpion often did. And of that, he was justly proud.

Afterward, they breakfasted and then left for the hunt, Frog feeling as springy and light as his namesake.

"See this indentation?" Uncle Snake brushed his fingertip against a cloven zebra print at the root of a nettle-bush, stopping it at a tiny break in the smooth, rounded edge. "It means that the hoof is cracked. He has been in dry land. Little water to drink. Walking over rocks. That crack means that he cannot run well. Track him. This one is ready go to the mountain."

Snake lowered his face to the ground and sniffed. "Tell me," he said. "What are the other prints?"

Frog studied the ground. He knew what his uncle was asking. A hunter had to stalk one animal at a time. If another beast was unlucky enough to come across his path, and in so doing to offer up its flesh and spirit, then so be it. A true hunter studied scat, prints, weather, territory and tools. He understood that the morning's wrestling was not merely exercise for the body but a way of knowing the strengths and weaknesses of his brother hunters as well. At a glance, he had to recognize the individual animals in a herd, determine their health and mood, and choose the ones who were the best bet.

Zebras were a mainstay of Ibandi cooking. Frog knew that they lived in groups, like men. Unlike humans, they loved the company of other animals: gnu, ostriches, antelopes and wildebeest. This was good: tracking a zebra meant opportunities for a fruitful, belly-bursting hunt.

Frog could not throw a spear as far as his fellows, or run as fast, but he remembered everything, and could separate tracks made one upon another upon another. What he learned here, he would never forget. "Oryx, kongoni, gazelles, eland and serval," his strong, wise uncle said, pointing out indecipherable impressions in a bewildering tangle of tracks. The eland tracks were a bit like the zebra tracks, the oryx's were more heart-shaped, and the serval's four toes made it easy to mark out.

Scorpion blinked. "How do you do that, Father?" Some of the other boys nodded their own confusion.

Frog kept his thoughts to himself. How could the others *not* see?

"Open your face-eyes. Practice," Snake said. "Who can tell me when zebras begin to mate?"

No answer from the other boys. Snake's single eye seemed to look right through Frog. *I know you know. Tell me.*

"The third spring," he replied.

Snake grinned and ruffled Frog's hair affectionately.

"How many young are born at a time?"

Frog did not answer, although the eyes of his fellows were upon him. *One,* he thought.

"One?" Scorpion finally ventured.

Uncle Snake nodded and led them on. Scorpion puffed his chest out. "See?" he said to his stepbrother. "You don't know everything."

"You are right," Frog said. "I still have much to learn."

Scorpion seemed to walk a little straighter and stronger for quite some time.


The sun was directly overhead as they crouched in tall brush, peering out at the dusty plain, a stretch of lightning-burned grass.

"How many in a group, Uncle?" Frog asked.

Snake squinted his good right eye. "One to four hands," he said.

A younger Frog had imagined all zebra to be much the same, but under Snake's painstaking tutelage he knew them to be of infinite variety, each with its own temperament, stripe pattern and length of mane. Each had a slightly different eating and sleeping cycle. Narrow, short, long, they were as individual as faces in the boma.

Some zebra had narrow and closely spaced stripes covering most of the body and extending down to the hooves. Mountain zebras, found in Great Sky's foothills, had narrower bars on the body than on the rump, like plains zebra. Some had little striping at all.

The flesh of plains zebras often sizzled on Ibandi spits, and their skins made broad-striped coverings for Ibandi huts. Their hues ranged from black to dark brown on a white to buff background. In some cases, there was shadowing on the flank and rump between the dark and white striping.

One precious day at a time, Frog Hopping learned his lessons.


·    ·    ·

Late that day, they came to the edge of a vast, burned clearing, and in that space Uncle Snake shushed them and had them hunker down to watch as, distantly, two leopards stalked four gazelles. The quartet faced the boys, chewing at the new growth while making certain the humans were distant enough to pose no threat. They seemed not to see the leopards at all.

The cats were to the side, mostly hidden in the grass. One breath at a time, they edged closer to their prospective meals.

"Watch carefully," Uncle Snake said. "The leopards are fast and strong but also smart. They do not waste their *num*. The leopards will get close before they spring."

Frog didn't know who to cheer for. The gazelles? The leopards? The cats edged around the burned grass, and by instinct or cunning they kept a tree between themselves and a gazelle with a slight limp.

Yes! To Frog's delight he realized that he had detected the animal's weakness, even without Snake's urging. He was a hunter!

When Frog's nerves were at the edge of breaking, the leopards sprang. The four gazelles all spotted the cats at the same time, and the chase was on.

Three of them vanished into the grass, but the fourth was cut off by the male leopard, and in doubling back fell into the claws of the female. The dust hadn't settled before Frog saw that its throat was in the female's jaws. More dust flew as its legs scrabbled. It seemed to Frog that the leopards were oddly gentle, almost as if they were protecting the terrified beast as it settled down into death.

"Sometimes the hunter wins," Uncle Snake said, watching, "and sometimes the prey."

"Uncle Snake, which are we?" Frog asked.

"Both," Snake replied. "We are both."


"The first to complete his bow wins a song," Snake said.

This was an important moment. Frog had been given bows before, but not allowed to make his own. Not until now. A hunter in the brush always brought his tools with him, but sometimes it was necessary to improvise.

Snake gave each boy a measure of dried and stretched antelope gut. Their only tool was the stone knife all Ibandi boys carried in their waist pouch. All the rest they were obliged to find themselves.

Frog searched until he found a sapling that spoke to him, whispering, *I am the one,* in the plant language a hunter could hear only with his heart.

With his stone knife, following instructions given by Uncle Snake and the other boma males countless times, he whittled it into the perfect shape and length. From his heel to his shoulder it stood.

He attached the antelope gut, looping it over notches at either end of the bow. He slipped the gut over one of the tips, set his foot against the secured end and bent it, slipping a loop around the other end. When he released the tension it sprang to life, filled with energy and power, awaiting his touch.

His chest swelled with pride. His first bow! It would spend more time unstrung than strung, of course. He did not want the life to leak out of the wood.

Frog presented his creation to Uncle Snake, who examined it without expression. Doubtless he would have enjoyed it if Frog had been swifter to complete his task. Instead, he was the fourth of eight. Scorpion had been faster, and Frog thought his bow looked better as well.

One at a time, Snake urged the boys to test their new weapons. Scorpion's eye and arm were strong: he hit the stump of a lightning-burned tree with little effort. Frog hung back, hoping that Snake would forget him, but had no such luck.

"Here is an arrow," Snake said to Frog. "Hit that rock."

Frog drew, aiming where Snake had indicated. He felt the sweat start from under his arms—not from the heat, although the sun was broiling them all. His cousins watched, eyes sharp and curious.

Frog aimed as carefully as possible, pulled the string back and let fly, missing the rock by a handsbreadth.

"Practice," Uncle Snake said. The right side of his mouth curled up in a smile. "Good, but no song."

After they had finished, Snake gathered the boys around. In the dust they drew images of buffalo and antelope, simplified so that they looked little like Father Mountain's four-legged except perhaps for the horns.

"I will show you special signs, signs you must know," said Snake.

"Why?" asked Lion Tooth, a boy from Wind boma. Lion Tooth wore a necklace of gleaming cat fangs, and chopped his hair so that it was short on the sides and high along the back of his head, like a lion's mane. Five years older than Frog, he had accompanied Uncle Snake on his outing as an assistant.

"Because tongues change, but the signs are more constant," Snake answered. "You can go horizon to horizon and farther still, meet bhan and other men. Those you meet may not speak as we do, but they will understand the signs."

The other boys nodded, but Frog repeated Lion's question. "Why?"

"Because all men live the same life," he said. "We are born. We grow. We mate, father children." With each of these words, his fingers traced lines in the dust, images representing these states of life. "We grow old and die."

"All men do these things?" Frog asked.

"All men."

Frog thought carefully. "Why do we have to die?" he asked.

With a hint of exasperation, Uncle Snake drew them around him in a circle, and beneath the full moon, he danced them a story.

*Once, a long long time ago, there was a tribe who lived beside a lake. They were much beloved by the sun and the moon, and by Great Mother and Father Mountain. One day after they had placed a beloved medicine woman in the ground they asked: "Why must we die?"*

*Father and Mother had pity on them and gave them the gift of eternal life. So they lived and they loved, and nothing could kill them, and they lost fear. When they lost fear they made mistakes while hunting, and often slept holding starving children, their swollen bellies protesting the lack of food.*

*Next, they lost love. When no one died, they lost the joy of new life, for the children. Husbands and wives no longer made love to each other, because they were busy exploring and playing games.*

*But as time went on, all that could be learned in life had been learned. There was nothing to do, no adventures to have. They cared not about one another, and they forgot their hunting, so that much of the time they were cold, and hungry, and alone.*

*They lived on, and with no fear of death their days at length lost their spice, and life lost its color.*

*One at a time they went to Mother and Father. They prayed in the shadow of Great Sky, asking Great Mother to give them any gift that would make them love and learn and taste life once again.*

*She gave them Death.*

*And this time, they understood, and were grateful.*

"Signs," Snake spoke in conclusion. "We hunt. We build fire. We fight against animals and men. We walk far. Each of these things we do, and all men do. If you know these signs, you can speak to others who have the knowledge."

"I will study," Frog said. "Who makes the signs?"

"They have always been."

"Could one make new signs?'

Uncle Snake looked at Frog with something close to suspicion. "Why? There are no new things. All that is has always been."

"Always?"

"Always." He stopped, and seemed to take Frog's question more seriously. "I tell you what. Find one of these 'new things' and bring it to me. Then we will speak."

## Chapter Ten

As the group turned northward, they retraced their steps such that Frog knew they would eventually pass the bhan boma a second time. Regretting his earlier, unkind thoughts, Frog promised himself to leave some bit of food behind, as had Uncle Snake.

Suddenly, without consciously understanding how he knew, Frog became aware that something was wrong. He sniffed the air, catching the scent of burnt wood and something else, something that churned his stomach. The wind shifted, and the smell came to him more clearly: burnt flesh.

It was only later that his eyes detected the first plume of smoke.

Frog's fists tightened as he glimpsed the first burned hut. Holes and gaps were torn in the thorn walls, as if some kind of desperate fight had raged within. He could almost hear the screams drifting in the wind. The stink of their terror drowned out that of their scat and piss. The burned and mutilated bodies of the small, strange, sickly people were sprawled around the sand as if life had never burned in their eyes at all. Men, women, children. All dead. Snake and the hunters entered so carefully they might have been stalking leopards. Only after they searched carefully did they allow the boys to enter.

"There are terrible things in the world," Uncle Snake said. The death on the left side of his face seemed to have distorted the right. "I am sorry that you must learn of them so young, but the time has come. Come, see." Frog retched, his mind and stomach overwhelmed. Some of the other boys also lost their food, and no one shamed them.

Frog walked so softly he barely left footprints, looking at everything, eyes wide as he passed the bloodied corpses. He had never seen violent death before, although he had seen dead babies, and Hot Tree's eldest daughter had succumbed to fever two summers past.

He gasped as he approached their hearth: someone had emptied his bowels atop the stones. No question: that was *human* scat lumped in the ashes. The insult was almost beyond imagining.

Frog poked at the dark lump with a dried willow stick. These invaders were human—judging by the size and texture of their scat, large men who ate generous portions of meat. His attention was drawn to a few interesting flecks of vegetable matter, which he probed with the tip of his stick. *There . . .* little white seeds speckled within. He didn't recognize them at all.

Frog examined the feces, their thickness, the dryness at the surface and the moistness within. Remembering the previous day's blazing heat, he decided that this violation had happened yesterday.

Then Scorpion yelled, "What are you doing, staring at shit! Come! Wounded man!" and Frog sprinted to the boma's torn gate in time to see one of the hunters dragging in a wounded bhan on a bloody zebra skin.

It was Silent Warthog, who just days ago had held a sick, flyblown baby in his arms and offered them shelter, however poor.

Scorpion was shaking. Frog had never seen his stepbrother like this, shivering and weak. Frog touched his shoulder in sympathy, and Scorpion took his hand, held it tightly.

The bhan's face was smeared crimson, masked in blood. Even in the fading light, the left side of his head seemed unnaturally flat. "Where did you find him?" Snake asked.

The hunter gestured toward the south.

Lion Tooth twisted his necklace nervously. "If this man's family is dead, he should be dead as well, protecting them."

Hawk Shadow shrugged. "Look at his wounds. He did his part. Perhaps they thought him dead."

"Run and tell the healers to prepare. We must take him to the dream dancers," Uncle Snake said at last. "We must know what happened to him."

Frog ran with Lion Tooth, struggling to match the older boy's effortless stride with his own shorter, weaker legs. By the time the sun had shifted a quarter in the sky, he thought he would die. Lion Tooth reminded him to exhale continuously, using hyena breathing's relentless *huh-huh-huh* to drive himself onward.

His eyes scanned the brush wildly as they passed. He could smell death all around them. Here? There? Where were the slayers? Behind them even now? Watching from concealment?

"Run," Lion Tooth said. "Breathe. You think too much, Frog. Thought steals your *num*."

So Frog ran until he hurt, and the pain drove the fear away.

They encountered a group of hunters from Wind and Water bomas, out on a friendly running game. Relaying their message, Frog and Lion could finally stop, heaving for breath as their cousins turned and ran back toward Spring Gathering, carrying the message to Great Earth.

Returning, Frog found that the others had already built a sled on which to carry the wounded Warthog, and begin moving him west toward Great Earth.

A mature dream dancer named Bamboo Flower intercepted them before the next morning's sun was fully born.


They took Warthog into Spring Gathering's healing hut, and while preparations were being made, the boys who had been on walkabout were allowed to observe.

Silent Warthog thrashed in slow agony. He bucked, body arching, every muscle pulled taut. Frog guessed that the bhan was dying, despite the herbs the dancers fed him and the liquid, red and thicker than blood, that he drank from a pouch made of eland skin.

After that last drink Warthog did seem to calm a bit. Then, with effort, he drew a symbol on the ground with his fingertip.

It looked like a stick-figure of a man, with a buffalo's horns. Then red drooled from the bhan's mouth, and he howled.

Hawk Shadow crouched to crawl through the door, coming to stand beside Frog. Hawk had grown into a proud, tall young hunter, his two parallel manhood scars newly scabbed upon his cheeks. Round-faced and more muscular even than Fire Ant, Hawk moved as silently as his namesake, and had a physical confidence that Frog could only dream of.

Hawk peered at the sign in the dirt with narrowed eyes. "What is this?"

Hearing him, the elders spoke. "Beast-men," they said. Break Spear nodded sagely. "We know that for moons, a clan of beast-men have camped on Great Sky's western slopes. We let them stay. Now, see what they do!"

Warthog's eyes seemed to focus a bit. He shivered but seemed no longer in pain. Frog wondered what ground and fermented miracle the pouch had contained.

His wounds were packed with herbs and bound with sweet grass. Snake and the hunt chiefs prayed and sang over him.

"Do I die?" he asked finally, as if it had taken all his strength to form those three words.

The medicine man looked at the elders and then back again. "All men die," he said.

Little comfort, thought Frog. Not all men would die before their next dawn.

# Chapter Eleven

The healing hut was a temporary structure of bamboo and grasses built at the center of Spring Gathering. Within its cooling shadows, T'Cori knelt and watched as Stillshadow crouched over Deep Dry Hole's thrashing body. The hunter from Fire boma trembled and gnashed at his lips, and a trace of white foam formed at the corners of his mouth. His *num*-fire was a riot of confused, jagged colors, like a fractured rainbow. T'Cori's terrified sisters stood back, awed by the sight.

Stillshadow wiped the hunter's forehead with wet leaves, then crushed herbs beneath Dry Hole's bulbous nose. And at length, late in the night, the hunter emerged from his fit, exhausted. Stillshadow sat cross-legged at his side, watching with narrowed eyes.

"Sleep," the old woman said, then motioned to T'Cori and Raven. "We must make medicine," she said. "Raven, you must teach her."

She said no more until they were outside the hut, where Dry Hole could not hear. "He has the holy disease," she said. "And has had it since childhood. Without the medicine, he might die."

"What shall I do, Mother?" T'Cori asked, holding her head high.

Raven's eyes glittered.

"Do not call me that," Stillshadow said sternly. "Go," she said. "Find the elephant's little brother, and bring his droppings."

T'Cori felt weak, her head still spinning. It was taxing to be in the company of one as ill as Dry Hole had been. Still, she understood why she had to participate. It was vital that she learn to heal others, and a healer must also be capable of healing herself. So, weak or not, she had to do as asked.

She and Raven gathered water gourds and some dried meat and set off. A quarter day's walk around Great Earth's slope stood a cairn of rock, marking the spot where the trail split off.

"Here," Raven said sharply, the first words she had spoken since they left the camp.

*She is very angry,* T'Cori thought. *She does not like it when I call Still-shadow mother.*

The two girls climbed until they were high above the ground. Raven was a good climber, as medicine women had to be in order to reach the rarest, most remote herbs. But as they moved upward, T'Cori saw that they were ascending to a dizzying height. High enough that the giant baobab tree was as small as her thumbnail. She smiled, but Raven was not so pleased. T'Cori could tell by the tightness in the way the girl moved that fear was in her body. She could see it in her limbs, their heaviness, that the fear was eating at the older girl.

T'Cori felt a certain lightness of heart at this. So! Great Raven was flawed after all!

The elder dancer ignored her fear, though, and led them onward until they had reached a flat place, a pile of rocks sheltered in shadow.

Little mouselike creatures skittered away from them as they approached. The rocks were covered in white droppings, and after Raven caught her breath, she motioned to T'Cori.

"Here," she said. "This is what we need."

"For Dry Hole's sickness?"

Raven nodded.

"Raven?" T'Cori asked. "You do not love climbing as I do. And you do not like me, I think. But you agreed to show me where the medicine is found. Why?"

Raven stared at her. "You want truth?"

T'Cori nodded.

"Then, no, I do not like you." She glowered down on the younger, smaller girl. "You want to take my mother. You want to take my position." She came closer to T'Cori, so close that the nameless one could smell her anger. "You will never take either," she said. "I will kill you if you try."

Two steps beyond T'Cori's heels, the level ground declined in a bone-breaking dropoff. Raven backed T'Cori up close to the edge, grabbed her shoulder and shoved her backward so that the upper half of her body projected over empty space.

"Do you feel it?" she said. "One shove. You would fly like a bird." She stared into the girl's face, looking for fear.

An eternity passed. Then Raven pulled T'Cori back, chewing at her lip.

She changed the subject. "These are hyraxes," she said, as if the previous moments had not occurred at all. "It is their scat that will make Dry Hole well."

They spent a quarter day scraping some of the ankle-high, sticky mass of dung and urine into a pouch, then gathering the other herbs and barks that Stillshadow sought.

Then Raven led the way back down. Halfway down, Stillshadow's daughter slipped, her arms spinning as she flailed for balance. Her foot could not find purchase, nor could her hands. Terror distending her face, Raven stared into the eyes of the girl she had so recently threatened.

She did not ask for help, even as the rock she clung to began to pull away from the wall. It was a very long way down.

"Give me your hand," T'Cori said, and Raven hesitated, until the rock beneath her foot began to give way as well. Then and only then she reached out.

"You will drop me," Raven said.

"Great Mother would see," T'Cori said, and Raven stared up at her, at the small, calm girl clinging to the rock face, and knew her meaning.

"Yes," she said, feigning calm. "Great Mother would see."

She took T'Cori's hand and with that purchase was able to find a safe place for her feet.

They made the rest of the descent safely, but when they reached the ground Raven was furious. "You will tell," she said. "You will try to use what happened to take my place."

T'Cori stared at her. "Is that what you would do?" she asked.

Raven ignored the question. "If you do, I will kill you."

Then she walked away.


It was good that T'Cori had fetched the medicine. Stillshadow used this as an opportunity to teach, blending the herbs and the scat together to make a broth for Deep Dry Hole to drink. The hunter was recovering, but still weak, and made faces as he choked down the gourd's contents.

"Finish," Stillshadow urged, and at length he did, then laid back against his straw.

T'Cori crossed her eyes slightly, until her vision blurred. Dry Hole's *num*-fire was still confused. How long would the healing take? Even as she asked herself that question, the outer layers began to slow, the smoky quality diminishing.

Powerful medicine, indeed.

The hunter seemed as if he had aged rains in a single night.

The other students were also staring at Dry Hole, and T'Cori saw that Stillshadow was studying them in turn. She watched T'Cori with special, approving interest.

Stillshadow whispered in T'Cori's ear. "What do you see?"

"Black and red," T'Cori said. "And . . . yellow . . . and white."

"Where is the white?" Stillshadow asked, voice suddenly sharper.

"Out here," she said. T'Cori's palms wavered a handsbreadth from her body.

"What else?"

"Things floating in the flame," she said. "Like moths hovering in the air. Some of them spin and some of them whine."

She heard a girl's voice behind her, murmuring agreement.

The old woman nodded gravely. "Very good," she said. "The black means he is very sick. The gold that there is still life in him. Stay with him." She addressed both T'Cori and the tall girl closest behind her, Sister Quiet Water. "Massage his hand- and foot-eyes."

T'Cori nodded, dropping into a woozy sort of semitrance. All through the day and into the night the healing continued, but the girls immediately surrounding T'Cori found excuses to leave more quickly, and when they returned, found places away from their younger sister.

Later still, Stillshadow spoke to them again, and this time some of the girls did as T'Cori had done, turning their heads and squinting. The crone was generous with her praise to each of them when she asked what they saw and listened to their replies.

As the day waned, they left the healing hut and went out to the Gathering, to join the trading and matchmaking and feasting. Stillshadow turned to T'Cori.

"What do you see?"

T'Cori mumbled her reply, eyes half closed, rocking back and forth in her solitary darkness. "So much. So many. Look! She is sick!"

A gray-haired woman limped slowly by. The edges of her fire-cloud flickered dark red.

"Yes," Stillshadow agreed. "She has been sick all wet season. She will heal now, or she will die."

"I think she dies," T'Cori said.

Stillshadow looked closely at her charge. "We will see," she said.

After night fell there was dancing and singing, but T'Cori stood to the side, as she often did, not part of the ancient patterns. Then, when no one was watching, she slipped away to be by herself, in the shadows between the huts. And there, where no one watched, she found her own dance, in her own way, and in her lonely world she spent the night.


In the morning, Stillshadow was awake before any of the others. . . .

Except one. She found T'Cori behind the huts, dancing by herself, as she might have done all the night long. The small, thin girl spun in circles, eyes wide but unseeing. It took several gentle shakes to pull T'Cori back from the dream.

"Back to us," Stillshadow said. "Back to the world of flesh."

The girl stopped spinning, panting as she did. It took ten breaths before she could focus on Stillshadow, and when she did, she seemed almost resentful that the old woman had pulled her back.

"Are we flesh and shadow?" T'Cori asked.

"And fire," Stillshadow whispered. "Every breath connects us to the flame that created all." She gestured at the newborn sun. "The hunters have their ways of breathing, and we have ours. Every breath is a song. Sing with me," she said, and began a tune.

The rendering was a sweetness. Although there had been no formal calling, the sisters crawled out of their huts, rubbing the sleep from their eyes. They gathered around at Stillshadow's urging, although the sight of the haggard girl was frightening to them. The crone gestured silently for them to come, as if to say, *Your sister needs you.*

They took up the song. It was an old and favored one. They easily remembered the calls and refrains, and yelled back to the crone as she raised and lowered her voice.

It was a song of dream, and of the thin walls between the dream world and this one, and of the dream dancers, those who risked their souls walking that narrow divide.

In transformations almost as magical as her healings, Stillshadow's voice now sounded like the wind, now like a leopard's call. She sang and sang.

At last a man appeared, and Cloud Stalker, grandfather of the hunt chiefs, joined her, accompanied by two of his sons—one of them the splendid Owl Hooting.

Stalker was a narrow man with hot eyes, his hair streaked with gray but knotted clublike so it lay against his neck. He was almost as old as Stillshadow, and although their stations in life prevented them from ever living together, it was said that they loved each other as much as two people could. They sat, legs crossed, and gazed into each other's eyes and linked hands as they sang, their deeply wrinkled faces smiling broadly.

He was Raven's father but not Blossom's. Raven watched the two of them together, her mother and father, and even T'Cori could see the love the girl had, understood why it was so desperately important to follow in her mother's footsteps.

Indeed, if Stillshadow had been her mother, she would have felt the same way. This was more than clan. More than family. This was an earthly reflection of Great Mother and Father Mountain, a bit of heaven here on earth.

They all sang, even T'Cori following along, although no one saw that as she sang the tears were streaking her face.

No mother. No father. And she would never have a husband.

That night it rained, and in that rain the thunder roared. Even if no one had ever told her, she would know that the thunder and lightning were Great Mother and Father Mountain, making love atop Great Sky, the eye-searing lightning their passion.

To have love like that, even for a moment—*that* would be worth dying for.

She hoped it would be worth living for as well. For if she could not hope one day to have such a thing, she was afraid that there would be nothing to live for at all.


It was early the next day that T'Cori first saw death.

Peering around Blossom, Stillshadow and three other gray old dream dancers, T'Cori the nameless watched as four hunters dragged a wounded man named Silent Warthog to the healing hut.

The old women had been called from their fire ceremonies to examine the wounded man. The eternal fire would be tended by apprentices. The bhan's life-flame was far more fragile.

There beneath the healing hut's shadowed walls Stillshadow and her apprentices spent much of the rest of the day around the dying hunter. His weakening moans clotted the air; his wounds oozed crimson ichor onto the sticky sand. The dream dancers did what they could to aid the spirits in facilitating Silent Warthog's healing, or easing his way to Great Sky. The task seemed hopeless, but they struggled anyway, snuffling on all fours as they attempted to summon Silent Warthog's totems, that they might aid their son. The dancers' skills were mighty. If he recovered, he might tell them what had happened to his boma.

The whole time, T'Cori watched Warthog's *num*-fires. While the others claimed merely to glimpse the life-flame from the corners of their eyes, for T'Cori it came easily. Light seemed to bend about his body, separating out so that it was almost like a rainbow.

A normal, healthy life-flame extended almost an arm's length from the body. She felt it as warm, saw it as bright, heard it as a low, pleasant buzzing sound. Illness was perceived as paleness, coolness, a high shrill sound or buzz like a bee. All of this she could see merely by squinting a bit, more than the other girls could see with teacher plants and days of fasting combined.

When T'Cori fasted, the world was a frightening place, more light than solid, and she felt as if she was walking on a pool of liquid, always in danger of drowning.

The outer layer of Warthog's flame was so pale she could see hardly any color at all. What little there was knotted with a cold, buzzing sound as the bhan shuddered in pain. Its edges darkened, then swarmed with black as if ants or bees were gathering. He shuddered and then quieted. Slowly, as the sun settled toward the horizon, his aura faded . . . and faded . . . and finally, in the early morning, went clear and then disappeared altogether.

The heat dissipated. The buzzing quieted. Movement stopped. Nothing.

T'Cori looked up at Stillshadow. "He is dead," she said.

Stillshadow and her daughters stopped their singing. As they stared at T'Cori, she could read the question in their eyes: could she have known the moment spirit left flesh to climb Great Sky even before the women did? Was that possible?

"Yes," Stillshadow admitted. "She is right. He is dead." Stillshadow leaned closer to the corpse, whispered some words.

T'Cori strained to hear but could not. What wondrous thing might Still-shadow be saying? What message would she have this man convey to their gods?

Stillshadow straightened and sighed. "We go to prepare his burial song. Do you wish to come?" she asked the nameless one.

T'Cori shook her head. "I will stay here," she said.

Stillshadow seemed to consider for a moment, but then nodded and left with Blossom.

The dead man lay slumped on the zebra skin, his half-open eyes staring up into the straw roof. T'Cori gazed at him, curious. So. This was death. This was the first dead man she had ever seen. It didn't seem so strange and terrifying. It seemed . . . peaceful.

Was he going to Great Sky? Could he perhaps take a message for her? No one knew who her parents were. Perhaps they were dead, and atop Great Sky with Father Mountain. Could she whisper in his ear, that he carry a message for her? He would see her parents, and perhaps his own, and many other loved ones: wife, children, brothers and sisters. All would dance, eternally, atop Great Sky.

She wished she was dead.

The straw and branches rustled. A boy eeled under the hut's edge, skinning his palms against the dirt. She backed up a pace, surprised but not alarmed. "What are you doing here?"

After a moment she recognized and remembered him. This was the small, thin one she had beaten on the Life Tree only days before. He was all knees and elbows and big white teeth. She had enjoyed the energetic way he climbed in futile pursuit.

"Who are you?" she asked.

"My name is Frog Hopping," he said.

"What do you want?"

"To see Warthog."

"You should not be here," she said, but made no move to call for help. By tradition, dream dancers were not supposed to be alone with common boys, but she knew that some of the other girls did not strictly obey the rule. This gap-toothed boy made her heart smile, and that was something she could use at such a time.

He grinned, reaching into the pouch at his waist. "I'll give you some springbok." Frog extracted a piece of blackened flesh wrapped in a leaf. In spite of her responsibilities, T'Cori salivated. It was a long time, too long, before the evening meal. She looked back at the door, and then snatched it from him greedily.

His life-flame was warm but not hot, dancing with blues and oranges and strangely bright around his head. The buzz was like a low song, like one of the tunes sung around the eternal fire at dusk, or the song the old women sang before dawn to birth the new sun. She liked him.

"How was it when he died?" Frog asked.

She chewed, bolting the warm meat as if afraid Frog might snatch it back. Antelope was one of her favorites. She could taste the springbok's frantic running and its fear of death, and savored them both.

"The fire died," she said. "His breathing stopped."

"Fire?"

She wolfed the meat down. "Silly," she said. "We all have *num*-fire around us, all the time."

"I have heard of *num*," he said. "They say it is a secret of the hunt chiefs. You know about it?"

She nodded.

"Teach me?" he asked eagerly.

"Maybe," she said. "One day."

Disappointment flattened his face. She wondered if he would understand, wondered if he felt the sky's pull as she did.

He squinted at the dead man. "Does it burn all the time?" he asked. "Why doesn't it burn me? Why can't I see or feel it?"

"You are only a boy."

He shrugged, touching the corpse. "He was hot before. He is cooling, just like any animal."

She split her attention between the meat, the body and this boy. He was a strange one. "All of the light and heat leaves our bodies."

"Why?"

Should she tell him? Would it not be sharing one of the forbidden mysteries? Still, it was an opportunity to talk with a boy strange enough to catch her interest. His *num*-fire was similar to that of most boys, except for the flame around his head. It was brighter, sharper, clearer. Interesting.

This was precious—she had little interaction with boys, and had many questions about them. "Our bodies are just husks," she said, recalling Still-shadow's teachings. "Our spirit makes them hot. When the spirit leaves, the body cools. The flesh melts from the body into the ground. The flesh goes down and down to Great Mother, who gives the spirit strength to climb Great Sky. There at the top, Father Mountain gives us our new bones."

"Oh," Frog said. He peered more closely at the corpse, poking his finger against the cooling flesh. "Can he see?"

"No. His eyes see nothing."

"Hear?" Frog asked.

"No."

He tilted his head to the side. "Perhaps he is asleep. Would he awaken if you said the right words or made the right dance?"

That, she had to admit, was a delicious idea. She could almost imagine such a dance. Was it possible? This boy said such strange, tantalizing things. "I believe what Stillshadow told me, and she said he is gone. I believe what I see, and I saw his fire cool. He is gone."

"How do you do that?" he asked. "How do you see such things?"

"I don't know. It is something I have always done. But I can tell you what Stillshadow said to us. Would you like to hear it?"

He nodded eagerly.

"Make a picture in your head," she said.

He closed his eyes. "Yes," he said, his forehead wrinkling. "I have done it."

"What is the picture of?"

"Of Uncle Snake," the boy said, "who married my mother and hunts for my family."

"Good," she said. "Now imagine that you are stepping into his body, as if putting on a skin."

His face tightened and then relaxed, as if he had never had such a thought before. "Yes."

"See what he sees. Hear what he hears. Feel what he feels."

The expression on Frog's face was almost ecstatic. In that moment, T'Cori found this strange, skinny boy beautiful.

Frog's fingertips probed the dead bhan's chest and arms. "But he was so strong, grown. He had received his scars, and talismans. If death could come for *him* . . ."

"It comes for all of us," she said.

"Aren't you afraid?"

"No," she said. "Are you?"

He puffed his little chest out. "No. I'm not afraid of anything."

A lie. This one reminded her of Small Raven. Raven did not like to climb high, or take food to the old women when they were sick. This one, like Small Raven, was afraid of death. "Then why should *I* be?" T'Cori asked.

"You're a girl," he said, as if that answered everything. He gazed for a few more breaths and then said, "I'm leaving. Are you going to tell?"

"Not if you don't," she said.

"We make a secret?" he asked, and smiled.

"Secret," she agreed.

He started to wiggle back under the flap, then stopped and looked back. "What is your name?"

Embarrassment and shame flooded over her, and she lowered her head. "I am T'Cori," she said. *I have no name.*

The girl expected the usual derision and laughter, but to her surprise, he offered nothing of the like. Instead, the boy gave her that smile again, and in its light she forgot she was in darkness.

"You will have a name one day," he said. "It will be a good name. I dream these things." A lie, she thought. Boys had no such dreams. But even his feeble attempt to comfort her she found warming. "But until then," he said, "I think I will call you Butterfly Spring."

A sudden flash of delight brightened her vision. "Why?" she asked, although she needed no reason at all.

"Because I only see you and your sisters at Spring Gathering, when the butterflies return." Another flash of his suddenly enchanting smile, and then he was gone.


In many ways, Frog's best friend was the orphan Lizard Tongue, the second word pronounced with a tricky click Frog could not always manage because of the gap between his teeth, so that he sometimes pronounced it "Lizard Head." Lizard was Fire Ant's age. His parents had been bhan, one of the groups who lived out in the brush, away from the inner bomas. Lizard had been found in a burned and shattered bhan boma and brought to Fire boma, when he'd only had about three springs. Bhan tended to be smaller, slighter, poorer hunters than Ibandi. Some said that they had been created from leftover clay when Great Mother birthed the real people, the Ibandi. Bhan were included in great hunts and encouraged to trade at Spring Gathering but were not true Ibandi—there was little intermarriage.

Lizard never fit in with the older boys. Like Frog, he was not particularly good at wrestling or running. His fingers were nimble at weaving, so even as a boy he spent more time with the girls than the other boys, and because he had no father or uncle to force him to be otherwise, he was left to make his own way.

"The man died," Frog told Lizard, and shook his head. "I've never seen death like that."

"It's always the same," Lizard said. "They grow quiet, and then still."

"You have seen it?"

Lizard nodded, "I hear them talk," he said. "They say there will be more death. That Father Mountain is angry that we let the beast-men hunt on His mountain."

Frog wondered if Lizard was lying. One of the things he liked about Lizard was his ease of storytelling, something most of his fellows lacked. Lizard could not see the faces Frog saw in clouds, but would lie and say he did. Frog liked that.

He turned, startled by a sudden rustling behind them. The girl from the healing hut had followed him. Girls made him feel itchy. The grown men said that one day he would understand, but he couldn't see why men seemed to do so much of what they did just to please or impress the women. It made no sense. Women were all right, he supposed, but unless they knew healing or good songs and stories, of what real use were they?

Something about the nameless one made Frog think she was lonely. He knew that feeling all too well, and hadn't the heart to turn her away.

"Who are you?" Lizard Tongue asked.

Frog didn't know why, but spoke for her. "They call her Butterfly Spring," he said.

Lizard puffed his chest out. "I am Lizard Tongue, son of Sand Flower and Arrow. Who are your mother and father?"

The nameless girl stared miserably at the ground, as if it took long breaths to muster her strength. Finally she raised her small chin, then thrust it forward aggressively. "Great Earth is my mother. Great Sky is my father."

That statement took Frog by surprise. He had heard that some of the most powerful witches in the medicine tribe had been sired directly by the divine mountain. Could it be true? "You believe that?"

"Of course I do."

Six Ibandi hunters ran by, hooting, flexing their arms and pretending to cast spears, hunching and standing in unison. They wore cheetah or lion skins around their shoulders. Dried grass was tied in bunches at their ankles. It rustled with each step, as they shouted their boma songs. They had started doing this as soon as the news came in about the slaughtered bhan, and the feeling was spreading. The younger boys imitated the running dance, play-fighting with one another, challenging, as if smelling something exciting in the air.

A clutch of those boys approached them. "Frog!" they said. "Come, practice spears with us."

Fire Ant and Scorpion came close enough to whisper. "We hear things. Our hunters have ceremony tonight. It is time to stop talking to the women." Ant said this with a significant glance at T'Cori. "Time to be a man."

"Isn't that the girl who beat you on the tree?" Scorpion said.

"You too," Frog said, his ears heating.

Lizard was edging closer to the other boys.

"That's the crazy girl," Fire Ant said. "Crazy dream dancer. Bhan girl."

She looked at Frog, expecting him to defend her. He knew what he should do, knew what was right to do, and couldn't bring himself to do it.

He stepped closer to his brother and brother's friends. "Crazy girl," he jeered. "Go away, dream girl. We are men and have no time for you."

She looked stricken, but he found something inside him taking a dirty joy from her distress. And found, even more, that it was good to be part of a group. And if the only way the others would accept him was by shaming her, then that was all right with him.

"Crazy girl!" he said. "Crazy, ugly girl."

Tears were starting from her eyes as the boy hooted and took turns with the others calling at her, insulting her, until she ran away.

Lizard shrugged his narrow shoulders. "Child of Great Sky? I could tell a better lie. That's just a story they tell to babies whose parents throw them away." Lizard laughed until he was about to fall over. Frog wasn't sure why, but he fell into it and laughed along, fell into the rhythm of it even as he knew he was being as cruel as cousin Scorpion poisoning a trapped lizard. He watched her short, thin figure as she retreated behind the lean-tos toward the healing hut. Too late, he fully realized he was taking away something fragile and precious he had offered her: friendship.

Frog heard a voice whispering, *Go after her,* but his feet wouldn't move. She had humiliated him on the tree not ten days before, and he was taking his revenge now.

He realized that in making her small he had somehow made himself larger. Frog was now safer and more secure, more closely held at the bosom of the tribe.

And Father Mountain help him, it felt good to be with the other boys, not different.

The nameless one hid behind a rock, watching as the others busied themselves. She observed the other children with their fathers and mothers. Their careless joy pricked her heart. *Butterfly Spring.* For one precious moment, she'd had both a name and a new friend. Then with a peal of boyish laughter, even that sliver of belonging had been wrenched away.

Tears streamed down her face. T'Cori knew she hated the boy as she had never hated anyone else, not even Blossom with her threats, switches, slapping palms and rough voice, or Raven with her sharp tongue and endless anger. She would show these boys, show them all. And one day, when she found the strength, she would join the gods atop Great Sky and leave all of this behind.

The young hunt chiefs, boys proven over time as fine hunters and wrestlers, and chosen in adolescence by the boma fathers to carry on the traditions of the great hunters, kept to themselves as much as the dream dancers did. The most splendid of them was a boy named Owl Hooting—tall, lean, with piercing black eyes and a lion's stride, two perfect scars emblazoned on each cheek. T'Cori's face burned whenever he was near.

As Owl passed, sharing easy laughter with his friends, a single bright idea pierced her darkness.

T'Cori sobbed aloud.

"Why are you crying?" he asked, only the second time he had ever spoken to her at all.

"That boy, Frog," she lied, thrilled that Owl cared. "He said that the hunt chiefs are afraid of the beast-men, would not dare fight them. That they let the boma hunters do their work for them and just tell stories for their meat."

His friends, strong young hunt chiefs all, stopped and stared. "What?" Their anger warmed her heart.

"And more—he came to me while I was alone in the healing hut. He tried to touch me."

She could see their eyes grow hot, and almost changed her mind, retracted her words, but her tongue seemed to have developed an evil life of its own.

Owl and his friends stormed off. Frog was still with his companions but saw Owl coming from a distance. His eyes went wide, as if he knew that this was trouble coming but didn't understand why or what to do.

T'Cori watched, delighted and a bit frightened by her own power.

Owl grabbed Frog's shoulder. He told Frog the things that T'Cori had said, and then asked, "Did you do these things?"

Frog looked as if someone had dunked his head in Fire River. Frightened. Confused. Owl was a head taller than Frog, and in comparison the boy seemed a child. "No! I would never!"

"She said you did. Are you saying that a sacred dream dancer lied?"

Frog's mouth opened and then closed like a beached fish. He searched for T'Cori and, finding her, seemed to silently beg her for mercy.

She wanted to laugh, but pinched her own arm to keep the tears flowing.

"Come to the wrestling circle," Owl said. "Father Mountain will reward truth with strength."

"I will wrestle the nameless one?" Frog asked, confused.

Owl growled contemptuously. "You would like to put hands on a dancer, wouldn't you? No. I am her champion. You will wrestle with me."

Once at the broad, dusty circle, the other boys gathered around, fascinated, their fear transformed into eagerness to watch the thrashing.

After all, any one of them might have been punished in such a fashion. There was endless speculation about the hunt chiefs, what they knew or did not know, what they were or were not.

The boys were eager to watch this, and perhaps learn a bit of the hunt chiefs' magic. T'Cori had seen the young and elder men of Great Sky almost every day of her life, so this was no mystery. Many times had she watched the young men entertaining themselves and each other at wrestling. But she could not remember watching one of them competing against ordinary boma folk.

This was going to be fascinating.

But in the end, it was not.

Frog tried this and that hold, and nothing worked. Owl was too strong, too quick, too skilled. He chuckled with contempt at Frog's greatest efforts. He threw Frog and ground his face into the dirt, and gave him a thrashing such as T'Cori had never seen.

"She is a dream dancer!" Owl said, his knee tight against the side of Frog's neck. "She is not for one such as you. You angered Great Mother, and Great Mother sent me to punish you. You will never even speak to her again, do you understand?"

Frog screamed that he did.

And then Owl left Frog crying in the sand. The younger boy picked himself up and ran, embarrassed, from the sight of his brothers, to where he might be alone, howling his humiliation and pain.

T'Cori was happy, and ashamed of herself for being so.

# Chapter Twelve

For a hand of days, the sky had opened the clouds, releasing a down-pour that drove most Ibandi into their huts. Frog thought the rain a perfect match for the miserable mood following his beating. The sight of Wind and Water bomas' folk dancing and cheering the downpour was wearying, and he was happy when, after three days, most of the others shared his opinion that the gods had offered them entirely too much of a good thing.

The dream dancers finally found the right song, sang it with enough heart and fervor to birth a sun strong enough to banish the water from the sky.

Then, under the critical eye of Uncle Snake and his hunt chief brothers, Frog practiced rolling and jumping in the mud, wincing at his sore back and shoulders. Still, he did the best he could and kept up with most of the others. There were many different types of play, all of them preparing the boys for wrestling: baboon jumping, snake crawling, elephant walking and more. They wrestled, practiced making their arrows and ran races.

But during this entire time the adult males were conferring in private, ar-guing and dancing their opinions beneath the Life Tree. No children were allowed near, but Frog knew from the location alone that something serious was in the offing. He could sense the fear in the camp as he had felt the weight of the sky before the rain drove them into their huts.

Something was wrong, and there was some momentum building, like a flow of rocks rolling down a mountainside.

The adult council was opened, so that all of the Ibandi, every adult and child who had come to Spring Gathering, was welcome to stand beneath the branches of the Life Tree and hear the words of their elders. Cloud Stalker himself, four scars on each cheek, wearing the skin of a lion and a mountain gorilla's skull tied to the top of his head, appeared in all his fearsome glory.

"We are here," he said, "to decide what is to be done about the beast-men. Shall there be peace between us, or shall we fight?"

Frog saw the men who nodded, and those who turned away, as if ashamed to admit their fear before their brothers.

Cloud Stalker danced, throwing powders that caused the fire to flare and smoke. He howled and mimed stalking lions and angry elephants, contorting his body so that the keloid scars etching his back seemed to come alive. Watching him, Frog forgot Stalker was a man, and instead saw far plains, strange beasts and deadly struggles beneath a pitiless sky.

But then he saw the chief's hand steal to the belt at his waist and stealthily slip out a small object. Frog's heart froze, a sudden understanding flashing into his mind. Hadn't he seen Snake making just the same move, distracting the audience with a sweeping motion of his right hand, while his left extracted a white stone from his belt?

So when Cloud Stalker held his hand up, pinching a white rock between his fingers, all the tribe roared with approval and awe.

Except Frog, who stood, dazed, realizing that a sentence of death had been passed not by the omniscient Father Mountain, but by mortal men.

One term was repeated over and over again the next day as two tens of men prepared their weapons. All the next day as they chanted in the men's hut he heard the sound coming from the walls. The term was "beast-men."

Frog was not told what was happening, shared no words with the hunters who took their weapons, embraced their wives or lovers and walked west around Great Earth's curve, murder in their minds.

Five of the men were from Fire boma. Snake and his closest friend, the short, thick-bodied Deep Dry Hole, split off, each seeking to bid farewell to his family.

Snake held Frog's mother, Gazelle, tightly, whispering something into her ear that Frog could not hear. She seemed to shrink. Snake held Scorpion, Fire Ant and Hawk Shadow each in turn, then Little Brook and finally Frog. Frog could smell the fear on his uncle, but stronger than the fear was anger. His heart swelled with pride. The beast-men thought *they* were killers! Well, the men of the bomas would show them, would spill their blood and brains. Frog could not wait to be a hunter, could not wait to experience the glory of fighting to protect the bomas.

Surely on that great day he would be a man.

When the men had gone, Gazelle walked back to their lean-to as if all the bones had been removed from her legs. Fire Ant took her arm that she might lean against him, Hawk Shadow on the other side. Frog was close behind, wishing that he was large and strong enough to help his mother.

"What did Uncle say to you?" Hawk asked.

Her eyes were hollow. "He said, 'It is time to wash the spears.' "


The men were gone a day and a night. Frog thought that they would return running and dancing, eyes bright, heads high. But the blood-spattered men who stumbled back to Spring Gathering seemed almost to be sleepwalking. Their words were loud and boastful, but their eyes . . . their eyes reminded Frog of Silent Warthog, the bhan hunter who had stopped breathing. Their eyes had lost life.

Snake would not speak fully of what had happened, but days later he took Hawk Shadow and Fire Ant out into the brush. They did not know, but Frog crept after them. He was very good at secret following. They did not see him as he overheard the things Snake said.

"We found their camp," he said. "We burned their huts to drive them out. Our arrows and spears were hungry."

"Are they large and strong?" Fire Ant asked.

"Yes," Deep Dry Hole said. An unhealed crescent bite mark scarred his right thigh. A bite mark? No arrow or spear wounds? "But they were cowards when faced by men. We are Ibandi!"

And then he would say no more.


The next day, the gathered clans prepared to return to their homes, to go their separate ways. In previous years this had been a happy time, a time to return to their lives having renewed acquaintances and made good trades for medicines and knives, and even marriage contracts.

But the Ibandi were quiet this year, faces long, as if some of the joy had been sucked from their lives like moisture drying in sun-bleached bones.

Fortunately, the marriages arranged during Spring Gathering were still joyous occasions. Marriages meant children, and the safety of increase. And this year it was Frog's own sister, Little Brook, who brought home a husband. To Frog's pleasure, that husband was the playful, courageous Lion Tooth.

Lion Tooth had seen seventeen rains, the same as Hawk Shadow. Frog thought him more than a match for the sharp-tongued Brook, and could hardly wait to watch them squabble.

That would be in the future: before they could be married, Tooth would spend at least a year in service to Snake and Gazelle Tears in Fire boma.

"Farewell," Tooth's father said to Uncle Snake. Tooth's father was a scarred and grizzled hunter from Wind boma to the north, and there was every reason to think that his son would prove as reliable a provider. "Watch my son, teach him, help him grow."

"I will hold him as my own," Uncle Snake said, and they clasped hands. It was a hunter's grip, strong, the free left hand forming into a fist to strike at the back of the other hunter's hand, hard, both at the same time. It was a show of strength, a thing done only between men.

Then the people went about their lives, and Frog returned to his own fire with his family and the new brother, Lion Tooth, with his happy songs and gymnastic dances.


Tooth's unfailing good humor swiftly made him a favorite. Tooth was folded into the games and life of Fire boma: the running and chasing and throwing and wrestling. Boys of all bomas played the same games, but Fire Ant, Lion Tooth and Hawk Shadow were usually the best. Ant and Tooth became almost inseparable, and Frog quickly found that Tooth was easy to talk to and good at keeping secrets.

Frog watched as the new husband-to-be worked with Uncle Snake, patching, hunting, carrying. Little Brook did not live with her man yet, could not even speak to him, but the air vibrated with a tension Frog's ten-and-two-spring-old body did not yet comprehend. Little Brook no longer seemed a miniature version of Gazelle, but more playful and eager, and in an endearing way nervous.

One day, Frog followed Lion Tooth down to Fire River's reeded banks, and as he suspected, Little Brook met him there in forbidden seclusion. "Hello, husband," Little Brook said shyly. At ten and five rains, both her body and mind were ready for marriage, but by custom they were compelled to wait a bit longer.

"Hello, wife," he replied.

She came closer to him and touched his arm. "You are very strong."

He rubbed his cheek against hers. "Strong enough to carry you and all our children."

Frog grinned, imagining Little Brook heavy with child. She wouldn't be quite so nimble with a switch then, would she?

"We will have many?" Her hand touched his rump, rubbing him.

He grinned. "If Great Mother blesses us."

She looked to see if anyone was watching. Frog ducked down, but snuck his head back up to see her press her mouth against the corner of Tooth's, a clumsy openmouthed smack. Then she dashed away. Tooth grinned, flustered. He heard hooting and turned to see Frog, rolling around on the ground, laughing helplessly.

He waved. "You wait! Your turn will come."

Frog scratched his head, doubting very much that such a day would ever arrive, and returned to the soft work of hard play. It was good to see his sister happy. She had ceased being such a nag, as if her coming wifedom had sweetened the sourness in her heart.

It was good to see and hear happiness in the camp. There had been far too little of that since the night of the thirsty spears.

Days rolled like the currents of Fire River. But despite the endless chores, joys and sorrows, the killing of the beast-men seemed to weigh on his people. Every day, there were times when Gazelle or Deep Dry Hole or Snake looked to Great Sky, and Frog thought he saw doubt in their eyes. Why? Not one of them seemed to have noticed that Cloud Stalker had pulled the white death stone from his belt.

It had been said that the tracks at the bhan boma were those of beast-men. Still, they were not sure. They were not certain. They had done all that could be done to protect their families, the ones they loved. But in truth, *they did not know.*

It hit him like a thunderbolt. Ibandi did not kill Ibandi. They did not kill bhan. Even to kill a beast-man was something that troubled their dreams. It was forbidden, but they had done it, and although their cause had been just, killing the beast-men had been like killing a part of themselves. Frog did not fully understand it, but there it was, a fact for all to see.

# Chapter Thirteen

Occasionally, the men of Fire boma hunted as a group. Twice during these times, Frog saw Deep Dry Hole's wife, Wind Song, sneaking off into the brush with Lizard Tongue.

Once he followed them, hiding behind a tree as they laughed and groaned for a time, then returned to the boma by different paths. He asked Lizard about it, but his friend only smiled.

Such dalliances were not strictly forbidden but could cause fighting between the best of friends. For a boy not yet a man to do such a thing was begging an invitation to the wrestling circle. A boy without the protection of father or uncles risked broken bones.

Still, the risk was one Lizard seemed happy to take.

Could sex be so wonderful that it was worth a sore head? Frog did not know, and could not wait to know, but such delicious speculations seemed a distraction from the pale, serious discussions conducted at the firesides, at the hide-scraping rocks down by the rivers, in the huts before sleep time.

There had been more attacks on bhan: bomas destroyed to the northeast. Men had disappeared on the hunt, their bones never found at all. The elders began to speak of things that had never happened in living memory—the Ibandi joining into a single unit in preparation for slaughter. Not two tens of men, but tens of tens. The idea was almost beyond Frog's imagining.

Uncle Snake used a word Frog had never heard before.

*War.*

"See this skull!" said Break Spear at the men's fire. Fire boma was hosting a group of southern hunters who had discovered yet another slaughtered family on the plain. He held up an orb of splintered bone, the skull of a slain bhan.

The men had the seats closest to the fire, ranked by age. Frog and Scorpion stood at the back, watching avidly. Frog could hardly wait until he had years and honor enough to sit next to the fire itself.

But even from such distance, he could easily see that a chunk had been torn or broken out of the skull. He shivered at the thought of such violence. "This is what the beast-men do."

"We fight again, kill more," said Snake, "or they will take our land. Fight!"

"We can talk with them," Thorn Summer said.

Fire Ant spit toward Great Earth. The Between was rarely criticized for his lack of scars, but speaking so at such a serious council was very nearly a transgression.

"You speak like a woman," said Water Chant, father of Water boma. He was a tall, lean man with the saddest eyes Frog had ever seen. They were touched with green, he noticed, much like those of the girl T'Cori. "They do not talk. They kill. And they will kill us unless we kill them."

"How can you say this?" Thorn insisted. "How do we know? Perhaps Father Mountain is angry, wants us to welcome new children. Our land is rich. We can share."

Break Spear snorted with derision. "They will kill us all. My father's father spoke of beast-men from the east. They did not speak our tongue. They did not look like us or share our ways. We let them come into our lands, and this is how they repay us."

The men drummed their feet against the ground.

"But—" Thorn began, voice plaintive.

Break Spear cut the Between off. "Where are the great hunters of my father's day?" Break Spear said. "Have the Ibandi grown weak and soft? Are we women, to let them come and take us? Perhaps *you* wish them to kill your daughters and bugger your sons, but we are men, and we will fight!"

They continued to discuss the ripe and rotten of the ideas until the moon began to sink below the horizon and the new sun was born in the eastern sky.


Later that moon, Little Brook left their boma with Lion, to join her new husband's family in Wind boma. Despite her harsh words and stinging slaps, Little Brook was his sister, and Frog was sorry to see them go. He had come to think of Lion Tooth as another brother. But Wind boma was only two days' run to the north. He would visit, and when he did, he could play games with Lion, and once again have the pleasure of ignoring Little Brook's commands.

She took his hands. "You will bring water, and scrape the skins well, and do everything Mother says, or I will come back and beat you," she said, tears sparkling in her eyes. Frog hugged her.

"I will miss you too," he said. She brushed her lips against his forehead, then turned to leave the boma with her husband. She seemed so sad, and yet so filled with hope for her future. Frog had a sudden, terrible premonition that he would never see her again, and blinked back tears. His only consolation was that, as yet, none of his premonitions had ever come true.

Of course, there was always a first time.

# Chapter Fourteen

The following winter brought the worst days of Frog's life. Hard rains were followed by a terrible plague of flies tiny enough to crawl up his nose and into his ears. It was not so bad in the boma, but as Frog, his uncles and brothers walked out on a five-day hunt, it got worse. Flies everywhere, in their mouths, biting at night. They encountered bhan in the outer circle completely overwhelmed by the buzzing plague, small, sickly men and women huddled in the corners of their boma, shivering, unable even to move.

Frog and his brothers inhaled clouds of insects, spitting them out when they could, choking on masses of them until they found a cave and set fires in the mouth, preferring to gag on smoke than that revolting living mass, dreading to become like the bhan, living there in the crawling cloud, their wailing children with maggots in their eyes.

They were forced to return home with empty hands, and it was of little comfort that the other hunters had fared no better. Indeed, it seemed that the flies had driven away all game, and as stomachs emptied, the Ibandi began to grumble.

And then finally, the word *curse* was spoken. It was Deep Dry Hole who used it.

"A witch!" Deep Dry Hole called, and pointed his finger at Lizard Tongue. Frog's friend recoiled. At times Lizard had been an object of mockery or suspicion, but never of direct accusation.

Dry Hole's wife, Wind Song, shrank back. Everyone knew that when Dry Hole hunted, she had slunk into the bush with Lizard.

"My hunt was for nothing," Dry Hole said. His eyes glittered with malice. "For days I hunt, and find only rodents and snakes."

Hot Tree tried to be reasonable. "This happens," she said.

"Not to me!" Dry Hole roared. "But I know why hunting has been bad. There is only one reason." He wheeled dramatically, fixing his eyes on the hapless youth. "Lizard Tongue! I saw him touching my spear. He pointed at me and mumbled."

Shock burned through Frog's bones. His friend was in trouble. Touching a hunter's weapons without permission was rude, even for a two-scarred hunter. But for one without a single stripe to do such a thing was a terrible breach and insult. And a bhan boy as well? Frog groaned.

"What is it you say?" Break Spear asked.

Dry Hole sneered, knowing that at last he had their full attention. "This is not a boy! Not a man, not even an Ibandi," he said. "This is a witch. He brings bad luck."

"No! It is not true!" Lizard said, panic in his voice. "I have lived among you since I was a baby. You know me!"

Dry Hole was scornful. "Any witch might protest as much. Witch, I say!"

Horrible silence followed, its own damnation.

"I say test him!" Dry Hole clenched his fists and screamed, spittle flying from his mouth. "Test him, or I will take my children and join another boma. I will not live in the same thorn ring with a witch, to wither my root and starve my spear!" Some of the others took up that call. Frog wanted to run and stand beside his friend, but Fire Ant's hand clamped hard on his shoulder. Despite his dismay, Frog was secretly glad for the restraint.

Fire boma's elders took to the meeting hut, where the door was closed and the children were warned to stay away. They remained, chanting and singing, until late into the night, when a grim-faced Break Spear emerged and said: "Accuser and accused must be tested."

Runners were sent racing toward Great Sky. Two days later, Cloud Stalker himself appeared. Although his spine was not so straight, Stalker was still the tallest Ibandi Frog had ever seen. His skin was more weathered than it had been just two springs ago, his hair now streaked with gray. But his muscles were still strong and full as a young hunter's, his eyes still sharp enough to drive an arrow through a hawk in flight. And he could still outrun most of the younger hunters.

Frog saw him speak to Uncle Snake. The hair on the back of Frog's neck burned. Earlier he had seen Dry Hole hand Snake a sliver of black rock wrapped with leather: a knife, and a good one, gained in trade with one of the eastern bomas. Frog's belly twisted. He knew that soon "the gods" would pass a decision, and without a word spoken he knew exactly what that decision would be.

"This is a serious thing you say," Cloud Stalker told them after he had rested awhile. He listened to their concerns, spoke to Deep Dry Hole and Lizard. Then after a smoke, he began to dance.

Lizard Tongue and Dry Hole sat in the men's circle, with the women forming another, looser ring outside them. Although Lizard was not fully a man of the tribe, with such a serious accusation all within the boma walls were granted protection of their laws. Challenger and challenged alike were equal in Father Mountain's eyes.

"I call a trial," Stalker said. "Earth, wind, water"—as he said them he danced to their directions—"and fire."

Lizard trembled. It seemed to Frog that Deep Dry Hole was hard-pressed to conceal his smirk.

"The fire trial," he said. The tribe moaned and swayed, agreeing, eagerness simmering beneath the surface. All the hunters had struggled recently. Ever since the washing of the spears, their luck seemed to have gone bad. Any change of luck was sincerely prayed and danced for. And if that called for the sacrifice of one terrified boy, then so be it.


First, as the elders beat the leather-headed drums, the men's fire was built into a blaze, then the coals and glowing ashes raked out in a long bed. Dry Hole and Lizard each had to scoop up a coal and then walk barefoot out on the glowing bed.

The rules were simple: they could throw the coals into the air again and again, but the first to drop it, or leave the bed of coals, would be he for whom Father Mountain felt no love.

Lizard scanned their faces, seeking compassion, and found it only within Frog's eyes. Even his lover Wind Song would not look at him.

For tens of breaths the two, Lizard and Deep Dry Hole, sat as the hunt chief danced before them with such liquid motions that Frog grew sleepy just watching, nearly entering the world of the dream even though his eyes were open.

Hot Tree and Thorn Summer brought forth ostrich shells filled with water. Dry Hole and Lizard were allowed to sop their bare feet.

Then with no apparent discomfort Cloud Stalker picked up two dusty, glowing coals from the bed and placed one in each of their palms.

"Dance," he said.

They stepped onto the coals and began their dance and chant. The steam hissed from their hands and feet. The water swiftly evaporated, and their chants grew louder, tinged now with pain as smoke rose from hands and feet.

Every eye in the boma was fixed upon them. All but one pair. Frog crept away, into the hut where Cloud Stalker had left his sack. And there, in the darkness, he opened Stalker's sacred belt, and committed a great sin.

By the time Frog returned, tears streamed down Lizard's swollen face. He screamed and stumbled from the coals, sobbing uncontrollably, pouring water on his burning feet. Dry Hole stepped off, sat on the ground with a thump and almost casually dribbled water on his toes, lips curled in a contemptuous smile.

Lizard rubbed water into his feet, trembling like a gazelle in a leopard's jaws. "Please," he whispered.

Cloud Stalker frowned. Did he want to condemn Frog's friend? Frog could not know. But he guessed that the knife that had passed from Dry Hole to Snake could now be found in Stalker's pouch. "I see stones in your body," he said, peering deeply at Lizard's chest.

Stones? Stalker turned and left them to go to the meeting hut, the flap closing behind him. Would Stalker discover what Frog had done? And if he did, would Uncle Snake's dead left eye light on Frog, blasting his soul? Frog shivered.

Stalker emerged, draped in his lion skin, wearing his gorilla skull. White bone marks were painted upon his face, as though his skin was transparent.

He did not walk back to them, he danced, one step at a time, singing a death song.


He held out a ball of dried herbs, opened Lizard's mouth, and forced it in. As the drums thundered, Lizard and Cloud Stalker danced together, Lizard struggling to match Stalker's movements as the hunt chief transformed himself into snake, and eagle, and lion, and gorilla. The herbs began to take effect, and Lizard fell to the ground, bucking and writhing, and calling out to the gods for mercy.

As the people screamed and sang, Cloud Stalker hunched over, seeming to reach into Lizard's abdomen. Did he, really? Frog could not see clearly enough to be certain, but the hair on the back of his neck itched, and his eyes opened wide, imagining such an intrusion into his own body. The boma folk screamed, and some of the women fainted, as Stalker howled and held his bloody arm aloft, holding—

*A black stone, signifying life.* Cloud Stalker's eyes widened with shock.

Frog sidled behind his mother, afraid to let Stalker see his face, lest his guilt betray him. What must the mighty hunt chief be thinking? Of a miracle, of the hand of Father Mountain in men's affairs? Or would he know that human will had determined hunt chief justice?

Frog snuck a peek at Uncle Snake, who looked at him, mouth thin with anger.

He knew. But would he speak, betraying Frog?

Cloud Stalker threw the stone down at his feet. "The boy is not a witch," he said.

"No!" said Deep Dry Hole. Frog saw his lips twitch, trembling. Finally, with venom enough to kill a man at ten paces, he leaned over Lizard, who was still curled, moaning on the ground, wiping flecks of foam from his lips. "You are a weakling. You will never be a hunter. The jackals will kill you for me." And stalked back to his hut.

Cloud Stalker's face was set grimly. "It is done," he said, and without another word turned and began his walk back to the mountain.

Dry Hole washed his burned feet with water, and glared at Lizard and then at his wife. Frog knew: regardless of Lizard's fate, Wind Song had earned a bone-rattling.

Had Frog sinned terribly against the gods in doing what he had done? For replacing the white stone held on the left side of the belt with a second black one? Was this an inexcusable sin?

Or worse . . .

What if there was *nothing* atop Great Sky? What if there were no gods at all? The thought hit him like a rock to the base of his skull, a thought so terrible and enormous that he dared not even whisper it to himself.

What if there was nothing?

# Chapter Fifteen

*Frog's eyes misted with tears as Cloud Stalker, Break Spear and even Uncle Snake declared him corrupt and evil. Lion Tooth, Lizard, Scorpion, even Ant and Hawk turned their backs. Under point of spear he gathered his meager belongings and wandered into the brush, until he was found, not by dream dancers or hunt chiefs or even bhan, but by leopards who sprang upon him, bore him to the ground just as he had seen one take down a springbok. And then, even as he prayed for Father Mountain to end his agony, they devoured him screaming. Horribly, nothing they did to him, no savaging of fang or claw, brought the healing arms of death and darkness. He lived through all, screaming until his throat tore.*

"My brother," Fire Ant said, shaking him. Frog could just barely make out his sibling's face in the darkness. "My brother. Frog. Wake up."

Frog came to waking slowly, like one swimming up through mud. He saw his brother's face in the moonlight streaming through the air hole. The bits of good-luck bone dangling from the willow branch ceiling swayed slowly in the wind, mocking his nightmare.

His mouth was sour with terror. In his dream, Frog had been unable to defend himself, to change their minds, and nothing could keep them from seeing him for what he really was. Beside him, Scorpion and his younger brother, Wasp, were rolled onto their sides, moaning with early morning visions. Gazelle was still fast asleep, but Uncle Snake's place at her side was empty. Hunters needed their sleep. Had his anguish awakened his uncle? Guilt added its weight to fear.

He clung desperately to his brother. "I am safe?"

"Safe," he promised. "What did you see?" Frog's dreams were still so real that he would have sworn the straw beneath him was slick with blood.

Despite his trembling, he thought clearly enough to ignore the question. "Brother," he asked, "have you ever been afraid?"

Fire Ant squeezed his shoulder. "I am too strong for fear, tadpole. In time, you also will grow strong."

Frog gripped desperately at his brother, lowering his voice so that young Wasp could return to sleep. "But I don't want fear!"

"Fear can be a gift. It makes us strong," Ant said.

"I do not want this gift," Frog said. "I will learn. I will grow, and learn enough, and one day I will never be afraid again."

Ant yawned and rolled over. "Go back to sleep," he said.

But Frog could not, and instead crawled up and out of the hut, squatting in the doorway and then walking toward the men's fire, happy for the solitude.

The boma was silent except for soft, burring snores. A hand fell on his shoulder, and Frog wheeled, startled, to find Uncle Snake behind him.

"Your friend is safe now," he said. "I could not sleep either." There was more to say, and both of them knew it. And knew just as well that those other words might never be spoken.

"Then why do I still feel afraid?" Frog said instead of the questions he really wished to ask. "I do not want fear, and it seems that no matter what I do, it just grows worse."

Uncle Snake shook his head. "If you ever learn how to stop it, if that day ever comes, I hope you will teach me your secret." He rubbed Frog's head. "You think if you learn enough you will not fear. Not die. Never be alone. It is not true."

"Why?"

"Because it is not the way Father Mountain made us. We are what we are, Frog. There are things that cannot be changed. Should not be done."

Frog thought that there was some hidden fire in Snake's eyes, a warning that he ignored. "Why not? How do you know?"

Uncle Snake shook his head and cupped the back of Frog's neck with his callused, powerful hand. The gesture started rough but then became more gentle. "Perhaps one day you will be a hunt chief and can brave the spirit world to ask Him yourself."

The two looked up at the dark, looming expanse of Great Sky. It disappeared in the clouds almost as if there was no top there at all. Did Father Mountain, from his awesome vantage, hate Frog for what he had done? Great Sky had taken Baobab before he could teach Frog to walk or talk, let alone to hunt or tie knots. Was it too much, was it too evil for Frog to cling to a friend?

There was only one thing he could think to do. One day, he would climb to the top of Great Sky itself, and ask his father. For if his own flesh and blood was angry with him, that was even worse than if the great god who made them all saw young Frog as unfit. In that case, he didn't know what he would do.

Or . . . perhaps there *was* no Father Mountain. Perhaps there were no spirits. Perhaps . . . perhaps . . .

Frog climbed back into his mother's hut and tried to sleep. But as he turned restlessly on his straw, he renewed his promise that one day he would climb the mountain. He could not quiet the part of him that whispered: *There are no gods.* Surely, such a thing as had almost happened to Lizard could not happen if Father Mountain watched and protected. No. No matter what the hunt chiefs said, there might be nothing, nothing, except darkness and death.

On the other hand . . . was it possible that he was Father Mountain's tool? Had he been fated, perhaps *intended* to save Lizard? All his life, he had felt that there was something different about him. Could this be it?

His head hurt. Could the hunt chiefs be lying? They knew so much. Everything that the hunt chiefs taught kept the Ibandi alive, kept flesh in their pots. They seemed so wise, so good.

Then why the pretense?

Frog vowed that he would not die without learning the truth of this, without climbing Great Sky to see if Great Mother and Father Mountain were things as solid as wood. Or were They more like shadows? Did the dream realm genuinely exist, or was it merely some strangeness in their heads, with no connection to the world of flesh and stone? There was no one he could say such things to, no one he dared ask.

So all he could do was swear to make the climb, as Uncle Snake had done, and learn for himself. At the top of the tallest mountain in the world, where, the wise ones said, their ancestors danced in dead water.

# Chapter Sixteen

In their dusty, cautious hands of hands, the herds had begun to return to the brush-dotted plains surrounding Fire boma. By their lameness or slowness or pretended unawareness some revealed their desire to return to the spirit world. Slowly, song and dance returned to Fire boma. No one spoke of what had occurred, but once again smiles appeared on people's faces. What remained unsaid was as important as what was spoken aloud.

Lizard seemed more pensive, laughed less often and stayed as far as he could from Dry Hole's wife, who limped for most of a moon after the trial.

The rest of the boma seemed to accept Lizard, and in so doing forgave themselves for sins real or imagined.

*We did what we had to do,* they said.

*We saved our children. Who can say we were wrong? The hunting is good. The flies are gone.*

*Life has returned.*

Then one day Frog went looking for his brother Fire Ant and could find no trace of him. He looked by the men's fire, in the storage hut and down by the banks of Fire River. Nothing.

"Where is my brother?" he asked his mother, Gazelle. She smiled wanly and turned away. He sought Uncle Snake and could not find him either. Anxiety blossomed.

"Where is Fire Ant?" he asked Hawk Shadow. None of the adults would speak to him about it, and it was later that he realized that Lizard, too, was gone.

"And where is Lizard?" he asked, and was given no answer. He was afraid. Had his actions been discovered? Had Deep Dry Hole or Cloud Stalker fulfilled the will of the gods after all? Could Frog have been so terribly wrong about the thing to be done? Hawk would not respond to him save to say: "Do not ask."

So Frog sat in a shaded nook behind his hut, knuckled his chin, furrowed his brow and tried to think. He remembered that the same thing had happened to his eldest brother, Hawk Shadow, the year before. Hawk had been gone for two hands of nights, returned briefly, then disappeared again for two moons. When he returned, he carried a gutted warthog across his shoulders. There was great celebration, and soon afterward he was declared a hunter. When Frog asked about it, he was told not to question.

Was this the unnamed mystery by which boys became hunters? Sometimes he thought that everyone knew the answer except poor Frog.

Fire Ant returned after a few days with a single scab-crusted scar on either cheek and a dazed look in his eyes. Frog felt great relief: Fire Ant had not suffered for Frog's sin! His joy was almost uncontrollable when Lizard appeared only a few breaths later, similarly scarred and dazed.

What had happened?

Ant barely spoke to Frog. Instead, he went to the straw nest built onto the side of the family hut and lay down to sleep. The next day Frog saw him speak to Uncle Snake, but again he had no words for Frog. He left the next morning, carrying nothing but a knife. No food. No spear. But he did rub Frog's head on the way out of the boma. That, at least, was a sign that he still knew his brother.

Lizard avoided him as well, did not meet his eye, would not reply to his questions. Frog could not understand, and at last went to his straw with unanswered questions in his mind. His stomach was as queasy as in his fifth spring, when he had almost died with fever.

Late that night, just before dawn, a stick poked through the side of his hut, scratching Frog's head and waking him up. At first he was disoriented, wondering what had happened, then realized someone had called for him, and crept out.

The older boy looked haunted and terrified. The single scar on either cheek had scabbed but still oozed fluid.

"What happened to you?" Frog asked.

Lizard shook his head. *I cannot say.* His lips twisted in a sad sort of smile. "Don't ever let them know."

"Know what?" Frog asked.

"Your mind." His fingertip brushed Frog between his eyes, a touch like a feather. "They would fear you if they knew you." He sighed, a huge, heavy sound. "All my life I have been different, as you are different," Lizard said. "All my life I have feared this day, and now it has come."

"Then stay," Frog said, feeling himself grow desperate. "You can be a Between, like Thorn Summer."

A flash of panic flared in Lizard's black eyes. "Dry Hole would find a way to kill me," he said. Then he straightened, perhaps trying to be brave for his young friend. "No," he said. "You should not have done it. Even if they had banished me, I would have found my way. There would have been something for me. I can feel it. I would have found another boma, or survived on my own. You have angered the gods."

It was a lie. Word would have spread to the outer bhan. Knowing he had been shunned, desiring the goodwill of the Ibandi, it was likely none would have taken Lizard in. So this was what their friendship had come to: a dance of lies. "I go, but Father Mountain goes with me," Lizard said. "They say that the night itself is the mountain's shadow."

There was a long pause, and for a time Frog feared that there would be nothing more to say, that those would be the last words they ever shared. Then a thought occurred to him. "Some say that the stars are the campfires of all the dead. I think them wrong."

"What are they, then?" Lizard said, so full of hope that Frog almost wept.

"They are Great Mother's eyes, I think. And they will see you wherever you go."

Lizard hugged Frog. "Only you would create a story just to comfort a friend. Only you could." He kissed Frog's forehead so softly it was like a whisper of wind. "Remember what I said. Never let them see. Stop speaking of faces in clouds. Don't ask so many questions. You have a mother, and an uncle and brothers to protect you, but still . . ." He was trembling now, and Frog did not think it was from the cold. "Fear kills," he said.

Then without another word, Lizard crawled through the gap in the boma wall and was gone.


In the days to come Frog hunted, kept his weapons clean, wrestled in the circle until he was exhausted. He helped the men burn the brush back from the boma walls, so that the leopards and lions could not sneak close. And as he did, the smoke blew back into his eyes and Frog was happy, because it meant that he could cry in front of his fellows, and no one would know.

Almost a moon and a half later, Fire Ant hobbled back into camp, leaning on a branch, his right leg badly cut and infected, the skin hot to the touch, swollen and running with pus. But despite his wounds and sore condition, a freshly slain antelope was draped across his shoulders. His chest was scarred. A deep wound bloodied his left arm.

The entire boma turned out to see the young man as, with one pain-filled step after another, he limped through the gap in the thorn walls.

Uncle Snake took his burden from him, and the other hunters helped him to the fire pit, where he was given water as they all clustered around.

Ant drank as if no water had touched his lips in days, his eyes sunken and haunted. When he had drunk his fill, he began to speak.

"I saw them," he said. "They were not beast-men."

Break Spear leaned in closer.

"What did you see?" he asked.

"It was after the first moon," Fire Ant said. "I had made myself a blind to hide, near a water hole, and I saw them come. They were big, bigger than us. They were faster, and stronger." For the first time that Frog could remember, Ant looked scared.

"What happened?"

"I watched them run down a springbok. They had not stabbed or poisoned it. They were that fast. It was quick, but they ran it down. Never have I seen the like."

"How did you hurt your leg?"

"After the night came, I crept out and ran away. I fell down a ravine and hurt my leg. I thought I would die, but at last it began to heal. One of my traps caught an antelope, and I came back."

They were amazed. Wounded, possibly hunted, frightened, and still he had waited to trap an antelope before returning. This was a hunter indeed, and Frog felt stronger just knowing Ant's blood ran in his veins.

To Frog's dismay, fortune was not with Lizard. He did not return, and after much argument and voting, the men decided to go in search of him. The nights after they left were filled with blowing dust, and Frog felt in his bones that their efforts would be in vain.

When Uncle Snake and Break Spear returned, their faces told the story. "We searched," they said. "And were almost lost in the storm. We were separated from each other, and knew that Lizard was gone. We came back."

Frog heard what they said, and suspicion burned in his heart. Had they really looked? Or worse . . . had Dry Hole found Lizard, quietly, privately, and . . .

Frog stared at him. Friend, neighbor . . . and something else? "But we found *these*," Dry Hole said, and laid out several crude arrows. The arrows were different from Fire boma's: longer, of thicker branches. He'd never seen such clumsy, almost childish workmanship. They were far too heavy for Ibandi bows. Except for the crudeness, they might have been constructed for Father Mountain Himself.

He crept away to where Fire Ant rested. Boma mother Hot Tree had tended to the wound and already sent for a dream dancer. Frog sniffed the mangled leg: the bad, rotten smell was not there, and for this he was glad, despite his brother's pain.

Fire Ant opened his eyes. "Frog," he whispered, and reached out to take his hand. Frog was relieved to find his brother's grip as strong as ever.

"Did you see the creatures clearly?" Frog asked.

He nodded. "They were not Ibandi, or bhan. . . . they were a type of beast-men we have not seen."

"Why?"

"They were larger," he said. "Larger than us." He turned his face away. "I was afraid," he said. Then exhaustion claimed him, and he spoke no more that night.


After two days, the compress of sweet grass and herbs had eased the pain in Fire Ant's leg. With the help of his brothers he was able to hobble out to the men's fire.

There, Snake and Dry Hole laid out the arrows once again.

"These arrows are crude," Break Spear said. "Perhaps the beast-men use them, and we have not seen."

*You slaughtered them and lost not one of our own people. There is something else out there, something more dangerous than any beast-man. You slaughtered the beast-men for nothing,* Frog said to himself, wishing that he could scream aloud.

Fire Ant nodded. "I could not see. There was no moon, and the clouds stole the stars. But once there was light, and I saw . . . something else."

"What?" Snake asked.

Frog strained to hear.

"I saw one of them jump, and he was like a monkey. He went farther than even a hunt chief can leap."

Did they leap like his own totem jumped? Frog wondered. He envisioned them springing in the moonlight on all fours.

Fire Ant bowed his head in shame. He was battered and bruised and scraped. "I should have followed them. Learned more. I was afraid and ran away."

Hot Tree laid her comforting hand on the youth's head. "There is no shame. You lived to bring us this knowledge."

Frog wanted to scream, *Let me go! Lizard may still be alive!* But Frog knew it was hopeless. His heart said that his friend was dead, and his mind knew his heart was right. He curled up that night and cried for his own sins. Cloud Stalker's stone had been black on the outside but white on the inside. Lizard's life could not be saved by human intervention.

Stupid Frog.

Stupid, stupid Frog.

He cried himself to sleep that night for his lost best friend, Lizard.

# Chapter Seventeen

In the time following Fire Ant's return, Frog Hopping came to a decision. Others, he thought, might be stronger or faster than he, but no one would work harder at his practice. As Frog grew older he was given more tasks and chores, but his primary purpose was to become a hunter, and every moment of his waking day was filled with knife-making, spear-throwing, stalking, hunting, all the men's skills. He had tried to be good with the bow, but despite his endless efforts, that skill seemed to elude him. With the spear, though . . .

That was very different. The spear he loved. And it loved him in return. Point. Shaft. Butt. He learned to use them all as weapons and tools. Frog learned to find the perfect bamboo shafts and tree branches, to harvest and sharpen them swiftly and surely.

The boys played games of their own, but other games were organized by the men. The favorite was the echo game: walking in each other's footsteps, mimicking one another's motion, walking silently in a circle, following one another up the sides of hills or creeping through the tree branches, placing each hand and foot where a cousin had placed his before. During the echo game, they practiced breathing in rhythm with one another, that they might gain greater connection with their brother hunters. They were also taught the shallow breathing that allowed them to stay awake for days at a time while lying in the dirt covered with biting ants.

And in between, they ran and wrestled and carried rocks or one another, becoming strong.

All of this preparation was about far more than merely becoming strong. It was knowing with every sinew the strengths and weaknesses of the other hunters, so that each could anticipate the inclinations and actions of his brothers. This was what was needed to succeed in the hunt. "A man alone is vulnerable," Uncle Snake said. "The boma together is strong. The Ibandi as a people are unconquerable."

Frog wanted desperately to believe that, but he had seen things, knew things now that caused him to doubt too much of his world. His brothers were secure in their trust and ignorance. Frog had knowledge, and that knowledge terrified him.

Hawk Shadow had returned home after his seasons away, bringing with him a bride named Flamingo from Wind boma, a graceful beauty already heavy with child. In spite of his new responsibilities, he took time to help Frog learn.

"Like this," he said. Hawk's round face set in a mask of concentration. He inhaled, swung up and back, then threw the spear twice as far as Frog had ever managed. "Now you. At that fever tree."

Frog's own throw, which he had so recently been proud of, went only half the distance, striking nothing but dirt. Hawk Shadow laughed and walked away, leaving Frog running after the spear. Frog practiced from first light to dusk. But at the agonizing end of that day he realized that he had done more running than spear-throwing.

He spent the next days crafting five spears. This was not an easy task: he had to find the right branches, of dark spearwood that effortlessly held the sharpest killing point. After he found his hand of branches, he stripped and sharpened them, built a fire with sober care and baked the tips to hardness while singing praise to the spirits of the wood. After that, when he practiced, he could throw one after another, seeking the perfect motion. At this point he wasn't trying to hit the tree or any specific target, just trying to throw so that each of them landed within an arm's span. Then, after throwing all five, he ran to collect them and began the process anew.

The eyes of Fire boma's hunters were upon him. At first those eyes were amused, but after some days he could reliably land all the spears within one arm's span, and their mirth gentled and became approving nods.

It was time to start refining his aim.

*Throw them. Fetch them. Throw them.* On and on he went, endlessly, until his aching muscles forced him to stop. In this fashion he filled any time he could steal away from other chores.

"Frog!" his cousins called. "Come play with us." Over the days the other boys had become impressed and perhaps even a bit intimidated by his practice. Did they see? Could they see that he feared he was as different as Lizard?

*Lizard.* That thought resurrected painful memories. What had happened to him, and would any of them ever know for certain?

"I have to practice," he said.

Stepbrother Scorpion, the largest of them, grabbed his arm, twisting. They all swarmed over him, bearing him away with them. "There is more than one thing to practice!" Scorpion said. "We wrestle!"


In the burned ring surrounding every boma was crafted a wrestling circle, raked earth ringed with stones. It was there that the young men found practice, competition . . . and occasional anguish. During Spring Gathering the various village champions contested for honor, rank, sport and sometimes brides. Every young man was expected to participate.

The rules were simple and relatively consistent from one boma to the next. The younger wrestlers were free to contest with one another, but could not ask older, more experienced wrestlers for informal practice: such were considered challenges. But older wrestlers could "ask" younger to roll with them. Such invitations were almost never refused.

Any wrestler who habitually thrashed younger, less experienced opponents swiftly became the target of the village's most senior wrestlers, who would teach him that there were infinite gradations to suffering. If that was not enough to dissuade him, hunt chiefs could be summoned from Great Sky, and their strong, sure hands generally resolved the matter. An additional correction was rarely required.

When Frog practiced with his brothers or one of the other hunters, he knew that they used only a portion of their strength. They were urging him to do his best, testing and encouraging.

Many times, Frog had watched spellbound as Fire Ant and Hawk Shadow wrestled with the older men. If the elders were still active hunters, they were usually better, and the brothers and other boys were encouraged to use all of their strength. But if the elders were no longer running with the herds, the younger men were expected to refrain from shaming the older men, whose days of strength and challenge were behind them.

During most practice one wrestled not just to win, but to "make pretty," to be graceful in the midst of struggle. To win "ugly" was less than to lose "pretty." This was something Frog strove to understand, and understand he must if he was to wear the scars.

This is how it had always been, and how it would ever be.

So they practiced with monkey rolls and baboon leaps, leopard-walking and all of the other exercises he had learned since he was a baby.

"Now," Scorpion said, "you can drive my shoulders down, or throw me from the circle, or make me cry Father Mountain."

Although trembling with fear and excitement, Frog's words were bold indeed: "And what if I kill you?"

The boys stamped their feet, applauding his bravado. "Well, then, you win!"

Frog put his head down and charged. . . . all the way out of the circle. The others laughed. He bounced up and charged again. Over and over again he was thrown out, but no matter how tired and sore he became, he never quit. Then Scorpion pinned him to the dirt and began twisting his arm until he was sure his shoulder socket would rupture. He screamed, "Father Mountain!" and the contest was over.

The boys cried out for the best of the young hunters: Frog's elder brothers Hawk Shadow and Fire Ant. One at a time the brothers entered the circle, and their strength and skill swiftly drove the younger ones into the dust.

To the side, boma father Break Spear was quietly watching every move.

Frog was fascinated by a twisting move that sent Fire Ant's opponent flying out of the circle. He had the next idea. "Now the two of you!" he cried. "Wrestle each other! Let's see it!"

His brothers grinned at each other. Some of the others in the boma stopped their work and drifted over. Fire Ant shook out his left leg, a flicker of unease floating across his face. Was the leg still bothering him? Hadn't it healed yet?

Whatever discomfort he experienced, Fire Ant hid it behind a face of stone. "You taste dust today, brother."

"One of us will cry Father Mountain today," Hawk Shadow said. "It will not be me."

Frog's brothers took their places on opposite sides of the circle and began to stalk each other.

The two collided in the center of the circle, each of them so well balanced and so well matched that, in straining together, their muscles leapt out in stark relief.

A flicker of pain crossed Ant's face. The injured leg again?

There was a fluid blur of limbs, a shout and a drop to one knee, and Fire Ant flew through the air. Hawk Shadow was the winner! Never had Hawk won so easily. Even now, a year after his injuries, Fire Ant was still diminished. Frog sensed that never again might Ant be Hawk Shadow's equal.

Hawk Shadow pounced, twisting his brother's arm. "Say Father Mountain!"

Fire Ant struggled, and twisted, and was unable to free himself. "Father Mountain! Father Mountain!"

A gigantic hand fell on Hawk Shadow's shoulder, lifting him off his vanquished brother.

It was the mighty Break Spear himself, breathing deep and slow and strong, vast belly jiggling, his eyes alight with mischief.

"Come, wrestle me." The hunt chief was squat and muscular, seeming to Frog to be as wide as he was tall. He was a gristly boulder of a man, his black eyes sheltered beneath shelves of bony ridge.

This was one of the most important moments in Hawk's life. It was a great honor indeed for the boma father to offer a younger hunter the right of challenge.

Next to Break Spear's massive form, Hawk Shadow's smooth, muscular body seemed almost girlish. Now it was his turn to shrink back. He was a handsbreadth taller than the hunt chief, but that made little difference. There was something . . . *quiet* about the broader man. This quality Frog had seen in some of the elders, a familiarity, a certainty born of experience. He had wrestled countless matches and knew every clever twisting move.

Hawk Shadow took a position on the far side of the circle, spreading his legs and planting his feet firmly.

Word spread swiftly through the boma, and the folk gathered to see what was about to happen between Fire boma's greatest hunter and its most promising young man. Hands of them gathered around. In a way that all understood, Father Mountain and Great Mother had granted the family a glimpse of seasons to come.

Three of the boma's old hunters hobbled happily to the wrestling circle, dragging their hollow-log drums with them. They planted themselves and began to stroke them vigorously, providing rhythm.

Hawk Shadow and Break Spear wore only twists of skins tied with knotted cord covering their genitals, but even if they hadn't, that tender target would have been taboo in a practice match. Mortal combat was, of course, different.

The drums throbbed with a beat that would have compelled dead bones to dance. Frog swayed and jumped, excited.

For the first time, Hawk Shadow stood in the challenge circle with the boma father.

There was no distinct call to begin, but the men surrounding the circle stamped their feet against the ground. Frog felt his pulse vibrating in his rump.

The two combatants responded to it, stepping to the beat, slowly walking the circle. As they tested each other, one gradual sliding step at a time, Hawk spiraled within reach of Break Spear.

Lines of sweat streaked furrows along their dusty skin and streamed from their hairlines. Hawk Shadow shook his head and flicked the salty droplets aside, never taking his eyes from his opponent. He raised his right hand to wipe the perspiration, and in that instant of diminished vision, Break Spear charged him. They were so close together that there was almost nothing Hawk Shadow could do.

Almost.

He sprang to the left side, planting his right leg in Break Spear's path. That trip might have worked with most, but Break Spear hopped nimbly over the obstacle, simultaneously uttering a trilling shriek that would have frozen Frog dead in place.

Hawk Shadow threw himself to the dirt, tumbling as Break Spear came after him. Hawk performed a perfect baboon roll, jumping to his feet in time to meet Break Spear's charge. The impact almost threw him out of the circle, but Hawk dug in his heels to resist.

In fact, as he tensed he not only stopped Break Spear's charge but pushed him back. Then the broader man stooped just before Hawk Shadow jumped in with another push, and Hawk Shadow sailed over Break Spear's shoulders.

Every man and boy around the circle groaned with empathetic pain. Hawk Shadow crunched into the ground, *whuff*ed air and rolled away— but Break Spear hadn't leapt in to continue the attack. Instead, he retreated a step and watched the younger man as he staggered to his feet, shook his head and prepared to continue.

The two fighters crashed in the center of the ring, slapping with openhanded buffets that tore skin and snapped heads to the side. Hawk Shadow charged in, suffering a mighty wallop along the way, slamming in his shoulder and grasping Break Spear around the waist, right hand gripping left wrist at the small of Spear's back. Grunting, he actually levered the heavier man from the ground. Break Spear linked his fists and clubbed Hawk Shadow's right shoulder.

The drums thundered, and the boma howled with sympathetic pain. Father Mountain, that must have hurt!

Frog snuck a glance at Hawk's wife, Flamingo, who watched with wide, worried eyes.

Hawk Shadow's eyes rolled up in his head. He staggered back a step but didn't release the older man. Instead he squeezed so hard that muscles leapt out from Hawk's arms and back. Break Spear's neck swelled with his own strain, but he still seemed measured and calm as he brought his fists down a second time, this time at the juncture of Hawk's neck and shoulder. Hawk Shadow groaned and sank to one knee, releasing his hold.

Swift as Hawk's namesake seizing a mouse, Break Spear attacked. Snaking behind Hawk Shadow, Break Spear wrapped his legs hard, locking his ankles, squeezing against Hawk's lower ribs.

This was a reversal of the previous position. Hawk's face purpled and puffed with blood. He struggled and twisted but was unable to free himself. Break Spear's grip tightened, so that Hawk could draw little breath.

His fingers clawed at Break Spear's strong arms. Frog sensed the exact moment that panic shaded Hawk Shadow's face, the moment he understood that he was finished. At that very moment Hawk Shadow gasped, "Father Mountain!" and Break Spear relaxed his grip.

Break Spear loosed his big booming laugh and released Frog's brother, slapping him affectionately on the side of the head as he did. Hawk's chest heaved as if he had run to Great Sky and back without stopping. His face was lowered in shame, sweat dripping from his forehead to puddle in the dust below.

Break Spear encircled the defeated boy with his arms, roared and lifted him off the ground before thumping him down on his heels. "This one is a great wrestler and hunter!" he said. "He will lead many hunts, kill many lions. I say he is to be honored!"

The boma folk stamped their feet against the ground, screaming their approval, Frog louder and harder than any of them.

The other men came to Hawk Shadow and slapped his shoulder, grinning. Then the younger boys approached more cautiously, touching him and then running away as if to transfer his power to themselves. Soon Hawk Shadow was smiling again, his breathing returned to normal. He basked in their admiration, grinning, big square white teeth shining as they congratulated him on surviving Break Spear. Although none of the women would ever stand in the circle, they fully understood the importance of what had happened. Some of the young girls gave Hawk appreciative side glances, nothing too bold. After all, Flamingo had run to him, embracing him eagerly, and flirtation might earn a boxed ear.

But that wouldn't keep them from accidentally touching him or cutting their eyes at him. Frog had begun to see something different and frightening and delicious in girls. He felt great envy and wished that he could be even half the hunter his brothers had grown to be.

Then he looked down at his own small hands, his thin weak arms, and was consumed with despair. Surely one so frail as he would never, could never, grow to be nearly so strong and brave and sure as Hawk Shadow.

He was feeling sorry for himself, but a sidewise glance at Fire Ant stopped the swell of sorrow. Fire Ant watched the celebration, and although he smiled, Frog knew that his heart must ache. Once, Ant had been Hawk's equal. Perhaps he had even been better: certainly he had been faster and more agile. But that injured leg had taken something away. He could no longer run shoulder to shoulder with his brother. That leg might never be the same, and without strength demonstrated in the circle, Fire Ant would never rise high in the boma, had no chance to be chosen as a hunt chief or become boma father.

So even as Frog rejoiced for one brother, he was sorry for the other. He loved both Fire Ant and Hawk Shadow, and to see the balance shift between them hurt his heart.


In respect for his struggles and courage as much as for his wounds, Fire Ant was allowed to marry Ember, a thick-waisted girl with laughing eyes, without the customary year of service. Her parents had but recently joined their boma from the north. This was a good marriage: Ember's father was Cloud Stalker's younger brother. Their children would be honored indeed, and it seemed to Frog that this very nearly satisfied Ant's ambitions.

Their marriage was performed at the next Spring Gathering by Cloud Stalker himself. Frog danced and feasted until the couple retired to their hut for their first night of love, then he joined Scorpion and their friends for races and games.

He noticed that something odd seemed to be happening, possibly because he was now the oldest unmarried brother. The girls were casting glances at him and flirting in a way that made his root throb.

He relished the new attention and flirted back, walking with his shoulders high and hips forward, strutting as if he already had his scars. The girls tittered appreciatively and made the small changes in their expression and posture that best displayed their beauty.

There were girls from all of the other groups, but as always, those who kept the fire were apart from the others, unattainable, untouchable. He saw the girl T'Cori, the one without a name. Despite Owl Hooting's prohibition he would have spoken with her, but she avoided him, made excuses and went away with the other dancers. In some strange way it merely made Frog wish to know her all the more.

Did she hate him? Feel guilty for her lie? He did not know but wished he could have asked.

He saw her several times over the days of festival. Owl Hooting was one of the finest of the young hunt chiefs, and T'Cori seemed to thrive when he came near, like a morning glory blossoming for the sun. Frog's back and shoulders still remembered the beating he had suffered at Owl's hands. He avoided the young man whenever possible.

Frog had to wonder: what kind of union could hunt chiefs and dream dancers share?

Whenever Frog glimpsed the nameless one, she was deeply involved in learning, going with the older women to hear their songs, watching their dances and studying their ways. At times she was with the fearsome Stillshadow, and she seemed to do exactly as Stillshadow did, following with eyes and body and facial expression, following in her footsteps as if she might absorb the older woman's wisdom through the soles of her feet.

On the last night of that year's gathering, a girl of the dream dancers approached Frog. Frog thought she was not particularly attractive, but her moon-shaped face was very clean, her teeth scrubbed brightly, her hair twisted up with sticks and daubs of mud into a morning-glory pattern. Beneath the leather flap her young breasts were small and high. He had seen her at the previous year's festival but had not experienced the same sensations when he looked at her. Was this what Lion Tooth had meant when he laughed and said that Frog would learn?

"Frog," she said. "Your name is Frog?"

"Yes," he said, somewhat dazed that one of these dazzling creatures knew who he was.

"I am Fawn," she said. "Come, help me find berries."

They were alone, away from most of the others, who sat circle. One after another, the men or women would enter the circle to speak, sing or dance their story. When one person was done the clan would smoke and discuss, and then another would take his or her place in the center, and the process began again.

There were many important things to be settled: territories, marriages, feuds and division of spoils. No one was paying attention to Fawn and Frog.

His cheeks burned, and he didn't know why. "I'm not hungry," he said.

She stared at Frog as if he was the stupidest creature in creation, then shook her head irritably and walked on.

Frog wasn't certain why she was angry with him. He heard a familiar laugh behind him.

"You see faces in clouds, but not what's right in front of you," Fire Ant said. "When a dream dancer asks you to go with her, you go."

Frog felt his face flush even more to know that his brother had heard and seen. "I didn't want berries."

"She didn't want berries either."

Confusion warred with anger, but some deep part of him already understood the answer. "No? What, then?"

Fire Ant grinned. "Why not go and find out?"

There was one part of Frog that wanted to leap on his brother and wrestle him to the ground, as Break Spear had done to Hawk. Another part, the one that remembered his humiliation by Owl Hooting, wanted to run away and hide.

Then there was another part altogether, and that bit of flesh was interested indeed.

Frog slid his chipped rock into the pouch at his waist and went running after the moon-faced girl. Her hips swayed, dizzying him so that he felt as if he viewed them from the top of the Life Tree itself.

He caught up with Fawn by the time she reached the riverbank. In most times wandering off by herself would be considered foolish, but festival attracted so many Ibandi and bhan that lions and leopards rarely approached.

*She doesn't want berries either . . .*

"I thought you weren't hungry," she said, her small white teeth nibbling at her lower lip. Somehow, she was becoming more attractive with every passing breath. His root's increasing rigidity might have had something to do with that.

"I thought that maybe I could help," he said.

Although she was shorter than he, in some odd way it seemed that Fawn was standing above him, looking down. "Perhaps. Come." Fawn reached out her hand for his and led him down by the banks of Sweet River, smaller than Fire River but known for its delicious sky-colored fish. His hand, clasped in hers, felt almost as if it had been chewed by fire. "Where do we go?" he asked. His voice sounded high and embarrassingly thin.

"Not far," she said. "This looks like a good spot." She led Frog to a place sheltered by bushes but lush with soft green grasses. From this secluded vantage, none of the major trails was visible. He could hear distant singing but could see no one.

"Where are the berries?" he asked, turning back to face her.

Fawn had slipped the hide covering from her breasts and lifted them in presentation. They were small and firm and beautiful. "Here are berries," she said.

He could but stare. Ibandi women rarely covered their chests. Young, old, large, small, firm, withered—he saw them all. Except for the dream dancers, whose breasts and sex-eyes were concealed from Ibandi view.

Fawn's exposure struck him like a blow over the heart. He could barely breathe. This lifting . . . the sensual softness of her mouth, the fact that he and Fawn were alone . . . perhaps the difference was in *him*. He was older now, and Father Mountain had given him more understanding of the world, as if the deities were rolling rocks aside to expose the mouths of secret caves.

"Pick them," she said.

He watched his hands reach out to her, fingers trembling as they touched. Her breasts felt like soft deerskins filled with warm water, or ripe fruit.

And there by the riverbank, one breath at a time, she taught him what his body could feel. Demonstrated that his own clumsy childish root-rubbing was nothing compared to a young woman's first feathery touch. That the touch of her tongue against his cheek, his chest, was like a brand of fire. When she pushed him back against the ground and mounted him, and for the very first time in his young life he felt the joining that made all other sensations pale in comparison, he knew that he had never known anything at all. With every movement of her body she urged deeper and deeper fire from him. Her eyes said that this was not the end, but merely a new beginning.

And he thought, after the time in which all thought vanished and he floated in a warm, calm current deeper than anything he had ever imagined: *Am I now a man?*

# Chapter Eighteen

T'Cori was often the first girl up in the morning, awake in time to listen to the old women clearing their throats to sing the sun to life. From morning until night the nameless one rushed from one task to another, tending the eternal fire and raising the coals back to full flame, cleaning and creating, teaching and learning. The world was opening itself to her.

T'Cori was beginning to remember more and more of her lessons, so that instinct was joined to knowledge. Even if she could not be a fleshly daughter, she could be Stillshadow's best student. Under the circumstances, that was a victory of sorts.

Even with no name, T'Cori was determined to be more than that, to be the most powerful dancer in her people's entire history. Some of the others laughed at her fantasies, but T'Cori was certain her eyes were open wider than any. And when Stillshadow deemed it time to open her sex-eye, as several of the other girls had done just within the last moon, she knew that she would understand and see farther than she ever had, and that would be a wonderful day.

At this moment, she carried a load of ground pigments down to the riverside, humming and deliberately stepping on rocks to hide her footprints, just for entertainment. A girl with no name should have no footprints, she thought, feeling herself in an excellent mood.

A nameless girl was not bound by the attributes of any totem. She might become anything she wished. Five times now Stillshadow had thrown the bones, and every time had failed to find a name for T'Cori. This was almost unknown. Six was the most times anyone had been denied a name by the gods. What might happen after that, no one knew.

At Sweet River, T'Cori would mix the pigments carefully until they were a mudlike paste. She would fill three gourds with this preparation, intending to bring them back to Stillshadow for her blessings and the addition of whatever final ingredients would transform this into the ceremonial paint that bonded their people together. These pastes would be given to the boma mothers. At certain times of the year, these powerful women would mix them with water or urine and use the pigments in their sand paintings, for their hunt chiefs, or when women wished to bless the unborn children sleeping in their bellies.

T'Cori was almost down to the river when a brown-banded ant caught her eye. This was a very special insect, one she'd never seen in the gathering grounds, but she knew it by the bristling black hairs on its rear. This was a smoke ant, known to make a very potent medicine when mixed with mint, lionroot and menstrual blood.

She followed the insect for several minutes before it encountered one of its sisters. The two brushed antennae and then traveled in different directions. Taking a chance, T'Cori decided to follow the second one. "I follow you, little brown," she said. "I find you, and I find your people. And when I find them I will grind their bodies to paste."

How happy Stillshadow would be with her! T'Cori crept on, following that second ant until it met a third, and a few moments after that, a fourth and fifth. Now T'Cori was following a trail, and if she was both careful and lucky, that trail would lead her to the colony. T'Cori would mark the location, then call the other girls, and they would spend a day drowning or heating the smoke ants out and killing them. When they were done, they would have medicine for the entire year.

The line of insects led through a stand of tall plants, and when she brushed them aside she could hear the gurgle of moving water and something else. . . .

Laughter.

She crept closer. What was this? T'Cori knew that it was rude to spy on her brothers and sisters, but her blood heated at the sounds of murmuring and cooing. She knew the things that some of the other girls did, the girls who were not promised to the hunt chiefs on Great Sky.

What she saw was a naked girl and boy, touching and playing with each other. She watched as they brushed lips and tongues, as the girl offered her breasts to his touch. The girl was Fawn. At first, T'Cori could not see the boy's face. Then it became clear, and she backed away.

It was that miserable Frog! He was awful, a terrible boy, and she was angry with Fawn for playing with one so low. True, she was not beautiful, but one must have standards. Stillshadow must have made a mistake in judgment, allowing Fawn to open her sex-eye so soon. T'Cori saw the *num-fire* flare around the two of them, and it was disgusting. Surely if Fawn wanted sex, one of the hunt chiefs would have done it with her.

At the same time, something inside her felt as if someone had twisted a thorn into her chest.

T'Cori bumped into Fawn's twin sister, Dove, who put her finger to her lips in caution as they backed away. T'Cori was shaking and felt a gnawing sensation, as if her heart had not eaten in days. She leaned her head against Dove's chest, tears scalding her cheeks.

"Why do you cry?" asked Dove.

"Nothing," she said.

"Do not lie," Dove said, and it was only then that T'Cori fully understood that the word she had spoken was far from the truth.

"They play," she said finally, surprised by the bitterness in her voice.

Dove smiled. "My seventh eye felt that someone was sexing. It is a good thing. You will know this one day."

Yes, they would play with boys, straddle the men of Great Sky and squeeze the seed from their roots. But never would T'Cori have a true family unless she left the dream dancers.

On the one hand, the honor and obligation. On the other . . .

T'Cori would never have a man of her own, and until that very moment, she had not realized how deeply she desired one. T'Cori gazed at Dove. Could it be that they did not share the same loneliness? She knew that one day a hunt chief would be the first to enter her. Her sex-eye would open, and T'Cori would come into her full power. He, or others, would give her children, so she would not mourn the lack of a man's touch.

But there was more. She could feel it. No matter what anyone said, there was the part of her that yearned to belong. To belong to . . .

Owl Hooting?

No.

She squelched that part of herself. That was not her path. And she reckoned that everyone, even those she envied most, had days in their lives they would rather not have lived. Even Stillshadow herself must have sometimes wished that she had walked another path.

But a dream dancer's path was not hers to choose. That was for Great Mother to decide.

Dove grinned at her. "Who was with Fawn?"

T'Cori gathered strength and dried her tears. "If we are very quiet . . . ," she said, and Dove nodded. The two crept on their bellies until the tall grass thinned at the clearing's edge. And there, for a time, they watched as Fawn ground her hips against Frog, urging him on or slowing him down, guiding his hands and lips and tongue.

They watched as the couple's *num*-fires flared and sizzled, as they flared brightly and then calmed again.

And they learned.

T'Cori heard Frog's cries and sighs. And as her ears burned she swore that one day she would be with a hunter. Not a scrawny one like Frog, but one possessed of great strength and beauty. She had breasts. She had hips and thighs. She, T'Cori, had full moist lips. And more important than that, she saw things that others could not. Heard and felt and saw the *num*-fire more easily than any of the others. She had premonitions that, given time, might ripen into wonders.

So she and Dove lay, and watched, and held each other, and laughed silently to keep the tears at bay.


That night, the nameless one lay in her hut, warmed by the breath of her sleeping sisters. Unlike most of the pilgrims down below, T'Cori slept in a permanent dwelling, not something erected for rapid raising and equally swift dismantling at the end of Spring Gathering.

She lay listening to their inhalations, trying to match their breathing with her own. This was the beginning of the pathway into their dreams. In dreams, the dancers leapt and swirled together in Great Mother's bamboo fields. She wanted to be a part of them, to join with her sisters in every possible way. But no matter what she did, every day it felt that she became something more and more different from the others. The others simply did not see. . . .

Finally, careful not to step on her slumbering sisters, T'Cori rolled up and crawled out through the waist-high entrance into the moonlight.

The moon was the sun's mate, as Great Earth was Great Sky's. Glimmering above, its pale, cold white light bathed the landscape with a glow strong enough to sharpen the shadows.

There in the darkness, she found a place of solitude. T'Cori leaned back against a rock a handsbreadth taller than she, gazing up and out. The eternal mists surrounding Great Sky's peak shimmered in the moonlight.

There, in some hazy place between sleeping and waking, T'Cori's seventh eye called to her. Her right hand slipped between her legs, beneath the loincloth. It was not the first time, of course: her sisters had taught her this trick long ago, for personal pleasure and in preparation for the eventual taking of a lover.

*You must find the flame within yourself, if you would help a man to find it,* Stillshadow said. Women who expect men to fan a fire they themselves had never kindled would be very disappointed by sex.

All of the girls pleasured themselves. Some formed pairs and relished each other. T'Cori had hugged and groomed and played with the other girls but never found it as satisfying as her solitary explorations. . . . or her dreams of love.

"No one wants you," she whispered to herself. "No one. What is wrong with your body? Will your belly ever swell with child?"

"Yes," Stillshadow said from behind her.

The nameless one leapt up, startled and suddenly ashamed of herself. "I . . . ," she began, and then merely said, "I did not know you were there."

The old woman shook her head, laughing. "There is no shame in your body," she said. "There is pleasure in touching it, yes. And even more pleasure in mounting a strong man, making him yours."

T'Cori hung her head. "What of love? Will there be no . . . love?"

"Blindness such as yours is rare in those who still have teeth." Stillshadow laughed warmly. "We have a whole world of love."

T'Cori listened to the words, their texture warming her. "What about you and Stalker?" she asked boldly. "I have seen the way you look at him, and he at you. Don't you yearn to share your hut with him?"

"I have, often. We've had our times," Stillshadow said. "He gave me five children, and I love them all. Blossom and Raven are here; the others were given to good families in the inner bomas. But I am the grandmother of all our people, as Stalker is the grandfather. As Father Mountain and Great Mother birthed the tribe. All things in the world are alive and in balance."

Stillshadow clucked empathetically. "You are daughters of Mother and Father," she said. "In our lives, there is little room for mortal men." She clasped T'Cori's shoulder. "Morning comes too soon. There is much to do tomorrow."

## Chapter Nineteen

When Frog awakened one summer morning in the fifth year past his tenth spring, something had changed. He could feel it in his bones, without the ability to speak its name. His ten-spring-old brother Wasp still dreamed. Little Brook had gone to live with Lion Tooth's family in the north. Hawk and Fire Ant had moved out long before. Hawk, the older, had built out on the side of the family hut.

Two years before, the spiders and pests had grown too numerous, and the entire boma had moved half a day's walk north, to an old boma deserted years earlier for a similar reason. In this new place, Fire Ant built himself a place separate from the rest of the family, but still nearby. The boma walls were disassembled and expanded outward, as had been done many times in the past.

The familiar dome of their living space was roomier now than it had been since he was a tiny child. But that was not the only difference.

Was it something in the sounds and smells? Perhaps, but that might not have been it either. Frog rolled over onto his side, listening. His thoughts were like stones skipping across the surface of Fire Lake.

Exiting the mouth of the hut, he looked out over the camp. Since returning from Spring Gathering, he had noticed that at times the adults seemed to demand more of him, increasing his burden of chores and requiring greater skill in his performance of them. It seemed that he could do nothing right.

His mother, Gazelle Tears, was already awake, preparing the morning gruel at their family fire pit. She gazed at him, her slender face drawn, upper teeth gnawing at her lower lip. Into the coals she inserted yams wrapped in leaves and grasses. She smiled, but he thought that a bit of sadness curled her lips. He counted new vines of white in her hair, and realized that his beloved mother was getting old. Her breasts, once full and fertile, now sagged as shrunken husks.

"Come, eat," she said, and rolled two of the leaf-wrapped yams over to him. He touched the spongy surface of the larger yam. . . . *hot!* Frog blew on his fingers to cool them, then pulled the tuber closer and unwrapped it, tossing it into the air whenever his fingers started to sizzle.

Uncle Snake crouched nearby, grinding points onto shoulder-length sticks, sharpening them one after another with long, calm strokes against a whetstone. After a while Wasp awakened and crawled out, rubbing his eyes and his plump belly, wandering his way down to the cook pit.

Wasp stamped and spit toward Great Sky. "Good morning, Father Mountain," he yawned, and then threw his arms around Frog's neck, leaning sleepily against him.

After a while the yam had cooled enough for Frog to nibble at its firm orange flesh, and then to gobble it down, sharing half with Wasp, who smacked his lips merrily. It was sweet, and sweetness of any kind was something of which Wasp never tired.

The knot of scar tissue in Uncle Snake's empty eye socket seemed almost to be watching Frog, judging him. "When you have finished," Snake said, "go to the river and bring water."

Frog almost choked on his yam. "But that is Wasp's job!" Frog had hoped to spend the day with the older boys, helping the men with their traps, learning songs and stories and the names of things.

"Frog!" his uncle insisted, without a hint of sympathy. "Wasp has other tasks. Go now."

Wasp stuck his tongue out at Frog, then begged their mother for more yam.

Muttering under his breath, Frog grabbed a stitched skin strung with hand-loops through the sides and sealed with acacia sap. It could hold a backbreaking load of water. Frog groaned, wishing that Wasp would hurry up and grow large enough to do his share of the work.

Fire River was fed by creeks running down from Great Sky and from streams farther north. Two days' walk farther east, it emptied into Fire Lake. The river was the lifeblood of the eastern Ibandi, bringing water to their boma and many of the eastern bhan as well. In years when the river dried up, they dug wells or found alternative springs. If such sources could not be found, and the game vanished as it did in the dry years, new babies might be exposed, sent home early to Father Mountain, to return in better times.

But in good years there seemed no end to the river's bounty. It brought them fish and turtles in abundance. Tubers clustered in the rich soil along its banks. It gave boma hunters cool places to lie in hunting troughs, awaiting the unwary zebra or pig. It gave Fire boma water for drinking and cooking and bathing and swimming and sport.

So many forms of plenty. Of course, the adults said it was fed by Father Mountain. Some said that the water was His tears, as He was crying for all the ways His children failed him. Uncle Snake said that it was His piss, and Uncle Snake had trained with the hunt chiefs, so he would know. On the other hand, Frog was never certain if he was meant to take that seriously. After all, both tears and urine were salty, and these waters were fresh and delicious.

He looked up at the mountain, wondering once again: Was there anything at all up there? Could the hunt chiefs be wrong? Could Uncle Snake?

The one thing to keep carefully in mind about the river was that Ibandi were not the only ones who benefited from it. Lions and leopards also appreciated its cool wet rushing depths and had been known to lurk along its banks. Best be careful, and be certain that he was not the target of those flesh-eaters! *We are both hunters and prey. . . .*

So he kept his eyes open, ears peeled back and nostrils flared as he filled the bucket.

It was probably for that reason that he was both mortified and frightened when the world suddenly went dark. A piece of leather brushed past his eyes, muffled his mouth, dampening the river sounds. Frog thrashed this way and that, to no effect. How could he have been so careless?

He felt no claws tearing his flesh, no fangs rending the skin of his back, seeking his vitals. Had he been seized by killer beast-men or Others? If so, was poor Frog destined for the same cook-pit that had doubtless claimed Lizard?

"What do you want with me?" Frog called.

There was no answer to his pitiful question. He was hauled to his feet, his hands lashed behind his back. Something unpleasantly sharp pricked his shoulder blade, followed by a shove with the flat of a callused hand. Frog lurched forward and began to walk.

For a half day he stumbled over broken, rock-strewn ground. His one comfort was the sound of Fire River guiding him, so he was always fairly certain where he was. From time to time the river sounds diminished. He was walked in a circle several times. When they finally stopped, Frog was spun around five times, so that he momentarily lost all orientation.

Then the warmth of the sun on his shoulder reminded Frog which way lay east, and the fear gnawed less painfully.

He heard Scorpion's voice, recognizing his stepbrother's plaintive whine before a hard slap ended the complaints.

His abductors walked him for another quarter day, leading him with a thong about the neck so that he did not stumble into a bush or tumble down a ravine. When he tried to ask questions, a rod lashed his shoulders until his mouth closed. The air cooled as night fell. Frog was pushed to the ground, and he slept cloaked in the same leathery darkness. There were new voices in the darkness as other boys joined them. He recognized some, but others he was uncertain of. Were those boys from the other bomas?

But even if he couldn't picture them from their voices, their smell was familiar. Fear spiced their sweat.

Frog slept in his hood, his hands tied. Again and again he awoke in the night, listening blindly to the harsh rasp of his breathing inside the bag.

Late the next day they were heading uphill, as he knew they would. The warmth of the morning sun on his back told Frog they were heading west. They were being taken to Great Sky, home of the hunt chiefs and Father Mountain Himself.

For the last quarter, Frog had staggered blindly up Great Sky's slopes, prodded by spear butts in the back.

When at last they stopped, Frog was so dizzy that he almost threw up inside the leather sack. He swallowed the sour mush back, unwilling to drown in such a humiliating fashion.

Something soft bumped into him, and he screamed, "Who's there?" only to be smacked sharply on the back of his head.

*Be silent.*

They were walking again, over uneven ground. From time to time one of the boys would speak, followed briskly by the sound of a slap or cuff or groan, and the voice fell quiet.

His stepbrother cried out in fear and despair. Frog heard a brisk thump, clearly the sound of a hand against a head, and Scorpion sniffled but no longer whined. In spite of his own misery, Frog smiled.

The air cooled as the slope began to steepen. They were surrounded by different sounds now. Running water again, and distantly, the chattering of blue monkeys, larks and sparrows.

The boys were led down a sloping path, bumping into one another and scraping their feet. Their captors stopped them and then pushed them down into a seated position. Finally, the skins were removed from their heads, and at last they could see.

They sat in a cave almost twice as tall as a standing man. Frog choked as he breathed in the fumes from torches jammed into the walls on either side of the room. Through the smoke he saw that the walls were covered with countless animal skulls, hands of hands of hands of them, all hollow eyes and bleached bone staring down on him as if daring him to be worthy of their precious flesh. In the dim light he could see that the walls curved like the inside of a gigantic bubble. And were they smooth as packed mud? He suspected that this place might have been dug, not discovered.

More than two hands of boys crouched or knelt next to him. Scorpion, Frog and Sunset represented Fire boma, and Frog knew Rat, from the west. All looked as disheartened and frightened as he felt.

As far as he knew, he was more afraid than any of them. But he realized then that he could be afraid without *showing* that he was afraid. It would not do to let them know!

Two hunt chiefs, masked with the leather faces of gorillas, stood with arms crossed at the only exit. For one crazed moment he considered attempting to overpower them and flee. The size of their muscles persuaded him that this was not the best course of action.

Then the idea of escape became moot, as six men filed through the narrow opening. Each wore a leather mask from a different animal: lion, leopard, antelope, oryx, buffalo, warthog.

The largest of them was a head taller than Frog, with wrinkled skin hanging from strong old arms. He wore an antelope face skin over his eyes and nose. By the gorilla skull lashed atop his head, Frog knew him to be Cloud Stalker.

The water threatened to squirt from Frog's root. He clenched it back, furious with himself for behaving as a little child! He would not disgrace his fire!

By their wide-eyed expressions, he guessed that some of the other boys did not understand what was happening to them. It was then he decided that he wasn't the strongest or fastest of them, but would keep his fear deep within, where the others could not see.

"You have dreamed of this time," Stalker said, his voice and presence swelling to fill the kiva. The antelope mask wavered in time with his words. "Trembled in fear of it. This is that day, the time when you must stand before the mountain to be judged." A few of their masks covered eyes and noses but not mouths. The lips he saw were flat and merciless, and it occurred to Frog that it was possible some of the boys might not survive this night.

He fought panic. No matter what happened, he would not soil himself. He would not disgrace his father and fire.

Despite the shared body warmth, the boys shivered in the underground chamber. He recalled stories whispered by firelight: this was Great Sky. This was where the nectar from rotting bodies flowed. Here dead flesh received new bones.

"What . . . what do you want?" Scorpion asked.

Cloud Stalker's head snapped around. "You will not speak unless spoken to!" he said sharply. Frog could do little save quake. But then, unexpectedly, Stalker answered the question. "You will run the gauntlet. You will show us how brave and strong you are," he said.

Scorpion asked the question in Frog's mind. "Will you kill us?"

Stalker came closer, looked at each of them in turn, so closely that Frog could not hold his gaze through the eyeholes and had to look away. "Perhaps. You do not have to do this. Perhaps all you need do is choose one of your brothers for the men to take away and use like a woman. Choose one of you. Just one! And the others will not have to fight. To run. Perhaps . . . die."

The boys stared at one another. Scorpion cast a stealthy glance at Frog, making the skin on his neck burn. Ridiculous! His fellows would never abandon him in such a way! It was not done!

Would they?

"Choose!" Stalker said. "Who sacrifices a brother to keep his own skin safe? Choose!"

"Frog . . . ?" Scorpion began weakly, and then hung his head in shame.

The boys shifted restlessly, glancing at one another and blinking back tears. Frog felt hands thrusting against his back and was disheartened to realize that some of his cousins might indeed have considered giving him up.

*As Lizard had almost been sacrificed?*

A bubble of protest welled up inside him. *No! No! Not me! Not any of us. Can't you see what they really want?*

The mighty Stalker examined their faces as if he could see beneath their skin, then turned and walked away.

Stooped with seasons, a gray old hunter spoke to the boys in a voice that burned. "Yes. Who is it that you reject? Who will you abandon? Who will speak his heart? Who will say: 'This one is not of the tribe. This one does not deserve the protection of the thorn walls! This one can have his manhood torn away!' "

Frog heard those words more with his heart than his ears.

The sharp pressure at his back had decreased. Frog was right: that *was* what the others had been thinking, and they were now ashamed of that stark truth.

They cast their eyes about, terrified and humiliated. . . . but also determined. Ibandi boys would not betray one of their own!

The animals with old men's eyes glared at them. "Remember!" one of them said. "What is done to others may be done to you. What is a tribe? Do we turn against one another in times of hunger or drought or disease? Do we?"

They glanced about wildly, seeking answers in one another's tear-filled eyes. Frog's nose wrinkled: the air stank of urine. Someone—Scorpion, he thought—had pissed himself.

"N-no," his stepbrother stammered.

"Do we desert one another to save ourselves?" Stalker asked. "Is this how you wish to be treated? Choose! Choose one of your fellows now to be taken and his ass set afire." Frog's anus clenched sympathetically, horrified by the implications. "Or you can stand together as *men,* and face your futures. Choose! Our women wish to know how many of you are men, and how many are little girls or Betweens. They await your decision."

Stalker's eyes blazed like coals. "How many of you are men?" he asked.

Here in this confined space, Frog was nearly overwhelmed with his brothers' powerful scent. He smelled their excitation, fear and something else . . . strength in unity.

"All!" they shouted, glancing nervously at one another, seeking support.

"How many?" Stalker asked, and raised his arms. Frog remembered when those limbs had been tight, the arms like tree trunks. The ravages of time had reduced his muscles to thick, slack braided vines beneath loose skin.

"All!" the young men called again.

"Who are you?" he asked them, and there could only be one answer.

"The sons of the shadow!" they said.

"Do we stand together?" he asked.

"Yes!"

"Hunt together?"

"Yes!"

"Die together?"

"Yes!" they called, shaking the mountain with their fervor.

"We are the family!" Stalker roared. "We are Ibandi! Rise, and face your future. All!"


A child had no scars. A man had at least two, one on each cheek. That first scar said that he was no longer a child, but not yet a man either. A hunter had two on each side, a hunt chief three. There were some who never won that second scar, and what happened to them was no fit fate for an Ibandi.

One after another the hunt chiefs had doffed their animal masks. Now each stood before one of the boys holding a wooden bowl filled with blood-red paste the consistency of mud. Frog smelled cayenne and something acid. Uncle Snake went last, and the web of scars etching the left side of his face made the boys gasp, although all of them had seen the wounds many times. Everything seemed more real here, of deeper significance.

Snake rubbed a bit of paste onto Rat's cheek. In the torchlight, it seemed that Rat bled already. The boy groaned, biting into his lip as the first incision was made, so deeply that a blood-vine crept down from the wound. Frog winced, suddenly fighting the urge to cry out in sympathetic pain. He would have sworn his cheek was already on fire.

Rat made no sound beyond the first groan, and Frog was proud. Other men worked with other boys, dividing the ten and two youths into three groups, two men tending to each.

When at last Frog's turn came, his heart drummed strongly enough to steal the strength from his legs. Uncle Snake somehow seemed to hold both of Frog's eyes with only one of his. "Breathe," Snake said so softly that Frog could barely hear it. "Run while standing still."

The first pulp Uncle Snake smeared on his cheeks felt like fire. That sensation faded swiftly, leaving numbed flesh in its wake.

Snake pulled a sliver of black rock from his pouch, its hilt wrapped in leather. Was this the blade Deep Dry Hole had given him? Frog could not tear his eyes away from it.

The surface of Frog's cheek felt thick and unresponsive when he probed at it with his fingers, but when the edge of the knife tore into his flesh, he was shocked at how much it hurt. He did not, would not cry out. Frog knew that eyes were upon him, judging and measuring him, and he refused to fail in this critical test.

When the rock sliver sliced his other cheek, Frog squeezed his eyes shut as hard as he could. When he opened them again, tears stained his vision. They spilled down his numbed cheeks, and there the cool, wet sensation disappeared. Snake's ravaged face nodded approval as he moved on to the next boy.

This was Scorpion, who only breaths ago had called for Frog to be driven out. He was shaking, and to Frog's great satisfaction, when the first cut was made his stepbrother cried out like a scat-smeared baby. "Please!" Scorpion said. "Don't cut me again. Not again."

"Be still and silent!" Stalker called, but Scorpion trembled as hard as ever. Blood flowed down his cheek, as did the water from his eyes.

"Don't cut me!" Scorpion pled.

Stalker glared. "Your father, and his father, and his grandfather back to the beginning all wore these scars. Do not shame us!"

Snake said nothing. Scorpion was the son of his flesh, but in this sacred space within Great Sky itself, no favoritism could be shown.

But something inside Scorpion had broken. He had lost his *num*.

Uncle Snake turned away from his son. If Scorpion could not do this, he would return to the boma. Frog had seen that, and now understood more clearly what he had seen all his life: boys disappearing, then returning, with cheek scars. Thorn Summer was one such. A Between. Such men would never hunt, never lead. They might not even mate. Life for such as these was pitiable. For the rest of their lives they were children who could sit with the old men or the women.

So many things about the previous moon were clear now! Whispers that had ceased when he approached, guarded comments and actions that had made no sense at the time, suddenly became clear in his eyes. Next year Scorpion would have one more chance to become a man. After that, he would either become a Between or be driven from Fire's protective thorn walls.

Frog promised himself that whatever came next, whatever might happen, that would not be *his* fate. The eyes of the other boys said that, terrified or not, all had made similar decisions.

"Will you stand?" Stalker's voice was a knife.

"I will stand," Scorpion said, but leaned back against the others, a hunt chief at either elbow.

The sliver of black rock went to work again, and the first scars were finished. The men rubbed berry pulp into the wound, as they had with Frog and the others, and then turned him to work on the other cheek. It seemed to him that the men were a bit more gentle with them now, less intimidating. Frog knew then that regardless of appearances they did not want the boys to fail.

But what of the threat of rape, so recently given? Despite the pain in his cheek, he knew that it couldn't have been real. It was another lie, a lie told . . .

*To help them be strong, yes.*

The other boys looked at one another as the men worked. Frog turned to Rat and whispered: "I thought Scorpion would be the bravest."

Rat nodded "If he is not the greatest of us . . . then, who?"

Frog smiled to himself. Still in pain, dazed with the cuts and the stinging, but the question still stood: if Scorpion was not the bravest and best of them, then, who?

Yes. *Who?*


When they were led up out of the kiva, a row of torches had been planted in the ground. More hunt chiefs stood in array, wearing their animal masks, their bodies festooned with feathers and leathers, torsos smeared with paint, singing and driving the butts of their spears against the ground.

Frog had his first view of the hunt chiefs' camp. There was no thorn perimeter, almost as if they dared predators to challenge them. Two hands of huts scattered around a clearing, each the same distance from a central fire. Trees had been hewn down for paces in all directions, but not quite in the shape of a circle. No. It took Frog a moment to realize it, but imagining he was an eagle, viewing from above he realized that the clearing was shaped like a man's eye, the kiva at the tear duct.

Frog and the others were escorted to a flat area between the trees. They clustered the boys together, then linked their own ranks into two rows. They held bamboo staves in their hands, and the nature of their intent was clear to Frog at once.

Only Cloud Stalker had not lined up with the others. He stood behind them. "Run!" he said, and struck them with his own stick.

One at a time the boys were forced to run. The lines of hunters struck at them, tripped them, beat them with sticks and kicked at them with callused, knobby feet.

Frog winced away from a blow, stumbled, fell and gasped as stroke after stroke bruised his shoulders, sides and belly.

Ahead of him, Rat fell. As the men beat him without mercy, Frog had to choose: did he run on or help his cousin? Ignoring his own peril, he bent, grabbed Rat's arm and hefted. Together, they ran on, although Frog was smote again and yet again, and his vision furred with sweat.

Frog was shocked at the speed with which he lost his wind. His chest heaved, despite the fact like all Ibandi men, he could run all day using the *huh-huh-huh* hyena breathing. He'd never experienced anything like this, all of the chaos and the screaming and shaking of spears, and the hideous painted faces and the torches.

Once through the gauntlet, they ran for the river, the hunt chiefs whooping close behind.

Frog fell, and immediately a spear haft struck his legs. He groaned, but no one helped him rise.

So be it. Frog helped himself up and hobbled on, and was one of the last to the stream.

They had survived, every one of them.

That was also the day Frog's eyes were fully opened to the death lurking within the game of wrestling. In pairs they grappled and threw each other, but now when one was down, instead of allowing him up so that the game could continue, the hunt chiefs stopped them and taught lessons. And the lessons were those Frog had heard only rumors of: How to cripple. How to kill. How to use rocks and sticks to thrust, to strike, to crush. How to smash knees and break throats. How to bite and tear and gouge.

Something hot and sharp flared within Frog's chest and at the back of his head.

"This is a terrible thing that we teach you," Stalker said. "But we may have to fight for our land. There are others coming. Perhaps they are beast-men. Perhaps something else. We know they have killed bhan, and even Ibandi. They dare enter Great Sky's shadow, and we must prepare."

The boys' eyes widened when they heard these words. The adults had never spoken to them so directly about the threat ahead. Both pride and fear flooded Frog's heart. Children did not hear such words. Only hunters, those who stood between the boma and the lion.

Or boys who, with the grace of Father Mountain, would one day wear a hunter's scars.

•    •    •

After three bruising days of wrestling came the most frightening ceremony of all.

Frog and the others were told to slip off their waistlets and present their roots. River Song, one of the oldest hunt chiefs, a man of calm, sober aspect, took Frog's root in hand and, as Frog fought the temptation to swoon, went to work.

The old one inserted a hardwood stick between the foreskin and the upper side of Frog's glans. Carefully, he rolled the tender foreskin back. With a sliver of glassy black rock he sliced the flesh along either side, creating wings. Frog bit back his cries of pain as River wiped away blood with a bit of moss.

Frog experienced an entire cascade of emotions: fear, humiliation, pride, embarrassment. The facial wounds had hurt less, and these were also more . . . intimate.

"It hurts," River Song said, reading Frog's mind. He touched the rolled flaps of flesh. "This will heal, and gather up under your root." He grinned toothlessly. "Your wife will like it."

Frog winced, struggling to remember that the deeper the cuts, the more powerful the man-magic.


Frog feared that his root would throb forever, or remain hideously deformed in such a way that no woman would want him to enter her body. Worse still, that he was so mangled he would never again be able to run and hunt. Despite those fears, after a hand of days of lying on his back, groaning in misery, he was able to walk without wincing and crying out.

During these times he learned new songs, and watched dances he was far too sore to perform.

If there was any solace to be found, it was in the fact that the other boys seemed even more deeply miserable than he, limping and crying out if their thighs rubbed against their wounded roots. What a fine flock of young hunters they were! Even rabbits would have little to fear from such a toothless pack.

As the other boys sweltered in fever or washed the pus from their new wounds, the hunt chiefs recounted endless tales of their own youthful days, and how soon after becoming hunters they had been singled out for possessing unusually strong or fast limbs. Recognized, the boma fathers nominated them to be hunt chiefs.

They also spoke of hunting secrets, and traveling far to acquire or practice them.

And they danced, oh how they danced at night, their bodies making the most expressive gestures, forming the most awe-inspiring shadows, and Frog was entranced.

"Small men are afraid of their brothers' power," Cloud Stalker said. "Big men raise their brothers up, that heroes may arise from our ranks. I tell you the story of a hero. It is also the story of the first bird on Great Sky."

And he began to dance.

*Once, a long time ago, there was a huge, shapeless monster, Kammapa, who spread terror through the land. He devoured every man and child on earth except one old woman. Without a man to give her seed, she birthed a child who was born wearing holy amulets. She named the child Mountain Walker, knowing that he would rise high and travel far.*

*"Is there no one but you and I in the world?" Mountain Walker asked his mother.*

*"My child," his mother said, "once the land was covered with people, but the monster who haunts the mountain has slain and eaten them all."*

*Hearing this, Mountain Walker knew that his name meant he would have to slay this beast. They fought, and Kammapa swallowed Mountain Walker whole, but with his knife Mountain Walker cut his way from inside the beast, releasing himself and all other people from its stomach.*

*Mountain Walker became grand hunt chief, but people were not happy, for they feared his power. So they decided that Mountain Walker should be murdered, and tried to throw him into a deep pit lined with stakes. Walker was too clever, and escaped.*

*Then his enemies built a fire in the center of the boma, and tried to throw him in. But in the frenzy, they threw in another man instead, and the screams were horrible, the smell driving the moon from the sky.*

*They tried to push him over a cliff, and to smother him in a cave, and always he was too strong and smart. But their hatred took the heart from Mountain Walker, and he grew weary of fighting them. So he let them kill him, and when he died, his body went into the ground except for his heart, which became a hawk and rose up Great Sky, and sits still on the shoulder of Father Mountain.*

The hunt chiefs told them of the climb to the top of Great Sky, to the world of the dead. Some of the boys who had lost parents or beloved cousins wept to hear the words, see the songs the hunt chiefs had carried back from the forbidden land.

They danced out tales of swirling, howling demons made of white powder, defending the passage to Father Mountain's home, and of heroes who had called forth the courage to overcome them. Frog had never heard such things and was confused. What should he believe: his eyes and ears, or the words of these awesome men? He was uncertain, knew only that he would give anything and everything, even his life itself, to see such magic.

He remembered the black and white stones in Cloud Stalker's belt. Did that, and what Frog had done to save Lizard, prove that there *was* no magic? Or had magic merely failed at that moment? Or could it be that he was an instrument of Father Mountain, and that the nature of magic was different than he had ever thought?

In this sacred place, this cave on the slopes of Great Sky, he could more easily believe.

But he swore to himself that one day he would climb the peak and see the gods.

Or see nothing.

Whichever there was.

Even these great men, and great they were, lacked the answers he sought. Perhaps at the top of Great Sky, he could ask Father Mountain. If the god existed at all. Frog no longer knew what to think. There was power here, and knowledge, but he also sensed an emptiness, just beyond the light of his knowing.

# Chapter Twenty

Frightened, but too proud to show his fear, Frog stood shoulder to shoulder with his healing cousins as the boys faced one another in a circle beneath a stand of wild fig and whistling thorn trees. "This is what you will do," Cloud Stalker said. "One at a time, each of you must step into the circle, and you will fight all of the others for as long as we chant."

"What are the rules?" Frog asked.

"There are no rules, except that you stay in the circle."

Frog watched as the largest and the strongest of them all, a boy named Baboon Eye from Wind boma, stepped into the middle. The men began to chant as the boys rushed him. Baboon fought back as best he could, but there was just no way to keep the strokes from falling upon him, and he was dragged down and thrashed. Frog gripped his own staff with sweating hands, wincing at every vibration as he thumped Baboon about the ribs and legs.

It was both exhilarating and frightening. What would happen when his own turn came? How would it feel? What would he do?

And so it went with the next, and the next after that.

In each case the men chanted for about ten and ten breaths, time enough for a generous serving of misery. Frog's stomach soured, and he could smell the stink of Rat's fear, and Scorpion's as well.

Scorpion did well, moving this way and that with the agility gained through endless days of wrestling and tumbling, but then he tired and was dragged down. He curled into a ball and wept as they thumped him.

And then came Frog's time. Old River Song stood before him, peering deeply into his eyes. "Into the circle," he said.

Frog felt very clear, very calm. They had devised the rules. He might use them in his own fashion.

The center of the circle was a very lonely place. All of his cousins faced him, their arms and ribs welted, knots on their foreheads and blood trickling from their noses. They blinked back sweat, chests heaving, simultaneously fearful and excited. Each of them had, in turn, suffered in the circle. They wanted to see how Frog would bear his pain, carry his wounds.

"Go!" River Song called. Instantly, Frog grabbed Scorpion, spinning him so that he was behind his stepbrother, arm around Scorpion's throat. The boy was so surprised that he hadn't time even to squeal. As the others attacked, Frog wheeled Scorpion around and around, using him as a shield. Strokes intended for Frog fell on his cousin instead. Frog felt himself going into a kind of trance, so that he watched the staves falling and it seemed that it was all a dream.

And then it was over. His shoulders and forearms stung a bit, and he felt swollen skin low on his back, but that was nothing compared to the drubbing his brothers had taken.

Frog swore that he saw the hint of a smile on Uncle Snake's ravaged face. "Once I told you to bring me a new thing if you found one, something no one has ever seen before. That," said Snake, "was a new thing."


That was the last thing they did before the hunt chiefs blessed the boys and led them back down the mountain path.

When Frog finally trudged through Fire boma's burnt clearing and through the gate, Wasp and Frog's younger cousins regarded the returning young men as awe-inspiring strangers. He saw his own face in theirs, longed to tell them what had happened to him.

And then realized that no, he did not want to spare them the terror. If *he* had endured it, why not the sprouts? He managed an exhausted smile at the thought. He now understood exactly why no one had ever warned him.

He could hardly wait until it was Wasp's turn.

Sweltering in the day's heat, any bit of shade was a welcome respite.

"Welcome home," Gazelle said, and offered him a gourd of water. He drank deeply, sighing with gratitude. In the loving, tender expression on his mother's face was the kind of pride that he had never seen before.

*My son is a man,* she was saying.

*Not yet, Mother,* he answered without speaking. *Soon now. Not yet.*

Frog crawled into his hut and collapsed onto his side, perspiring and shaking.

He thought he would not be able to sleep, and rest did elude him for a time. Then suddenly he found himself in the world of dreams. In that mystical place trees pranced, and gazelle were rooted to the ground. Everything in his world had changed order, position, perspective. Nothing in Frog's world was the same as it had been. In all likelihood, nothing would ever be the same again.

Frog awoke sweating from a dream in which hunters hunted animals who in turn hunted fleeing boys. He could not see his own face anywhere among them. Was he hunter or prey?

*We are both,* Snake had said.

When he crawled back out of the hut, the sun was heading toward the western horizon. He saw Scorpion creeping around behind the huts, but when their eyes met, his stepbrother flinched.

What next?

Gazelle gave him a gourd filled with mashed yam and pieces of fish, and a folded leaf with a few chunks of hot blackened zorilla meat. The flesh of the small black-and-white furred four-legged was usually one of his favorites, but today . . . today it seemed that every taste and texture was far stronger. All the colors, the smells, the flavors . . . everything so stark and strong that it was as if he had never eaten at all.

His hearing was sharper as well. He could hear every soft, grinding stroke as Uncle Snake slowly and methodically sharpened a knife. Frog stared at his stepfather, and it seemed somehow that he was looking not just at Snake, but at the Snake that he had known as a child. Many, many younger Snakes, with firmer bodies. And then an even younger Snake, one that Frog had never known. His face was unscarred. Both eyes were whole and firm.

A Snake no older than Frog himself. A flash of clarity illuminated Frog's mind, a sudden, strong sense of where he, Frog, fit into the order of things.

He, Frog, would also grow old—if fortune smiled upon him. If he was wary enough to evade the leopard and the lion, he would grow old. If Frog was lucky and wise and strong and good, the reward was to live long enough to watch his body rot.

Was it possible the only reward for a lifetime of work and risk was deterioration and disease? The naked eye of death itself seemed to fix him, the terror that none of his fellows seemed to fear, because unlike him, they *believed*. And if that was true, then who was really more alive in the mind? He who saw through the tricks and lived in constant fear? Or one who succumbed to the mirage and lived his life in joy?

And if there was nothing but the struggle of life, then what good was it all?

Uncle Snake seemed to have been studying Frog through his one good eye, almost as if he could know Frog's mortal thoughts. "You go," he said. "Stay until two moons pass, then you bring zebra. Or boar or topi. Understand? When there is meat to share, you come back."

There it was. He had always known this day would come, but had had no idea how it would feel. It felt as if a precious part of himself was dying. And yet, and yet . . . there was great excitement as well.

"Uncle?" he said. There was so much more that he wanted to say, but dared not. Did Uncle look at him, see in him someone like the boy he once had been? Did he know what Frog had done to save Lizard?

Why could he not wrench his thoughts away from death?

Frog felt as if a mist had cleared away, as if for a brief breath he had clarity that no Ibandi had ever known. There were no gods, no magic. Just men, and animals, and plants, and dirt.

And that was all.

Then the mists closed back in again, and that clarity was gone.

*What if he was wrong?*

Uncle handed him the black rock knife and gave him a hard smile. "You are my brother's son," he said. "Since you were a baby, you have been mine as well. You will succeed."

The knife. He had seen Deep Dry Hole hand Snake that knife. Had Snake accepted it as payment to influence Cloud Stalker? And when the stones had been given, did Stalker return it? Was it a cursed blade, its intentions foiled, and did it now live only to fail poor Frog at some crucial moment?

Frog wanted to wrap his arms around Snake, to feel his strength. *Do you love me, Father? Am I worthy? Am I a bad thing?*

But then, for the first time in memory, Snake simply turned his back, as if Frog had offended him. Snake flicked his hand toward the opening in the boma wall.

A question, a plea rose in Frog's throat, one swiftly repressed.

Frog turned to his mother, Gazelle, who would not look at him either, choosing instead to stare at the ground. Tears dropped from her eyes, puddling in the dust.

So, then. This was goodbye. Young Frog Hopping, the boy he had been only days ago, was dead to them. His heart rumbled in his chest. Today was the beginning of all things! He wanted to be worthy, to make his family proud.

More than anything beneath the sky, more than life itself, he wanted that.

Frog carried nothing but that knife as he walked through the gap in Fire boma's thorn wall. He looked back over his shoulder and saw Scorpion approaching his father. Frog sensed that Scorpion's behavior on the mountain had angered Snake, that despite the bond of blood, Scorpion would have to earn his father's love with a good walkabout. And yet when Scorpion's eye briefly met Frog's, there was no resentment there.

It was fear that Frog saw. And that, he could understand.

What was about to come was terrifying enough to drive petty concerns from Scorpion's mind. They were both in this alone, together.

# Walkabout

# Chapter Twenty-one

"Moon-blood is special," said Stillshadow from the height of her sitting stone. Several of the elder dancers were seated about her, but it was to the younger girls that she directed her words. "It carries in it a living being. It is like a tree. Before bearing fruit, a tree must first bear flowers.

"Moon-blood," she continued, "is like the flower: it must emerge before the fruit—the baby—can be born. Childbirth is like a tree finally bearing its fruit, which the woman then gathers." She was most directly addressing the four girls who had recently begun to bleed: T'Cori, Fawn Blossom, Dove, and Sister Quiet Water. Fawn and her twin sister had already had their seventh eyes opened.

The Ibandi ceremony for the coming of moon-blood was called Tinaalá. It was considered the most important of their religious rituals. Its purpose was to make sex holy and fruitful. During this time, the menstruating girls were secluded in the Tinaalá hut. For one full moon the other dancers sang and celebrated the new women, as T'Cori and the others contemplated the changes within their bodies.

When a woman was in her moon-blood, she was among the most powerful beings in the universe, temporarily raised in status. At such times it was vital to isolate herself so that she would not waste her energy on everyday matters or have her concentration broken by members of the opposite sex.

"Here is the tale," Stillshadow said, and began to dance. The depth, extension and pace of her motions all told the story more eloquently than words.

*Great Mother birthed a blessed daughter, who loved and protected all the animals in the shadow of Great Sky. Angry at a group of hunters who killed more than they could carry, she followed them until, gorged on the flesh of her beloved, they fell into a stupor and slept. She slew each of them in turn, and then appeared before all of the people covered with blood. She grabbed a live antelope with one hand and wiped her other hand over her vulva. She wiped this hand on the antelope's nose, and twisted its nose, and then let it free. From then on, it knew the smell of man. From then on, it was hard for men to hunt the antelope.*

Stillshadow paused, and although the dancing had been impeccable, T'Cori saw that she was more than out of breath: she was shaking. "To the moon shelter," she panted, and Blossom helped her mother to her rest.

Within the Tinaalá hut, T'Cori learned that all of her energy should go toward meditating on the purpose of her life and the gathering of her *num*.

During her days crouched naked in the sweltering hut T'Cori used a special willow stick instead of idly scratching herself with her fingers. It was important to focus her whole attention on her body, to become aware of even the smallest natural actions. It was her duty to study her own body the way hunters studied their prey. The other girls groaned and smeared the sweat with their hands, but T'Cori pulled deep inside herself and was content.

When she emerged from the women's hut, T'Cori watched the world swirl around her, and had to sit on the ground with her head between her legs, waiting for it to slow. When she was ready, Blossom led her to the circle of the eternal fire, a sacred spot protected by a tumble of rocks and ringed with berry vines. She had never been here before. From time to time the old women threw a handful of powders into the fire. When they did green sparks and a sharp spicy aroma rose into the night air.

Some of her sisters were grown now, with children of their own. With Stillshadow's approval, some of those children would become the next generation of dream dancers. Others would marry or be adopted into the inner bomas. Some were younger than she, girls who had been given to the dream dancers as infants, just now entering the circle. Not all born to the dream dancers became medicine women. Every woman who yearned to be of the circle had to be approved by Stillshadow. With some, Stillshadow sorrowfully looked into their hand-eyes or face-eyes and said: "This one does not have the fire."

And for those, when the butterflies returned and it was time for Spring Gathering, families were found to take them in. Tears stained Stillshadow's cheeks when one of them left, but she wiped the water away quickly, and never knew she had been seen.

The younger girls gazed at the older ones with an almost worshipful awe.

Stillshadow strode among them, tired, perhaps, but still powerful as a gray-muzzled old she-lion. Her voice rang from the rocks. "We live lives apart from the others, apart from the normal women. But this is not a loss. We are the soul of the Ibandi! We are the heart beating within their chests. Only as long as we, the dream dancers and the hunt chiefs, are whole are we a true people. Only so long as we sing is a new sun born every morning. Only as long as we keep the fire does Father Mountain know we are here, and protect us," Stillshadow said.

Raven bowed her head. "It is sometimes lonely," she said.

"Yes!" Stillshadow replied. "It is lonely, but that is our place. And it is only lonely to she who does not feel the warmth of the mountain's shadow, who does not hear Great Mother's voice. The mountain calls to some of our sisters now."

Immediately, the girls around the fire began to buzz. What did this mean? Were some of them to be blessed in such a fashion? Stillshadow spoke to each of them in turn, explaining what they must do to earn power and honor. To T'Cori and several others, Stillshadow nodded. "And it is your part to bring back healing herbs."

"Which herbs?" T'Cori asked.

"Close your eyes," the old woman said sharply, but then softened her voice. "Close them!"

They complied.

"Now think of this: imagine that the hunters of Earth boma are leaving to seek flesh. They are gone for many days, and when at last they return, four have been tusked by an elephant. Of those, you must heal those who are able to heal. Some will return to the mountain. You must help them die without pain. You have learned much by now. Go, and find those things needed to make this happen."

T'Cori thought about this, understanding what was being asked. *Heal those who can heal, and provide* num-*chilling potions for those who are beyond healing.* She knew of poisons, of course, as did the hunters. But the idea of using them on her own people was sobering indeed. "Could I start with thistleroot?"

"Do not ask me, girl," the old woman thundered. "Have you not watched and listened these years? Your men rely upon you."

"When shall I go?"

"Tomorrow. But not just you. Your sisters also." Then as if the speech had emptied her, Stillshadow sighed deeply, and sat.

T'Cori searched her feelings, seeking the meaning in those words. She, T'Cori. Fawn. Dove. Sister Quiet Water. Could they do this? They were being asked to function as women of the tribe, with all the freedoms and responsibilities that that implied. Her next words emerged as a whisper. "Where must we go?"

"The best thistleroot can be found to the west, beyond Father Mountain's shadow," Stillshadow said.

Dove blinked hard. "I . . . saw thistleroot in the rocks near the stream. . . ."

Stillshadow smiled at Dove's feeble attempt to influence her fate. "Oh, no," she said. "A baboon pissed on that. We need *new* root. Do you understand me?"

T'Cori nodded, trembling. "Yes, teacher."

"Go," Stillshadow said. "Prepare for the morning. And then sleep."


Although the camp was unusually quiet that night, deep sleep evaded T'Cori. Fawn Blossom and her twin, Dove, were even less fortunate. Twice during the night the nameless one awakened to hear them tossing and groaning, muttering to themselves as if afraid they would be devoured on the morrow.

And perhaps they would.

When sleep finally came, T'Cori dreamed of colored bands bending and bonding around her, of a sun blazing fire tracks in the sky, of a moon little more than a hole torn in the darkness, a tunnel to all the secrets of this world and the next. She was restless, but excited as well.

This was her chance.

T'Cori swore she would make Mother Stillshadow proud.

She glanced at Raven. Could the girl hear that she had called Stillshadow mother, even in her mind?

No, of course not.

Still, it was always best to be careful.


.   .   .

In the morning, T'Cori began her cleanliness rituals. After all, they were voyaging out as brides of Great Sky, with faith that the mountain itself would keep them safe from harm. They had to look and feel the part.

So they washed and prepared themselves. Stillshadow made a mush of red berries and urine. With it she painted stripes and swirls along their bodies. Then she made white markings with a lump of chalk, sketching the bones and skull beneath the flesh.

The chalk tickled, like a furry caterpillar crawling up their legs, but not a giggle escaped the girls. There had been no moment in their lives more serious than this, and every one of them knew it.

When this was done Stillshadow drew the girls around her, and there spoke to them plainly. Her flame was cool and calm.

"One day my flesh will flow up the mountain," the old woman said. "My daughter Raven will keep the fire, but you will be at her side, and some of you will stand high."

"How will you decide?" Sister Quiet Water asked.

"Your dreams will tell the tale," the old woman said. "One at a time, I will come to each of you. In the night, in the dream time, I will show you a dance. Display these steps for me, and you are the one.

"Dance in your dreams," she told them. "Live in them. Come to me, although you are far away. The one who can dance my dance in dreams is the one who will follow me." She paused, the very silence adding significance to her words. "Great Mother speaks in dreams," she said.

Alone in the cool of her hut, T'Cori knelt and with ritual precision gathered her bundle, rolled it in a zebra hide, and slung it over her back. Within was a sleeping skin, as well as dried meat and a pouch to carry whatever herbs and medicinal plants the girls gathered. Within it she would also carry foodstuffs or small creatures her guides might trap and kill. Every small motion, twist of wrist, and flex of her shoulders was as controlled as a dance. Softly, she sang a sacred journey song.

Whirling Pool, a slender stick of a nine-spring, scurried up to her. "How long will you be gone?" Although young, Pool knew the name of every plant on Great Earth, and could repeat a dance after seeing it only once. She spread her arms and turned in a circle, dancing her name.

Some of the fear T'Cori had not allowed herself to feel last night finally made itself known as a sour taste in the back of her throat, a tightness in her legs. "I don't know. Days. Nights." She paused. "A moon, perhaps. I am afraid."

"Don't be afraid," Whirling Pool said, perhaps peering into her flame. "Mother would not send you if you were not ready."

"I hope you're right," T'Cori said. "I'm not sure I'll ever be ready."

Pool hugged T'Cori, then ran away. T'Cori realized that the words of encouragement were not actually meant for her. Whirling Pool was actually speaking to her own older self, knowing that one not so distant day it would be her own turn, wanting to believe that when that day came, things would be fine.

When the girls were ready, they gathered together. Stillshadow blessed them, sprinkling a pinch of powder over each bowed head. Then, together, they started down Great Earth's slopes, heading southeast.

"Why must we do this?" Fawn pouted.

"Because it is the path," T'Cori said.

Fawn glared at her. "Aren't you afraid?" she asked.

"This is everything we have trained for. We have protection—the hunt chiefs are with us, and we are on Great Mother's work. When we return, we will be women." She felt Fawn's fear and frustration, but knew that strong words could stiffen a weak spine.

Dove spoke for all of them. "We'll be fine if we stay together. It's a test of trust."

T'Cori prayed that that was true. But as she descended the path and glimpsed the two armed hunt chiefs who would accompany the young women, all strength seemed to abandon her. What was she doing? Didn't Stillshadow know that there were risks out there, beyond the shadow? And why did she, T'Cori, imagine she could do such a thing?

Then the taller of their guides turned. Owl Hooting smiled at her. And at that moment, she knew that all was right with the world.

# Chapter Twenty-two

The four young dream dancers walked away from the rising sun. The girls carried slender bamboo walking sticks to help them across uneven ground and steep grades. Throughout the day they kept a steady pace, stopping occasionally to rest, study the plant life, or test the wind for unknown smells. Their escorts remained ahead of them far enough that it was all too easy to imagine themselves utterly alone.

They proceeded in a strange fashion. First the girls decided upon a destination near the horizon, and then the hunt chiefs led the way until they had reached that spot, and the girls chose again.

The nameless one found herself incapable of taking her eyes from Owl Hooting as he led the way. She found Owl's loose, easy stride as dizzying as any of Stillshadow's potions.

T'Cori found it impossible to ignore the flex and play of muscles in the small of Owl's back. She could not stop looking at the clustered scars, rewards for his skills and ranking among the hunt chiefs.

When the sun was directly above them, Owl held up his hand, signaling for them to stop.

"What is it?" Sister Quiet Water asked.

"Lion scat," he growled.

"Lions?" T'Cori asked.

"Perhaps," he said. For two hands of breaths they waited as he tested the air, then his tight shoulders relaxed, and he waved them onward.

They encountered the actual droppings only a little later, partially covered in sand. Owl Hooting bent, speaking with his fellow about the antelope fur fuzzing the gummy mass, speculating upon where and how the hapless animal had been run down.

After the setting sun smote their eyes and the evening sky purpled, the girls stopped to camp. Owl and his brother cut thornbushes to make rude walls and vined them in a circle around their fire. T'Cori and her sisters ate some of their dried antelope meat. Not too much—it had to last until Owl and his brother made a hunt or until they found nuts and turtle eggs for a meal. Then the dream dancers lay down to sleep, trusting in the hunt chiefs to tend the fire and protect them.

In the morning T'Cori ate more, and the girls made their toilet. Then they continued on, traveling southeast.

The flat savannah was dotted with brush, patches of spiky green grass and trees with gnarled trunks. Herds of drowsy zebra and dusty wrinkled elephants lumbered past, usually ignoring the humans, but occasionally glancing and trumpeting in warning, protecting their calves.

Kites and hawks and buzzards weighed down the top branches of the trees, and although some fled as the humans approached, other birds and animals simply watched the procession, judging the newcomers to be no threat.

They saw evidence of both life and death: carcasses splayed in the sun with vultures or crows pecking, others that had crumbled to insect fodder. Dung beetles rolled away balls of half-dried elephant droppings in their path. Within days, nothing would remain.

From time to time, each of them looked back in the direction of Great Earth. Already, the only home T'Cori had ever known was swallowed in a blur of clouds.

"I have never been so far from home," Dove said.

The sense of loneliness was swelling within them when Quiet Water called, "Look! Thistleroot!"

Instantly the mood shifted to one of excitement. "How much should we bring back?" Fawn asked.

Dove paused, fingering the green, minty sprigs. Thistleroot grew in knee-high bunches as large as a woman's hand. "Should we divide this? Or should it all go to Sister Quiet Water, who saw it first?"

T'Cori clucked at them. "I think that it is more than that. Mother wants to learn how we are together. Do we work together? Who makes the way smoother?"

Fawn scratched her head. "You should not call her mother. Raven would beat you."

"Raven is not here," T'Cori replied.

## Chapter Twenty-three

For half the day now, since long before dawn, Frog lay beside the wait-a-bit bush, struggling to keep his breath calm. Late the previous day he had detected the nyala tracks leading down to the water hole, and remembered one of the first things Uncle Snake and Break Spear had told him of the art of hunting.

*Look for them at dusk and dawn. It is then that the four-legged go to the watering holes, knowing that many meat-eaters hunt at night and men hunt during the day. Dawn and dusk are the times when elands and nyalas hope the lions and leopards and men are asleep and unaware. This is when you will find them.*

He'd spent the first day walking west, away from the places of possible danger. It took Frog three days to pass Great Earth and Earth boma, finally breaking into the bush beyond the Circle. Until this time he lived on fruit and nuts gathered as he went—all of this territory was known to him.

Singing songs of hunts and knots and whittling, he kept his eyes open for anything that he could use. A bleached buffalo skeleton, tumbled in a dry wash, triggered his imagination. Frog broke the rotted old ligaments to tear a shinbone free. *This,* he thought as he slipped it into his sack, *a clever boy could find use for.*

The following day, Frog walked until he found new water, and then soon afterward found the branches needed for a fire-bow and spears. The happy discovery of a knobby stand of fill-cactus gladdened his heart. As he hacked out its heart and scraped pulp into a folded leaf, he swore he would not need it. . . . But on the other hand, if hunting went poorly and hunger bared its teeth, he would be happy for the respite.

He made and set snares, determining to return the next day to check his luck. Now then . . . where *was* that poison-grub bush Uncle Snake had been so happy to find? A quarter later he located it, and dug up thumb-long, wiggling red-ringed crawlers. Grinning, he simply squeezed the grub's guts directly on the tip of his spear. Uncle Snake probably wouldn't approve, but then again, Uncle Snake wasn't here, was he?

The previous night Frog had thought not to have fire, figuring that the smell of smoke sometimes scared off prey: fire was friend only to man, not animals.

But tonight he longed for the comfort of the leaping tongues, needed to remember home. He brought together the materials for a fine blaze, thinking that tonight he might very well cook chunks of a potential kill. Of course, he would have preferred to bring a coal from the family hearth, but Uncle Snake had watched him carefully. He would have to make his own fire. If he did not, if he *could* not, Frog Hopping was unfit to provide for a family.

So he took stock of his gathered resources. Most important among them was a flexible green branch as thick as his finger. It was both strong and springy, and about as long as his arm.

As he went to work, all disappointment drained away. The sun was near the western horizon and would be down shortly, only the stars and the moon above providing light. Time was vital.

Using his stone knife, Frog cut notches in the ends of the branch, then tied tough woven vine around the ends. This was an important skill: choosing the vines, weaving thin ones together tightly to make a strong, pliable cord. The texture was also important. Select the wrong vines, and there would be too much or too little friction, which was not good.

When the bow was bent and the vines tight, he tested the stretch. This had to be just right, and feeling the tension of the vines was another skill that took time to learn.

The vine was the right length, the bow tight. He was a little afraid that it might break, so when he inserted the drill stick he looped it once, rolling the bow back and forth, testing. Then he stopped, started over by adjusting the length of his makeshift twine, then tried again, this time satisfied that the flex of the branch made the vine snug enough to provide good traction.

Frog required two other pieces to build a blaze, and he had spent the earlier part of the day making these ready. One was the fire trough, and the other was a cap for the stick. Two pieces of wood were sufficient, but it had taken a quarter to find the right pieces.

Already, his efforts had gouged a furrow in the wood now flat against the ground, and braced between his knees. As he slipped the stick into position, Frog tested the friction and draw by rolling the bow back and forth. This time, he managed to make it turn evenly.

It was important to begin with a drill stick as straight as possible, about as thick as one's small finger. If the drill stick was not straight, it would wobble and become absurdly difficult to control.

The fire trough was the buffalo shinbone Frog had discovered in the ravine. Uncle Snake told Frog that his father, Baobab, had always preferred bone to wood. The stick was cut to a dull point—not a sharp one, as he had seen some of the other boys make. Uncle Snake had judged that a bad idea. It could actually burn a hole in the bone, and where would he be then?

Frog braced his knee against the shinbone and nestled the stick in the depression. The bowstring was set facing his leg, with the bow wood horizontal and away from him. The piece of wood capped the stick, and he leaned down on it just enough to make the proper contact with the tip of the stick and the bone.

Then, humming a fire song to keep time, Frog began a gentle sawing motion, as he had been taught by Uncle, and as Uncle had been taught by *his* father, back to the first sons of Father Mountain.

Placing the bone over the log, Frog sawed smoothly, back and forth, back and forth, not letting the vine catch, a little worried that if it did, it might break. There was a perfect rhythm to be found here, and Frog searched until he found it. The smooth play of his muscles, leaning on the stick, turning it with each bow stroke—all of these melded together until he smelled the first smoky wisps. He continued for a few more strokes, until the smell grew stronger, then stopped and looked at the little coal glowing in the depression of the wood.

Although he added only a few tiny pinches of tinder at a time, Frog accidentally smothered the coal, and it died. He did not lose heart: this was a skill in which he was reasonably proficient, even if perfection continued to elude him.

He would continue. He would open the door between the human world and the world of fire, and it would come. It would.

With infinite patience, Frog began again. This time when the first spicy curl of smoke tickled his nose he smiled and continued. He sprinkled a pinch of shaved wood and dried moss into the depression, and continued his stroking until the smoke darkened, the sign that it was almost there.

Frog took away the bone and bow, and brought his lips down close to the glowing embers, blowing carefully, adding a few more scraps of dry moss, until the first tiny tongue of flame appeared.

It was easy to build on that initial success, and in a few hands of breaths he had summoned a healthy fire and was feeding it scraps of stick. When it could eat those handily, he gave it larger sticks, and then carefully stacked rocks around the edge of the fire pit, adding wood as it felt safe to do so.

And when he had summoned a fire-spirit fully to life, and it accepted his offerings of sticks and shavings with a grateful crackle, Frog lay back, ate nuts and berries gathered during the day and went to sleep with a reasonably full belly and a contented smile on his face.

Just Frog and the fire, two predators in the night.


Awakening the very next morning, Frog knew the ancestors were pleased with him. Through the tall grass he spied, just within spear-casting distance, the gray-brown flank of a grazing antelope. He was as silent as he had ever been rolling up, setting himself and making a good throw. The spear struck the antelope in the belly, driving fist deep. The wounded buck bucked and tried to run, but made only five steps before toppling onto its side.

*Thank you, Father Mountain,* he thought as he cut its throat. Fresh meat, and so soon after beginning the hunt! But it was too soon to take the carcass back to Fire boma. His people needed to know that he could survive in the bush for at least a moon.

He had to dress the antelope immediately, remembering the lessons learned from Uncle Snake. The sooner the organs were removed, the faster the meat would cool, delaying putrefaction.

Hands shaking, Frog ripped and sliced the liver free from the steaming guts and ate it raw, savoring the hot blood spilling over his chin.

Then Frog got down to business. It was important to keep dirt and foreign objects away from the exposed body cavity. Removing the scent glands was not absolutely necessary, but the hunt chiefs saved the glands for use as cures while hunting. Removing the glands carelessly could taint the meat.

He rolled the carcass over on its back, placing the rump lower than the shoulders, and spread the hind legs. With his uncle's obsidian knife Frog made a cut along the centerline of the belly, from breastbone to base of tail. First cut through the hide, then through the tough belly muscle. To avoid cutting into the paunch and intestines he held them away from the knife with his left hand while guiding the stone sliver with his right.

Frog cut through the sternum and up the neck as far as he could, looking to remove as much of the windpipe as possible. The windpipe rotted rapidly and would taint the meat before he could eat or cure it.

He cut around the anus and drew it into the body cavity, so that it came free with the guts. Very very careful here. Piercing the bladder would be an unpleasant mistake: no hunter wanted a dead antelope pissing on its own flesh!

Frog loosened and rolled out the stomach and intestines, then cut around the edge of the diaphragm, which separated the chest and stomach cavities. He split the breastbone. Then Frog reached forward to cut the windpipe and gullet ahead of the lungs. This allowed him to pull the lungs and heart from the chest cavity. The heart was good meat, a nugget of pure chewy flavor the size of his brother Wasp's fist.

There were important decisions to make. He could hang the corpse from a tree, using spice to keep the flies away, but he had no spice. Frog wasted no time longing for what he did not have, choosing instead to make himself a slow fire, enveloping the meat with smoke. This would both cook it, dry it and add a savory smoky flavor.

That night he ate well, and was satisfied with himself. No mere berries and nuts tonight! Young Frog was off to a very good start indeed.

Two days later, Frog smeared his flanks with zebra dung to hide his scent, and crouched out of sight in the brush. If the animals came down here, then he would kill with his spear. He had made two more spears, but the fire-hardening was not yet complete. Still, it just might be enough.

In a moon he would return in triumph, as a full-fledged Ibandi man, and earn his second scar. His root was still sore but improving with every passing day. He could run without lightning bolts of pain lancing through him. Then at the next Spring Gathering, one of the eligible women might ask her father to pick him, and his life would begin.

For two days Frog had seen no other human beings, just endless horizons of brown and green grasses, low bushes and flat-topped trees below a fleece of thin white clouds. Against that placid background loped giraffes, herds of zebra and the occasional waddling warthog. In midday he passed a lake pink with storks and white with lazy, sleeping ibis. Although he was more completely isolated than he had ever been in his life, Frog was too excited to feel lonely.

A sound tickled his ear. Antelope? *No.* Nosing its way over the crest of the ridge came a single pig, dark gray against the predawn. It snuffled the air carefully, perhaps searching for predators. To his delight, Frog remembered that that was what *he* was. A predator. One who brought death to the unwary.

His heartbeat quickened.

"Come, little pig," he whispered, so softly that in the tremor of a breeze that stirred the grasses, his words were lost. "Come to mighty Frog. My spear is thirsty."

The pig wandered down, snuffling to itself, and finally reached the pool. It looked around again. Did it smell the zebra dung? If so, did it wonder where the zebra itself might be? He wondered if leopards ever rolled in dung to mask their scent, and thought it unlikely. Frog had seen the cats hunting, at rest and at play, and they usually seemed fastidious, pausing to lick themselves or groom each other whenever any kind of soil mucked their fur.

So his plan *might* work. Only a few steps closer, and the pig would be near enough for a cast. Frog held his breath, as he had been taught, making his breathing shallow enough that he himself could not hear it. Some of the old men said that pigs could smell your breath, but he didn't know if he truly believed that.

It was closer now, and soundlessly, he drew his spear back.

He could hear Uncle Snake in his mind. *There is great magic in the casting of a spear. The hunter must feel the connection between himself and the prey. He must find the animal heavy with life, ready for death. And when the animal's heart hears the prayer spoken by the hunter, it decides whether this is the time and place for it to return to the mountain.*

He remembered all of this, acted out at the fireside by his uncle and cousins. They would perform pantomimes in the boma, and at Spring Gathering, when the tribe's experienced hunters shared their tales. The young men listened and dreamed of the days when they would have their own stories to tell.

If the hunter's heart was true, and he made a true request of the prey, and the prey was ready to die, then a line of light connected them. One needed only to guide the spear along that shining path, and the prey was food for the boma.

But as Frog very carefully, very slyly pulled his arm back, the shaft brushed against the grass, making a *sshhhh*ing sound. Instantly, the pig glanced up from its drinking. The sudden movement of his target startled him, rushed him, and the young hunter cast the spear just a moment too soon.

His prayer went unheeded, or his heart was weak, or it was not the cursed pig's time to die. Frog's spear grazed its side as his prey reared around and bolted. He was out of his hunting hole instantly, but not fast enough.

The pig was charging back up the hill, madly pumping its absurdly stubby little legs. Frog threw another spear, this one sighting by eye and not by heart. Predictably, it didn't even brush his target's flank. With a shake of its delicious rump, his dinner disappeared into the brush.

Frog's arms and legs trembled and he sank to his knees, drooling disappointment into the soil beneath his knees. Retrieving both spears, he trudged back to the little rock crevice that served as home.

At least he had what was left of the antelope. He had wrapped the smoked meat in its own hide, and then rolled rocks atop it. . . .

As soon as he reached the rocks, Frog knew that something was wrong. The rocks had been pushed aside, the dirt scrabbled up in a rooting frenzy.

The dirt was a blur of four-toed hyena tracks. He knew *exactly* what had stolen his food, could almost hear the scavenger's yipping laughter as it dug up his prize.

Frog changed his lodgings that night, cursing his carelessness, his stupidity. Most of all, he cursed the rumblings of an empty stomach.

## Chapter Twenty-four

As his campfire crackled and cast leaping shadows in his little alcove, Frog sipped water from his gourd and thought back over the day's events. "What did I do wrong?" he whispered. "Fathers, tell me. Was I not fast enough? Not strong enough?" His thin arms' weakness haunted him. "I must try harder tomorrow. Harder," he whispered. "I cannot fail."

Beyond the mouth of his little resting place, he watched the stars as they emerged in the night sky. Each of them *did* seem to be an eye. Perhaps what he had said to Lizard had not been so false a tale as he had feared.

The ancestors gazed at him. Measured him, and found him wanting.

All of his doubts and fears, kept at bay by his fire-making, rushed back to plague him. "Perhaps I am not good enough. Not a real Ibandi. Perhaps I am only bhan." He paused. "Perhaps not even bhan," he said. "Perhaps only beast-man."

This, at last, caused a chuckle. But the sound lost its humor rapidly and he quieted. Frog crouched closer to the fire, and despite the warmth, he shivered.

With all his will Frog bore down. He refused to allow despair even the tiniest victory. "I must do better tomorrow," he said, and resolved to do so.


In the morning Frog performed a few monkey stretches and baboon rolls to work the knots out, and ate his remaining food: a handful of nuts. He needed to hunt, and the hunt needed to succeed.

The idea of returning home in empty-handed disgrace did not sit well with him. He remembered what happened to failed hunters. He had watched Thorn and some of the other Betweens at Spring Gathering sitting with the gray-hairs, weaving and repairing tools. It was not a pleasant thought, and the women who sexed with such men were far from the most desirable.

The thought of Fawn writhing atop him, drawing fire from his eggs, doubled his resolve.

So after he soothed the knots from his bones, Frog spent the day making deadfalls and snares. While unlikely to reap a large meat animal, such traps just might keep him alive long enough to learn whatever it was he needed to learn to survive. When his empty belly growled at him, Frog reluctantly chewed pinches of fill-cactus pulp, and hunger's cries softened into whispers.

He would hunt. He would trap or fish. He would learn.


As the sun climbed in the sky, Frog moved cautiously across the plain, stopping frequently to sniff the air, filling his nostrils with a heady blend of scents. He smelled green, live plants as well as their rotting parents and cousins. In addition, the air roiled with the scent of live and dead animals . . . but leaf-eaters, not the strong nose-wrinkling meat-eater's scent. Frog was a meat-eater as well, but his fangs and claws were smaller than those of the great cats. He strove never to forget that. That mistake had cost the lives of far too many good hunters.

That very mistake may have cost his father, Baobab, his earthly existence. Cost Uncle Snake the left side of his face.

Frog came to a place where the water trickled up out of the earth and ran down to a clear, cool, rock-rimmed pool. He knelt close to the earth, looking slantwise so that the light would best reveal the footprints: antelope, gnu, baboon, the tiny elephant hyrax.

The thought of a juicy baboon haunch made his mouth water. The hooting manlike beasts were especially tasty, one of his very favorites.

A hunter had to decide what to hunt. If he came across other acceptable prey, only a fool declined the gift of fresh meat, but only a fool hunted without knowing what he was hunting *for*.

"Could this be a place to wait?" he asked himself. It did, indeed, seem a good place, a place Uncle Snake or Fire Ant might have chosen. He stopped to see if he could hear their voices in his head; he could not, but he did see the lean and honorably scarred faces of his forefathers.

By the warmth of their smiles, he knew this to be a good place.

So Frog dragged branches, scooped earth and made himself a hunting trench. He lined it with his antelope skin and burrowed in, covering himself over. Here he would wait. Here, he hoped, he would finally find what he sought.

And if not, his two hands of snares might yield a hare, doves, or a small pig. Tonight he would eat fresh meat and, in continuing to learn about this area, find a way to hunt and kill even larger creatures. It would be good.

By late afternoon the blazing sun was sinking toward the horizon. A quarter of daylight remained, but . . .

Then Frog caught the first meaty, acid whiff and froze in the trench. Hands of hands of heartbeats passed, and then spiky sheaves of grass parted and an immense, wedge-shaped yellow head thrust slowly through. The hungry eyes scanned the water hole, blinking slowly as they slid back and forth and back again. For a dreadful moment the eyes seemed to fix on him. Frog was certain that the lioness had seen him, but then the great head turned away.

He was frozen, unable to move; he felt like a stone. His nose still wrinkled at her rank, meaty scent.

Frog felt the wind blowing against his face and beseeched it. "Please, wind. Do not change. Please, do not bring my scent to the lion," he whispered. "Please. Please."

She lapped languidly, perhaps thinking to wet her throat before a fine meal of fresh young Frog. She seemed about to turn toward him, but then came a gobbling cry from over the rise. Baboon. The she-lion looked directly at Frog. No question now: she saw him. He was quite certain that she was going to circle the water hole and eat him, but instead, with a single languid switch of her tail, she turned and stalked away.

Drained by tension and relief, Frog sagged in his trench. If a ripe deer had appeared at that very moment, Frog couldn't have summoned the strength to spit.

"Father Mountain," he whispered, trembling, "you let me live. You must give life for a reason. Let me die, or help me find my way."

# Chapter Twenty-five

Two days had passed.

Blood seething with fill-cactus, Frog felt no hunger but remained desperate for nutrition. Despite his best efforts, his traps were as empty as his belly. He began to consider walking home. Five days' walk, without meat for strength, but he would find plants as he traveled, and perhaps turn up logs for grubs. He would survive. Shame was better than starvation.

Wasn't it?

He lay in his hunting trench, the heat of the day broiling him so that from time to time he had to creep out like the frog he was and lap water to replenish his strength. Then he would creep back and take his position again. And wait.

During that time, although he lay in the shade, the very heat nudged him into an odd place between sleep and wakefulness. And in that strange time, he found himself dreaming of many things, among them the girl he had once called Butterfly. He found himself thinking of her hair, tied in those exquisite dream dancer knots. Of her green-flecked eyes and delicate hands.

And how she had climbed, that day on the tree! He remembered now, but in that memory he found himself gazing at her legs and the play of the long, powerful muscles of her thighs.

He shook his head.

"Why do I think of the nameless one?" he asked the clouds, but although they had faces, their mouths remained silent.

Frog struggled to remember one of his brief interactions with T'Cori, so long ago. He almost never saw her except at Spring Gatherings, of course, but he had seen her at those for as long as he could remember.

What had she said to him?

*Make a picture in your head.* A picture. He closed his eyes, and the dark space in his head shimmered. Something began to stir in that darkness. Something. But what?

Was his mind just bringing him images of something he had already heard? Or smelled? Or . . . ?

There was the image, bright in his mind, clear at last, as if smoke had blown away from his mind. A fat, juicy warthog, trotting in his direction. His mouth watered at the thought. Oh, if only. He remembered a great feast at last Spring Gathering, when a tasty hog had been rolled into a cook-pit lined with glowing stones.

After the men had eaten, oh, the steaming flesh that had been his to enjoy! What he wouldn't give for another feast such as that one!

Frog opened his eyes, and . . .

*Snuffle, snuffle.*

Waddling down the path toward him was the plumpest, tastiest pig Frog had ever seen. Its coloration was different from what he had imagined: almost black, instead of light brown. Still, he was dizzied by the sudden sense of power and magic. Certainly, if gods there were, then Father Mountain had given him a vision, and this was the fulfillment of that vision. And when such a blessing occurred, it was up to the hunter to be sure that his arm was strong and his aim true.

"Come to me," he whispered. "Come to me. Wet my spear. If you will die for me, I will honor you always. I will tell my children and my children's children that *you* were only the second to come to me, who gifted me with blood and flesh that I might become a man. Please."

He could feel it now, the naked yearning to earn his scars so powerful that it dizzied him.

Sniffing the air, the warthog came closer. . . .

Frog's hand tightened on the haft of his spear. He felt his own heartbeat, imagined extending his *num* until it touched his prey's. Then, as it lowered its head to drink, he threw his first spear.

Struck in the left front leg, the hog squealed in pain. Frog leapt from his blind, putting everything he had into the charge. Only at the very last instant did he remember how dangerous warthogs could be.

At that moment Frog swiveled aside. The hog charged at him, drawing a line of blood from his belly with its left tusk. But Frog did not feel fear, as he would have expected; rather, those endless days of practice saved his young hide. He weaved and leapt simultaneously, driving his second spear into the wattled black flesh of its throat.

*Yes!*

It reared back, squealing in agony. Frog snatched at the first spear, wrenched it out. Blood gouted, spraying the pig and Frog as well. In almost the same breath he stabbed it again, alongside the first wound.

The pig was not yet done. Blinded by its own blood, it spun. Pain split Frog's world like a bolt of lightning in the summer sky as the pig's tusks ripped into his right hip, tearing skin. Panic flared, but Frog's mind clamped down on it: now he understood the pig's movement, realized that he was faster than his foe, and the joy blossomed in his heart.

It tried to run, but its stubby legs gave out and it collapsed. Exhausted and dying, it gazed up at Frog. Its front legs scrabbled at the dust a bit. Then it just lay there, blinking, ribs expanding and contracting, blood running from its side.

And then, as Frog stabbed it again, its breathing stopped.

That night, Frog gorged on flesh that was half raw and half burnt. Between mouthfuls he bounced to his feet, waving his spear at the sky, prancing in total joy, shouting his pleasure to the moon. "Who is the greatest hunter beneath the sky?" he called. "Who is the greatest? I! Frog! Frog of the Ibandi!"

He screamed and swayed. From far across the savannah came an answering scream, baboons perhaps . . . or men pretending to be baboons.

Hunting calls.

Fear shivered away Frog's joy. He dampened his fire, and squatted down in the darkness beside the cooling embers.

Perhaps Frog was a great hunter. Perhaps not. Either way he was certain of one thing: the night held creatures far more frightening and dangerous than Frog, and it was an incautious hunter indeed who ignored that sobering reality.

# Chapter Twenty-six

T'Cori and her sisters had spent the first days away from home gathering as they hiked, then finally they set up camp in a fissure in the side of a ravine. Yellow and red vines strangled the wall. Fat black-and-yellow bees busily traveled from flower to flower but didn't molest the humans who made their camp in the shelter of the granite gap.

It was Sister Quiet Water, graceful and placid as her name, who had carried the coal from the eternal fire. She and T'Cori shared the honor of awakening and fanning it to greater life. This was a holy process: removing the coal from its leather sack, awakening it from its bed of clay and leaves, blowing on it until it glowed, feeding it until it smoked, building it up until the flame sprouted forth once again.

The nameless one was absurdly happy in both work and leisure. Whenever her eyes rested on Owl Hooting, her heart raced in her chest.

This was her chance, and she knew it. It might well be the only opportunity she would ever have. Stillshadow would be angry, the gods and her ancestors likewise, but T'Cori wanted to pick her own first time. And if she dared to take her fate in her own hands, to decide when her seventh eye was to open, then she would choose this fine young warrior. The only question was when.

Both guards were strong and tall and excellent with their spears and bows, the pride of the hunt chiefs. Owl Hooting and his brother Leopard Claw were two of Cloud Stalker's many sons, sired with women of Wind and Earth bomas. It was widely thought that Owl might well follow his father in leadership of the great Circle.

The males kept their distance from the dream dancers, occasionally pointing out sights of interest or tracks that portended danger. They remained alert, but as day faded slowly into evening, they kept to their own fire, hunched low and singing together of snares or tracking or whatever concerned young hunters in their prime. T'Cori did not know, but longed to have such a man in her own hut, one to share her life with, to listen to as he told his stalking stories. A man to share sex with, making love and children together.

But that was not her path. So with the other girls she sorted her herbs, tended the fire, and made their meals.

On this night, they had finished a meal of fish and berries when a wavering call went up from the brush beyond their firelight's liquid limits. It was a high, ululating cry that rose and fell and rose again before dying away. The girls glanced at one another soberly.

"A soul returns to the mountain," Dove said.

They stood and left the cave. Their guides outside had set up a thorn barricade, one by no means as extensive as a boma wall, but enough to give a leopard pause, or force it to make noise as it crept through.

"Did you hear that?" T'Cori asked.

Owl Hooting nodded and pointed toward the southern horizon. "A lion kills a baboon," he said. "One dies. One eats." He shrugged.

She longed to extend the conversation, but a sudden wave of shyness shushed her. T'Cori stood on a log until her head was above the thornbushes, and peered out to the south. Certainly she had heard such cries before. Never had they frightened her as this one had. Never had it been so easy to imagine that she herself might have been that baboon, howling beneath bloody claws.

The shadows were deeply purple, dark enough to steal all of the light. She could see nothing.

She turned slowly, searching in the other directions as well. She was about to step down when her eyes focused on something flickering just at the edge of her vision, almost beyond her ability to resolve the image.

"A fire," she said, and pointed.

One at a time the other girls and then their male guards peered out toward the distant light. At times it seemed to die completely, but then it happened again, twinkling like a star at twilight. "A campfire," Leopard Claw said.

"Who is that?" Sister Quiet Water asked.

"I wonder if it is a brother," T'Cori said.

"Perhaps it is one of *them*," Quiet Water said. The emphasis made it clear she meant one of the murderous beast-men, or whatever creatures might be even worse.

"I think it a brother," T'Cori said hopefully. "An Ibandi brother. If it is, that is *our* fire, and it warms us too." The other girls glanced at her as if they thought that a strange comment, and the men did as well. "Now I will sleep better."

They returned to their cave and its own small fire, adding a few pieces of wood to grow it, to increase the warmth, and perhaps the light as well.

T'Cori slept curled on her side, mind racing. A lone hunter sought prey in the night. An Ibandi? Probably. Who would dare challenge the Ibandi within the mountain's shadow? A beast-man? Possibly. Certainly something new and terrible had been happening in the last years. T'Cori could feel it in her blood, see it in the *num*-flames surrounding Stillshadow, in the voices of the old women as they sang the sun to life.

So . . . it *could* be a member of another people, but her heart said it was one of their own. What did she know about the men of her tribe? Usually, unless they were close to home, they hunted in groups. Were her kinsmen hiding and hunting out there?

But if it was only one, and that fire was far from any of the outer bomas, then she thought that it might be one of the young men out on his solitary journey, proving himself worthy of his second scar. What could he be feeling? Never in her life had she been alone. Journeying away from Stillshadow and Great Earth, even with two strong hunters, still plunged her into a darkness beyond her powers of description. Fear haunted her as it rarely had.

In that darkness dwelled her own inevitable journey to the mountaintop. Was this where she might begin it? Was this the place where she would find Great Mother and be lifted up to Her mighty bosom?

Oddly, the thought of death triggered warm, moist thoughts of Owl Hooting. Perhaps she and Owl were intended for each other. Perhaps this was the time that they would become lovers. Small tongues of heat licked at T'Cori as she envisioned their entwined limbs.

He behind her, his hip bones nestled against her naked buttocks. She above him, dancing a sex-song, making the baby-rhythm to draw forth his seed.

True, he could never be hers. But they might still share the things that other couples shared, do what others did, for at least a little while.

As she lay there in the darkness, her hands crept between her legs. Once the touching began, she slipped a finger into her wetness, seeking the places that created the greatest pleasure, concentrated the greatest heat. Owl's face appeared. She tried to change the face she saw above her, behind her, beneath her into one of the clean-limbed younger hunters Stillshadow might choose for her.

But it was to Owl's face that she returned, again and again. Owl who smiled, who licked at the hollow of her neck and whispered love songs in her ear. So great was her yearning that when she found the rhythm that took her to that place of fire, it seemed like a trip to the summit of Great Earth. It was Owl who had guided her every bit of the way, Owl whose smiling face had taken her to the place where even the stars themselves shone less brightly than their passion.

# Chapter Twenty-seven

The next morning T'Cori rose stretching and yawning, amused that the very first thing she did was peer out across the valley floor to where she had glimpsed firelight.

Nothing to be seen now. Even the distant ribbon of mountain itself shimmered in the heat, like fragments of a dissolving dream.

What of the connection she had felt? *All in your mind,* she told herself, however real it might have seemed in the moment.

It took a few breaths for Fawn to fan the previous night's coals into flame, and then she fed them until they could be certain that their campfire would be strong in the evening. Fawn stayed behind as the rest of them went out to perform the day's scavenging. Blossom and Sister Quiet Water had found most of the herbs and plants needed to heal or bring painless death. Here, no more than three days' walk from home, lay a hilly swatch of fertile ground that seemed ideal for their purposes.

So T'Cori was able to spend the day gathering. A quarter day of searching yielded more banded ants. As she had been taught, she followed them to the nest, catching hands of hands and biting their heads off, tossing the bodies into the pouch. She could barely keep her mind upon her work. Tonight would be the night, she was determined. Her first night of love with Owl. Even without Stillshadow's permission, tonight Owl would open her seventh eye, and she would be a woman at last. T'Cori could hardly keep her mind on the task before her. There was more than one way to make the medicine, but the ants were a blessing from Great Mother and would make the final result more powerful than ever.

In fact, wasn't there a love potion that used the banded ants? Mightn't she coax the recipe from Quiet Water and slip it into Owl's drinking gourd?

It was with a sense of pride and expectation that at the end of the day they found their way back to the cave. And it was on the way back that Leopard Claw waved his hands, bidding them to crouch and stay down.

For many breaths T'Cori remained so, and finally she saw the reason: a pair of deer approaching the water hole from uphill.

The male watched as the female drank. After a while they seemed to exchange roles, she watching as he lapped from the pool. Yearning for fresh meat, T'Cori dared not even breathe. Leopard Claw crawled away from them, disappearing into the grass. Then, suddenly, he stood erect and threw his spear so straight and true it might have been an extension of his arm.

It struck the male's right flank, wounding but not killing it. The buck tried to escape, but the gash transformed the run into a wobbly limp. The doe gave a single plaintive backward glance at the male and then disappeared into the grass. Her mate limped no more than a dozen strides before Owl Hooting's spear struck it in the throat.

So intense was her excitement that T'Cori could barely breathe. If they had not been under strict orders, she had little doubt that her sisters would have rewarded their guards at once, in the most intimate manner possible.

They ate well that night. Her sisters seemed flushed and cast frequent glances at Leopard Claw.

"Tonight," Dove whispered to Fawn, "let us both go to Leopard."

Her sister seemed shocked and delighted. "Both of us?"

Dove nodded. "Yes. I have heard some of the old dreamers talk, and they say the hunt chiefs know how to pleasure two women at once."

Fawn looked as if she wanted to melt.

And at that moment, T'Cori decided she could wait no longer, that she would give herself to Owl. Tonight, she would capture a man's flesh with her own.

Even the thought sent chills and heat through her body. The air felt thick in her lungs.

After the meal, they talked and laughed by the fire a bit, and then as fatigue from the day's gathering gnawed deeply into their bones, they curled up in the cave's sheltering shadows for rest.

.    .    .

T'Cori slept quickly and awakened sweating, her dreams of touching and being touched only grudgingly receding. At first she wondered if she had fallen asleep at all. She raised her head and looked around at her sisters. When she had last seen them, Fawn and Dove had not yet settled down. But now all three of her sisters lay without moving, making soft, burring sleep sounds.

Perhaps now was the time for her to awaken Owl.

When she'd first closed her eyes, the fire was still licking up the sides of the logs. Now she could barely see a glow. What had awakened her from slumber? T'Cori could just make out Owl Hooting's silhouette. He was lying on his side just outside the cave mouth, sleeping by the fire.

*No. Not sleeping.*

His *num*-fire was cold and slow, a thin wavering like a heat mirage, like a collapsed skin. No lights. Little motion. No warmth.

Owl was not on guard. He was not sleeping. He was *dead,* killed mere moments ago.

Something horrible had happened. The dread of it clawed at her like cold fingers at her throat.

Sudden movement rustled out at the cave mouth. She glimpsed something man-shaped, but larger than a man. For a moment she felt relieved, and wondered if she was being foolish. *Oh! This is a dream—*

She smelled something rank, and suddenly realized the air in dreams always smelled like the air around Great Earth. This was different. Strange. No dream. Then perhaps it was just sleep-fogged eyes blurring the image before them.

*No.*

Instinct burned, assuring her that the silhouette was not an Ibandi male's. It was heavier, thicker through the upper body than the familiar, graceful lines of a male Ibandi body. She *heard* something as well. Grunts and pops, more like an animal's growl than Ibandi speech.

The light of a half-moon shone brightly into the cave, so as the shadow moved farther in, the light diminished.

T'Cori was unable to move or close her eyes, or take her eyes away. The silhouette loomed in the cave mouth, staring at them. Staring at *her.* His eyes burned, blazed, shriveled her *num.* The cave's darkness seemed so deep and oppressive she might have been trapped within Great Mother's heart itself.

Then torchlight flared. Two more figures appeared behind the first one.

The thing in the cave mouth screamed at them. She finally grasped that they were words, not monkey babble. Words, even though she could not comprehend them. It did not matter. She felt them in her marrow, knew what they meant even as her sisters awakened with wails of distress such as she had never heard and hoped never to hear again.

*Wake up! Move. Or die.*

And then the Others were among them. These were not the less courageous beast-men. There were three intruders, each twice as thick through arms and chests as Ibandi males. Bhan were smaller, more slender, more timid than Ibandi. As bhan were to Ibandi, beast-men were to these giants.

Fingers hard as stone seized her legs, dragged T'Cori out of the cave into the moonlight. Her head spun at the sight of Leopard Claw's crumpled skull and Owl Hooting's bloodied corpse. What had happened? This could not be!

The largest of them had a face like a shelf of rock. His fat fleshy nose was broader than those of her own people. He was the largest male she had ever seen, immense across the shoulders and through the chest, with legs that looked as if they had been hewn from logs. And oh, the stink! Never had she smelled a man or a woman with such a stench. But it was not a stench of feces or putrefaction. This was a scent like a rutting beast, pungent and vital.

What were these creatures?

Quiet Water squared her shoulders. "You don't dare touch us! We are mountain daughters!"

Without changing expressions, Flat-Nose clubbed her with the back of his hand. Quiet Water fell to the ground as if the blow had removed her bones. She lay where she fell, making mewling mindless sounds, shuddering, blowing bloody bubbles between her bruised lips.

That single violent act seemed to break the paralysis. T'Cori wobbled to her feet, running for the break she now saw in the thorn wall. The place where the Others had crawled through to do their murder. Her heart ached, but that ache only spurred her to action.

Flat-Nose reached out almost languidly, and his forearm crashed across T'Cori's chin so that her feet flew out from beneath her. She tumbled to the ground and lay dazed, listening to the screams and pleas as her sisters were forced onto their backs, their hands bound behind them with rawhide strips. When it was her turn, T'Cori struggled against their attackers to no effect. She might as well resist Father Mountain Himself.

They were pulled to their feet and prodded out of the thorn wall. T'Cori stole one last glimpse of the proud Ibandi hunters who had sworn to protect them. Had they awakened at all? Had she slept through some futile, silent struggle? Owl and his brother sprawled like tired children, lying there in the shadows of night, eyes open and glazed, fixed upon the world to come, the ancestors and gods who would call them to account and demand explanations for their catastrophic failure.

In the chill of early morning's darkness, the four girls limped along toward their unknown destination. By the time the sun's glow appeared along the eastern horizon T'Cori's legs burned and shook. She stumbled but did not fall. Her bound hands challenged her balance, and she struggled to stay erect.

The three Others walked them at a pace just below a trot, alert as lions on the prowl. Despite their ferocious strength and power, their captors were wary. Not fearful—when she read their *num*-fire, the red was mixed with black: an awareness of death without terror of it. These creatures *lived* in the space of death. Knew it as no Ibandi hunter she had ever read. They simply were not like Ibandi men.

Fear drove thought from T'Cori's mind, leaving nothing but dread of their fate.

What was to be their fate? Were they merely fresh meat, as some of the clansmen thought? Or were other, even more terrible hungers to be satisfied?

On and on southward they walked, through most of the day. With every passing step the southern mountain ridges grew just a hair closer, and any remaining bits of hope drained away. Her sisters were all but dead. Their heads drooped, shoulders slumped in exhaustion and despair. They had had a few rest breaks, sufficient time to chew on scraps of dried deer meat thrust into their hands by their captors.

Anytime one of them tried to speak, they were all cuffed. Only silence and sobbing were allowed.

Twice that first day they had stopped to sip brackish water from stagnant pools. Flamingos bloomed like bamboo stalks on the far side of the pond, balancing upon their single sticklike legs. Shaded in pink and white, the birds watched them incuriously. A delicate gold-and-green butterfly landed on a flower not an arm's reach from T'Cori as she drank, but for once its beauty failed to lighten her heart.

*Butterfly Spring.* Yes. She was a butterfly who had seen her *last* spring. Tears streamed from her eyes.

That night the girls were allowed to sleep, but T'Cori's hands were tied to a flat-topped acacia tree. One of the Others—she called him Notch-Ear because of a jagged wound on the left lobe—remained awake all the night long. It was easy to understand why. Considering how they had so recently slaughtered two Ibandi, these hunters would have little taste for risking the same fate.

And that, strangely, she found comforting. Despite their strangeness, these were men, not demons. Men who sought to avoid death.

T'Cori opened her mouth to whisper. "Dove—" she began.

The girl shivered, and kicked her leg with a thump. T'Cori could barely see Dove's face, but her eyes shone with terror in the darkness.

*Do not speak.*

Dove closed her eyes tightly.

The others were no better: T'Cori could see it in Quiet Water's slumped shoulders, the way Fawn had curled into a ball at Dove's side.

Her sisters had already begun to abandon hope.

She would not. Could not.

And then, just before midnight, she was dreamlessly asleep.

# Chapter Twenty-eight

The next day T'Cori was forced to walk until her legs ached and her head spun. Whenever she tried to stop she was prodded on with blows clearly intended to inflict pain but not injury. Her sisters dragged their feet, making what timid and pitiful resistance they could. With every passing quarter day, with every step they trudged south, their *num*-fields burned cooler and lower, drained of life.

Near dusk on the second day, they entered another small valley, little more than a large defile. Climbing up the other side, they entered an arid, shallow basin, with a long low floor that stretched away into a horizon shrouded by heat mirages. The shimmer made some of the distant images vanish, ripple and then reappear. She shaded her eyes, trying to resolve the image more clearly, and could not. This was different from the land that she knew. If this terrible place was the womb of the Others, she feared for her people.

Why hadn't they realized the true threat? Why had they blamed the beast-men for what the Others had done? Had they not left tracks enough, sign enough? Why hadn't Father Mountain warned His children?

A terrible thought occurred to T'Cori: perhaps the Others had gods who were *greater* than Father Mountain. In her present despairing state, it seemed possible.

As they came closer to the camp she saw more Others, males and females. These males were as large as any of her captors, with the exception of Flat-Nose. But the females were no larger than she, and in many cases smaller.

The males averaged a full head taller than their females. With relief, and disgust at her relief, she noticed that they were well fed.

*They are great hunters,* she heard a voice in her head say cajolingly, as if seeking a rationale for surrender.

What could she do? If she ran away, was she even strong enough to reach Great Earth? She knew the direction, yes. From time to time when the light was just so, she saw Great Earth's shadowy outline, floating in the air like a leaf floating in a lake. But could she cover the distance by herself?

T'Cori was herded into a thorn-walled pen. Seven other females cowered there in the fold, and they did not have the look of Others, more nearly resembling bhan. Was this how the Others increased their numbers, by killing males and capturing females? Were they expanding north into Ibandi lands?

Flat-Nose gave a sharp, nasty laugh as the thorn gate scraped closed behind them. His companions yipped back in response.

The Others built up the fire carefully, and through the thorn brush T'Cori watched them spit the back half of a bongo and set it to roasting. The females served the males with downcast eyes, never meeting a man's gaze directly.

Fawn, Dove, and Quiet Water squatted sobbing in the dust, clutching one another. T'Cori held them too, but there was one part of the nameless girl that floated above all of this, and in separating from her body was not clutched by the same terror that crippled her sisters, who wailed until the Others beat them with sticks.

One of the other women approached them, scuttling like a spider. T'Cori recognized her from Spring Gathering. Rings of ritual scars around her eyes, hair straggly and unbraided, small pretty shoulders with strong arms. Willow, she thought the short woman called herself. She'd seen Willow trading with the women's circle, exchanging eastern black glass for herbs and potions. Burning Willow. Willow was not of the Circle, but of eastern bhan, with whom the Ibandi traded.

Willow no longer burned.

"Stop," Willow said. "No yell. He hurt you bad." The words seemed to penetrate, because Quiet Water suited her actions to her name and fell silent.

"Who are they?" T'Cori whispered.

"They Mk*tk," Willow replied, her tongue making a soft clicking/popping sound between two harsher syllables.

"Mk*tk . . . ?" T'Cori said, trying to fit her mouth to the sounds.

The gate scraped open, and the Mk*tk males threw chunks of sizzling, smoking meat into the pen. Her sisters fell upon it like hyenas. T'Cori scrabbled as quickly as any, although she never quite lost that sense of being separated from herself. She watched herself doing it, calm even as her hands dug frantically into the dirt for scraps of meat while the males watched and laughed.

Her fingers curled around a splintered leg bone with flecks of pink flesh clinging to it. She gnawed the meat off like the famished animal she was. When the bone was clean she sucked frantically at the marrow. Her body was so moisture-starved that the slightest drop of juice flowed like nectar down her parched and dusty throat. As she ate the males entered and examined the women one at a time. The other women shrank back from them. When it was T'Cori's turn she continued to gnaw, as if she couldn't see them at all.

She knew, floating there above herself, that she should beg, plead, abase herself, but it was all she could do not to spit in Flat-Nose's eye.

*You killed our men,* she thought, wishing that she could say it to him. *You killed Owl Hooting, who was to be my first.*

*I swear one day I will watch you die.*

His wet fleshy nostrils flared, and he bent closer to look at her. His breath was heavy, hot and pungent, as she imagined a lion's meaty breath might be.

Next to T'Cori, Fawn stared down at the dirt, whimpering. Flat-Nose leaned close to T'Cori, grinning . . . then grabbed Fawn's arm and dragged her out of the pen.

With sickening clarity, T'Cori understood. Always she had thought Fawn to be the least attractive of the dream dancers. But in a way that was completely unanticipated, Fawn was the most appealing to these creatures.

The horror of it gripped Dove's sister until she shivered like an antelope in a leopard's jaws. She clawed at the ground and screamed plaintively, hopelessly, her sister pulling at her arm, pleading, begging.

Throughout that long, terrible night laughter and screams mingled with obscene intimacy, even when those shrieks died into exhausted whimpers.

With every cry, each ragged plea for mercy, new tears burst from Dove's eyes.

One of the giants lumbered into the corral, burning them with his heavy, dull eyes. As his gaze slid up T'Cori's limbs she spit into the dust at his feet. They might take her body, but she would show them an Ibandi woman's spirit was not so easily stolen.

Without reacting, making a sound or taking another of her sisters, he closed the gate again.

Sister Quiet Water whispered to her: "What do they do to her?"

"You know," T'Cori said, appalled by the flatness of her own voice. "We all know."

But Dove could not believe the evidence of her senses. "But she is a mountain daughter. How can they?"

T'Cori had no answer, but Quiet Water did. "Because we have displeased Father Mountain, and he has forgotten us."


In the last quarter of night, Fawn was thrown back into the pen. Stinking of blood and sweat and other fluids, she curled shaking, naked in the dirt. She turned away from them, too filled with shame to meet their eyes.

"Do not look at me," she sobbed. "I am no longer Ibandi."

Then Fawn wept, great gobbling gouts that seemed to surge from an infinite well of grief within her. She slipped her thumb in her mouth and sucked, squeezing her eyelids tightly shut.

Dove and Quiet Water huddled around the shrunken girl, seeking to comfort. Despite her lack of traditional Ibandi beauty, and her occasional awkwardness, she had been so clever and quick to learn dances, beautiful when lost in the play of the drums. T'Cori touched her arm. The small, quick, grasping fingers clamped hold of her, but Fawn was still lost in her own private world of pain and shame.

T'Cori crawled away into her own corner, watching the futile efforts to comfort, and then whispered to herself. "Father Mountain, why do you not hear us? We have been faithful daughters, always. But you do not hear us. Are we so distant from you? Do you care so little? Tell me. Show me. Please, before we lose hope."

Was this Great Mother's punishment? Was she angry with the girls for choosing their own first time for sex? Because T'Cori had entertained her own sinful, shameful thoughts and plans? Could their beloved gods be so petty and cruel? She thought not, prayed not. But it was possible.


The next night the giants came for Dove. Her cries, resounding through the thorn wall, made Fawn's seem like girlish laughter in comparison.

"Dove!" Sister Quiet Water cried, but she was not really speaking to her friend. Quiet Water was speaking to herself, knowing that she would share the same fate tomorrow, or the next day, or tonight.

Or it could be T'Cori's time. She prayed it would be one of the others, and was ashamed of that prayer.

Halfway through the night Dove was cast carelessly back into the pen. She would not meet their eyes, even those of her own twin. Finally Fawn went to her. The two wrapped their arms around each other, whispering, crying, two bodies sharing a single lost and tattered soul.

The Mk*tk males worked T'Cori's bones to dust the next day. Miraculously, she considered the fatigue a gift. Mind focused solely on her aching body, it was easier to forget what might lay ahead of her that night. She and the other girls were forced to scrape fat from hides with rocks, to scrub dirt from roots at the side of a nearby river. To work their hands raw pounding tubers, berries and strange small orange fruits into a mash. As they worked, the men poked and prodded at them. Without effort, from time to time her fire-vision blossomed, and she saw the life-flames of the girls cooling beneath the attention, watched the fire surrounding the Mk*tk's seventh eyes flaring dreadfully.

Several of them watched T'Cori. She tried to float away to that place in her head, but realized that she was babbling to herself: "Not me, not me, anyone but me . . ."

In despair she realized that she had failed in her attempt to retreat to that odd place within her. The Mk*tk *saw* her. *Knew* her.

And laughed.

Tonight, she knew, would be the night.

*Not like this. Not like this.* For all her life, T'Cori had dreamed of becoming a woman, wondered what it might be like to join bodies with a strong young hunter, to suck his root into her body and milk him dry. To open her seventh eye. To have a man who would be hers to use, their seed, and progeny, belonging to the tribe.

But the coming violation was something she had never dreamed of. Never had she imagined that her seventh eye might be savaged in such a horrific fashion. As she thought about it, and desperately tried to find the part of herself that could float away, panic swarmed her senses.

All her life, T'Cori had felt suspended between this world and the next. Since childhood she had fought to increase her sense of rooting in the world of two- and four-legged. But now this world had become her vilest nightmare, and she wished for nothing so much as release.

So as the day went on and they were walked back to the pen from the river, T'Cori took her chance and fled.

Here along the trail the ground was pebbles and sand, the grass high and dry and brown and spiky. Her vision collapsed into a tiny bright spot in the midst of a dark field, so that she saw nothing except the light directly ahead. In that state she couldn't see her guards but could *hear* them, yelling at her, hooting like baboons and roaring like lions and laughing like hyenas.

No matter which way she turned, there they were. Their cries and motions herded her so that she lost hope and fell. She forced herself up but could no longer pretend that she was not near swooning with terror.

The grasses came to an end. Ahead of her stretched only rocks and dirt and then open air: a cliff. At the bottom of the cliff, she thought, would be rocks. Certainly if she reached it, she could throw herself over, and if Great Mother's sheltering hands caught her, then this was good. And if they didn't . . .

Then wasn't death deliverance of a kind?

She reached the edge and teetered there, gazing down, overwhelmed by fear and shame.

Didn't she want to die? How many times had she asked Great Mother to take her, had she longed to fly to the arms of the only one who loved her? And now, in this terrible nightmare, didn't she have even more reason to release life?

Where was her faith?

At that moment, T'Cori knew herself fully. Knew that she lacked the courage to end her life, to throw herself off. With all the desperate skill and strength in her arms and legs and hands and feet, she began to climb down. The Mk*tk pointed down, jabbering in their odd tongue. Good. They didn't know what to do. Just perhaps, those huge bodies were useless for climbing.

But in the next instant even that hope left her as they clambered down after her, agile as apes. She commanded her hands to release their grip, to just surrender and allow her body to drift down to a certain death in the ravine, but they would not obey. The urge for life was too strong.

T'Cori cowered as they descended like spiders around her. She couldn't even look at them as they wrapped her arms around Notch-Ear's neck, then lashed her wrists with a leather thong. Trussed like a freshly slain deer, T'Cori was lugged back to the top.

At this range she could not only see his *num*-flame, but feel and almost taste it.

T'Cori was beyond shock, spiraling into a territory where her mind was losing its ability to function. These men—if men they were—were simply stronger and more nimble than Ibandi. If they were expanding into the north, she feared her people were already lost.

All the way back to the camp, she screamed. As they untied her hands she sank her teeth into Notch-Ear's meaty shoulder. That, at last, evoked a response. Notch-Ear pulled her around and hit her in the mouth, just once, quite hard.

The world went white and then black, then slowly spun back into focus. T'Cori staggered back and blood gushed from her mouth, and she stared at the ground, unable even to move. She wiped her mouth with the back of her hand, spit out the fragment of a tooth. Her world was pain and fear.

That night they came for T'Cori. As their hands closed upon her, she tried desperately to find that secret place outside herself, a place where she might be able to elude the horror. She tried to dissolve the world, to escape into the realm of light and fire.

And failed.

They dragged her into a hut made of lashed, straw-covered willow branches. A low fire cast only a dying glow before Notch-Ear threw an armful of branches on it, coaxing it to crackling life. They pulled her over a log in the middle of the hut, tying her hands to stumps. She pulled and twisted but could not free herself. T'Cori craned her neck to look back over her shoulder and watched Notch-Ear approach her. His shadow was a man's, but the *num*-fire glimpsed from the corner of her eye was monstrous. His seventh eye was like a burning brand, flaming with purples and harsh, muddy green.

She wanted desperately to faint, to die, but could not.

*Shadows are part of the waking dream.* So Stillshadow had said a lifetime ago. If she could bend his shadow, she might bend his body. She strove desperately to make the magic come, the magic she had been taught, the magic that had always been a part of her existence.

Sudden, vital pain ripped this final hopeful fantasy away. She bleated as he pushed his way into her, screamed as her flesh tore. T'Cori prayed to Father Mountain to spare her, to take her away, but her prayers were drowned out by her own groans.

This man, in this place, was T'Cori's first. He howled and shuddered within her, and then withdrew, and was replaced by another.

But now, thankfully, Great Mother finally heard her prayer and accepted her, trembling, into darkness.

When T'Cori came fully back to consciousness, she was being dragged along the ground. The Mk*tk tossed her into the pen. She collapsed, feeling filthy inside, as if something precious had been stolen. Fluid built up over and over again in the back of her throat, and she hacked and spit, trying to breathe.

All the rest of that night, she sobbed. T'Cori closed her eyes, trying to visualize Great Earth, but could not. She felt that she had lost something she could never regain. Her seventh eye had been ripped open and then blinded.

"I am nothing," she whispered. Her fingers grooved the dirt beneath her. Four small troughs, graves long and wide enough to bury the fragments of her shattered *num*.

And not all her sisters' comforting touches could brighten her darkness, all that endless, lonely night.

## Chapter Twenty-nine

As a ripple of faint echoes rang through the night, Frog awoke from sleep. Darkness still enshrouded the hills. Here, so far from the land he knew, he was very careful where he set spark to tinder. He did not want enemies to see it, and he had come far enough west and south to know he'd reached lands unknown to all but the bravest hunters.

There was danger about: that much he could sense. But on the other hand, risk would make whatever victories he had all the sweeter. What stories would be his to tell!

But . . . what was that sound he'd heard upon awakening? Faint, grief-stricken echoes of . . . what? He raised his head. Had it been merely a wisp of dream? Had it been something of this world?

Frog lay very still, ears straining to catch another wisp of sound. Nothing. *Only the wind,* he thought. *Nothing but the wind.*

The night seemed uncharacteristically cold. He fed a bit of wood to the dying fire and pulled skins over himself more tightly.

Frog loved the grasslands. Most Ibandi had a name for everything. Frog Hopping had five. Not just *dik-dik,* "tiny antelope," but *spotted, close-eyed, quick-dik, tiny giant* and *sour.* Not just grassland but *sweet grassland, lion lair, soft-soil, water-rich* and *spiky.* He knew that he should have felt more fear: there were so many ways to die. But when his eyes and ears were fully alive he felt as transparent as water, as if he could not be seen at all.

If he recognized a fruit and knew it to be good, Frog would stop to eat it. If he didn't recognize it, but saw monkeys eating it, he took the risk. One greenish sweet fruit he munched through happily, and then stopped to examine with greater care. The seeds were small and white and three-cornered. Where had he seen such seeds before? It came to him with shocking suddenness. He had seen them in the scat he and Scorpion found in the shattered bhan boma.

That meant that whoever had killed the bhan folk had come from this direction. Could such fruit also be found in the north, where some thought the beast-men had originated?

It was wetter up in the north, and the green fruit plant's deep roots and tough skin suggested a drier clime. That lent weight to the idea that whoever had destroyed that bhan boma had come from the south, eating this fruit along the way. Perhaps the killers had dried some for eating while on the move.

Fear and excitement mingled as Frog felt his senses opening more widely, the entire world becoming a stream of smells and sounds and sensations, his human mind sorting through them, comparing them with everything that he had ever known, and drawing conclusions about what might come next. It was a sense unlike any he had ever experienced. A hole opened in his mind, a portal to a world undreamt of.

He was no mere boy, to be protected by his relations. He was a man, a hunter, as his father and his father before him, and he swelled with the thought that this was *his* time.

This was what his people had sent him out to find. *Himself.*


Clearly, Father Mountain smiled upon young Frog. A young ostrich had succumbed to his spear, and his traps had caught two rabbits. With hunger and fear as instructors, he was learning. If you paid attention, life itself was the greatest mentor.

No longer did he consider his walkabout to be torture. It had become a fierce, demanding and dangerous adventure.

Visible first as a man's skeleton with outstretched arms, a dead, hollow old baobab tree rose on the plain before him like the ghost of a slain giant. Its gnarled, ashy exterior said it was much older than the sacred tree at the grounds of Spring Gathering. The hollow was as tall as two men, and wider than Frog could spread his arms. The interior stank of bat scat, but he found bits of bone, scraps of carved wood, and the remnants of a fire as well. So.

Someone had been here before. He looked at the tumble of burnt wood, and guessed that they were not Ibandi. It showed no deliberate banking of the fire. His entire body tingled, as if lightning had struck nearby.

His first contact with the Others!

There was no way to be certain of how long they'd been gone, but Frog knew that all hunters repeated successful behaviors and discarded unsuccessful ones. Anywhere a hunter found prey once, he was likely to return. When and if that happened, Frog did not want to be there.

So instead of sleeping in the tree, Frog backtracked, being very very careful to wipe out his footprints. Then he burrowed into the grass.

And he waited.


A quarter of the night passed, during which it finally occurred to Frog that this might not be quite the splendid adventure he had hoped for. It occurred to him, in fact, that this might have been the single stupidest thing that he had ever done.

In the distance, baboons hooted.

Frog had very nearly decided that the smartest thing he could do was to run north as fast as he could, when there was a disturbance on the other side of the clearing.

Out in the waving field of yellow-green grasses, something stirred. A baboon? Perhaps. He couldn't make it out, but had seen the stalks rustle. It happened once, and then again, and both times the wind had been still. Then something . . . some*one* emerged from the grass. A great, hulking figure moving with unnatural lightness. To his considerable surprise, Frog was less terrified than fascinated.

His Ibandi brothers moved with formidable ease and power. And of course the hunt chiefs ran and wrestled like gods. But this creature and those that followed it walked more like apes than either men or immortals. They loped, occasionally pausing to sniff the air. Instantly, Frog began circling downwind of them, knowing that if they smelled, saw, heard or sensed him in any way, they would kill him.

Their backs, chests and shoulders were more tightly curled with hair than the smooth Ibandi torsos, and more thickly muscled as well. They entered the clearing, snuffling, and then approached the tree. He counted: two, three, four of them. One of them climbed into the baobab, so lightly that their arms must have been stronger than Frog's legs. The others took up position outside, keeping guard.

What were these strange creatures doing? He did not know, but they spent less than a quarter at it, and after they were finished they sniffed the air again, then trotted off to the south.

After they were gone, Frog looked into the tree. A few things had changed: a small bleached dik-dik skull, an antelope skull, and a baboon skull with scraps of hairy flesh still attached had been placed in a circle. Something . . . mud? Ash mixed with water or urine, perhaps, had been used to scrawl a mark in the middle of the circle, something that looked vaguely like a half-moon.

He stared at this. Hunting signs? Messages for others of their kind? Or communications to their god? Overcome with sudden chills, he backed away.

As Frog stood staring into the tree, he realized that he was about to do something suicidally stupid. He was going to follow these creatures.

"Uncle Snake said to bring back meat," he whispered, so softly that he could not hear his own words. "But what if I bring back knowledge of the Others? And the hunt chiefs use that knowledge to defend us? Then I will be the greatest of hunters."

And that is how he came to follow the band of Others as they traveled south. They loped along at a brisk pace, still very alert to the grass and wind. Although the pace made Frog pant, it seemed entirely casual for the Others. They never seemed to tire, and if they hadn't stopped from time to time to dig into the earth or scratch bugs from each other's pelts, Frog might have become winded. By the time the day was half gone, he was praying to a Father Mountain he was no longer certain of that one of them might break a leg. He kept circling right and left to stay downwind, or too distant to alarm them . . . he hoped.

# Chapter Thirty

T'Cori's days had melted into a blur. First, the pain of the broken tooth had kept her from sleeping, sent her into a constant frenzy of weeping until Quiet Water, tapping some unknown well of strength, gathered the grasses and herbs necessary to compound a poultice for her to bite down on. Within a quarter the pain faded. She tried to thank the tall girl, but it almost seemed that Quiet Water was floating in a dream, had been able to help T'Cori only at the cost of emptying herself out. For after that one final act of kindness, Sister Quiet Water drifted away for the last time.

Flat-Nose, Notch-Ear and several more of the Others attacked the dream dancers in their degrading nightly ritual. After a few rotations there was no more ceremony about it. If they wanted a woman, they took her, and seemed little concerned whether it was one of their own flat-faced, ugly women or one of the new acquisitions.

Already the abuse had numbed her three sisters. In ways it seemed that T'Cori was in the same sort of daze, but she had finally found her way into a waking dream state. Stillshadow had often spoken of such a trance.

*It is not sleeping. It is not waking. You have had dreams where you were awake, yes?*

*And you know of sisters who walk, but still sleep, yes?*

*This is the place I speak of. This place where you feel no pain, where you see what others cannot. Where all the world is magical. It is sleeping, walking, awake. Do you understand?*

She never had. But now T'Cori did.

The Mk*tk seemed to consider the four dream dancers new members of their tribe. As long as the girls did not try to escape, they were treated without undue cruelty. They were fed, allowed to bathe in the waters of a river just a short walk away from the cage. If they tried to run away they were beaten, but not badly enough to reduce their ability to perform their daily chores.

T'Cori watched helplessly as her mind began to die. She heard voices within her head, dull, damning voices she had never heard before, speaking in a chorus. She yearned to summon her ability to see *num*-fire, and could not. The world spun until she teetered perpetually on the edge of nausea. Constantly weary, the girl just wanted to roll over and sleep, but she was afraid to close her eyes for fear of nightmares even worse than her waking terror.

As she had many times before, T'Cori tried to speak to one of the Mk*tk women. The woman was heavy-lidded and stank of fear, and also possessed a deep feminine scent almost like moon-blood, although T'Cori did not think she was on her menses. "We have to escape," she whispered. "Help me. Help me."

The woman's eyes were dull and dead. T'Cori recognized this mind space, had seen it in the eyes of the poisoned deer.

She gave up and crawled over to Dove and made the same plea. "We have to escape!"

But Dove was no longer the same girl who had once laughed and sung and danced so joyously. Terror and shame had transformed her into a creature of small, startled movements, twitching at the slightest unexpected thing.

Dove stared at T'Cori as if it took great effort merely to recognize her sister. Then she said, "There is no escape. We were wrong about Great Sky," she said dully. "*This* is the land of the dead."

"We are alive!" T'Cori protested. "We feel, we dream. We will die if we don't act."

"No. We will live if we please them. We must please them." Dove's voice broke when she said this. Her eyes shifted to the side, as if wondering if a Mk*tk was coming. Then she scuttled away and would speak to T'Cori no more.

On the tenth day after her first assault, T'Cori saw a terrible thing, a thing that never left her memory for the rest of her life. It happened like this:

While their lives were confined to a narrow cycle of waking, eating, gathering, cooking, rape and sleeping, they were allowed to go to the river to wash themselves and the gathered food every few days. Fawn seemed to have regained just a bit of her strength. When Dove faltered, Fawn helped her twin carry her basket of tubers, whispering to her to keep strength.

On this day, as the women washed, several new Mk*tk hunters had joined the group. T'Cori had the impression that their current habitat was some kind of temporary boma, that Flat-Nose was their chief, and that others of his people were gathering slowly, perhaps for a push northward.

T'Cori's mind was drifting away again when a sudden, panicked scream tethered her to earth. She twisted around in time to see a crocodile lunge up from the water. Almost as long as two of her, its pebbled moss-green flesh dripped water, rows of gleaming teeth flashing as it buried them in Fawn's arm.

Suddenly awakening from her trance, Fawn twisted, struggling desperately to tear herself away. Blood gouted over the crocodile's snout as it dragged her into the water.

With one great despairing wail, Fawn disappeared beneath the surface.

Dove screamed, a sound like a throat being torn out with hooks.

T'Cori heard herself scream, the shock rooting her in place.

Fawn surfaced one more time, eyes impossibly wide, her distended face glistening with water. Her mouth jetted blood and a single wet scream, and then she was gone.

Her basket of tubers floated away in the current.

The Mk*tk ran about, jabbing ineffectually at the water with their spears, confused and perhaps even frightened. When they finally grasped that there was nothing to be done, they pulled the other women back from the banks and to the cave.

T'Cori felt nothing. She struggled to find some shred of emotion, but it seemed that the pain of the last days had burned something out of her heart. She heard the screams, remembered her sister's distended face, saw the blood slick on the muddied banks . . . and felt nothing.

All she could think of was that a crocodile's teeth were not the worst possible instruments of death.


T'Cori had wound her way to the world of waking dream, a safe space, very different from the hellish state of Dove and Quiet Water, who had screamed and sobbed and then yielded into a dull, beaten, barely human state. She escaped into this distant world when Flat-Nose came to sex her.

As terrible as it was, on some other level she began to grasp that Flat-Nose was not actually trying to *hurt* her. Rather, he was trying to make her a woman of the Others, pouring his seed into her that she might grow heavy with child.

*His* child.

She could only pray that his seed would fail to root.

She looked down at her body, trying to see her *num*-fire. Should she have been able to see it? To sense whether or not she was pregnant? Perhaps once that ability had been hers, but not now.

Slowly, the dream-world became a place of refuge to her. On successive nights she came to know it well. It was a world of feeling and symbol and memory, and it welcomed her into its depths.


*She dreamt of Mother and Father, She deep within the earth, He atop Great Sky, T'Cori's imaginings of what such a being might be, and what might protect His kingdom. A fearsome dream.*

*She did not see Great Sky as mountain or as not-mountain. This dream had come before, and never, upon awakening, could she be certain what she had seen or experienced. Never could she relate her knowledge to others. It seemed that there were no Ibandi words for the new perceptions, and without words, she could not hold on to the experience.*

*She sensed more than saw Their mighty presence. In Their way, with dance and gesture of arm, leg and hand rather than words, Mother and Father spoke to her. "Who are you, my child?"*

*"My name is T'Cori, of the Ibandi," she said.*

*"And why do you come to Us?"*

*She spoke to Them with the yearnings of a child who has never had a father or mother, one who dreamt that perhaps the greatest of all parents would be those loving Ones. "I have been captured. Our hunters were killed, and I am badly used. Please help me."*

*The darkness roiled. For a moment she saw something resembling a nose and a face. Could this be truth? Could human eyes see Great Mother and Her mate? "Your fate is yours, and you must walk your path. But there will always be a safe place for you," She danced. "Here, with Me."*

*"Can I please stay?" Even to herself, T'Cori's voice sounded small and still.*

*She looked down from the mountain's mystic heights. She saw a small girl from Great Earth bent over a log. Her hands were lashed down. The giant Flat-Nose stood behind her, pushing rhythmically. His hands clutched her hips, his head thrown back as his thighs slapped against her buttocks. His fellows watched and laughed and clapped along in time with his thrusts as he rutted for his own pleasure and the entertainment of his brothers.*

*Behind him were two other Mk\*tk, impatiently awaiting their turn.*

*"Please?" she begged.*

*Her mighty voice was filled with regret. "It is not more than you can bear," She said.*

*"How can you know?" T'Cori whispered.*

*No answer.*

*Worse, she had begun to fragment. The single voice in her head was becoming a confused, frightened chorus. She was being pulled back into the world of pain and shame. "Help me!" she pled. "I don't want them to take me again."*

*Great Mother took her hand. "I won't let you go. Stay with Me awhile."*

*She enfolded T'Cori in Her arms. And in that mighty embrace T'Cori slept, safe at last.*

# Chapter Thirty-one

When she returned from the dream time, the violation had ceased. T'Cori gathered herself together and pulled her skins up, exiting the hut to rejoin the other women.

Dove looked at her, eyes heavy-lidded and dull. "They are rougher than our hunters," she said. "Their roots are larger."

T'Cori said nothing, wondering how many men Dove had sampled.

"We need not be strong, if we can yield," Dove said.

"It is our fate to yield to powerful men," said Quiet Water.

"We will make strong sons," Dove said, as if her words made perfect sense. And T'Cori knew then that Dove's mind was dying, even if her body still breathed.

Then at a grunted warning from two Mk*tk, they wandered off to cook and mend.

T'Cori closed her eyes and prayed. "Great Mother," she said, "thank You for Your strength. Please, please give that strength to my sisters. They need it more than this daughter."

Notch-Ear cuffed her hard, lighting her vision with fire, crashing her to the ground. He barked a string of gibberish, containing only one word that she now understood: *"kord,"* work.

The blow caught her by surprise, but another did not follow. She rubbed her ear, waves of pain making her nauseous. The Mk*tk bent and put his face close to hers, licking his teeth suggestively. With his fingertip he motioned toward the blazing orb now dropping to the horizon. Then he grinned.

He squeezed her breasts roughly. T'Cori squirmed, not daring to turn away or resist.

He spoke another word, this one, for the first time, in Ibandi. "Tonight."

He brought his face close to her. His rank smell and overwhelming physicality numbed her mind, but she still managed to whisper, "No."

Notch-Ear hurled her face-first to the ground. She tasted dirt, wheezed as the breath was slammed out of her, but to her surprise, felt no fear. He hunched down, flipped her over and snuffled between her legs. T'Cori tensed, suddenly flushed with an emotion: disgust. Something more than annoyance crossed his face: she detected hurt as well.

From a pile of discards he selected a stick as thick as her thumb. He whipped it across her back, each stroke like a flash of lightning in a night sky. The beating seemed to last forever, until she was reduced to a shuddering heap.

"Tonight," Notch-Ear said again, his mouth shaping the Ibandi word so rudely that she hoped never to use or hear it again.

Her sisters gathered around and sought to comfort her as he stalked away. "Do not fight the Mk*tk," Dove begged. "If you do, you die."

"We help you," said Quiet Water. "Forget Great Mother and Father Mountain. There are no mountains here."

T'Cori curled herself knees to chest, biting her lip. She would say no more to her sisters. They were lost to her. But to herself, she repeated over and over again, until she thought she would go insane: "Great Mother, help me." Her fingers scrabbled at the earth beneath her. "Forget Dove and Quiet Water, if they have forgotten You. But do not forget me."

Notch-Ear returned and grabbed her arm, dragging her behind a bush. But now she knew how to crawl into the special place in her mind, and she did, closing her eyes. When her eyelids opened again, they exposed the whites of her eyes, and nothing more.

T'Cori lay curled in one filthy corner of the thorn-walled pen. Her single overwhelming sense was one of being soiled inside and out. Dried fluid scabbed on her thighs, sticky as raw egg. Despite that, she had a small feeling of triumph. They had raped her, yes, forced her to satisfy their appetites. But they had held her hands instead of tying her down, taking turns. And this time, in the darkness of the hut, the Mk*tk had made a mistake.

So eager had they been to sex her that someone had dropped a partially completed knife in the dirt not far from her hands. How long had it been there? Which one of them? Could it even have been a trap? She didn't know, but could not afford to miss the opportunity. So this time, she pretended not to struggle, even raising her hips to invite their penetration in a way that pleased them and made them hoot and jostle to be first.

In the midst of all of it, she managed to get hold of the knife, flattening it against her forearm. And when they were done with her and sent her off with her little bundle of skins, they didn't see what she had, or know what she had done.

She hid the blade in a corner of the pen, covering it with dirt. She dared not tell her sisters of her small triumph. In little more than a moon, the other girls had begun to creep closer to the fire. No longer was there much difference between them and the Mk*tk females. Even as T'Cori watched, Dove displayed one of her legs, postured so that the long muscle on the inside of her thigh glowed in the firelight. One of the hunters nodded appreciatively and threw her a piece of meat.

T'Cori did not react. She fought to keep her balance, but the world began to swirl and she shook almost uncontrollably.

Flat-Nose appeared above her. He reached down.

In her eyes she was suspended in a blackness filled with stars and moons. She floated there, away from everything and everyone.

"Great Mother," she sobbed, "send me a sign. Help me, or I die. If You will, save me. If You can save me, I will be yours always, until the end of my life. Send me . . . something. They've taken my sight."

Silently, falling one precious droplet at a time, her tears puddled into the dust. It was at that moment that she knew the path ahead.

She would have freedom or death. And what greater freedom than death could one like T'Cori hope for in a world such as this?

# Chapter Thirty-two

Five days later, T'Cori and the other women were at the river again, washing dirt from the roots and the stink from their own bodies, busy scrubbing the soil away from their rudely crafted baskets of tubers. She studied the rushing waters, troubled that she did not know where and how the waters terminated. But she had seen Fawn's bundle of roots washed down the river, and that was when T'Cori got the idea.

Was anyone watching? The other women worked, but also flirted with their guards, waiting until one of them was watching to slowly roll her hips, flexing and relaxing to draw his eye. Thinking, no doubt, of extra food or lighter duties.

This was her time. Three Mk*tk guarded, but only Notch-Ear was watching them closely. Such an opportunity might never come again. She checked to see that she had her little knife, the sliver of black rock wrapped in leather. She had thought perhaps to use the knife to open her veins, but now that there was the slightest chance of escape, that idea died like a coal in water.

T'Cori unwrapped part of the leather thong and jammed her fingers through the loop.

She turned and smiled at Notch-Ear, wriggling her hips at him seductively. A wide grin split his face, and he grabbed her, pulling her back behind a bush next to the river, out of sight of the others. T'Cori dropped to all fours, raising her hips in invitation. Notch-Ear fumbled with his loincloth, seeking to free his root. Still smiling, she helped him, and felt his body stiffen in pleasure as her hands found his rigid organ, its repulsive warmth pulsing against her palm.

And the smile never left her face as the knife dropped into her hand, and she slashed. Notch-Ear's eyes and mouth opened in astonishment, but before he could scream she stabbed him in the throat with every bit of strength and speed in her tiny body, so that the scream was drowned in blood. Blinking rapidly, seemingly unable to comprehend what had happened to him, Notch Ear sank to his knees, fingers pressed futilely against the gushing wound.

T'Cori paused just long enough to spit in his dying face, then ripped the blade out, turned and leapt into the torrent, and was washed away.

Only an instant after the waters closed over her head, the first moment at which she could not draw breath, T'Cori regretted her action. The current was rough and stinging cold, filling her mouth and nose. She swallowed foam, and fought blackness, squeezing her hands tightly so that she would not drop the knife. The current wrenched her this way and that as if with vines attached to her arms and legs. She tried to cry out as her hip banged into a rock, and merely swallowed more water. The shock almost made her lose her grip on the blade, but the fear of being utterly weaponless tightened her hand again. When her head surfaced, she flailed toward the shore. Panic took her as soon as she began to choke. She could barely swim! The rivers and lakes around Great Sky had never attracted her as had Great Earth's heights. While some of the other children had learned to splash and swim, she could barely paddle her legs in still water, let alone in this maelstrom! Madness! What had she been thinking of? Surely it was better to live under any conditions than to die. . . .

But then T'Cori felt a calm, warm place within her, a place that said no, it was better to die and remain who she was than to change and live on as some shrunken, sallow creature neither Ibandi nor Other.

Resigning her soul to the gods she had served since childhood, T'Cori surrendered to the current.

Twisting, gasping, she glimpsed the Mk*tk leaping from rock to rock, attempting to grab her arms. They called to her, brutish faces twisted with confusion that she would decline to take their hairy hands, unable to comprehend that she might prefer death to being a receptacle for their seed.

Into the central channel T'Cori tumbled. Here the rocks were less plentiful, but the current ripped along at a faster pace. She was out of the reach of the Mk*tk, but still they called out to her.

Here there was peace, to which she surrendered at last.

*Peace.*

This was, no doubt, a calm before the storm of her passage to the shadow realm, but she kept her head above the water and floated with the current. So peaceful. What had there ever been to fear? Her ears filled with a sudden churning sound, and for the first few moments she didn't recognize it. Then the water's roar was closer, the torrent itself rougher and more violent. Suddenly T'Cori was in midair, swept over a waterfall, falling weightlessly in a world of wet sound. *Great Mother, Your arms . . . ,* she thought, and then was gone.

The fall seemed to take forever. She was weightless, suspended in a roaring so immense and enveloping it resembled silence. Then came a sensation like being smashed with a great flat hand as she thundered down into the pool at the base of the waterfall. She plunged deep, but then thrashed her way back up, vomiting water as she broke the surface.

Shock, relief, fear and excitement all mingled in her heart.

Alive! She was alive!

Knife still in hand, she spit water, oriented herself and struck out toward the shore, suddenly panicked from that placid, accepting place by the reality of a violent whirlpool formed by the current and the falls. T'Cori swallowed more water than she thought she had ever drunk. She struggled to keep her head above its surface and thrashed her arms and legs frantically. A final wrenching effort extracted her from the whirlpool's grip. A few more moments in which it felt that her lungs would burst in her chest, and then she was free and crawling into the shallows.

Utterly exhausted, T'Cori pulled herself out onto the riverbank.

She was destroyed, nude of flesh and spirit. Her skirt of twisted leather had been washed away, along with every bit of strength that remained. She heard approaching footsteps, and knew only that she would never allow herself to be taken back, that she was very close to losing her mind.

No strength remained. Now, there was only shame. Shaking, she exhausted herself raising her arm. She needed both hands to point it at her enemy, her teeth bared.

Then she saw his face. The single unhealed scar on each cheek. The gentle brown oval, the mouth set in a quizzical, concerned curve, the gap between his gleaming front teeth.

Great Mother be praised, *she knew him.*

Small, thin, but with a gentle Ibandi face and those bright, bright eyes, that thin, smiling mouth now turned down in a frown.

Her dizzied mind raced, searching for a name. *Frog.* It was Frog.

Was he a phantom, and this some cruel mirage? Had she perished in the plunge? If so, perhaps she had finally found the path to the mountaintop, and she would gladly travel it. She pulled herself onto her knees. "Ibandi boy," she said, "please. Help me."

He hunkered down at her side, studying her with curiosity mingled with awe. "You are the nameless one. One of Stillshadow's dream dancers."

T'Cori's vision began to fade, and it took everything she had merely to plead: "Help me."

"What are you doing out here?" he asked, looking nervously to right and left and then behind him, as if worried that someone or something might have been playing a trick on him.

"The Others," she said. "They took me." She bowed her head, made the posture of submission. "Shamed me."

Instantly, Frog became more alert. He squared his shoulders, straightened his back, seemed no longer the gangling boy she had bested on the tree, or caused to be beaten by poor dead Owl. This was a young Ibandi hunter, brave and true. By custom and breeding, he would die to protect her. That thought both comforted and frightened her.

Frog scanned the hillside for trouble. "Where are they?"

"Beyond the rise," she said. "Hurry. If they find us, they will kill you."

"They will kill *us*," he said.

"No," she said. "They want my sex. You they will kill."

"Not easy to do," he said, puffing his chest out. "I am Ibandi!"

She thought of Notch-Ear, so horribly strong and agile, and found hysterical laughter bubbling up from her gut, felt her mind bending, twisting. Floating away.

"What happened?" he asked.

"They killed Owl and Leopard. Took us. They . . ." She tried to tell him more, and could not force her mouth to repeat such wickedness. T'Cori crouched, her hand outstretched palm up, making obeisance as she never had to the Mk*tk. "Help me, Ibandi man."

# Chapter Thirty-three

Even a skilled and observant hunter might have walked past their little shelter and never seen it at all. Which was, of course, Frog Hopping's entire intention. His makeshift boma was snuggled into a cluster of wait-a-bit thornbushes, their spiky brown branches cut away and then vined back into place as doorway and camouflage once Frog had hacked out a central chamber large enough for himself and the nameless girl.

Frog had worked with feverish speed and limited options to complete the boma by nightfall. Predators of two legs, four legs and no legs haunted the darkness.

If necessary he would cheat sleep all night, watching for human foes. On the other hand, if he and the girl were discovered, it might not matter whether he was awake or asleep. The enemy had slain Owl and Leopard, hunt chiefs. Poor Frog would stand no chance at all. When the Mk*tk ran, they ran like the hyena, with endless endurance. Or as the cheetah, with irresistible speed and power. He could barely imagine how it would feel to face one in the wrestling circle.

Or in the brush, where there were no rules at all.

For days before finding the nameless girl, Frog had trailed his enemies at a distance. Not by preference, but because that was the only way he could. He could not have kept pace with them even if he'd possessed their skills and strength. Not even a hunt chief could have done so while remaining hidden.

Frog dared not follow at night, worried that the Mk*tk—as the nameless

girl called them, with a glottal click between harsh syllables—were noctur-
nal hunters, or that he might stumble across their encampment. And Frog
further swore to himself that if footprints indicated that they had been
joined by others of their kind, he would make a retreat. He had no great sui-
cidal urge to be trapped in enemy territory.

So after rescuing the girl, Frog knew he that if he did not control the fear-
flame, it would burn a hole in his belly. How best might he return her to
Great Earth? Where exactly had she camped when the Mk*tk killed the
hunt chiefs and stole the dancers away? He did not know, but guessed that
if he headed directly back for Fire boma, they might be safe: the Others
might move to intercept them based on where they had originally captured
the nameless one. Even if they tracked him, found his footprints with hers,
they would not know which Ibandi group he belonged to, and would have
little hope of anticipating and intercepting him.

Or so he told himself.

On the other hand, they might be hunters with skills beyond those of
even Cloud Stalker. Perhaps they could merely glance at his footprints and
know his origins. Then his foes might circle around to intercept him, lying
in wait with spears and arrows and slings. . . .

But there were other problems: after pleading for his assistance, the girl
had collapsed, swooning with some weakness.

When he found the nameless one on the riverbank she had been naked,
the leather waistlet gone, the zebra-skin flap that normally covered a dream
dancer's breasts nowhere to be seen. He had fashioned a covering for her
from one of his pouches and a bit of warthog skin, tying it around her so
that his eyes would not take that which was hers alone to give.

She lay sprawled on her back beneath the sheltering thorn branches, a
small, firm-bodied girl of ten and five years. Her braids remained, but he remembered also tight coils held in place with beautiful shells and bones.
They were gone, and in their absence she seemed frayed and disarrayed.

Her eyes were open and staring at nothing. She crawled blindly, mewling.

"What do I do?" he asked her.

She seemed blind, unable to see or even hear him, and spoke words that
were no answer to his question. "I see fire," she said. "Fire and blood . . ."

Was she dying? Or perhaps filled with some evil spirit? Or could this be
a sign that Great Mother was reaching through her child and trying to speak
to him? Both terror and awe burned his veins.

And he also felt the stirrings of something else, an attraction to this strange girl, sensations troubling in the extreme. He tried again. "Tell me what to do." No response. He took a desperate gamble. "Tell me, Butterfly Spring."

At that name, given to her in jest so many moons before, her eyes fluttered, focused. Her hand snapped out and gripped his wrist with surprising strength.

"Don't leave me." Her voice cracked with desperation.

Uncertain what to do, he enfolded her in his arms as he might have sheltered a child, somewhat discomfited both by his compassion and his stirrings. This was the strange, wild one who had followed at Stillshadow's ankles. Frog didn't know what to do with her. She wasn't a child, and he couldn't really look at her as a woman, so what was she?

"I see things," the girl he called Butterfly Spring whispered.

"What do you see?"

"Days to come," she said.

This was all entirely too strange for a simple hunter like Frog. Perhaps the wisest thing he could do was to leave her here. True, this mad girl would die, but no one would ever know he had found her. And even if they learned the truth, who could blame him? If he tried to take her with him, they would probably be caught and killed. Better one live than both climb the mountain.

*Wasn't it?*

But even as he thought those things, he knew that she sensed his ambivalence. "I go, but I will return."

"Go . . . ?" She clutched at him. "Where do you go? *Why* do you go?"

"I . . . I must hunt," he said. "For both of us." The lie twisted his tongue.

The girl gazed at him, finally managing to focus her eyes. "I see things," she said.

Curiosity halted him where compassion had failed. "What? What do you see?"

"That if you save me, you will be a great hunter."

Several long breaths passed. Frog felt as if someone had brushed his scalp with a burning coal. "Great?"

"I see that if you stay with me, one day you will be grand hunt chief."

He paused. "Grand chief?" Beyond the cave mouth, the wind whistled: *She lies.*

She held his eyes, unblinking. "In the shadow of Father Mountain," she said, "I cannot lie."

Could she read his mind? "We are not in the mountain's shadow."

"The night is the mountain's shadow," she replied.

He listened with his heart. Yes, desperation weighed her words. But did that mean she lied? He leaned closer. "We will both die," he said.

"Not if you are a true Ibandi." She tried to smile, and failed. The effort exposed a cracked, broken front upper tooth. Her lip above it was swollen. Oddly, like Uncle Snake's wounds, the scar did not diminish her allure. Swiftly and clearly he envisioned her fighting for her honor, struggling to escape her brutish captors, and his respect for this nameless girl soared.

There was no doubt: she was Ibandi, blood and bone.

Her words seemed heartfelt, but . . . could he believe this girl? She would say or do anything to keep him with her. She was helpless on her own, as were all the dream dancers. "What happened to your sisters?" he asked.

"Fawn is dead."

He shook his head, disbelieving. Fawn! The smiling, round-bottomed, sensual Fawn, who had been his first lover. The name brought back memories of that time by the river, with the grass pressed against his back, Fawn showing him the way to pleasure a woman. "What else?" he asked.

"Sister Quiet Water, and Fawn's twin."

"Dead?"

She shook her head. "Worse. The Mk*tk made them their women. Help me. I beg you."

From birth, she had been raised to consider her own flesh above his own, that it was natural for him to risk, or give his life to preserve a dream dancer. And yet . . .

Was she wrong? Were her gifts not more vital to the Circle than his own?

*Grand chief?* Absurd. He was not even a hunt chief. Could not run or jump or fight as should a hunt chief. Many boys were better, stronger, faster than he. And yet . . .

And yet *those* boys were not here. *They* had not followed the Mk*tk. They were not the ones with whom a dream dancer pled for her life.

Frog Hopping squatted beneath the thorn branches, brooding. "You can see the future?" he asked.

"Yes." Her eyes shifted to the side.

*Liar.* He was sure she lied. If she had told the truth, perhaps he would have remained. Instead, Frog decided to abandon her to her fate. The relief of that decision flooded him like a warm, clean tide, sweeping away doubt. His smile was not kind. "If you can see the future, you should be able to tell me: will I return?"

She looked at him, and to his shock he felt himself losing balance, felt himself falling into the infinite brown depths of her eyes. In that instant he felt that she *saw* him. Knew him as perhaps no one else ever had.

"Yes." Her voice trembled, but she did not blink. Her eyes did not shift, and Frog wondered.

*Grand chief.*

Then without another word, he left.

Frog the hunter skulked upon the plain, stealthy as a spider monkey as he scrambled to a ridgetop. From this concealed vantage he could peer down on the bouldered plateau. There was little to be seen save acacias and wild fig, candelabra and a fever tree or two. The moon squatted low and swollen on the horizon. The night was very clear.

There within the darkness . . . was that a greater, deeper shade? Was that the shadow of the mountain? A moon shadow? It seemed almost to point at the very clump of wait-a-bits where lay the terrified, exhausted Butterfly. From time to time out on the heated sands, he dreamed dreams of floating phantom mountains, shining, vanishing, reappearing at the whim of the moonlit clouds.

He should run. He should leave the husk of a girl in the boma and go home. No one would ever know he had even seen her. In that way, at least he would live, and one day marry, and have children. . . .

"Chief," he whispered.

*The nameless one tossed and turned beneath the lashed branches, lost in nightmare, her eyes clouded with bloody visions.*

*Again she stood on the cliff above a distant, raging river. Afraid to die, shamed by the inability to simply release her grip and fall into Great Mother's arms.*

*Gigantic, implacable, motivated by hungers beyond her ken, the Mk\*tk crept toward her, hand over hand along the rocks. Their alien smell drove thought from her mind, so that she slipped and tumbled. . . .*

Gasping, she sat up, raking her cheek against the thorns. For a few breaths she was disoriented, unable to remember where or even who she was. Then a primal wave of hunger banished the confusion. The glorious aroma of roasting animal flesh filled her nose.

Frog squatted in the boma's entrance, turning a spitted, skinned hedgehog over a bed of coals.

He was still with her? Had not fled? She was so astonished she could not speak.

"Eat," he said. He wrapped a steaming half carcass with a banana leaf, and tossed it to her. She caught it, passed the steaming meat hand to hand until it cooled, and then put her teeth to work.

"I wish to see if your dreams are real," he said. "Or if you are the crazy girl everyone says."

So immersed was she in gnawing the flesh from the small bones that she could not even think of words to answer.

He gazed at her soberly. "If we both die, I will know you were wrong."

At that, she felt the corners of her lips turn up. It was the first glimmer of happiness she had felt in a very long time.

Frog and T'Cori lay in shadow, looking down the hill at a group of three Mk*tk below them. They were larger than Ibandi, muscled much more heavily, with more body hair and flatter jaws, broader noses beneath shorter foreheads. The three looked in all directions and at least once appeared to look directly at the two Ibandi.

Beside him, T'Cori stiffened and started to crawl back, but he gripped her arm. He himself might have bolted, if not for the memory of the lioness: *The predator can look directly at you and not see you. He is not Father Mountain or some all-powerful demon.*

The Mk*tk sniffed the air, scratched at the dirt in search of sign and then trotted away.

The girl had described the place where she and her sisters had been captured. It dried Frog's throat to realize he had been just across the valley from his people's desperate struggle.

Could he have helped? No. If Owl Hooting and his brother had been killed, poor Frog would have been squashed like a melon.

In the easiest decision of his life, Frog decided to stay far away from them. It was possible that these creatures would anticipate his actions, but he was following his own, lesser *num,* which told him to trust the girl. Every evidence suggested that the Mk*tk were stronger and faster and more aggressive than he. He could only hope that he was smarter. If he had not even that advantage, then the two Ibandi had no hope at all. Better to simply lie down and die.

After the Mk*tk below them moved off to the east, Frog and the girl continued west.

Every shift of wind increased the risk of discovery. Every strange smell or echo promised disaster. Despite her small stature and mannered ways the girl seemed sturdy enough, and surprisingly nimble. She knew nothing of hunting or trapping, but from time to time she would stop and point out a plant or animal, and tell him of some function of which he had never dreamed. She pointed to a cairn of rocks and dung perched on a cave shelf above them. "Hyrax," she said.

He knew the tiny mouselike creatures well. "Not much meat," he sniffed.

"Their scat makes a tea, good for the shaking sickness," she said.

She seemed thoughtful when she said that, and he wondered if there was a story to tell. She didn't continue, and he remembered when Deep Dry Hole had collapsed, frothing at the mouth. Three times in a moon this had happened. The dream dancers had come and given him a thin soup to banish the shaking sickness. Afterward he had suffered only one more, and then none for as long as Frog could remember.

"Mouse shit?" Frog asked. "This is the medicine Dry Hole took?"

She looked at him proudly, seeing nothing humorous at all in the secret ingredient.

"Tell no one," she said. "It is our secret."

"No one," he lied. Frog simply couldn't wait to tell Dry Hole the truth. Perhaps he would wrinkle his nose, or if Frog decided to speak while Dry Hole was eating, he might even spit up his food.

That would be entertaining to watch. All the more reason to survive to reach home once again.


He heard the river before they reached it, and rather than merely fording its rushing waters, Frog thought to see if it might offer up nourishment. He shushed her and together they lay flat in the grass, watching the water at a slant so as to reduce glare. For half a quarter they waited, and then . . .

*There!* Frog glimpsed a flash of life beneath the surface.

"Butterfly, quiet," he whispered, and crawled onto a jutting flat rock, close enough to the water to see his own reflection. She bit her lip and hunkered down obediently. Ten breaths he waited, and then ten more. When he saw the moving shadow, he lunged.

Frog was not strong, and many were faster afoot than he, but Frog's hands were quick as his totem's tongue. He lunged, slipped from the rock and fell into the river. Then he sat up on the rocks, sputtering, holding a flapping blue fish high in both hands. Never before had he seen its like: pink speckles against pale blue flesh with flat black eyes. But it flapped mightily, and anything that fought so for its life must be tasty indeed.

Both he and the girl laughed delightedly. She stood and ran in a circle, flapping her arms like her pretended namesake, thanking its spirit for the gift of flesh.

It was the first truly good moment that they had shared.

Another day's walking, and Great Sky was now a misty gray ghost before them. Or was that Great Earth? Coming from the south, the two mountains were in line with each other, so that what appeared when the light was just right was a vast cairn of green-dappled gray rock. This was the outer range of Ibandi hunting territory. The nameless one seemed more at home now as well. Occasionally she dug tubers and plucked fleshy seed fruits with cries of happy recognition. Gradually their camp transformed into a place of joy and promise. Where they found caves, he used them, except one that had clearly been used before by Mk*tk. On that occasion they moved on, as he had with the baobab tree.

Two days from home, he was about to step out of the grassland into an area blackened and still smoldering from a lightning fire, when the nameless one pulled at his hand. "Wait," she said.

"What, Butterfly?"

She smiled at the play name, then grew serious again. "Something is wrong," she said. At first Frog thought to question her, then a voice within said, again, *Trust the girl.*

Were they being followed? But if that was true, why hadn't the Mk*tk simply killed them? Certainly the monsters had little to fear from a single Ibandi boy.

Not that, then. Perhaps something else. Perhaps . . . perhaps their enemy was closer than he thought. Occasionally, as the wind shifted, his nose had wrinkled at a strong, alien scent.

So far, he had seen nothing: no tracks and no visual sign.

Perhaps he no longer believed in gods or a life beyond this one, but he had to trust something sometime. Why not trust himself, the skills taught him by Snake and his brothers, and this strange girl?

Yes. Trust.

What to do? Frog and T'Cori couldn't circle any farther west. If Others were genuinely on their trail, then they might be driven into lands completely unknown. On the other hand, considering the nature of their enemy, if pursuit was that tenacious, no hope remained.

*No.* There was always hope. He was an Ibandi hunter, and the Ibandi would not be driven from their own lands.

So very cautiously, he began to move T'Cori farther east, backtracking and then searching for footprints.

And then at last he found sign, one brutish, splay-toed Mk*tk track, with wide thick toes and deep, heavy heel-print. A green centipede lay crushed in the impression, its pus sac mostly dried but still a bit gummy to the touch. From that wetness, Frog estimated the Mk*tk to be a half day ahead of him.

Letting caution rule him, Frog circled around the field of short blackened grass, camping in the bush without a fire. They followed on at daybreak when once again his eyes could distinguish between eland and elephant.

The wind wrinkled his nose. Frog stopped them, crouching to examine a sprig of broken grass. Then he simply remained still, and motioned her to follow his example.

"What are we doing?" she whispered.

"They may be close," Frog said. "We take no chance. A hunter's ally is stillness. My uncle Snake told me to be like a rock. All men, all animals want to believe all is well. Tell the world that you are harmless, and most will pass at peace."

The girl nodded, and remained silent and still until he rose and motioned her to follow, which she did, dumbly, head down. But a quarter day later she said: "You are following him. How do you know he is not also following you?"

The idea burned. The thought of one of these terrible two-legged in the bush behind them, growing closer by the breath, was almost more than he could bear. And yet he wondered: Could that have happened? Could the Mk*tk have backtracked, just as he had? Found their signs? Even now come close enough to cast a spear?

No. Frog was slower and weaker than his brothers, but he trusted his mind. He *had* to. It was, and had always been, his sharpest weapon.

But with every step, that possibility gnawed at him.

*Grand hunt chief. What if she was right? What then?*

Frog began to cut glances at the nameless one. Again, he considered his motivations for remaining with her. Because she was a sacred dream dancer? Because there was a chance that T'Cori saw things that he did not? That she had actually seen a future in which he rose high in the Circle? He did not know how such a thing could be, but she claimed to see it, nonetheless. He had always suspected the dancers possessed such power. Snake said that Stillshadow could see the future. Could the nameless one?

So Frog doubled back on himself. For a quarter, he circled back, until he cut his own tracks again.

And there they were. Mk*tk tracks. Larger, deeper than Ibandi tracks. More weight on the balls of the feet, as if ready to sprint at any moment. "Do you trust me?" he asked the girl.

She nodded. "With my life." Frog took her up into the rocks, very careful to brush away her footprints and any other sign that he and the nameless one had passed this way. "If I don't return, it will be because I am dead," he said. "If I die, would you rather die or have the Mk*tk take you back?"

Her expression told him all he needed. For his broken-winged Butterfly, death would be a comfort. Frog nodded. "Then here is the rest of the food," he said, laying down the leather sack in which he had carried their supplies. "I will come back."

There was a pause of several breaths in which neither of them spoke. Tears shone in her eyes, making them like twin summer moons reflected in the waters of Fire Lake. "Butterfly Spring," he said. Her lips turned up in a sad little smile, and she spread her arms, flapping. Frog replied with his own little hopping dance.

Butterfly. Frog.

*Family.*

He started to turn away, but she called to him and threw her arms around his shoulders, holding him so tightly that he could barely breathe.

Again, he felt himself growing aroused, and was troubled. He had sexed with Fawn, a dream dancer, and now Fawn was dead. Other men and boys had lain with dream dancers, and it had brought no grief. Frog was confused, not knowing what was right or whether Fawn had been wronged in lying with him. He knew only that he did not want to sin against Great Mother twice.

It was almost embarrassing to pry her away. But the gratitude glowing in her eyes told him everything that he needed. This was right. And regardless of what happened, in her eyes he was a hero. As were his brothers. As Uncle Snake was. As he, Frog, had always hoped to be.

"I'll be back," said Frog. And then he was gone.

·    ·    ·

Whenever the way was clear Frog trotted, slowing down whenever the brush might offer concealment to an enemy. He crouched to examine the grass ahead, saw that it had been bent and broken only a quarter before, and increased his pace once again. If he could even *once* glimpse his quarry, it might be possible to design some kind of ambush. But even if he did catch sight before the Mk*tk detected him, how would he get into a killing position?

He was just thinking this when an impala buck bounded out of the brush behind him. Golden, slender and graceful it was, with a flash of white at hooves and flank. Its curved brown antlers swept back as if windblown. Wide-eyed and startled, it bounded off in another direction when its wide brown eyes glimpsed the human hunter.

The flesh along the back of Frog's neck itched terribly. What had just happened? Was the appearance of the buck a coincidence? A sign from Father Mountain?

Or had the impala been disturbed? Driven from behind?

And if it had . . . ?

The impala fled, but Frog sprinted after, cocking his spear arm, aiming, feeling the sense of sacred connection, praying that it was the impala's death time. He threw, blunt end first.

The spear flew true, striking the impala hard at the rounded back of its skull, stunning it. Frog unslung his second spear, swinging it as the impala staggered to its feet, smashing it along the side of the head. It collapsed onto its side, bleating.

Then Frog scrambled away, wiping out his tracks, stepping on rocks whenever possible, until he was concealed at a safe distance.

The impala fell silent.

A hand of breaths passed. Frog felt a fool. Then again, better a live fool than a dead hero. Or a dead and *devoured* hero. Who knew what terrible things these Mk*tk did? T'Cori had not spoken of them eating human flesh, but that did not mean they eschewed such fare. Young Frog would make a tasty morsel indeed.

Frog heard something stirring in the brush, and a silver-backed jackal emerged. Its black-peppered tail twitched, red flanks and legs devoid of fat, pale chin and lips flecked with saliva. He was about to throw a rock to drive it off, when a second sound tickled his ears. The jackal's massive head flicked around to face the direction from which the sound had come.

The imposing bulk of a solitary Mk*tk emerged from the brush. The jackal took one look at the Other, snarled, and despite its obvious hunger decided not to contest the meal. It ran, yipping in raucous disappointment.

The Mk*tk faded back into the brush, becoming just another shadow among the fronds. What was that shadow thinking? Was the Mk*tk as cautious as Frog had been? Then his enemy crept farther forward, close enough to examine the stunned impala. Frog was glad that he had downed it without leaving an obvious wound. What might the Mk*tk think about the gift? Had they mind to consider such things, or would belly overrule head?

The Mk*tk sniffed the air. Frog prayed that the wind would not shift and betray him. With a black-bladed knife wrapped with a leather thong the Other cut the impala's throat. Even before the buck's feet ceased flapping, the Mk*tk was slicing strips from its body.

Unwelcomed thoughts swirled in Frog's head: Did the Mk*tk trade with the coastal people? Or rob them? Or did they have their own sources of black rock?

*Quiet,* he told his mind. No time for the endless rattling of unanswerable questions.

Frog raised his spear point-first. Felt the stretch in his shoulder as he drew his arm back. Careful. Careful . . . and then he released the tension, hip twisting, chest pivoting, and then shoulder, the last segment of what the hunt chiefs called *The Bamboo Whip,* the movement that released the spear to flight. Almost as it left his hand, Frog sprinted after it, knowing that if it missed, the Mk*tk would catch and kill him.

But it did not miss. The spear struck the Mk*tk squarely in the back beneath the left shoulder, driving into the lung. The giant staggered, roaring in pain and rage as he reached back and clawed for the shaft, gripping and wrenching it loose. Screaming a string of sounds Frog did not comprehend, the Mk*tk hurled it to the ground. The spear's fire-hardened wooden tip was smeared with crushed poison grub, but even if there was enough to kill the Mk*tk, it might take another quarter. Frog did not have a quarter.

One or the other of them would die this day.

The Mk*tk spun, arms wide, eyes bloodshot and lips pulled back from his mouth exposing great, flat, thick, yellowed teeth. Shrieking challenge, it charged him.

Frog stood his ground for a breath and then jabbed his second spear at the left ribs, wove out of the path of a grasping arm and jabbed at the right, swift enough to nick the Mk*tk, but almost slow enough to be grabbed as his foe clawed for him. The Mk*tk wrenched the spear from Frog's grasp, spit on it, then cast it aside.

Frog ran for his life.

Twice the Mk*tk's fingers scraped the back of Frog's neck, but the boy twisted this way and that, and he managed to stay ahead. Never had he run so! On and on he went, through reeds and rushes, across open and bushy plain, arms and legs pumping, the Mk*tk roaring in pursuit, barely ten paces back. His heart threatened to burst, his lungs burned as if he had swallowed fire, but he never slowed. At last the giant began to drop back, and Frog knew that the wound was finally weakening him. Perhaps the poison was beginning to work as well. But Frog was almost exhausted and had run out of clear ground: the Mk*tk had trapped him against a tumble of boulders and spikey wait-a-bit bushes. The giant scrambled up over the rocks after him, his eyes burning in the waning daylight.

Then Frog was cornered, and the Mk*tk's hands were upon him, hissing as Frog slashed at him with his knife, tearing at the boy with fingers so strong they ripped at his arms and thighs like an animal's claws.

Frog stabbed again, angling his blade at the heart, and *now* the Mk*tk screamed, a terrible sound. Despite the pain and the weakness from the wounds, the Mk*tk's mighty fingers closed on Frog's arm, crushing muscle against bone. Frog screamed and leaned in, pulling down, working the knife side to side. The Mk*tk caught him a bone-cracking blow with the side of a balled, giant fist. Frog felt as if Father Mountain had fallen on him.

He was thrown to the side. Frog hit the ground and rolled as much as he could, but the breath had still been slammed out of him.

The Mk*tk pawed at the knife buried in his side, and screamed more words Frog could not understand. The giant tried to pull the weapon out but his hands were slippery with blood, and couldn't secure enough of a grip. For the first time a real expression of pain and dismay creased his flat, blunt features. He coughed, a thick bright red bubble blossoming at the corner of his mouth. He wiped at it, glaring at the crimsoned palm with a confused expression. Again the Mk*tk wrenched at the knife, for a moment turning his back on the young hunter almost as if he had forgotten Frog was there.

Frog jumped onto that broad back, twining his arms around his enemy's neck, raking at the eyes with splayed fingers. The strength in the Mk*tk's body staggered and disheartened him. He was unyielding, unbending. Nothing Frog did seemed to make any difference at all. The fact that he was wounded and stunned, stabbed, smashed in the head with a rock, and poisoned . . . all of that, and this much power remained? Was this a man at all?

Then the Mk*tk fell backward, his weight almost crushing Frog. Frog screamed and pulled the knife from the Mk*tk's side, slashing at the bigger man's throat, sawing and tearing until thick, hot, salty blood spurted and flowed back into Frog's eyes and mouth. He gagged, fought his own stomach's spasms and held on. For a moment the struggles grew more violent, hammering Frog back against the ground so that he feared he would lose consciousness.

Frog's ears were filled with a roaring sound. The Mk*tk's screams? His own? To the end of his days he could not have said.

And then . . . the giant was still.

It took Frog almost as long to push his way from underneath the Mk*tk as it had taken to kill him. Covered with gore, he stared at the bloody corpse, unable to believe that he himself was actually alive.

He stopped shaking, suddenly understanding the implications.

*He was alive. And the Mk*tk was dead.*

Frog Hopping had slain his first man.

## Chapter Thirty-four

Heart pounding, Frog sawed off the Mk*tk's hairy ear, then found his way back through the brush to the nameless one. Every step was agonizing. What manner of creature had he slain? Fire Ant had been right to creep away. Survival against such a foe was victory in itself.

T'Cori was crouched shivering in the darkness. She groped around her, unable to see.

"Frog?" she gasped.

"It's me." His chest still heaved. How strange: to be exultant and nauseated at the same time. His kill had been a man, not a four-legged. Somehow, it was different.

"What happened?"

"There was only one of them."

"And?" she asked.

"I live. He does not."

She threw her arms around Frog and tried to press her mouth against his face. Embarrassed, he pried her away. "It's late," he said. "We can camp here."

And so they did.

Frog decided not to summon a fire. If the Mk*tks found their cousin's body, they might be raised to a fever pitch of rage. Did such beasts love one another? Did they play? Would they seek revenge? It was hard to put his mind into theirs, to imagine what thoughts and feelings they might have.

As they rested the girl clung to him for warmth. And more than warmth.

Late in the night, after he thought she had fallen asleep, she began to circle her hips against his buttocks. "Ibandi man," she whispered, lips close against his ear. "I would have you, if you want me."

Although his root was growing more interested by the breath, Frog drew back. Fawn had sexed Frog. Fawn was dead.

"It is not done. You are mountain daughters."

"The Mk*tk made me one of their women," she said, her voice pinched. "Your seed can make me Ibandi once again."

The southern men had satisfied their hungers with her, and now she begged Frog to sex her. Did the dancers' secret teachings say that would make her part of the great Circle again?

Regardless, he could not do it. It was not safe, not seemly to sex with her at such a time. The entire situation confused him, and confusion at such a time was an invitation to disaster.

But still, his belly was warm to her. "You are a dream dancer," he said. "You have courage and strength."

Sullen at the rejection, she pulled away. "No man will ever want me."

"You are a mountain daughter," he reminded her.

She lowered her eyes. "Great Mother is ashamed of me."

"Father Mountain loves courage," he said. "Doesn't Great Mother as well?" And although he stuck with his decision not to share sex with her, he held her close until morning, and that much, at least, was good.

He was glad, though, that her fingers did not stray to feel his root, which was now fully awake. Regardless of the decisions he had made, it had its own notions of right and wrong.


The next day brought more walking. T'Cori and Frog reached a place where he could climb high and look in all directions. The wind was sweet-smelling, and from their position they could spot winding game trails through the grass. Here and there and there, ibex and nyalas and bongos had made way in single file, blazing a path for their fellows.

There he waited for half a quarter, looking. No one. Nothing. He and the girl had been very careful with their footprints whenever possible, walking in water, on rocks, doubling back, wiping out their tracks. Frog used every trick that he knew or could invent, and at last was convinced that he had thrown their pursuers off the scent. Perhaps one escaped woman was not enough to motivate their enemies to follow them so deeply into Ibandi territory. But if the Mk*tk found their slain kinsman . . . ?

At this point, they began to move with more confidence, trusting in speed to succeed where stealth might fail.

On the fourth day they reached a steep decline leading to a long, open stretch of savannah. He looked down, spotting an abandoned campsite. Frog was relieved to see that the method of arranging the fire pit looked more Ibandi than Mk*tk. They were nearer home.

They were forced to descend a steep ravine, where the rocks looked more secure than they actually were. Twice he slid and almost fell, catching himself, but T'Cori shamed him by descending with a lighter, surer foot. So her tiny stature was good for something after all!

At that thought, Frog lost his footing completely and fell, remembering his monkey rolls only at the last moment, contracting into a tight ball and thumping his way down the rest of the ravine. He was lucky not to have split his head on a rock!

He dusted himself off, peeking back to see if she was laughing. Her expression was nothing but concern, and he felt he had maintained sufficient dignity to continue on.

The camp looked childish, as if the camper lacked complete hunter skills. But then, what was he doing so far from any encampment, something that was usually reserved for the most experienced hunters?

Frog dug around the campsite with his spear's blunt end, and found bones. They were human bones, and had been gnawed. Scraps of dried and twisted ligament and sun-cured skin bound the bones together. Not all of the bones were here. Some had been taken away, for ease of consumption elsewhere.

"What happened here?" the girl asked.

"Blood," he said. "And fire." Frog looked at his companion, wondering. Should she have foreseen this? He dug into the ashes and found a skull. He did not know skulls well enough to be certain, but he thought it was a bit small for an Ibandi hunter. The back of the skull was cracked, as if someone had struck it from behind, he thought.

Running from a foe? Wrestled to the ground and pounded with a rock?

"Recent?" she asked, interrupting his thoughts.

"No," he replied. "The bones are bleached. For many moons. Someone camped here. At first I thought it was Ibandi, but now I am not certain. A young Mk*tk, perhaps."

She shook her head, pointing. "Not Other," she said. "Not Mk*tk. They make their fires on level ground; they do not dig pits."

Frog squatted. "This is dug," he said. "Not well, but . . . smart." He set the skull down and pointed. "See the windbreak? This one watched and learned. He did not know, but he thought." Frog looked even more carefully, walking around the bones, feeling a certain degree of respect for the unknown hunter.

"He was afraid," she said.

"He?"

"Women are taught to build fires with the rocks in a broken circle. This is a man's fire."

"Ah," he said. "And how do you know he was afraid?"

T'Cori closed her eyes and spoke softly. "He was staring out into the savannah as he made this. He wasn't careful to make a circle. It was as if he built it only to protect himself, with the rock at his back."

"How can you see that?" he asked.

She shrugged. "It seems obvious."

"Well, it didn't work," he said. After he examined the site a bit more, Frog added, "He was young."

"Young?"

"Yes," he said. Despite his fatigue, he was enjoying their talking together. It was unlike conversing with his brothers, Uncle Snake or even Break Spear. Something about the way she spoke made his own thoughts clearer. "The men teach basic knotting, but all elders have their own way. Only the children tie knots the exact way they are taught. This one didn't have time to develop a knot of his own. He was young. And afraid."

Frog peered more closely at the bones, studying. Then his mouth opened, and his spine flamed with utter horror.

"What is it?" she asked.

He could find no words.

"You knew him," she said. It was not a question.

Frog killed the flash of emotion, shut it away deep inside, hoping she could not read his expression. She touched his arm, but he shook her hand off. "I have to bury him," he said.

She opened her mouth as if about to speak, and then seemed to recognize something in his face. She remained quiet.

Surrounding Frog were the last vistas his old friend Lizard had ever seen. These dry rutted hills, endless fields of brown grass trees with spiky, jutting leaves. Had the dust devils danced for him, then, as they danced for Frog and the nameless one now?

If Father Mountain had been real, Frog might have cursed him.

"They might be close—" she began.

"We bury him," he repeated, his voice like stone. Frog felt a pain in his gut, a sense of loss so intense that it frightened him. Always his heart had known Lizard was gone. But seeing his bones . . .

All the last few days' dreadful events seemed to well up within him at once. Frog sank to his knees, unable to speak.

T'Cori knelt beside him, carefully taking the bones from his grasp. "He has new bones now," she said. "He dances with his ancestors on Great Sky."

*How can you know? What if you're wrong?* he wanted to say, but could not. In peering into her clear, placid face he seemed to find strength he'd not possessed a moment earlier. "Yes," he whispered. "He has new bones."

Together they clawed a trench in the earth, gathered what bones they could, and covered them with sand.

As Frog knelt, T'Cori danced and sang for Lizard. "Your bones are dry already," she said. "So I know your flesh has made its way to Great Sky, there to dance with our fathers."

Frog nodded. "I will see you again one day, my friend. And when I do," he whispered, "you will tell me your tale."

He stood, grateful to her, but unable to find the words to voice that gratitude. So instead of trying they continued on their way. And later, when Lizard's death came back to him and the tears started from his eyes again, she took his hand, and they walked that way together for a time, in silence.

Frog found tracks the next day, spent tens of breaths examining the brush and studying three-toed aardvark and four-toed serval tracks near a stream, and for the first time since the burial T'Cori thought her protector seemed happy.

He carefully selected a wild fig tree, saying, "These branches are thick enough. Up!" and she followed his commands, climbing up into the makeshift blind.

From that secure place she watched as, through the afternoon, he used a flat rock to dig a pit, and his black obsidian knife to cut stakes to line the bottom.

"Can't I help you?" she asked.

"No." He panted, drank a bit of water from his gourd and offered her a sip. "I have to do this myself."

Frog took the gourd back, slung it around his neck, and then wiggled his way into tall grass near the water hole, waiting.

Throughout the day flies buzzed, and little biting mites swarmed in the fig tree. Their jaws were large enough to irritate but not to draw blood. She examined them more closely. "Spice mites!" she said, and using her fingernail crushed one with a pleasure quite unbecoming for a dream dancer. "Stillshadow needs you for her fever brew. I will lead my sisters back to you. We will make soup," she said. It was probably her imagination, but the mites bit her less frequently after that.

Three quarters passed before the boar appeared, snuffling toward the water. Suddenly, Frog sprang up hooting and waving his spear. The pig bolted blindly. At the edge of the pit it seemed to recognize its danger and clawed at the dirt for purchase, but slid in and tumbled down onto the stakes.

It squealed in agony, and had torn itself half free of the stakes when Frog jumped to the edge of the pit, spear in hand. He thrust down into the pit many times, and finally the boar stopped bellowing.

Frog puffed and strained and gasped as he rolled the boar's pierced carcass out of the pit, but after he did, his lips curled in a broad smile.

Low white clouds boiled slowly above them. The wind whistled, rousing a tribe of dust-folk into their eternal dance. It was a good day, a very good day indeed.


He pulled the pig to a clean spot, and turned it over onto its back. He made the first cut at the sternum, at the center bottom of the rib cage.

He cut out the kidneys from against the backbone, cut off the eggs and root. Frog grinned at T'Cori as he hacked out the liver. "This is the best," he said, and handed the gory chunk up to her. "Only the hunters get this,"

She took a tentative bite, then tore into it with relish, blood running down her chin and reddening her smile.

They wove vines to create strong, useful straps. Frog crossed branches to make a sled on which they mounted the boar. Then, their mood truly light for the first time since the burial of Lizard's bones, they used the straps to drag the sled home to Fire boma.

· · ·

Half a day out T'Cori and Frog met the first of his people. "My cousin Little Slug!" he grinned.

Slug was perhaps two years older, taller, with a huge smile. Slug danced to see him, hooting, fat belly jiggling, artfully dragging his leg behind him to leave a trail. "We thought you were lost!" Slug said. "Scorpion came back many days ago. We sent out hunters to look for you!"

"I am Ibandi," Frog said, straightening his shoulders. "I bring meat."

Coming closer, they encountered a few more cousins, and then more as he and the nameless one approached the boma walls.

As the thorn walls became visible, his cousins surrounded them, shouting greeting.

"Frog," they said. "You return!"

"With meat!" he said, dropping the sled.

T'Cori knew his legs and back ached, and admired the way he concealed his weakness from his people. What a fine hunter he was!

"And there is more!" Frog threw the scrap of Mk*tk flesh on the ground.

They gawked, silent, and then Break Spear plucked the ear up. He examined it cautiously. "Who was this?"

"An Other. They are called Mk*tk," he said. "I rescued one of the dream dancers from them, and I know. This one has seen their camp." He took a deep breath. "They are not beast-men. They are larger, stronger than beast-men." He paused, trying to think of a way to explain it. "As we are to bhan, the Mk*tk are to us."

Fire boma's people stared as if he spoke monkey-tongue, then nodded, although he knew they did not really understand.

An old woman shuffled forward as well, leaning on her stick. T'Cori knew her—this was Stillshadow's younger sister, Hot Tree, Fire boma's mother.

"Who is this?" Hot Tree asked.

This was T'Cori's time to conceal her weakness. She and Frog had walked in off the savannah, with game and the ear of a dead enemy. The people's eyes were worshipful. "I am the one with no name," T'Cori said. "I am protected by Stillshadow herself."

"What do you do here, girl?"

How could she even begin to tell them? The girl Frog called Butterfly hung her head, but he jumped into the conversation. "She was taken by the Others, the ones who call themselves Mk*tk. I saved her. I killed my first man."

He pointed to the scrap of severed flesh in the dust. Already, ants were testing it with their jaws.

Hot Tree looked at him closely, and then peered at T'Cori as if she had never seen a dream dancer before. She picked up the ear and held it up closer to her eye. "He speaks truth," she said.

"There is more," Frog said, sadness thickening his voice. "I found my friend. I found Lizard's broken bones."

Runners were sent to fetch Stillshadow. A day passed, during which the nameless girl slept in Hot Tree's hut, discovering new and unexpected depths of fatigue in her bones. Her dreams were of silent giants clambering down a rock wall, mocking her.

The messengers retuned with two young hunt chiefs and the crone herself, leaning heavily on her cane with every step. T'Cori ran to her, clinging desperately. The old woman returned the embrace for a long fierce time, and for the first time in any of their memories, tears started from her eyes.

"The other dancers . . . ?" she asked her sister, as if the implied question tore her mouth. "Quiet Water. Fawn. Dove?"

Hot Tree shook her head.

"My girls," Stillshadow said, her voice barely audible. "Poor Lizard Tongue. Terrible."

The old woman turned and faced Frog, who had watched it all. "And you are the young hunter who brought my dancer home."

"Yes, honored one," he said, swallowing nervously.

She touched his forehead. "You are a fine one. There is something in you. You are Frog Hopping. I remember naming you. I saw something special then, and I see it now. You and I will speak again," she paused, and then added, "Great Mother is pleased with you."

Then, smiling, she turned to her apprentice. "You must come home now," she said. T'Cori nodded gratefully.

And so they left Fire boma. T'Cori looked back over her shoulder as they headed toward Great Earth, and there, in the gap in Fire boma's wall, stood Frog. He waved to her, and T'Cori waved back.

From time to time she continued to look back at the boma. And he was there every time, until the time came that she could no longer see the gap, and could not have said whether he was there or not.

But something in her heart hoped that he was.

# Chapter Thirty-five

For the next two days, T'Cori slept and ate and drank and slept. When she finally crawled out of her hut, the morning's fierce sun was shaded by noon clouds, and she felt more wholly alive than she had in over a moon.

Small Raven greeted her, and for once, the older girl's expression contained something other than disdain. To T'Cori's surprise, there was actually a measure of compassion in her eyes. "My mother wishes to see you," she said. "Find her at the sitting stone."

Wobbling a bit but feeling stronger by the step, T'Cori made her way down the path until she spotted her teacher, perched atop the boulder, knees drawn to her chest, smoking a pipe.

"Come sit with me." Stillshadow patted her palm against the stone.

"But . . . no one but you sits here." The girl could not even meet her mentor's eyes.

"This is a special day," Stillshadow said, and held her hand out. "Come sit with me, girl."

They sat there alone for a while, looking out on the valley floor and at Great Sky's misted expanse.

"You are a woman now," Stillshadow said. "Not the way I had planned, but the way it was intended."

"But how could that be?"

"Do you think anything happens that Great Mother does not plan?"

"But why?" the nameless one asked.

"I can tell you things, but they would all be lies," the old woman said. "I do not know the way of all things. But I believe there is a plan. Look at me. Tell me what you see."

T'Cori considered before answering. "I see the woman who has always cared for me."

"Yes. Do you see my *num*-fire? Look, as I have taught you."

T'Cori shaded her eyes, squinting as she peered at Stillshadow. She tried and tried, but the fire would not materialize. T'Cori threw her arms around Stillshadow's shoulders.

"I see nothing!" she cried. "Nothing at all."

Stillshadow's ancient face sagged, overwhelmed with pain. T'Cori shivered like a small, trapped animal.

"So," the older woman said quietly. "The Mk*tk, is that what you called them?"

The nameless one nodded, shuddering at the memory.

"The Mk*tk hurt your sight. But, girl, they cannot take that which only Mother can give. If She wills so, your vision will return."

"Is that true?"

"Yes." Stillshadow's warm dry hand clasped her shoulder, an attempt to comfort. "You must be strong for your people."

"And if I can't?"

"Then your sisters sacrificed for nothing."

"I left them behind," T'Cori whispered. "They're still there. Still—"

"Silence," Stillshadow said. "We have this, now. The rest is dreams. You may dance all of that out, as the dreams come to you. But life is for we who live. My other students are dead." Her mouth quivered, and for just a moment T'Cori glimpsed the almost unimaginable depths of the old woman's guilt and pain. How must it feel to be the old medicine woman, to know that she was the one who had sent the dancers out to disaster? "Dead to us," she said. "You are alive and must be strong."

At that moment it seemed that the weight of all the world had suddenly descended upon her chest. "And if I can?"

"Then you might sit at Raven's right hand," Stillshadow said.

The words, doubtless intended to comfort, sent a cold shudder up T'Cori's spine. "I'm afraid, teacher."

"Your sisters failed their test," Stillshadow said. "But Great Mother brought you back."

T'Cori covered her face with her hands. "I failed the tribe. I could not keep them from my body." She sagged. "I am a weak and wicked thing."

"No!" Stillshadow roared. "You are an Ibandi woman. A mountain daughter. There is no one, nothing strong enough to change that."

T'Cori looked down at her belly. Was there a monster within her, even now? "But . . . if their seed grows within me?"

Stillshadow's face softened. "You are skinny but strong. Your strength is hidden, like Great Mother's. Like the strength of women. She will turn their seed to ours."

Stillshadow slid down from her sitting stone, opened her leather pouch and crouched to throw the bones for the eighth time. "I have a good feeling," she said.

T'Cori could see nothing in the jumble of bleached monkey bones. Then again, she had not been trained to see, and hope blossomed within her. "Is there a name?" the girl asked.

Stillshadow remained crouched. When she straightened, her mouth was twisted in an uneasy smile. "What was the name that that boy called you?"

"Butterfly Spring," T'Cori said.

"Perhaps we will call you Butterfly for a while, until Great Mother sends you a name."

T'Cori shook her head slowly. "Thank you," she said. "I love you for what you try to do. But Great Mother delivered me. And I will stand by Her choices, whatever they are. I will wait."

Stillshadow turned her face away, wiped at her eyes without speaking. For a time there was no sound but that of birds and monkeys. "Tell me," she asked eventually, "did you dream while you were away?"

"Yes," T'Cori said. "Many dreams."

"Were there dances in those dreams?"

T'Cori shook her head sadly. "No."

"Did you see animals? Clouds? Water?"

"Clouds," T'Cori said after a pause.

"You saw clouds. Did they move?"

T'Cori squeezed her eyes tightly. "Yes."

"Stand," Stillshadow said. "And show me the cloud dance."

T'Cori paused, uncertain, and then climbed down off the rock. Slowly, nervously, she spread her arms and began a shallow gliding motion, then spun in a circle. She stopped and blinked. "That is what I can remember."

Stillshadow smiled broadly. "That is what I sent in the dream," she said. "Truly, we are blessed that you have returned. Truly, you are a dream dancer."

T'Cori ran to her and buried her face against Stillshadow's chest. "Thank you, thank you, thank you," she murmured again and again, as if the old woman's words had saved her life.

Stillshadow closed her own eyes and leaned back against her sitting stone, feeling the girl's heart fluttering against her chest. *Such a small lie,* she thought. She was certain that Great Mother would understand.

# Chapter Thirty-six

Word of Frog Hopping's adventure passed through the bomas like wild-fire. News of the Mk*tk traveled to Great Sky itself, where it came down from high that Father Mountain Himself had proclaimed the war with the beast-men concluded, and forbade any of their people from molesting them in any way.

This, as much as anything, made Frog proud, almost as proud as Cloud Stalker himself giving Frog his second scar, with the small keloid dots beneath which meant "man-killer."

The boma children would run up to him, touch his hand and run away again, laughing. When he encountered girls from other bomas traveling through their territory, they knew who he was, fluttered their eyes at him and turned away shyly. On two occasions, parents attempted to open marriage negotiations with Gazelle, but his mother pretended not to understand, and they went away.

Come the next Spring Gathering, life changed again for young Frog Hopping. On one fine, sunny day Uncle Snake and Gazelle sat him down with Earth boma's father and mother. With them were a small man and a woman almost twice the man's size, of great beauty and smiling aspect. Between them sat a young girl, of perhaps ten and three summers, compared to Frog's own ten and five. Her back was to Frog, so he could not see her face.

He could see her back, however: her skin was smooth, and there was a trio of keloid scars in the sign that meant *dawn*.

He found himself imagining her touch. For almost a quarter his uncle and mother spoke of Fire boma's fine heritage, and the great hunters living within its walls.

The small man spoke of his wife's strength and great wisdom and loyalty, and the woman herself spoke of the ease with which she had brought seven children into the world. At the end of that time, both spit once on the ground, and then again in the direction of Great Sky Mountain.

Snake and Gazelle took Frog away, and Snake sat him down. The rest of the Gathering buzzed around them, but young Frog heard none of it. He had, all his life, waited for the words that Uncle Snake was about to speak.

"You are a man now," he said. "And we have chosen you a wife. She is a fine girl, of a good Earth family. This marriage would bind our families together. As is our custom, you do not have to accept my choice, but if you do not, then we cannot support you, and you will have to make your own way."

These were more or less the ritual words. An obedient son, Frog had always followed the guidance of his parents. He sat with his spine as straight as the path of a dropped stone, with full respect. "I know you want the best for me, Uncle." Frog lowered his voice to a whisper. "Is she pretty?"

Snake grinned. "She has a face like a warthog," he said.

Frog's heart filled with anguish. The girl T'Cori had not been beautiful, not really, but she was hardly a warthog. He certainly would have been happy to find her in the marriage ritual. . . .

The thought stunned him. Where had *that* come from?

Snake saw Frog's confusion and perhaps misinterpreted it as anguish. "Did you not see her mother, Smoke Leaf? My nephew," he said, "I would not curse you with an ugly woman. Your root must grow strong when you dream about her, that you give the boma many fine hunters."

In the midst of their shared laughter, Hot Tree hobbled over to join them.

"Come with us," she said.

Together they led Frog to Hot Tree's lean-to, and he bowed down to crawl within. Seated at one side was a dream dancer he had seen before, a slender beauty named Small Raven. She was, he had heard, Stillshadow's daughter, Hot Tree's neice.

Seated on the other side of the hut was his future bride. Her face was turned down, but when she tilted it up, he saw that she was indeed a pretty thing, with a round face, smooth warm-looking skin the color of a pepper pod, and eyes so bright they glistened. Her hair was braided with carved bits of bone and shell.

"Her name is Glimmer," Hot Tree said. "She will be your wife. You take her from her family, and so must give back to them. You will live with them in Earth boma until she is of age to make children."

The knowledge that she would be his made his root burn. He also thought of Fawn, dead Fawn, the first woman his body had ever known, and felt an odd mixture of joy and sadness.

He had not seen a dream dancer since his return from walkabout, and sensed a sadness about them he had never detected before now. How could it feel to be one of them, to know that somewhere out beyond the horizon, your sisters had been turned into Mk*tk women, and that there was nothing to be done for it? How did one make peace with such a reality?

"Until Glimmer is a woman, do not enter her," she said. "Her mother will tell you when."

"What if she *never* gives permission?" he blurted out. The girl smiled in a way that gave him warm tremors below his navel. Fear, passion, need, caution, eagerness . . . all warred within him.

Hot Tree, perhaps noticing the way he fidgeted, gave a knowing laugh. "Boys! So eager to be men. Of course her mother will try to postpone. She wants your work, your hunting for as long as she can. But she also wants strong grandchildren, and knows that until the night you enter her daughter, you can choose another mate. Or may sleep in the hut of a widow, or older woman. She will not want this. She will tell you when."


And so the deal was made.

At Gathering's end Frog gathered up his spears and arrows and knives and traveled west with Glimmer's family to his new home. What wonders might this new life hold? Or troubles? As custom demanded, he had not so much as exchanged a single word with his bride-to-be. What if they hated each other, like Dry Hole and his witch of a wife?

Frog sighed. He had to have trust, trust that this would be best for him, as every decision that Uncle Snake and Gazelle had made had been good for him.

But as he walked with them on that different path, he saw the eyes upon him, the whispers saying what a fine young hunter he was, the stories about the Mk*tk he had slain, the dream dancer he had rescued. With every telling, the story of his adventures upon the plain had grown. Frog began to sense how stories of gods and heroes were born. One distant day, his grandchildren would dance Frog's tale by firelight. In those leaping shadow-plays he would be as tall as two men, a great hunter who had slain three Mk*tk with his bare hands.

He carried himself strongly, shoulders back, strutting as befitted a man-killer, the husband of a great beauty, a girl of good breeding, whose wide strong hips would produce many children.

But there was something that he did *not* see. What he did not see was the girl that he had rescued, watching him with wistful eyes, watching Glimmer with her parents, watching him disappear to the west, off to his new family. Off to be married.

A girl who, for a short precious while, had danced to the name Butterfly Spring.

# Chapter Thirty-seven

For the most part, Earth boma was the identical thornbush ring, the same combed ground and scorched circle, the same familiar cluster of huts around two central fires that Frog had always known. Still, more than a moon passed before he became accustomed to seeing Father Mountain standing in the northeast instead of the northwest. In other ways the terrain was much the same, save for a network of ridges farther west that he suspected might provide good hunting.

Frog stopped himself. He was a man now, no longer a stripling. For was that not what one became when one took a wife? And only a boy spent endless quarters climbing and frittering away the days while the adults mended, gathered and tended traps. He would go find out if those hills were plentiful with four-leggeds. And if he did a bit of exploring in the process, well . . .

Day by day, he became more a part of Glimmer's family, his new family, sharing their tasks, but sleeping in a solitary hut at night while he gathered and hunted for them during daylight.

Glimmer's mother, Smoke Leaf, was a woman so large that the boma often joked about her lovemaking with her husband. "Don't crush him, Leaf!" they would cry when the two hugged.

She was of good nature and infinite patience, smelled always of burnt herbs, and loved her daughter, seeming only to wish that Glimmer's husband see her for the flower she was . . . and also feel love for her parents.

When not stalking, Frog maintained their tools and weapons and began building a hut for himself. This task was harder than he had expected. Frog had helped his brothers build, but had never done it entirely on his own.

Finding the proper vines and willow branches, stripping them, bending them and shaping them were the most important things. Frog had to soak the branches to make them more flexible, bend and dry others to take specific shapes, and perform the hands of other small tasks that led to the creation of a suitable long-term dwelling.

And he had to do this after his day's work for Glimmer's family was complete. During this time, his access to her was extremely restricted. She was always a presence at the periphery of his awareness, but there were limitations on how much time they spent alone. As yet, they were not even supposed to speak.

But at other times he would have sworn Glimmer had never heard her family's dictates! Or if she had, she intended to ignore them the very first chance she got.

If Frog had feared that Glimmer would prove cold, their first stolen moments together out behind the storage hut calmed his troubled mind. She pressed her mouth against his salty shoulder and licked. Behind her cool eyes raged a scalding heat. If after tingling his root she ran away like a child, he knew that, in time, the moons spent in winning her would seem short indeed, and sweet.

And her father certainly seemed to understand that. He watched with approval as Frog did his chores, few of which required skill. Frog considered most of them to be tests more for his back than his mind.

Frog was happy to note that his body was beginning to develop, that Father Mountain had seen fit to bless him with muscles that day by day grew harder and larger.

Long Arrow was as skilled with that hunting tool as his name suggested. He tested Frog at every occasion, perhaps satisfying himself that his future grandchildren's father would be a good provider.

At first, Frog was embarrassed: he had always been better with the spear. But in time, Long Arrow ceased chiding him, and showed Frog little adjustments of stance and choice of gut that made his bowplay far more respectable. In time Frog's accuracy of aim seemed to be improving, so that he felt that on a good day he could have rivaled Fire Ant, an impressive feat indeed.

On one occasion Frog staggered back to the boma, bent under a heavy stack of sticks, while Glimmer's father hardened his spear over hot coals, being careful not to burn or scorch the wood. Beside himself, Smoke Leaf watched Frog struggle with the branches, a bundle that might have tested a hunt chief. "You are strong," Long Arrow grunted. The man himself was small, but his back was as broad as a hut.

As Frog tripped, caught himself, and struggled erect again, Long Arrow nodded approval. "Boy! You are to be my son. You will work hard to earn my daughter."

To this, Frog recited the ritual response. "She is a flower worth the wait," he said.

Long Arrow nodded his gruff acknowledgement. "Do you take me as a father?" he asked.

"Second only to he who hunted for my family."

"Do you take me as your mother?" Smoke Leaf spoke up. She had asked on numerous occasions, always seeming to forget that she had asked the question before.

"Second only to she who birthed me."

Smoke Leaf nodded, then gave him a mischievous grin. "If I had borne you, it would be a sin for you to be with my daughter. But as a son of the shadow, you and my daughter can make strong children, who will protect the tribe. I accept you as my son."


Sore from an impossibly long day of hunting and hauling, Frog crawled into his small and solitary hut. The sky had barely darkened, but he was already completely exhausted, rolling over onto his back to prepare for sleep.

Frog lay there staring up at the ceiling, mind roving over his body, seeking a muscle or tendon that did not ache, and failing to find one. Leaf and Arrow had sorely tested him, but had confidence that things would be easier after the moon was full again. After all, they didn't want to work the father of their future grandchildren to death!

There came a sudden, sharp rustling from outside the hut. A shadow grew darker, and then broke away from the door, coming close. It was Glimmer. Even in the darkness, her smell and heat dizzied him. She gazed down at him. Her eyes seemed to have absorbed what little light there was to be had, reflecting it back like twin moons in a cloudy sky. They both knew that she was not supposed to be there, that it was a taboo. Never had they been alone together, and her body radiated heat like a hearthstone.

She sniffed at him, not exploring, more as if trying to remember something. Her nearness triggered a response from his body more powerful than anything he had ever known, even when actually playing sex with Fawn. His dimmed vision swam, and he felt feverish and swollen-headed.

He started to speak, but she silenced him with her fingers against his lips. Their eyes met, and he felt he was falling into their depths, as if Glimmer was the gateway to mysteries undreamt.

And then, without touching him, she left.

He thought that he would never get to sleep, so engorged was he. He spit in his palm and began to pleasure himself, stroking until the heat he felt through all his body began to concentrate itself in his root and he finally burst. Frog wiped himself clean with grass, then rolled over thinking about Glimmer, until sleep took him.

# Chapter Thirty-eight

Boar Tracks had two tens of springs, was the fastest runner among the hunt chiefs and was the best wrestler among the young ones. His laughter rang from the rocks, and he could throw a spear to pierce a butterfly's wings at three tens of paces.

T'Cori knew that she should be happy when he appeared at the door of the little hut she had spent almost a month building. He was tall and triple-scarred on each lean cheek, lean-bodied and silent in motion.

"Tomorrow is full moon," he said, his eyes lingering upon her. "I return to Great Sky." She noticed that his usual casual manner was somehow off-kilter, like a rock balanced on its edge. She could not read his fire, and felt a desperation. Would her sight never return? Or was that what the Mk*tk had torn away from her? Better they had plucked out her face-eyes.

"Is there something wrong?" she asked.

He seemed uneasy. "The mountain," he said. "We feel it rumble beneath our feet, and Father Mountain talks to us. I do not know what he says."

"Travel safely, hunter."

"Tonight," he said, "Stillshadow says I am to stay with you."

Always, she had known this time would come. Without hesitation she gave him the ritual response. "You are welcome at my fire, and beneath my roof." Was it possible that Stillshadow knew what she was doing? If Boar Tracks lay with her, might her magic return?

Boar entered her hut. He was a strong, fine hunter. The other girls winked knowingly.

"Bring me meat," he said.

She served him. As she bent over, from behind her he ran his fingertips up the inside of her right leg, his touch like a trickle of warm, soothing water. She gasped as a wave of fire blazed up almost to her navel. *Yes!* This was the feeling she had waited for. This was the way it should always have felt. His touch shifted her *num*. Perhaps . . . perhaps . . .

"Is it good?" she asked as he ate his meal.

"Very good," he said. "Now come to me, woman of the mountain."

"Great Mother smiles on us," she said.

There were two ways that sex-play usually occurred among the Ibandi: the rear entry, and a woman lowering herself upon a man. Boar Tracks made his own preference swiftly known, turning her around and bending her forward.

She held her breath and then released it, relaxing the muscles of her sex, and then tightening again as he slid inside her, squeezing rhythmically as they moved together.

They breathed together for a time, but then his breath quickened and he made his seed. She knew that some of the girls learned to move in rhythm with the men, so that their fires caught at the same time. This joining had been too swift, too fast.

But in a short time his root regained its firmness and he reached for her once again. This time he took longer. Not long enough for her own fire to ignite, but it was better, sweet enough so that she never once thought of the Mk*tk during their union.

Then with a grunt of satisfaction he slapped her rump with the flat of his hand, rolled over and slept.

Her eyes wide, T'Cori lay staring at the wall. Was that all? True, it had not been painful, as sex with the Mk*tk had been, but neither had there been fire. She rolled over and looked at the man whose body had so recently been joined to hers. Could she see so little, even under such ideal conditions?

If she squinted, T'Cori could see the very slightest trace of fire flaring around him. Not much more than she might have seen around a rock, if she had squeezed her eyes in a similar fashion.

Her gift was gone.

The moon was high when T'Cori climbed out of her hut, gazing across the plain at Father Mountain's mist-enshrouded majesty. There was something about the mountain that roused her curiosity. The clouds up around its peak seemed to be somehow . . . *changed.* They glowed differently in the pale light, and seemed almost to be oozing from the mountain itself. Strange. Did this have anything to do with the voice of the mountain, the shaking in the ground? The words whispered by Father Mountain?

As far as T'Cori knew, of all the Ibandi, only she was awake. "Great Mother," she whispered, "I do not wish to sin. I know that this fine hunter is filled with Your spirit. I could give him my sex, but not my heart, which is too heavy for me to lift. My heart is still out on the savannah. It has not healed, and I cannot give what I do not have. Please forgive me."

For a moon after T'Cori's return, the women of Great Earth had wailed and torn their hair and asked Great Mother why their daughters had been taken. And then their lives went on.

The girls worked and studied and played. T'Cori remained a bit separate from the others, living deep within herself, in the secure and sacred space she had discovered while with the Mk*tk, a place the outer world rarely touched.

She awakened and made her toilet in the place out beyond the huts, where it would not poison the water, the place where the dung beetles swarmed. She stamped her small foot upon the ground. "Good morning, Great Earth!" she cried, and then spit toward the north. "Great Mother, Father Mountain," she called. "Good morning!"

From time to time she watched the odd clouds around the peak of Great Sky. It made sense that Father Mountain could make clouds, but why had she never seen it before?

She cocked her head to the side, listening. She wondered if she would be able to hear Father Mountain's voice, as Boar Tracks claimed he had done. "And what would you have me learn today?" she asked.

"What did the mountain say?" Raven said, coming up from behind, sounding both curious and irritated.

"Can't you hear Him?" The earth beneath her bare feet rumbled. T'Cori could feel the slight tingling, a pleasant sensation against her toes.

Raven grimaced and shook her head. "Stillshadow protects you. She's a sweet old woman, but one day she will be gone, and then you will deal with *me.* With *this* world."

"It is not Stillshadow who protects me," T'Cori said, and spread her arms as if she had never heard the threat at all. "It is Great Mother who protects us all."

"Great Mother sees *me*," Raven said. "*I* am the one. I see the way you are. What you try to do." She paused. "I will strangle you before I let you take the boma, as you tried to take my mother's love."

T'Cori remained calm, although Raven was almost a head taller. "I take nothing that is not given."

"Use all your eyes," Raven said. Before the moment could grow dangerous, Stillshadow approached, and the larger girl retreated.

"Wise mother," T'Cori said.

"Do not call me that," Stillshadow said, but she laughed.

"But you are."

"Perhaps," she admitted. "But do not let Raven hear you. She hates."

"Because she fears," T'Cori said.

Stillshadow regarded her with curiosity. "You no longer see the fire, but still see many things," she said. "I am not certain you see your own danger."

"I see." *Mother,* she added silently.

Stillshadow wagged her head as if she had heard the unspoken word. "Once, she was jealous of your vision. Now, of your strength."

"My vision is gone," T'Cori said. "Why does she hate me still?"

Stillshadow placed her hands on T'Cori's shoulders and then gathered her for an embrace. "I wish I had more to give you. But all I have is all the world."

Despite her distress, T'Cori managed a smile. "Then I suppose that will have to be enough," she said.

With that Stillshadow left, leaving T'Cori to begin the first task of the day: preparing a new gnu hide for tanning. But as she scraped, and later prepared the tanning herbs, she found that she was humming a little herb song to herself. The corners of her mouth were turned up in a smile and she felt well pleased.

# Chapter Thirty-nine

After eight more moons passed, Glimmer's mother, Smoke Leaf, came to Frog's hut, crying, holding a bit of bloodstained grass in her fingers.

She held her face calm, but he could tell that there was sadness and loss there, as well as acceptance. "The child is a woman," the big woman said. "The child is a woman, and must sleep in her husband's hut."

Glimmer's father, Long Arrow, came to Frog's hut, carrying a gutted white-tail antelope. Glimmer walked three paces behind him, her face painted white, eyes down.

As the entire boma watched, Glimmer and Frog made a roasting pit together, fed the fire, tended the coals, spitted the antelope and cooked it. Each member of the boma brought food—roots, fish, greens, spices—and there was a noisy, joyful time as all shared the meal together. When the meal was finished, her mother and sisters cleared the preparations away. Then, without another backward glance, her family returned to their huts.

This was their first night together, the first time when it was permissible for them to be alone. Glimmer sat cross-legged on the straw mat, eyes cast down. "Please," she said. "Please, husband, be kind. I am afraid." He almost laughed, certain that Glimmer actually felt excitement, not fear. This was all part of the ritual.

He did not approach or move closer to her, although he felt his body burn. *This is what a man is,* he thought. *He knows what he wants, what he is entitled to, but he is not an animal.* He can wait.

"You need not fear me," Frog said, and laid his spear down on the mat between them. "I will not cross the spear."

So he lay on his side, and she on hers. Although he could hear and feel her breathing on the other side, and could hear when it slowed and became warm, and knew that she was deciding whether or not to let him have her, this was her choice to make: he would not cross the spear.

And she decided to let the sweet torture continue another night.

The second and third evenings passed the same way: they slept side by side without touching. Finally, one night, that patience was rewarded. The scent of fresh fruit and sweet grass wafted from Glimmer's skin, and he knew that sometime during the day she had decided. She pulled the spear from between them, and cuddled closer to him in their hut. He waited breathlessly to see what she would say, what she might do. "My husband," Glimmer murmured at last.

"My wife," he replied.

She nestled herself against him, and he knew that their time had come. "What happens now?"

"Now you open yourself to me," he said. "And our lives begin."

"I could wait no longer," she whispered.

Her words and actions were as one. She reached for him, stroking between his legs until his root grew as rigid as a raw potato. He pulled himself to a seated position, copying her own pose. She mounted his lap, then gasped as she lowered herself onto his root, having to push and sigh and wince, as if he was too large or she too small. Their kisses were first dry, clumsy, then with licking and tasting each other's sweat, a mutual exploration as the energy built between them. He could feel her passions rising but could not control his own, exploding before Glimmer remotely neared her own climax.

"I . . ." she whispered.

He traced her face with his hands wonderingly. She shuddered.

"What is it, wife?" he asked. "Did it hurt? You cry."

"It hurt," she said, "but there was more than pain. There was something else."

"What?"

"I do not know. Like a small fire in the darkness, perhaps. I want more." She managed to smile.

"You will have more," he promised.

"When?"

He grinned, feeling the blood already returning to his root. She had, indeed, been worth the wait. "Now."

She lowered herself onto his lap, and then rolled him atop her, so that her legs were locked together around his waist. When they were well joined and moving slowly together, there were shared breaths and gentle lickings, their hot-eyed wonder illuminating the darkness. Virgin she had been, but Glimmer grasped the way of it swiftly. "I will give you the food you need," she whispered, lips brushing his ear.

His hips rose and fell with hers like some warm, gentle wind. "We make children now. Our children."

"Our children," she repeated. "You are my man."

There were no more words. This time, she controlled the depth and angle of the thrust. She found her way to a time of gasping and shaking, clutching, crying out, and they held each other through it all.

They lay on their sides afterward, touching in wonderment, the air heavy with their mingled scent. Then, not long after, the rhythm began anew, as if it was something that had lived before them and would survive their deaths, something with its own will that carried men and women like feathers in a whirlwind to some unknown and unknowable place of peace and fire.

# Chapter Forty

Frog's year passed with aching slowness, then suddenly was over too soon. Frog bid goodbye to Glimmer's mother and father and returned home as a man of his tribe, a two-scarred man-killer escorting a beautiful mate to Fire boma. Although he had walked through the thorn walls more times than any man could count, it seemed now that he passed the threshold with new eyes, a new man.

His cousins welcomed him with smiles, cries and little dances. Uncle Snake and Gazelle Tears met them at the gate, warned by boma runners. His mother smiled, lowering her eyes in ritual acknowledgment of her son's manhood. His uncle clapped his shoulder. "You bring a fine daughter to our home."

Gazelle Tears said, "I would warm myself at your hearth."

Glimmer said in ritual response, "I would gather beside you and have you teach me the ways of Fire."

"Welcome, my daughter," Gazelle said. "Come, work." She led her toward the place where the other women busied themselves, and sang and cared for one another's children.

Glimmer's round lovely face shone at Frog, seeking swiftly granted permission. Once she went on her way, Snake came to him. "Come, work."

Work is life. Life is work. The same countless tasks supported all the boma now, as they had before he left, and would long after Frog's flesh returned to the mountain. He was content to have returned to the place of his childhood, happy to see his old friends and cousins once again.

As he had hoped and as his uncle had promised, Glimmer was a fine wife.

Their days were filled with labor, their nights with song and story and love. Frog found no greater pleasure than lying with Glimmer beneath the stars, dreaming of the children they would raise together. They spent quarters and whole nights there, gazing up at Great Sky's unimaginable heights or into the eyes of the ancestors themselves. He tried to point out the faces in the clouds above them, but despite his patient teaching, she never saw them. Still, he was content.

At such times, whether gods existed or whether the dead lived again atop Great Sky mattered little to Frog. What mattered was this life, here and now, in this world of earth and blood. It was all he could touch, so it was all that he chose to care about.

And far more than a younger Frog would have believed, it was good.

One day two moons past Spring Gathering, T'Cori followed three paces behind Stillshadow, striding in her mentor's footprints, as she traveled to Fire boma. It would have been impossible for the novice healer not to see Frog and his new wife, Glimmer. She had not seen her rescuer in almost two years, but despite the intensity of the time they had shared, they merely nodded to each other as the dream dancers went about their healing and teaching.

Still, no matter how she tried to lose herself in the ritual ceremonies attending Stillshadow's work, T'Cori could not stop from glancing at the young man and his wife.

*That is not your world,* she reminded herself again and again. But as she danced, sang, healed, told the stories binding their people together, blessed Fire boma's children and taught the women of herbs and sacred six-legged, again and again Frog came into her mind. And all her training and prayer could not stop the pain.

In Fire boma's meeting hut, T'Cori and Stillshadow shared sleeping and storage space, and a cook-fire for the preparation of food and medicine.

As she knelt, preparing their evening meal, T'Cori fumed about Frog. Despite her best intentions, she fantasized about killing his ugly little wife, Glimmer.

"What is it, daughter?" Stillshadow asked, noting her student's distraction.

T'Cori ground her teeth. "I wish to see her dead."

Stillshadow pushed a leaf-wrapped yam into the ashes. "And how would this happy event come about?"

"Poison," T'Cori said, happily contemplating her rival's agonized contortions. "I am good with poisons."

"Ah," said Stillshadow. "Grubs? Sour berries? Sunfruit root? There are many good choices. Her suffering would be long."

"Or I could wait until she goes to dig yams."

"And what then?"

"Lie in wait," she said, unable to conceal her grin. "I would make a knife of a lion's tooth. Or a spear. And I would kill her with it, and all would think that she was slain by a cat."

"That is very clever," Stillshadow admitted. "And would you then devour her, as would a cat?"

T'Cori sank down, miserable. "Or perhaps I should just run away into the brush. No one would miss me."

"No, my dear," Stillshadow agreed, poking the coals with the tip of her cane. "No one."

T'Cori sighed, allowing her pain and jealousy to run out of her like diseased milk.

"Or I could stay with you?"

"Yes," the old woman said. "You could."

"And become the most powerful dream dancer who has ever lived." T'Cori stamped her feet and managed to conjure a smile. "How angry Raven would be!" They laughed together, but then T'Cori glared at Stillshadow. "Don't you feel anything?"

"I feel many things," Stillshadow said.

"Didn't you ever want a man of your own?"

"Who would want such a smelly, useless thing as a man around after his root has softened?" she said. "I am content."

T'Cori considered carefully. Was her life so poor? In truth, the dancers were the heart of their people. These were her sisters. They laughed, and cried, and danced for one another, and made songs. For many, there was love as well, and if that had not yet been a part of her sexual life, who could say what the future held? "Then I, too, will be content."

"That is probably best," said Stillshadow, and handed her a basket of potatoes and greens. "Make soup."

## Chapter Forty-one

In recent days the zebra had been slow and fat, the baboons suicidally curious. As a happy result, there was meat for all to share. The arrival of Stillshadow and her apprentice had energized Fire boma, and the boma reciprocated with all the hospitality it could muster.

Mothers carried their children to listen to the wise women and study their wisdom. They learned tales from the other major bomas, and demonstrated the dances learned in dreams.

Frog lurked around the edges of those gatherings when he could, watching the strange small girl as she swirled and angled her body for story-spinning, remembering their time together out on the savannah. And his new wife, in turn, watched him.

Glimmer prepared a delicious dinner that night, baking yams and spring hare in a clay ball, breaking it open only when he sat down to eat, so wisps of savory steam nearly overwhelmed him.

He ate greedily, and as he did he noticed that Glimmer merely nibbled, as if she had no appetite. Over the moons he had become sensitive to her moods and ways, and knew his wife had something to say to him. Sure enough, when he was half finished with his yams and fish, she cleared her throat.

"You know that dream dancer," she said. "The small one."

"Yes," Frog said in cautious reply. "I know her."

"You know she can belong to no man."

"That is true."

"She is also ugly," Glimmer offered. "Her tooth is broken in front."

"Compared with you," said Frog, "all others are ugly."

Glimmer made little effort to conceal her smile. "If she tried to sex you, I would stab her."

"Her womb is dry with fear," he said. She bumped him with her hip, and seemed to relax. They finished their meal in companionable silence.

As if sex had somehow ripened her, Glimmer's hips and breasts were now a woman's. But he wondered if she felt secure in his love. Did he not bring her meat? Jealousy was not a stupid thing. More than one man had abandoned his woman to seek another, leaving the jilted one with no hunter to fill her pot and share her straw. Still, most wives and husbands tolerated each other's lovers unless they were indiscreet indeed.

Perhaps Glimmer could sense emotions that he himself hid deep within. But Frog had never played sex with the nameless one and probably never would.

Moons waxed and waned, as moons always did. Uncle Snake was beginning to show his rains. Hawk Shadow spent moons on Great Sky, and his wife, Flamingo, often ate with Frog and Glimmer during these times. She and Glimmer grew as close as sisters, and when Glimmer held Flamingo's children, Frog often thought they seemed to be her own.

Every time Hawk returned from the mountain, he moved more silently, saw more clearly, spoke more like one possessed of great vision. Frog was very proud of his brother at these times. Even Fire Ant hid what must have been great disappointment, and danced with Hawk as they did when they were children.

Once upon a time, Fire Ant and Hawk Shadow had been as alike as turtle eggs. Now, Hawk Shadow was clearly superior with the bow, with the spear and in the footrace. Fire Ant was an excellent and experienced stalker, but whatever secrets the hunt chiefs taught Hawk were transforming him into a formidable hunter indeed. He demonstrated it with every tireless stride, every grip of his suddenly irresistible wrestling. In every way he had become something wonderful.

Even though Fire Ant could no longer run as swiftly as Hawk Shadow, the two were above the boma's other young men in almost every way. Frog could only dream of such prowess. Uncle Snake no longer ran with the hunters, and when he wrestled, the young ones no longer tried their hardest to defeat him. Instead he spent more and more time passing on his knowledge of nets and spears to the younger ones. It was increasingly common to see him sitting with the elders, fixing and sharpening spears, telling and embellishing tales.

Frog sometimes whittled with him. Snake would squeeze Frog's shoulder affectionately and hand him a length of wood, and teach him tricks with a knife point that turned branches into walking sticks for the old ones and toys for the children.

Snake could lose himself for whole quarters in such a fashion, speaking little or not at all, and that was a good and peaceful thing to Frog.

Stepfather and stepson had been sitting that way since the sun was directly overhead, and now the shadows were long.

"Another sun gone," Snake said.

"To be reborn tomorrow, if the dream dancers sing."

"They always sing. The sun is always reborn," Snake said. "I wonder if they could sing for me."

"What do you mean?" Frog asked.

"A cold wind whistles in my bones," Snake said, watching the dying sun with sad eyes. "I remember my father when he first came to sit here. And then the last time he spoke to me." Snake paused, setting the tip of a sharp rock against a soft chunk of wild fig, gouging out curls of wood in a sun pattern. "He said that his life seemed so long before he came to the old ones. And that after that, it seemed to pass in a heartbeat." He blew at the wood curls, scattering them like lazy butterflies drifting in the wind. "I am not ready to be old," Snake sighed. "But I suppose old age is ready for me."

The dead left side of his face was a web of white lines against brown skin. Sometimes it was difficult for Frog to read Snake's mood unless he was close enough to smell him. Now, however, the right corner of his mouth curved up. "You've been a good son," Snake said. "Scorpion is a good boy too. Once, he was cruel." Frog started to protest, but Snake waved him off. "I saw it. I think that he blamed the world for his mother's death, and saw no beauty in it."

"He doesn't hurt things anymore," Frog said.

"No. And I think that is because you are his brother," Snake said. "I thank you. And thank you for being my son."

Frog stared at his stepfather, waiting to see if Snake might say more. He did not, and Frog made peace with that, finding that what had already been shared and said more than filled his heart.

.    .    .

The day came when Frog returned from the hunt to find Glimmer at the small fire pit before their hut pounding yams into an unusually fine mush.

"Come, husband," she said to him. "Sit with me." And he did.

He waited, thinking that perhaps there were things that she wished to say to him, but she continued mashing with her wooden pestle, humming a cooking song.

Frog took pleasure in watching the smooth, regular strokes, the grace of her body, the beauty scars on her shoulders and back. He remembered tracing his fingertips over them when they loved, and hungered to do it again.

"Life comes," she said to him finally, not looking up.

He sat up straighter. "What?"

Smiling, she pressed his right hand against her warm, smooth, rounded belly. "Life comes," she repeated. "Your seed has taken root."

So stunned was he that the sounds of the world seemed to fade away altogether. Glimmer bore his child?

He was a father?

Frog held her until they both dissolved with laughter, and he ran to tell his mother.

He found Gazelle at Fire River with Snake, weaving reeds into a fishing basket. Gray streaked her hair now. Her skin was loose, the flesh at her throat wattled. But in Frog's loving eyes her grace and beauty were undiminished. Frog watched Gazelle and Snake before they saw him, watched the way they joked and worked together. With the passage of years, it seemed that their circles had come closer together.

Children, male and female, played together.

The adult men and women lived in different worlds.

And then, with age, they seemed to join again.

Frog blinked hard and scratched his head. This was another of those moments when it seemed that the universe was surrendering a mystery to him. Then the mists, so recently and deliciously parted, closed again, and the insight vanished.

He had intended to tell Gazelle and Uncle Snake of the baby. Instead, he took his pleasure in watching them. So peaceful and comfortable with each other. Was that what he had to look forward to with Glimmer? If so, then all the hardships of life, all the doubt and pain and loss, were worthwhile.

They would raise their children. He would hunt, and she would cook, and they would grow old together, as had Snake and Gazelle.

And that, in some strange way, told him that Great Mother and Father Mountain might be watching after all.

.    .    .

In moons Glimmer's belly swelled as if she had swallowed a melon seed. His brothers and uncle watched Frog with great amusement as he strutted about the boma. His root was strong! He would be a father!

Hot Tree and the other village women gathered around the hut when birthing time came. As always, Thorn Summer ran errands, carrying herbs and water for the women, the Between still the only man who could enter a birthing hut without losing *num*. His belly protruded and sagged over his belt now, and great folds of flesh bunched at his neck and cheeks. Still, he loved bringing babies into the world as much as he ever had.

Frog sat with the men outside the hut, puffing a pipe and rattling off an endless stream of jokes and stories, so that his mind would not dwell on the screams from within the hut.

Why was it taking so long? And why did the howls sound so terrible? When had a birth ever taken so long? A full day passed, and the women came and went, shoulders sagged, feet dragging. They smiled at Frog, but he could smell their fear and concern.

All night he crouched outside the hut, Fire Ant and Hawk at his side, fat worms of smoke rising between them as they spoke of anything and everything except the only thing that mattered.

Near dawn his brothers finally tottered off to sleep, but Frog, energized by the moans from within the hut, sat and waited.

Near noon of the second day, he heard a baby crying, and his heart leapt. Hot Tree crawled out of the hut on her hands and knees, levering herself up to her feet with great effort.

"You have a son," she said. Her eyes told him that his joy would be diluted with sorrow. "Go, and see your woman."

Frog crawled through the doorway of their home. The air within was thick with sweat and blood and other fluids. Gazelle and Hawk's wife, Flamingo, knelt at Glimmer's side, removing damp grasses from beneath her, replacing them with dry. Glimmer seemed shrunken, like an emptied water skin, but still seemed somehow to reflect more light than streamed through the slats in the ceiling.

Nestled against her breast, silent and suckling now, was his son. Tiny, not much bigger than Frog's two fists. Wrinkled and still moist, mostly bald with a few strands of black hair. Minuscule pursed lips locked on Glimmer's breast, suckling in frustration. The baby began to cry again, and Flamingo gently took him away, and put him to her own full breast.

"I will take him out," Flamingo said.

"Let me hold him," Frog said. "For just a few breaths."

His son seemed to weigh nothing at all, more spirit than flesh. *Is this how life begins?* Frog thought, dizzied. All his life he had seen babies, but still it seemed that he had never known one before. His life. His flesh. The future of his seed. He trembled as his lips touched the boy's forehead.

Frog traced his fingers over the tiny chest, the rounded tummy, noting the knotted umbilical still projecting a thumb's thickness from the infant's belly. It would fall away in time, but now it seemed that his son was a precious piece of fruit, plucked from some divine tree.

"Frog. Frog. Hurt. So weak," Glimmer said, crying and tossing.

He handed his son gingerly to Flamingo and turned back to his wife. Hot Tree was wiping her forehead with a bundle of moss, whispering healing songs in her ear as she did.

"Save your strength," he said, and touched his lips to her forehead. "You must heal."

Throughout the day Hot Tree offered what medicines she could, but she was unable to reverse the draining of Glimmer's strength. The boma mother shook her head, eyes worried above her wrinkled cheeks. "My herbs and dances are not enough," she confessed. "We must ask my sister for help."

"Can you hold on?" Frog asked his woman. "In another moon, our son will have a name. If you can live that long, you might live for many rains. You might live longer than me."

She smiled, laughed shallowly, but the effort strained her. "I hurt. . . ." Her eyes rolled up, exposing the whites.

"You gave me a strong son," he said, struggling to keep light and hope in his voice. "How can such a woman be weak?"

"Frog," Glimmer whispered, "love our child."

"Always."

She clutched at his hand. "You are a good man. I do not see what you see, or hear what you hear." Despite her pain and weakness, she managed to laugh. "My husband talks to the clouds!"

"They do not answer," he said, trying to keep his words light, but choking on them. "You are a good wife." Was there nothing more, nothing better he could think to say? His mind, once his pride, failed him utterly.

Glimmer seemed to be mustering her strength for an answer, but then sank down into unconsciousness.

.    .    .

Flamingo had had her third child only two moons earlier, and her milk was strong. Her child and Glimmer's nursed side by side as if they had shared space in the same womb.

With that stress relieved, Frog could concentrate on nursing his wife.

Twice more during the next night, Glimmer awakened and spoke. For a moment she saw him, looked through him, almost as if the last moments of her life were destined to be the most lucid.

At times they spoke of small, simple things, and she seemed to be growing stronger. But when morning came and he could see her face more clearly, it seemed that the flesh was almost melting away, that he could see the bones beneath the skin.

She spoke again, twice, during the next night, but as time passed it became more and more difficult to understand what she was saying.

*She is going to die,* Frog thought.

And for the first time since childhood, he cried.

# Chapter Forty-two

The moist black soil on Great Earth's northwestern slopes was perfect for the multitude of berries and fruits the dream dancers used in meals and ceremonies throughout the year. The nameless girl had been there all morning, picking the fingernail-sized purple fruit Stillshadow used for dye. Her fingers were thorn-pricked and blue-stained, but she had filled two baskets and felt content. Young Whirling Pool waved her arms in greeting as she ran along the eastern trail, and T'Cori stood to greet her.

Pool's little round face was neutral, hard to read. "The boy who saved you," she panted.

"Frog Hopping?" T'Cori asked, and straightened, wiping perspiration from her forehead. She thought of his gap-toothed smile, both warmed and worried. "What has happened to Frog?"

"It is his woman," Whirling said. "Her baby tore her, and she bleeds. They have called for a dancer to heal her, or ease her way."

T'Cori hesitated. Since losing her special sight, she was no longer confident in her ability to heal. Perhaps it would be better to send another—

"He asked for you," Whirling said.

"Then I must go," T'Cori replied. She would go and do her best. And the rest would be up to Great Mother. *Please, Mother,* she thought. *Let me do this good thing. I owe him so much.*

And another thought: *And I wished for his woman's death. I am chosen. This is my chance to undo an evil thing. Let me atone for my sin, please.*

.    .    .

T'Cori and Whirling were at Fire boma by sundown of the third day. She stood at the boma gate with their hunt chief escorts until they were seen, and thumped her staff upon the ground. "The dream dancers are here!" she called, and the people gathered around.

Hot Tree herself and a woman named Gazelle took them to the hut, where an exhausted Frog crawled out to meet them.

Frog collapsed to his knees before her in the dust. "Please," he said, "save my woman."

"If it is Great Mother's will," she replied. It had been almost a year since she had last seen Frog, but not a day had passed that she had not thought of him.

Perhaps this was why Frog had remained so powerfully in her heart. Perhaps what she had thought was love was the urging of her heart, telling her to be strong so that she could repay his kindness and courage as only a dream dancer might.

By saving his woman.

That would be a proper thing for a dream dancer. Surely that would be the gift Great Mother and Father Mountain needed to give her back her sight.


As Whirling Pool stood by silently, T'Cori studied Glimmer's sweat-streaked face.

Once she had considered this girl her rival. Now she was merely another patient, and by all the oaths of the dream dancers, T'Cori had to consider her a sister.

How satisfying and frightening to hold the girl's life in her hands. She, T'Cori, could either send this girl up the mountain or heal her and thereby prove her own mettle.

Glimmer was a sister. T'Cori's own tragedies and needs had no place in this room.

T'Cori inhaled strongly, then let the breath out slowly through her nose, allowing her sense of self to drift away. The human T'Cori had no place in this room. This was a place for Great Mother, and Great Mother alone. T'Cori could be but a riverbed conducting Her healing waters. And here, at last, having no name might prove an advantage.

*Let the nameless one be gone. Let Great Mother manifest.*

*If Frog cannot be my man, he can be my brother. Then his woman is my sister, and I have chosen the path of love. Please, Mother. Give me the strength to be weak, to step aside and let Your wisdom flow.*

For the next three days and nights sleep was but a distant memory. She danced, she waking-dreamed, with the greatest of difficulty she read the *num*-fire flickering above and around Glimmer's body. But no matter how she pled, what she tried, how she massaged Glimmer's hand- and foot-eyes or how she pressed her own body against the girl, trying to share heartbeats, Frog's wife's continued to weaken. Her chest's rise and fall grew more and more shallow, and then imperceptible, and then she simply stopped breathing.

At first, T'Cori couldn't quite believe it. It simply could not be. Great Mother would not, could not fail her in such a way. Certainly her prayers and songs and shadow-play had reached the depths of Great Earth and the top of Great Sky. Surely the gods would reward their daughter with this most precious victory.

No.

Glimmer was gone, cooling even as T'Cori's tears welled and fell. A vast emptiness opened in the nameless girl, an abyss so deep and wide it recalled her terrible days with the Mk*tk. She clutched her fist over her heart and wailed.

T'Cori closed her eyes, picturing Great Sky's summit, as she had seen it just the last dawn. Mighty, beautiful and a bit strange now, oozing plumes of cloud-stuff. Was this where the girl would go? Despite what Stillshadow said, some whispered that the dead remained beneath the earth. Others swore that they danced atop Great Sky. She prayed that one day, however distant, she might learn the truth.

But what were these new clouds? Were all clouds born from a mountain womb? But . . . why not Great Mother, then? Were clouds more like Father Mountain's seed? Then . . . where did clouds go to mate? Her head spun.

She felt an overwhelming sadness, knowing that these thoughts existed for but one reason: to distract her from the pain of failure, her anguish at Glimmer's death. Frog had saved T'Cori's life, and she had rewarded him by letting his woman die.

Namelessness was not her greatest curse. She was also useless, and worthless.

She had once prayed that Glimmer would die. And now she had. Surely Frog would see her complicity in her eyes. Surely he would hate her now, as she so richly deserved.

In defeat and misery, T'Cori gathered her tools and herbs together and left the hut.

The people of Fire boma stood outside the hut, forming a double line for her to pass through on her way from the boma. She faced them, found it difficult to swallow, even harder when they drummed their feet against the earth: their dance was one of loss, but they sang of gratitude, gratitude for T'Cori and Whirling Pool, who had tried to save their kinsman's wife.

T'Cori stood between the lines for a time, so numb with fatigue and sorrow that she could barely feel anything at all. Then one step at a time she walked toward the gap in the boma wall.

At the end of the line stood Frog, his tearstained face glowing. For just a moment, a barest moment, she saw his *num*-fire shining about him, and it pierced her to the core. There was nothing but bright, clear yellow there. Nothing but gratitude.

Just for a moment she saw it, and then it was gone, as if the gods, in one moment of kindness, had lifted the obscuring mists enough to give her the knowledge she so desperately needed.


Following his people's custom, Frog dug a trench with his hands and, after wrapping Glimmer in skins, laid his mate within it. He burned sweet herbs atop her grave, then added twigs and finally built a fire atop it, so that the heat would drive the flesh from her bones.

Fire Ant and Hawk stood beside him, Uncle Snake and Gazelle behind him. Little Wasp held Snake's hand, his eyes never leaving his adored big brother. Scorpion chanted and danced the funeral dance in a little circle, voice sad and strong.

Flamingo handed Frog his son. The boy had no name, would have none until at least another moon had passed. Then Hot Tree or the dream dancers would throw the bones and find his totem.

But now . . .

Poor boy, Frog thought. Poor boy. No name. No mother.

His nameless son's wrinkled face seemed impossibly small. How could a hunter grow from such a small and helpless thing? The tiny eyes opened, focused on Frog's face, and held it for a moment before wobbling off. Frail moist fingers clutched at him, gripping at Frog's arm.

*My mate is gone,* Frog said to himself. *But my son lives.*

His son, who needed both a name and a father. Frog swore that the boy would get the very best of both, if his life or skill had any say in it at all.

Frog was afraid of crushing the boy as he clutched him, but the smell and feel, the small strong heartbeat, the wet pursed lips, all combined to create a shock like a kick over the heart.

*This is life. Not the worst of your nightmares or the best of your dreams. We live. We love. We die.*

Above him, Great Sky's slopes rose slowly up from the plain, so huge that the incline could barely be felt until you suddenly realized that the bomas lay impossibly far below. Today no clouds cloaked its white-shrouded peak. Today he could see it clearly, and to his eyes, nothing lived atop the great mass of rock and mysterious white.

Perhaps there were no gods. There was nothing.

And yet . . . and yet . . .

As never before, Frog hoped that he was wrong. How wonderful, he thought, it would be to be wrong. If gods there were, then perhaps his father was there. And grandfather. And his good friend Lizard. And his beloved Glimmer.

Frog stood, handing the baby back to Flamingo. *You never tasted your mother's love,* he thought. *But you will know your father's.*

*I swear.*

Then, his family singing the death song, Frog returned to the boma.

# Great Sky Woman

# Chapter Forty-three

Moving gingerly and leaning on her bamboo cane, Stillshadow walked her young students south around Great Earth's curve, their four hunt chief guards ever looking to right and left, laughing and speaking of men's things as the women they accompanied busied themselves with dream dancer work.

Stillshadow seemed aware of everything and nothing as she walked. She talked and told stories, demanding that the tales be repeated back, correcting for accuracy. But while listening to every word, she remained on the lookout for roots and berries and herbs.

T'Cori knew that sometimes Stillshadow made her potions to heal, and sometimes to aid her dreaming. At other times she seemed to compound smoking or drinking mixtures merely to entertain herself. On such occasions she became more jovial, less apt to sink into one of her sour moods.

The third night Stillshadow lectured the girls until they were about to fall over from lack of sleep, then took one of her potions and spent the rest of the night ranting at the moon.

T'Cori tried to sleep, but due to Stillshadow's ravings, it was almost impossible to do so until near dawn.

Then, finally, the effect of the herbs seemed to die out. Stillshadow remained unconscious until the sun was directly overhead, then dragged herself up to a sitting position and joined them.

"Why do you do this?" T'Cori asked.

"You do not ask me questions!" the old woman said. Her wrinkled face puckered, as if immediately ashamed of the outburst, and grew thoughtful. "Father Mountain speaks," she said after a pause. "I confess I do not understand what he says. I must learn. I can feel that he is . . . disturbed. And I do not know why or what it means."

"What must you do?" Small Raven asked.

"I will have to go into the shadow," the old woman said, "where I am closer to death than to life. It is there that Great Mother speaks to me."

"But isn't that dangerous?" T'Cori asked.

She thought that perhaps the old woman would scold her, but instead Stillshadow nodded. "Yes. The dream dancer's life is not for cowards." She sniffed. "Men think that they are the brave ones, the ones who hold the power of death. But we hold the gift of life, and if we do not keep that gate open, all the thorns in creation cannot protect us. We place our bodies between our people and the forces that would destroy."

She leaned closer to T'Cori, smelling of pepperspice. "We are the ones who stalk death. *We* are the real hunters."

"What is that?" T'Cori said, pointing up at Great Sky. Its peak was wreathed in thin white clouds. They seemed to ooze from the mountainside itself.

Stillshadow shook her head. "Only this past moon have I seen their like." She frowned. "I ask my dreams, but so far they say nothing."

All the next day T'Cori felt the ground rumble through her soles. Several times they saw more of the strange white clouds up far on the mountainsides. When Boar Tracks came to her hut that night, after the sex but before sleeping, he told her that birds were winging away from Great Sky's slopes in the hands of hands of hands. "The world is strange," he said. "Five days ago we saw beast-men creeping out of the sacred caves. Once we would have chased them out. Or hurt them. Now we dare not do a thing."

The elder women rebuilt the eternal fire, moving the stones out into a larger circle. They sang more loudly, danced with more dedication, hoping to learn the meaning of the mountain's signs.

Even more disturbing, the waters of Fire River reeked with a strange salt-bitter aroma, becoming barely drinkable. They worried that it might sicken the bomas and the bhan . . . but then it grew clear and flavorless once again.

That night Stillshadow took several more of her herb concoctions and rolled onto her hides to enter the world of dream. The girls took turns watching over her.

When T'Cori's turn came, she entered the low doorway to Stillshadow's hut on hands and knees. The air within smelled of spices and smoke. Bits of bone and sacred rocks dangled from the ceiling, swaying in a wind she could not feel. Every handsbreadth of the hut's wall was painted with magical symbols. Half the dirt floor was mazed with sand paintings, leaving only a narrow path to her straw. Even Stillshadow's dream space was one of learning and teaching.

As the night passed, Stillshadow moaned, growing more restless as morning approached.

The girls whispered among themselves, worried.

"She is sick," Blossom said.

Raven was not so certain. "I have seen her this way before. Always she heals herself. She can raise the heat in her belly and burn the poison away."

"But never has she taken so much," Willow said.

"I do not understand," T'Cori said.

Raven sneered, as Raven often did. "Because you do not have the magic anymore," she said. "For all her power, my mother is only human. She was wrong about you."

Before T'Cori could reply, Stillshadow opened her mouth. She curled, gagging as brown mush gushed forth to spatter on the dirt, obliterating a stick-figure elephant.

As the others stared, T'Cori jumped to her feet. "Help her!" Before their eyes, their teacher's skin was growing ashen.

"What do we do?" asked Whirling Pool.

Stillshadow feebly pointed to the south, through the body of the mountain. Although her voice was very weak, she managed to speak. "They are there," she said. "Beyond the ridge. They are close. They watch us. Only Father Mountain keeps them away."

The young dancers were startled and frightened. "The Mk*tk?"

Stillshadow continued. "They bring death," she said. Her eyes were glazed, unfocused, as if the old woman only partially inhabited her body.

"When will this happen?" Dove asked.

"For moons they watch us," the crone said. "Measure us."

Stillshadow's eyes slid up. Her head rolled back, and she was unconscious.

"She will heal now," Raven said, but the tremor in her voice said otherwise.

T'Cori was not so certain. "And if she does not?"

Raven raised her head proudly. "Then, I will take her place. I am her daughter. I am the strongest." T'Cori had known this girl all her life, and despite the bad feelings between them, she sensed that Raven's words were not mere ambition—they were an attempt to protect the lineage, an attempt to assure the other girls that the work of the dream dancers would continue, no matter what.

Despite this, she could not stop herself from blurting out, "But she is *dying*!"

"If it is Great Mother's will," the older girl said, perhaps already accepting what she considered inevitable.

As T'Cori suspected, despite the bluntness of her words, Raven did not sleep, barely ate and did everything in her power to help Stillshadow. T'Cori's respect for Raven's medicine skills increased greatly.

The other girls did the best they could to make their mentor comfortable.

But this was another matter to T'Cori. Even if she could never openly call her such, Stillshadow was the closest thing to a mother she would ever know. Even if she had not grown in her teacher's womb, she could not accept Stillshadow's death without attempting to prevent it. And so that night, T'Cori crept to Stillshadow's side, as she often had as a child.

*Mother,* she said in her mind, and felt as if she had become an infant once again. If only she could, mightn't Stillshadow hold her in her arms, sing to her, perhaps even regain her former strength?

"T'Cori," Stillshadow murmured.

"You die?" she asked, glad that she could still frame it as a question.

"And you will not?" Stillshadow rasped, managing to smile at her old joke.

"Please," T'Cori begged. "Help me save you."

At that, the old woman chuckled without humor. "You cannot," she said. "You can only lose your own life." The old woman's hand gripped hers. "Live, child."

Hot tears ran from T'Cori's eyes. "You gave me life," she said. "You are all I have known. I'm not ready to lose you. If you die and I have done nothing to save you, my heart will cool."

At this, Stillshadow seemed to find some mote of strength and struggled to push herself up from the straw. "You must not! Raven has my voice now." Her eyes flickered to T'Cori. *I'm sorry,* she seemed to say. "When I go to the mountaintop, she will be the one. You must obey her."

For the first time, T'Cori openly defied her. "No," she said.

Stillshadow grew stern. "You will be cast out."

"I don't care," T'Cori said.

Stillshadow's next words were whispered. "I cannot help you."

"Tell me a story, as you did in the old days."

For a hand of breaths they shared the darkness, and then Stillshadow's withered fingers stroked T'Cori's cheek. "Yes. A last story. These old bones are too weak to dance. I must talk this one." Stillshadow sighed deeply, then seemed to quiet herself. "In the beginning the universe was whole, and all things were good to eat. But the sins of man and animal threw this world out of balance. When the body loses balance, it dies."

This was rambling, as random as a cluster of berries. Somehow she had to squeeze the precious juice, find the essence of the message. "Is this what poison is?" T'Cori asked.

"Man and woman. Human and animal. Animal and plant. Sky and earth. All in balance. Things of sky and earth. Beneath the sky. Beneath the earth. Life is heat. Death is cold."

Suddenly T'Cori glimpsed a deeper meaning. "What are you trying to tell me?"

Stillshadow gave a painful smile. "Use your *num,*" she said.

T'Cori peered deep into her mentor's exhausted face. "Tell me how to save you, Mother."

The crone closed her eyes, too weak to chastise her. "Use your *num,*" she said again.

"All things in balance," T'Cori whispered. "Sky and earth. The things under the sky . . ."

"And beneath the earth," Stillshadow said, repeating what she had said before.

"Is there something beneath the earth that can save you?"

Stillshadow turned away, tears welling in her eyes. For the first time T'Cori saw that the old woman, too, craved life and feared death . . . but could not say the words. It was not done. She could not encourage T'Cori to disobey Raven. And worse—to disobey Cloud Stalker and perhaps Father Mountain Himself.

"Beneath. Within."

Understanding dawned. "Something . . . in the caves?"

Stillshadow was talking about godweed, the most precious of her herbal mixtures. One vital component was the sacred mushrooms found in caves on Great Earth's western face.

But Boar Tracks had told T'Cori that beast-men hid in the caves. Father Mountain had forbade them from interacting with the creatures. What was she to do?

Again, Stillshadow turned away. "Use your mind, child. I cannot tell you how to destroy yourself." Her cheeks slicked with tears. "I am ashamed," she whispered.

"Do not be," T'Cori said, and stood, wiping the tears away from her own cheeks. "You gave me life. Saved my heart and *num*. If I do not try to save you, I am no Ibandi woman."

# Chapter Forty-four

Night had fallen across the bomas, the mountains and the teeming savannahs. While some Ibandi slept, others made ceremony, watching the moon or the mountain. The hunt chiefs kept guard, sang, danced and taught, as they always had . . . except now they found it hard to take their eyes off the strange clouds wreathing Great Sky's peak. From time to time the ground trembled, and there was not one of them who did not wonder if their god was awakening from some long slumber, that perhaps soon they would see the face of Father Mountain Himself.

But while they fought to understand, the nameless one crept out of the dream dancer boma, slithered beneath the ring of thorns, and made her way out of camp.

For the rest of the night T'Cori walked, and the next day, picking her way west around Great Earth's lower slopes, until she reached the narrow, rock-strewn trail leading to the sacred caves.

Gigantic and implacable, Father Mountain rumbled, an angry witness to her sin.

From time to time over the years T'Cori had glimpsed the beast-men. They were hairier than Ibandi but less so than monkey-people. Taller than the average Ibandi and with longer arms, they loped in an ungainly fashion rather than sprinting with a hunter's speed and grace. She was certain the beast-men caught sight of the Ibandi as well, but ran or concealed themselves in fear.

Could it have been fear of a greater threat, perhaps the Mk*tk, that kept the beast-men within Ibandi territory despite the terrible price they had already paid?

She could only believe that if they caught her alone in their territory, they would kill her. She had to be very cautious now. The footpath ended in a cliff wall festooned with morning glories and creepers. The cave mouth would have been easy to miss if she hadn't heard it described countless times. Chewed and broken bones were scattered about the entrance. T'Cori paused there, making herself very still and small, until she could barely hear her own breathing.

Her eyes, adjusted to the darkness, detected slight motion. There was something alive and man-shaped in the cave. She heard snoring, but knew that that did not necessarily mean that all were asleep.

*If they catch you, they kill you,* she reminded herself.

Even just breathing, she smelled and tasted them, and felt as if she had slipped into a waking nightmare.

Perhaps these people were not murdering beasts like the Mk*tk, but they were filthy. They slept here near their own scat. This alone would have been sufficient reason for the Ibandi to avoid them.

All night and day, circling Great Earth, she had felt her anxiety threaten to swirl out of control. Once, she might have run back to the dancers, screaming. But many things had happened to her in the last years. T'Cori was no longer a mere girl—the Mk*tk had stolen that from her forever.

But now, if things went wrong, she might be driven from Great Earth. By this time, certainly her sisters knew that she had gone. If Stillshadow died and Raven learned T'Cori had disobeyed orders, she could be cast out. And then what would she do? She supposed that some bhan hunter might want her as second wife, but such a life might be worse than no life at all. Might as well simply wander out into the tall grass and call a leopard.

On hands and knees, T'Cori felt her way around the cave's edge. *Things* lurked in the darkness. What kind of things? She wasn't certain, but decided that this was not the time to learn. She willed herself to be a part of the night. One with the night.

"Be as rock," she whispered, so quietly that she herself could not hear the words. "Your ally is stillness. Know what the hunter knows." Hadn't Frog Hopping said that? Hadn't he said that it was difficult to remain fearful, and that we try to believe that all is well? If so, couldn't she use this truth to her advantage? *Be harmless, and pass at peace.*

Something stirred in the shadows, and she fought an almost irresistible urge to scream and flee. Just before her nerve broke, T'Cori glimpsed some faint light farther on, perhaps a hole in the ceiling through which moonlight glimmered. The glow revealed a silhouette.

Man? Ape? The trees around Great Earth were alive with red, black and brown monkeys. Baboons seemed aware that they were unfortunate enough to be tasty, and usually gave the human encampments a wide berth. During her life she had even glimpsed one or two of the much larger apes, creatures often considered mere phantoms in tales told to frighten children into obedience.

But what was this? She wasn't sure, and was afraid that her eyes might become clear. If *her* eyes could work here, then certainly *theirs* could as well. The figure stood and made wet, snuffling sounds. A second reclining shadow grasped at the first and pulled it down. The two merged, and dull wet, smacking flesh sounds echoed between the walls.

The smell of sex, combined with the beast-folk's stench, was enough to turn her stomach. She fought nausea and vowed to move on.

The light beckoned ahead. She moved around the edge, careful not to step on any of the sleepers. Great Mother! Was Raven right to think her crazed? Then T'Cori thought of Stillshadow's kind face and infinite wisdom, and knew that she had no other choice.

She reached the glow by hugging the wall, trying not to let herself be outlined against the light. Could this outcropping of pale, shining fungus be the same plant used in the godweed mixture? She'd never seen it growing before, and had to rely on description, hope and instinct.

Fingers shaking, she tore a chunk of fungus off the wall, and stuffed it into her waist pouch.

At the very instant she closed the pouch, the ground rolled beneath her feet. The rumble stirred her bones, like a deep voice in the earth calling her secret name. It was like nothing she had ever experienced, save only the earlier, weaker trembling from a few days before.

And she was not the only one who heard it.

The mountain folk were awakening. She could not go back the way she had come, and only one other option remained. She could retreat more deeply into the cave. Was there another way out? Or a place she might hide until night enfolded them once again?

But as she moved deeper into the darkness, her keen eyes caught a glimmer above her, a pale blue, a promise of dawn's first flush.

The sky. Morning. There was an opening above her.

Taking a deep breath, T'Cori began to climb toward the opening. She was only halfway up when an even more violent rumble shook the stone, dislodging a rock that fell spiraling into the darkness. An ugly babble wound up from beneath her. There was little she could see down below, but she was able to make out dim shapes shambling about.

Had they arrows? Spears? Might her first clue be a grip on her ankle and a crippling bite?

The opening narrowed to the point where she could brace her back against one side and scramble up with her arms and legs braced at spiderish width. The sound of something coming up from beneath her made acid splash into her throat. Her grip failed and she slid back down, ripping skin from her back and hands as she did.

T'Cori choked back a sob. Was Great Mother so furious with her?

Then a thin wind drifted down from above, carrying a sour, burnt aroma.

Her hand grasped a loose stone, and she pulled at it until it wobbled. Then, once she had climbed above it, she stomped with her heel, bruising her foot but sending a chunk of rock tumbling down into the darkness. She heard the thump as it struck meat, a howl and the sound of someone . . . something . . . falling, and far beneath, a sound of breaking bone as the body smacked against the cave floor.

Her sin was complete. She had caused harm to these people, against whom the Ibandi had committed murder. She would pay for this. What that price might be, she could not begin to say.

T'Cori was blowing hard now, sweat burning her eyes, dripping from her nose, matting her hair. The muscles in her arms and legs were cramping into knots, but she closed her mind to the pain and kept going.

*Something* was coming up from beneath her.

She was so close . . . almost close enough to touch the sky above her. Something brushed her ankle. A furred hand? She remembered Notch-Ear's hand, his hot wet breath against the back of her neck, and she screamed. T'Cori climbed more rapidly, splintering fingernails against the rock as she scrambled toward the stinking sky.

T'Cori was panting now, near exhaustion. A snarl just below her made her bite her own tongue. Close. Too close. Then she slid down again. Her rump struck something solid. Her ears rang with squeals as another pursuer tore free from the wall and plunged down. Teeth gnawed at her leg, tearing. She wrenched it away, sobbing, and continued her climb as her third victim fell howling down into the darkness. She could not see beneath her, and considered that blindness a blessing. If she knew what followed her from the underworld her heart might fail, her hands slip.

She was bleeding, exhausted and terrified, but there was something else too. Deep in her heart, T'Cori imagined herself to be her tribe's great hero. *She* would bring back the medicine, and *she* would be called the greatest of them all, and at long last be loved. . . .

That dream crowded out the ugly thoughts, kept her going. Panting and wheezing, she clawed her way out onto the cave's roof. It was a small opening, just large enough for one of T'Cori's size, not large enough for the beast-men, and she squeezed through.

Dawn splashed blood on the horizon. She looked back. Something else reached the top. A hairy arm stretched out, bent at the elbow, reaching around, clawing at the ground, howling and grunting in frustration.

The ground was shaking more severely now. The sky above was filled with billowing white clouds, casting down a dry, powdery rain, an acid, ashen substance that burned her eyes and skin.

She watched, her eyes wide, and then picked herself up and ran as fast as she could, through the forest, down Great Earth's haunted slope, hoping that she would be forgiven. But if the cost of saving the only mother she had known was the loss of her own place atop Great Sky, then that was a price she was prepared to pay.

# Chapter Forty-five

Once upon a time, sleep had fallen from Cloud Stalker as rapidly as a snake-eagle taking flight. Now the hunt chief's dreams were sticky, clinging things, and his limbs felt like stones for almost a quarter after awakening. On this early morning, however, he shed sleep as swiftly as a young man.

At first, he wasn't certain why he had awakened at all. Then he felt Father Mountain's growls and rolled up to sitting.

Emerging from his hut, he stared up at Great Sky's mist-shrouded peak. His toes curled into the dirt as it shuddered against his bare feet.

Since boyhood he had lived here, given over by parents convinced of his gifts by the former grand hunt chief, Leopard Eye. Since those early days he had explored its slopes, hunted in its ravines, climbed the great strange cliffs of cold dead water they called ice.

His gut told him that something terrible was happening to his home, but his wildest imaginings could not have anticipated just how terrible it would be.

*Over hands of hands of hands of years Great Sky's ice pack had grown thicker than two tens of men standing on one another's shoulders. The volcanic gases and steam blew chunks larger than whole bomas into the clouds above. Magma gushed from the earth. In an instant, the searing heat converted a mountain of ice into boiling water.*

*The seething mass mixed into a slurry of ash and pumice and dirt. It tum-*

*bled down the mountain slopes, reaching a speed far faster than even the fastest hunt chief.*

*Within half a quarter, the landlocked tidal wave swept down the slopes, crushing trees, slaughtering mountain goats, lemurs, zorillas, antelopes, leopards and baboons in numbers beyond counting, plowing up enough ground to fill a valley, gaining heat from new fissures in the ruptured and rupturing earth.*

*The fiery cloud gushed from the mountainside, wrenching trees up by the roots and tumbling them like straws in a cyclone. A blistering flood of water and rock carried with it everything from sand and gravel to boulders taller than two men.*

*As it rushed down, its size, speed and volume constantly changed, tearing rock and brush from the sides and along the river valleys it entered, creating a cascade of boiling water mixed with mud and rubble, devastating anything in its path.*

*Debris flows cut across streams, damming them. The water continued to rise until the dam was breached.*

*As the flow dissipated, the action of the wave reversed as it redeposited the debris. The heaviest objects dropped out first. As the flow continued to lose energy, progressively smaller and smaller fragments dropped out until the wave faded out of existence.*

*But by that time, the damage had been done.*

River Song, Laughing Buzzard, High Tree, and the other hunt chiefs emerged groggily from their huts, witnessed the approaching devastation and tried to flee. They ran the race of their lives, as swiftly as any human beings had ever moved, but the mass of searing water and tumbling logs caught up with them in moments.

Some hunt chiefs were killed by collapsing huts or flying debris. The rest were engulfed, the bodies of some contorted and crushed against trees, other suffocated by mud as it forced its way into eyes, mouths, ears and open wounds. The pressure of the mud against their chests slowly choked those buried to the neck. Some were burned, some drowned.

There was only one thing in common: all died.

Men, animals, hunters, prey, all a divine unity there in the holy place. All at terrible peace in a white hell on earth.

They died in their hands of hands, knowing that their god had not only deserted them but singled them out for destruction. Or perhaps their god, the very force that had created the world itself, was dying.

They died, but not one of them cursed the mountain. And of that, at least, Stalker would have been proud.

A tower of ash blotted out the dawn. The mountain's death cry was heard where the land met the sea, farther than a man could run in ten days, where bhan ceased their fishing to look back west at the clouds darkening the morning sky. Ash fell over mountains so distant the Ibandi had never dreamed of their existence.

Despite the dream dancers' desperate singing, the blessed morning sun was never born that day.

Everything exposed to air was covered with a pall of white. Everything, as far as the eye could see and even where it could not, was transformed.

Heaven was gone.

In the face of such a catastrophe, it seemed even death itself might die.

Cloud Stalker, mate of Stillshadow, leader of the mighty hunt chiefs, opened his eyes a final time. The tumbling wall of mud had somersaulted him over and over again, stones suspended in the mass grinding his bones to splinters. His head remained aboveground, but jagged, broken ribs pierced his lungs, so that with every passing moment they filled more deeply with blood.

In his last moments, gazing up into the sky, in the billowing, swelling cloud above him, Cloud Stalker finally saw the mighty visage of Father Mountain.

He tried to move his lips, to whisper a prayer-song, but could not. But by then he was too weak for even that frustration to upset him.

With the face of his god burned into his brain, Cloud Stalker closed his eyes and died.

# Chapter Forty-six

For most of the last night of his old life, a morose Frog Hopping had enjoyed the company of Little Brook and her husband, Lion Tooth. The pair had made the four-day walk from Wind boma in the north to comfort him in his loss. They had prayed and danced and eaten with him. Little Brook finally scolded him enough to coax out a reluctant smile, then convinced him to tell them stories of his time with Glimmer.

For the first time in a moon, the pain in his heart lessened. Parting from them even for slumber seemed a sacrifice.

Frog was still dreaming of Glimmer's soft braided hair, the clasp of her smooth warm thighs, when the earth began to tremble.

Shaking sleep from his eyes, he climbed out of his hut and gazed up at the mountain that had been a comfort all his life. The night was clear, and unspeakable horror seized him as a cloud larger than anything he had ever seen or imagined sprouted from Great Sky's side. It writhed and coiled like a ball of snakes, flashing with lightning, although there was no rain. His cousins fled their huts, gazing up in slack-jawed disbelief.

They dashed mindlessly to and fro, tore their hair out, clawed at the ground and howled. "Father Mountain is dying!"

Hawk Shadow's wife, Flamingo, appeared before him, naked and wild-eyed, a baby beneath each arm. She thrust his son at him. "The end of the world!" she screamed.

Frog sank to his knees, clutching his unnamed infant son to his chest. Nothing that he had ever seen or imagined prepared him for such chaos. He felt beyond himself, outside himself, completely detached from his world. He no longer believed in gods, but at the moment there seemed no contradiction in his conviction that he was watching one die.

The cloud swelled and billowed, and in it he saw Glimmer's face, and Lizard's, and trembled at the sight. The others saw fire and dust and smoke and stars disappearing from the sky. They dropped to their knees, gnashing their teeth, tearing their hair and wailing, begging forgiveness for sins real or imagined.

Forgiveness, but not grace. They were witnessing the death of heaven, something no mortal eyes should ever see.


For a day and a half T'Cori walked and ran and staggered without rest, until her head swam and her limbs were like stones. She had now gone almost three nights without sleep. All that kept her stumbling along was the fear that her mentor might already be dead.

Ash rained from the sky, transforming the entire world into something alien and foreboding. She felt so numb, so shocked, that it was all she could do just to put one foot before another.

Was this her doing? Had her transgressions caused this, the end of the world?

Should she go back, return the fungus?

The world swam around her as she reached the familiar trails and began to climb, ash coating her skin and the trail. It felt less like coming home than like presenting herself for judgment.

But whatever might happen next, she would not quail. She had done what no one else could or would do.

When Blossom and two other women blocked her path on the outskirts of camp, T'Cori finally stopped, heart thundering in her chest. The thick-bodied Blossom's eyes were wide and wild. The bamboo cane in her right hand might have been intended as a weapon, but to T'Cori it looked as if her former wet nurse needed it to keep herself erect.

"Wh-Where are you going?" Blossom stammered. There seemed no way to prevent a confrontation. Slovenly Blossom might have been, and slow of mind. But she was devoted to her mother and sister.

T'Cori said nothing.

"Where have you been?" she asked again, only then noticing the pouch on T'Cori's belt. "Our mother is almost dead. You are too late. If you have something, give it to me. I will give it to her."

T'Cori's stolen stone blade was in her hand almost before she knew what she had done. Exhausted and frightened she might be, but the blade reminded her of something: she was the girl who had escaped the Mk*tk. Who had slain an Other, and walked many days to rejoin her clan and bring them knowledge. She was not a mere girl to be intimidated by anyone, even Blossom.

All her life she had feared her gigantic wet nurse. She remembered the boxed ears, the slaps and pinches when no one watched, the feeling of helplessness in the grip of the stronger, larger, older woman who had nurtured her body but starved her spirit. But her concern for Stillshadow and her own fatigue and guilt had accomplished something unexpected. It had driven her fear into the shadows.

T'Cori no longer cared what Blossom thought or tried to do. The sense of freedom was extraordinary.

"Touch it," T'Cori said, brandishing her spar of leather-wrapped obsidian. "Touch it, and I will cut you. You think I am small? You think I will not fight? Small things have sharp teeth," she said.

The other girls were speechless, shocked by the sudden change in T'Cori's demeanor. Blossom's heavy jaw worked side to side, and then she nodded. "Raven will deal with you," she said, and sent a runner off to find her sister as T'Cori pushed her aside.


Stillshadow lay collapsed on her zebra skin amid the shadows. The air reeked with a sour, damp aroma. T'Cori could just barely make out Stillshadow's shrunken silhouette. She seemed dead already.

T'Cori came closer. Although her teacher's breathing was slight, the withered breasts still moved up and down with each exhalation.

Most of Stillshadow's preparations were made fresh, but a few, like godweed and other healing or ritual herbs, were made in batches. T'Cori searched among her teacher's pouches, sniffing and judging textures until she found the right mixture, recognizable by a sharp, stinging scent. Now she needed to add the glow mushroom, the most powerful component of godweed. How much? She had never learned, and unfortunately, now it was too late to ask. She knew only that she had to do what she could.

For a moment the mixture glowed slightly in the lean-to's darkness, and then the glow died. Half-dead from lack of sleep, fatigue and injury, T'Cori propped Stillshadow's head on the crook of her arm, and tried to feed her a bit of the mash. The old woman's jaws did not move.

What to do? She suddenly remembered something she had seen Still-shadow do. The young woman took the medicine and slipped it into her own mouth, chewed until the sour, tingling mash was all one texture, then pressed her lips against Stillshadow's. T'Cori pushed the wet pulp into Still-shadow's mouth with her own tongue.

Very slowly, the old woman's mouth began to work, taking the mash, and then chewing at it. Swallowing.

"Mother," the girl whispered. "I am here. I am here. I got it. Please. Please take this from me."

Stillshadow finally began to eat a bit, managing to consume two mouthfuls.

The old woman's hand rose, as if to say, *Enough.* Her withered lips curled in what might have been a smile, and the eyes fluttered open just long enough to fix on T'Cori and then close again.

T'Cori waited at her side for a few moments, then slipped out of the hut.

Raven stood just outside the doorway, face strained. "You disobeyed Father Mountain," she said, and pointed toward the northern sky. The ground still shook. Clouds still fountained from the mountainside. The sky rained ash, not water. "Look at what you have done."

The lining of T'Cori's mouth tingled. When she looked at Raven she saw not a girl but a shimmering shadow. How strange! Was her vision returning? No . . . the edges of everything in sight began to blur. The world swirled painfully. She could barely stand, but she knew a truth, as surely as if she could still read the *num*-fire.

Raven was afraid of her.

*A nameless child will be born. And that child will end the world and cause the death of gods.*

A power shift had just occurred, like a stream changing level at a water-fall. The chosen one was not happy. There was ritual, there was tradition, and then there was the holy woman they all loved. Every dream dancer in the camp knew that she should have been willing to do anything to protect Stillshadow, who had raised and protected them all.

"I did what I had to do," T'Cori said. Her tongue felt swollen enough to block her throat. In that moment, T'Cori ceased to hate Raven. The girl was a bully, but not evil. Fear was the destroyer. Raven didn't know where she fit in the world any more than T'Cori did. All she knew was the rules, and how to keep them.

"We must follow Father Mountain's will," Raven said. "You will see, stupid one. You will see."

Sky, mountain and grass swirled, changing places. She staggered, but no one helped her. T'Cori tripped, pulled herself to her feet again, then managed to wobble as far as her hut before collapsing again.

She lay there in the dirt and looked back over her shoulder. Her sisters, young and old, watched without moving. They spoke among themselves, but she could not hear a word.

A row of white-haired old women came and stood in front of her. The sun-singers held hands and stood with spines straight as bamboo. Then they dropped their hands and gave their judgment. *She has the godweed in her,* they danced. *Foolish girl! The nameless one has not the strength or knowledge, has not undergone the rituals, to stop godweed from draining her* num. *It is between the nameless one and the immortals.*

*If the gods still live.* That last was both question and prayer, a plea for Father Mountain and Great Mother to heal sky and earth, once again revealing Their bounty to faithful children.

T'Cori managed to crawl into her hut, but then darkness claimed her.

# Chapter Forty-seven

White was the color of death, and all about them was white. The people of the inner and outer bomas held one another and shivered as smoke and ash spewed into the sky above them. White, all of them. Corpses, all. Before their eyes, the land itself had died.

The land, the animals, the trees, the rocks and the dirt.

All about them, the balance between life and death had sickened.

A hand of days later another eruption darkened the sky. This time they watched fire dance around the mountain's peak, smelled smoke from burning trees, covered their ears to protect themselves from the peals of thunder. Only after another hand of days did the sky begin to clear.

On Great Earth, the three hunt chiefs who had protected the women surveyed their home and trembled. They dared not go to see what had happened to Cloud Stalker and the others.

They knew in their marrow already. Their *num* told them what their eyes could not yet see, and their hearts feared to confess.

So instead of going up to Great Sky, they danced in the ash, praying and singing all of the songs they knew or could devise, hoping that one of them might heal the mountain or please their gods.

Or perhaps simply spare their lives.


When T'Cori first clawed her way back to consciousness, Stillshadow knelt beside her. The old woman was drawn and thin, but her eyes burned bright.

She dipped leaves in water from a gourd and wiped them slowly and smoothly across T'Cori's brow.

Raven sat cross-legged in her hut's doorway. T'Cori's eyes refused to focus, but she would have recognized that disapproving form and posture in the midst of the wildest hallucination.

"It was wrong for her to help you," Raven said. "This is why the gods are angry. Why They abandon us."

"We do not know this," the old woman said, her forehead slick with sweat. Only then did T'Cori's fevered mind comprehend that the woman tending her was still sick and weak.

"No," the nameless one said, slipping her feverish hand into Still-shadow's. "Save your strength."

She heard herself say that. *Try* to say that. But from Stillshadow's puzzled expression, T'Cori realized that she had only mumbled.

"Rest," Stillshadow said.

"Mother," Raven said, "you need to save your strength, to heal." What was that in Raven's face? It was too dark. T'Cori could not see, but she could hear her sister dancer's voice. Was that anger? Shame that she had not had the courage to do what T'Cori had done?

"I will care for her until she is well," Stillshadow said, and dipped the leaves again.


With the passage of days T'Cori did grow strong enough to crawl away from her straw to empty her bladder. She ate nothing and thus produced no solid waste, for which she was grateful.

In between these brief bouts of strength she collapsed back on her straw, dampening it with sweat and vomit. Amid the agony and filth, the plant children gifted her with visions.

*It seemed to T'Cori that she walked a path of light, a path like a log fallen across a yawning crevasse. It grew thinner as she walked. The nameless one fought to stay balanced, to not fall off to either side. It felt as if she was taking forever. Then she reached a wall and began to climb.*

*Along the way up the rock face she came to a place where a woman sat cross-legged. And now it was strange because for a moment T'Cori was not in the dream place. Rather, she was in her hut, and it was Stillshadow who came to her, hushed her, gave her grasses and herbs to eat. Was it real? Had Stillshadow come to her hut, helped her? She could not say. All she knew was that those few moments of grace saved her mind, if not her soul.*

.    .    .

In time, T'Cori's eyes began to focus on things of this world, and she returned to her senses. No one could say why this happened or what it meant. Perhaps because she was righteous in the eyes of Great Mother. Perhaps because she was young and strong.

And perhaps because Stillshadow and the mighty One she served loved her.

T'Cori lived.

And miracle of miracles, the eruptions had ceased.

Weak and wobbly, T'Cori emerged from the hut. Some of the other women seemed a bit afraid of her, as they had not been after her previous adventures.

Was it possible that her sight had returned? She looked at her sisters, hoping. Nothing. Slanting her eyes sideways, she could detect a bit of glow around them, but less than the average dream dancer saw. She was alive, but the thing that had once made her special was still gone.

Still, some whispered that T'Cori was Raven's only competition for leader. None of the older women was strong enough to lead after Stillshadow went to the mountain, none would live long enough to raise a new generation of dream dancers. They could sing the sun to life and tend the eternal fire, but not lead.

Only Raven could lead. Raven, or the nameless one.

But the very idea caused other talk, for what was death itself now that heaven was gone? Now that, as some whispered, Great Mother and Father Mountain had died?

And so it was that T'Cori went seeking Stillshadow and found her resting in her hut. "Teacher," she said, "did I do wrong?"

"Very wrong," she said. "But if Father Mountain had wanted you to come to Him for judgment, He would have summoned you."

"Why?" the girl asked. "Why am I alive?"

"Use your *num*," the old woman said. Then T'Cori brushed her lips against Stillshadow's brow, and left her to rest.

# Chapter Forty-eight

A warm rain had washed the white death from the ground. Pygmy geese, kites and fish-eagles winged the sky again as life began to return. Still, the Ibandi spoke in hushed terms, as if speaking loudly might awaken whatever demon had smote their god. But people must eat, and hunt, and the Ibandi had returned to the process of living.

Every day Break Spear performed ceremony and sacrifice, begging the ruined mountaintop to give signs. Every day someone suggested that they send a delegation up Great Sky to see what might be seen.

The proud hunters of the Ibandi met one another's eyes only with difficulty. Instead of climbing they sacrificed antelope, burned the flesh of their catches, begged Father Mountain to send the hunt chiefs back.

But they did not return. And no one climbed the mountain to see.

"Frog!" Gazelle called. In the last moon she seemed to have grown thinner, and it seemed to Frog that his mother gazed up at Great Sky almost wistfully, as if longing for the day when her time came to receive new bones. "Your mate is gone. You must find a new one. It is not good for your son to have no mother. Find a woman and take her to your hut."

Frog paused in the maintenance of his spears and sighed. "I do think about such things."

"This is good." She nodded. Her hair was thin and almost completely white now. Her cheeks, once plump, were sunken. "I have spoken to the women," she whispered to him. "This world ends soon, and we will be taken to the world beyond. There, we will be asked what we did, asked if we lost faith." Panic dwelled behind her eyes, an emotion that had crept into all their lives, into every motion, every word. It was almost as if the Ibandi he had known were dead. "Your child needs a mother. You need a helper."

How could she think of such common things at such a time? Then he realized that it was by thinking of the continuance, the unbroken thread of their seed, that his mother managed to hold on to her sanity.

"There is one in my heart."

"Good," Gazelle said. "A widow, perhaps, with children. You will need one to nurse your boy. Or you will need to bring food to a woman who has milk, and ask her to feed him." She spoke in a singsong, a tone he had heard from her only once before, when she was sick with fever.

"This woman has no children," Frog said, hoping that Gazelle would not ask more.

"Has she been married?"

After a pause, he said, "No."

Gazelle smiled. "Then go to her parents. You are a good hunter and will be a welcome son."

Frog avoided her eyes. There was no way around it now. "This is not needed. She has no parents."

"An orphan?" Gazelle brightened. "Better still. You can bring her home at once. Where do her people camp?"

"On Great Earth."

A pause.

Now Gazelle seemed to emerge more fully from her partial slumber. "She is a dream dancer?" Sudden comprehension blossomed. "She is this nameless one you saved?"

"Yes," he said.

Gazelle's face hardened. "It cannot be. Wash it from your heart."

"Mother—" he began, his thoughts interrupted by a sudden screaming and shouting from the far side of the boma.

Before they could continue, it seemed that half the boma was running toward the gate, hunters and women alike. Frog sprinted over to see a young boy from Water boma, his feet swollen and bloody. He was exhausted and ranting. Dried blood and sweat masked his face.

"They kill us," he panted.

"What happened?" asked Hot Tree.

"We were hunting to the east," the boy said, "and had speared a fat zebra. We were making a sled to pull it home when they set upon us."

"Who?" Break Spear asked. "Who did this?"

The boy's torn face tightened with fear. "The Mk*tk," he said. That word had spread through the bomas in the past year.

"They killed you all?"

He nodded, his eyes utterly haunted. "They hurled stones at us. Shot arrows. Killed all but me." The boy whimpered, finally abandoning all pretense of courage. Tears streamed down his cheeks. "They let me go. I do not know why."

"So we would know, and fear," Break Spear said.

Break Spear was old for a boma father. That he had kept his position so long was testament to the fact that his men, indeed the entire boma, loved and trusted him.

Now he called to his young, strong hunters. He was not a hunt chief, not one of the almost superhuman beings who had lived on the mountain, but he was still their champion, still the one to whom all turned in time of need.

"What do we do?" Deep Dry Hole asked.

Break Spear threw his shoulders back and stretched to his full height. The other hunters responded to the silent challenge by straightening their spines as well. This was a day for courage! "It is time to call the bomas together. Run to find the clans. At full moon, the hunters meet at the gathering place."

Frog watched the folk as they clutched their spears or mates or children, grumbling nervously. The mountain had vomited. The land was poisoned. And now the Mk*tk had attacked the men of a boma openly. Who could need more sign that the end of the world had come?

"What of the hunt chiefs?" Scorpion said. "Should we go to the mountain?" His voice broke on the last word.

Deep Dry Hole spat. "Do you wish to lead the way?"

Scorpion hung his head. They turned and looked at Great Sky. Once again, clouds swirled up around its peak. Although the ground had not trembled in many days, they could see where the white cap had been torn away, so the mountain barely resembled the peak that every one of them had prayed and dreamed and spit to, for lives without counting.

In teams of two and three, Frog and the other hunters ran to the inner and outer bomas, hyena-running *huh-huh-huh* to gather the hunters together for a war council, something that had never happened in the memory of any living Ibandi.

By next moon almost half the Circle's hunters appeared at the Gathering site, hands of hands of hands of men. To their surprise, five hunt chiefs had survived the disaster. All had been walking the Circle, visiting boma women or teaching wrestling and trapping. All were young men. None carried themselves with the confidence Frog had always attributed to the chiefs. They looked frightened, uncertain.

There was discussion of war, and dreaming, chanting and dancing. But from the time Break Spear coaxed the first ceremonial fire to wakefulness, everyone knew something dreadful was happening.

Morning Spring, the bamboo-thin, white-haired father of Wind boma, was the oldest man who still ran with the hunters, and therefore was given a place of respect at the council, even mighty Break Spear bowing to him. The five hunt chiefs sat around him, but by their refusal to seek the fate of their elders on Great Sky, they had lost all authority. Their fear hung about them like a mantle of shame.

"We have legends of war," Morning Spring said. "When I was a boy, the hunt chiefs"—and here he spared a disdainful glance at the young men at his feet, who cringed at his displeasure—"said that there were legends, tales of a time when the Ibandi were forced to stand together. We did it then, and defended our land. We will do it again."

"How?" Scorpion asked. "How did we do this thing?"

"Did the gods help?" Lion Tooth asked.

"They are not dead!" Spring said. "This is a test of our faith. Those who believe otherwise are fools." The last word brimmed with both venom and hope.

The old man seemed to blaze with fire. Even Frog felt uplifted by his words, and the others stirred. Could the old man be right? Could there be hope?

"You will see," he said. "We must prove ourselves worthy, must stand tall. Perhaps we redeem ourselves by facing this threat. But you will see. The hunt chiefs will return to us, strong and transformed!"

He raised his voice when he said this. Now he seemed to be inspired. "Yes!" he said. "We saw not the death of heaven but the birth of a new, greater world. And when the hunt chiefs come back to us, clad in feathers such as we have never seen, those of us who are worthy will dance, and sing, and celebrate. Our gods were here before the first of our ancestors were born, and they watch us now to see who will falter!"

The Ibandi beat their heels upon the ground, stamped and cheered.

"Now is no time for weaklings," Break Spear declared to the group. "This is the day you have prepared for."

"I am ready," said Hawk Shadow. "All my life, I have prepared."

"And I am ready," Fire Ant joined in.

"We will wash our spears with blood," said Uncle Snake. But it seemed to Frog that he was not so confident as he wished them to think, as if he possessed some secret knowledge.

Morning Spring, perhaps, knew what Snake was *not* saying. "Their spears will drip red as well! None of us has known war! War is not trees standing still so that you may cast your spears into them. You have slain lions and leopards. Lions and leopards cannot kill at a distance. They do not think as men, or attack in waves, or call the fire people. War is not antelope who seek only to run, to survive. I am old and remember my father's stories, stories that his father told him, about a time when a tribe came and tried to take our land, a time when we were forced to fight. War is death, and pain, and fear."

Their young men began to murmur.

Fire Ant seemed angry. "Are we not strong?"

"Morning Spring is right," Uncle Snake said, throwing aside his uncertainty. "Strength is not enough. Brave hearts are not enough."

Fire Ant stepped in. "Tell us what we must be," he growled. "What we must have, and that is what we will give to you."

Lion Tooth seemed to quail before Fire Ant's courageous speech. Was the Lion afraid? With such a mighty totem, who could fail to stand proud?

Wind boma's father stood again. "It is good for you to speak so," he said. "You must go to fight as if already dead. We do not ask for your muscles, your skin. Give us your bones."

This triggered an even more disturbed murmur.

"What do you mean by this?" Scorpion asked.

"Many will die, even if we win," Snake said. "If you try to save your life, you will turn and run, and you and your brothers will be slain. I want no one at my side who seeks to live." His eyes flamed. "Seek to die for your tribe. All others stay with the women!"


To Frog's pride, not a single Ibandi hunter turned away from the bloody task ahead. All joined the line to climb up Great Earth to seek blessing from Stillshadow and the dream dancers. All day they ran, and long into the darkness. They reached the dream dancers near noon of the third day, but it seemed that the women had been awaiting them.

Frog was shocked by how weak Stillshadow appeared. Always she had seemed aged to him, but now she seemed beyond ancient, as if the last moon's terrible events had drained her flesh. She seemed animated now by nothing save spirit.

Her eyes were clear enough, in fact they burned, but she did not speak. Her every inhalation seemed, to Frog, a small miracle.

His Butterfly Spring stood to the crone's left, while Small Raven stood to her right. Both dancers bowed their heads slightly. So: as he had anticipated, the girl he had rescued on the plains had risen high among the dancers. This, he thought, was a good thing for the Circle in its time of need.

Stillshadow seemed almost half asleep. Twice, as he watched, she reached into a pouch at her waist and extracted a small pellet, pushing it between teeth and gum. Soon afterward, she seemed more alert and aware. She heard their plea: that in the absence of the hunt chiefs, Stillshadow herself would ready them to fight for the Circle.

She had not spoken a word in all of this, but after they finished she simply said, "Yes," in a harsh, weak whisper. "Come to us at dusk. Prepare to die."

Then she hobbled away, a dancer at each arm.

# Chapter Forty-nine

"War comes?" T'Cori asked after the hunters retreated.

"Yes," Stillshadow said.

"What if our men die?" asked Raven. T'Cori watched her rival from the corner of her eye, careful not to show that she was watching. Did Raven's hand tremble? Was she afraid? Yes. So she and Raven were sisters in fear, if nothing else.

"Then," said Stillshadow, "all of you will bear children for the Others."

"I wish I was a man," Blossom moaned.

Stillshadow shook her head sadly. "And many of them wish that they were women, that they would not have spears twisted into their guts." She leaned so hard upon her staff that T'Cori thought it would splinter. She knew that the old woman was still burning with fever, the spirits of life and death warring in her veins. She should have been lying in her hut, to await the outcome of that battle. Instead, Stillshadow had dragged herself forth to meet with the hunters. Soon, she would perform ceremony, draining herself of the precious *num* all men and women needed to heal.

"We are afraid," Raven said.

"You think they are not?" Stillshadow pounded her walking stick against the ground. "They piss themselves with fear. They fight for you! For your smiles, hoping you will think them brave. And what would you have them see in your faces? Fear? If so, they will know you think them too weak to win, too weak to protect you."

Stillshadow's daughter shivered. "I cannot help it. I know what they did to T'Cori."

"You do not hear me!" Stillshadow's eyes narrowed. "Women put the strength into men or rip it out of them. Any one of you who cannot be strong, tell me now! I will not have even *one* of our men go to battle without knowing their women's hearts are with them."

The young women exchanged sick, worried glances. Raven trembled. T'Cori saw her moment and pushed herself up to full height.

"I will stand with you," T'Cori said. "I will be strong for our men."

Raven glared at T'Cori, furious that she had spoken first. Finally she nodded. "I will as well. It is my place." She whispered to T'Cori: "Sit down, *ugly.*"

T'Cori's hands crooked into claws. "Sit me down," she said.

Raven was larger, stronger, but her eyes only narrowed. "In time," she said.

*"Now,"* T'Cori said. "For years you have ruled me. If you have something to say to me, make it now, in front of our sisters."

"You are not sister," Raven snarled. "You are bhan. Mother found you where your own parents had thrown you away."

T'Cori's face burned, but she refused to back down. "Perhaps we die soon. Today is as good a day as any. If so, I am ready. I will not lie awake nights waiting for you to find my back."

"Silence, both of you!" Stillshadow hissed, as if emptying herself. "Is this what you wish the men to see? The women they love, the women they dream of, fighting among themselves like monkeys? *You* are why they are willing to die! Be prizes worthy of that sacrifice, or we have nothing."

The two girls fell silent.

"As you say, Mother," said Raven, lowering her head.

"Yes, wise one," T'Cori agreed, angry and ashamed, and angry for feeling ashamed.

"Go and prepare yourselves," the crone said.


Together in single file, those fertile dancers currently not with child walked to North Stream, the largest body of running water within a day's travel. North Stream flowed from the heights of Great Earth in the wet months, slumbering in the dry.

T'Cori and Raven strode in the lead, and the others followed them as they doffed their leather waistlets and breast flaps and bathed themselves in the cool waters.

The other dancers looked at T'Cori. Once she had been special because of her sight. Now she was special because of the way she had lost that sacred gift. She had, after all, been a Mk*tk captive, raped by beasts. She had killed one with her own hands. She was the only one who knew what their men would face.

"Tell me of the Mk*tk," one girl requested.

"Were they fierce?" asked another.

"Like two-legged lions," T'Cori answered. When she said that, she thought what she did not say: that her body remembered their smell, and the taste of their blood.

Her sisters whispered and murmured among themselves, frightened.

"I knew it," the first said.

"But I killed one, and I am only a woman!" she said. "Do you understand? Ibandi women kill Mk*tk men!" They cheered her, lifted her up on their shoulders and carried her around in the river.

Small Raven watched as the others celebrated, nodding. Finally she slapped her hands together. "Enough! We must prepare!"

They cleaned and washed one another, scenting one another with juices and fixing one another's hair. Then they walked in line from the river, each one passing Raven in turn. When T'Cori passed Raven, there was a moment when the older girl's disdain wavered. She licked her lips and said in a low voice: "You really killed one? It is no tale?"

"Yes," T'Cori said. "And Frog Hopping slew another. The Mk*tk hunted us. And then we hunted it." Raven searched her face, seeking lies, finding none. "I believe Stillshadow. Our hunters will be as strong as we make them. As strong as *we* are." She hesitated a moment, then spoke her truth. "And you are strong, Raven."

Stillshadow's daughter studied T'Cori, still seeking evidence of dissembling or mockery. Finally she nodded. "You are fit," Raven said.

T'Cori walked on. *You are fit.* She savored those words, the first kind ones that had passed between them in many springs.

As the sun died in the west, the hunters from Earth, Wind, Fire and Water bomas hiked double file up the narrow trail on Great Earth's north face. "Tell me of the dream dancers," Fire Ant said to Boar Tracks.

The young hunt chief seemed shrunken. Once Frog had thought him a giant, one of those human gods who had thrashed him with such contemptuous ease. Now his eyes were hollow and weak, unable to long avoid the sight of the transformed Great Sky. This question changed his aspect, so that he suddenly seemed to remember who and what he was. "How do you mean?" he asked.

"As women," Fire Ant said, and Hawk Shadow laughed. All found themselves listening to this conversation. "How are they as women? You have been with them."

"Yes," Boar Tracks said, suddenly seeming to remember who and what he was. "I have."

"And?" Fire Ant asked.

"Worth dying for," he said.

Hawk Shadow thumped the butt of his spear against the ground. "I will be a great hero," Hawk Shadow said. "They will seek me out and give the gift of their fire."

The other boys and men spoke in turn of the great deeds they would do, and for a time Frog's heart was lifted. For a moment he thought he could see T'Cori's face in the clouds surrounding Great Sky, there among the gods and ancestors. Was that sunbeam the slant of a broken tooth?

Then the faces began to drift and dissolve. The clouds roiling around Great Sky's peak seemed dark and heavy, whipped by the wind, crawling even as he watched them.

His stepbrother Scorpion noted Frog's expression and looked back over his shoulder. "Are our ancestors in those clouds?" he asked. "Do they speak to you?"

Frog shrugged. "They are just clouds," he said.

Sometimes, when the sun was just right and the clouds had parted, Frog could see up to the very top of the mountain. The shape of the summit had changed, as if unimaginable quantities of the strange dead white stuff had been torn away.

"Father Mountain is angry," Fire Ant said.

"He has much to be angry about," Lion Tooth said. When Hawk looked at him sharply, he shrugged.

"He took our hunt chiefs," said Hawk.

"No," Snake said nervously. "I say the Others did this."

"Then they are too powerful to fight!" Hawk said, and shuddered.

"Not so," Snake replied, brushing a fern frond out of his way. The path to the dream dancers' boma was well trod but still overgrown. "Magic is like water. You can sip or guzzle from a skin, but there comes a time when the skin is empty. If they did such a powerful thing, surely their water sack is now dry. After all, Frog killed one. The nameless girl killed one. They are men, not spirits."

"They are beasts," Lion Tooth said, glancing at Fire Ant, who knew.

*They are beasts, and they are men,* Frog thought. One of them, just one Mk*tk, poisoned, stabbed and slashed, was still stronger than any hunter he had ever known. And now they faced an entire tribe?

In response, Fire Ant shook his head. "Father Mountain is enraged," he grunted. "Angry with the Mk*tk. Angry that they would challenge us on our own ground."

"Silence," said Snake. "We are almost there."

The narrow trail wound across a sharp rise, and then they arrived at the dream dancer camp.

Snake seemed to shake himself out of some kind of trance and began to speak. "When I was with the hunt chiefs, and we went to the mountaintop—"

Suddenly, Stillshadow was there, leaning heavily on her bamboo walking stick, flanked by her daughters Blossom and Raven. Blossom seemed to be carrying most of the old woman's weight. The crone's face was ashen, her eyes sunken in her skull. "Why come you to me?"

"You know why we come," Snake said. Both hope and grief shimmered in the air between them.

Though she seemed unable even to stand without help, her eyes burned. "I see only dead men before me," she said with satisfaction. "This is as it should be. Come," Stillshadow said. "Present yourself to your tribe's dream dancers."

As they entered the clearing, Frog saw the boys and men from the other bomas who had arrived before them, rows of tens of tens of hunters: young, mature, and some gray and stooped, all prepared to die for their people. Some were painted, some plain. Some wore feathered headbands or had tied the tails of foxes to their spears.

The young hunt chiefs stood behind her, watching. Stillshadow and Morning Spring presided.

"These are the daughters of the mountain," Stillshadow said. "They are for Father Mountain alone: Father Mountain, and those found worthy in His sight."

Arrayed in their splendor, freshly washed and their hair braided in tight spirals, the ripe young dancers faced the tribe's bravest hunters, their bright eyes and moist mouths an invitation to boil the blood.

One of the young hunters whimpered, and Stillshadow roared in response. "Our great god is not dead! You saw His anger, because He knew that this filth would come to our land, and that His children would feel fear instead of rage! He is disappointed with you, and you must now earn your place in His shadow."

Snake turned to the boys, who shivered in their ranks. "Say the words!" he demanded.

"We are dead already," they chanted, as they had been instructed by the hunt chiefs, by Snake and Boar Tracks.

"Let us see your bones," said Stillshadow, the walking ghost. Frog could not meet her eyes, was happy when those burning hollows floated past him. He was filled with a sense that he, and all of them, stood in the presence of the living dead.

And with that the girls went out among them with bowls of white paint, smearing their ribs and legs with smooth stripes.

T'Cori slid her way in front of another dancer, standing just two hand lengths away. Her fingers dipped into the white paint, and with their tips she drew bones on his skin. The wetness felt to him like fire. "Frog," she whispered. She did not look at him. Ordinarily, the nearness of her smooth body might have made his root stir, but there was something else happening here, something more than sexual. This was a flame he had never known.

If faith he needed, it was here that he found it.

"Come back," she said, a tear glistening at the corner of her eye.

"I will return," he assured her.

She nodded.

They finished the ritual, and Stillshadow stood. "You are our hunters! We, the Ibandi women, kneel before you." Stillshadow suited her actions to her words, bracing herself with the bamboo staff as she lowered herself first to her left knee, and then her right. The sight of this phenomenal woman kneeling before him was hypnotic.

"You are strong, and we are weak." Her voice, ragged and trembling, carried both a current of spiritual strength he *felt* rather than heard, and an aching need. "We beg you to protect us. Know that we are yours, and yours alone." Gathering her strength, she called to them, "Gaze upon what the Mk*tk would ravage!"

As the older women stood in a half circle and sang to them, the young ones drew the hides from their breasts and waists, standing nude before the men, rolling their hips in invitation. The breath caught in Frog's throat. Rarely did the dream dancers reveal their pubic hair or breasts in public, rarely did they behave in an overtly sexual fashion, and never, ever as a group.

It was almost more than his mind could comprehend. "Father Mountain," Frog murmured, "save me." Now he felt the physical response, as if his eggs nestled in a bed of coals.

"We await your return," Stillshadow said.


The very moment that the last of the men was out of their sight, the crone collapsed to the ground, spent.

With Raven and Blossom's help T'Cori plucked her up and tenderly carried her to her hut, laying her on her straw pallet with the greatest care.

"What now?" Blossom asked. T'Cori noticed that Blossom didn't seem to know where to turn for leadership: to Raven, or to T'Cori?

Raven stepped forward, blocking Blossom's line of sight to the nameless one.

"Now we wait," Raven said. "We wait, until it is time to mourn the dead."

"Many of them will die?" Blossom asked.

"All are dead already," Small Raven said. "Now come. Back to your tasks."

T'Cori looked after the path where the men disappeared. She closed her eyes with a sigh and offered prayers to their dead gods.


Stillshadow lay on her side, listening to the chattering from outside her hut. She managed to turn onto her back, exhausted by even that simple motion. The crone stared up at the ceiling, unblinking, a single tear brimming from her eye to slide slowly down her withered cheek. "All gone," she said, to herself and the darkness and the dead mountain. "All gone. Everything gone." There was silence for a long moment, and then she said, "We die."

For all time the Ibandi had lived here in the shadow. Could her people sustain even a dream of leaving? It was possible that they would choose to die here, close to their gods. And if that happened, then all of the generations that had come before them had lived in vain.

She wanted desperately to call out to them, to say, "There is something you do not know," but realized that this hidden truth would give her people no strength. Better to keep it to herself. Better to wait . . .

She closed her eyes, spiritual strength failing her at last, *num* expended. Only the slenderest of vines connected soul and body, a vine that seemed to grow more frayed with every harsh, shallow breath.

# Chapter Fifty

A day's run south of Water boma, the open savannah yielded to tumbles of rocks and ridges overlooking brush and trees stretching all the way to a distant horizon. It was here, far from their homes, that the Ibandi hoped to face the Mk*tk in mortal combat.

The hunt chiefs and tribal elders chose this position after a full night of debate and deliberation.

Their reasoning seemed sound to Frog. Because the days had been unusually hot, the southern route required even more water than usual. If the Mk*tk followed the water holes as they came north, they would have to pass this place, which the Ibandi hunters vowed to transform into a killing ground. The grasslands below, wavering with their bamboo and slender peacock flowers, would soon be drenched with Mk*tk blood.

Boar Tracks returned from his scouting expedition, clambering up over the rock shelves with apparently effortless strength. Despite the dire circumstances, Frog still took pleasure in Boar Track's serpentine grace and power. But the hunt chief seemed nervous as he approached the brothers, to have trouble meeting their eyes. Was he ashamed of his fear? "I was close enough to smell them. There are many."

"How many?" Hawk Shadow asked.

"Hands of hands, I think," Boar said, still not meeting their eyes. "They move through the rocks, there." He pointed down toward the grasslands.

"We will meet them near the fig trees," Break Spear said. "Go and light the fire."

Together, Boar and Lion Tooth strode out onto the plain, built a fire and lit it before retreating to the highlands. The Ibandi had incurred the wrath of other tribes in days past. In most instances, troubles had been averted by the offering of meat and fruit, left in the midst of these grasslands south of Water boma. This time, they knew, such offerings would prove useless.

The fire was lit from the dream dancers' eternal flame. *If the Mk\*tk will not have peace,* it said, *then the fires of death will consume them utterly.*

Strong thoughts. Frog hoped that he could live up to them.

Surrounded by his brothers, Frog crouched up in the rocks, their rough grain scratching his belly. In the darkness, they could see nothing save the fire's glow, but they knew the Mk\*tk were somewhere in the grasslands below. The wind shifted, and he swore he could *smell* them, felt his eggs clench up tightly in response to their alien aroma.

Their mortal enemies were nearby, waiting, as the Ibandi waited, for dawn.

"Do they feel fear?" Lion Tooth asked, stroking his necklace with a nervous thumb.

Fire Ant turned to Frog. "My brother knows. When you drove your spear into the mud-man's belly, did he shriek?"

He saw the plea in Fire Ant's eye. *We must put courage in our brothers.* For the first time, Frog truly felt that he was one of them. He was a man.

Why, then, did the memory of the Mk\*tk's animal strength still make his legs weak?

He bared his teeth and lied with all his heart. "He begged as I drove in the spear. He crawled, trying to escape. He was weak, and I was strong!" Frog pounded his spear into the dirt. "I was strong because I am Ibandi!"

"Ibandi!" said Scorpion and Lion Tooth and Hawk and Ant.

"We are all Ibandi!" Frog said.

"Ibandi!" they chanted, joining in.

"This is my little brother," said Fire Ant, with great pride. "Many here are stronger, faster than Frog. He and a girl slew Mk\*tk, and they were alone and afraid! Be as he was, do as he did, and you will return to your huts."

"We are Ibandi!" they chanted.

"Now sleep," Fire Ant said.

They curled up in their hides. Frog found an open spot near Hawk and Ant and Scorpion and nestled down. "Did I do right?" he whispered.

"You were perfect, little brother," Fire Ant said.

"I am afraid," Frog confessed.

Hawk Shadow nodded. "Fear is here now. Stay close to me tomorrow."

Fire Ant agreed. "Stay close to us. You will make us proud. Let me see those little fangs again."

Frog bared his teeth.

"I am frightened already," Hawk Shadow chuckled.

They wrapped themselves in skins and curled up, waiting for sleep.

Frog lay there, eyes open. He studied the bones painted on his skin.

"Already dead," he whispered, and closed his eyes.

# Chapter Fifty-one

Even as the Ibandi hunters prepared for battle, a small Mk*tk raiding party had circled behind their lines for a raid on the defenseless Water boma, slaughtering women, children and old men, and setting the huts ablaze.

By the next day, refugees streamed into the dream dancer camp on Great Earth. The dancers ministered to them, made certain that they had dried meat, a handful of nuts and water gourds.

As word of the coming battle spread, healers from the entire Circle clustered on Great Earth, hoping to help with the wounded. One of them was a Between from Fire boma, a big, loose-bellied man named Thorn Summer. He helped T'Cori bring water to the refugees, including an old man with a gashed left shoulder and two fingers severed from his left hand. Whirling Pool ministered to him under Blossom's direction. Despite his pain, the wounded man stared at T'Cori in a way that made her stomach sour.

"I've seen your eyes before," he said. "Who was your mother?"

"Great Mother is my mother," she said.

He nodded, but continued to stare as Pool tended to his wounds. "What is your name?" she asked.

"Water Chant," he said.

T'Cori wandered away, puzzling. "What do you know about him?" she asked Thorn.

"His wife, my sister, was killed in the raid," he said. "It was very sad."

She agreed it was, but could not stop herself from thinking that there was something familiar about the man.

"Do you know him?"

"Yes. I helped with the birthing of his third daughter."

"How many children did he have?"

"Seven," Thorn said. "Three died as babies. Two died since. He has living daughters in Earth and Water bomas." He nodded, as if agreeing with himself or summoning a difficult memory.

"It was said that one of his daughters disappeared. It was a time of drought. She was born blind, and it is said that he exposed her."

Something like a lightning bolt crackled up the nameless girl's spine. All her life she had wondered who her father might be, and now it was possible he was only a few steps away.

She turned back to the old man. Should she say anything? She realized that she did not need to. He could not take his eyes from her.

"Do I look like your wife?"

Water Chant nodded. "Where is your father?" he asked hoarsely.

"Great Sky is my father's home," she said.

He mumbled, unable even to speak, and then wandered off by himself. How appropriate, she thought. How dare he face her, a weakling, a coward who had fled his village, a broken man who hadn't even been able to protect his own wife. And yet . . .


Just before dawn, their sentries roused them from sleep. Runners dashing in from the brush claimed that they had heard or seen Mk*tk.

Frog had made himself four spears. "Stay here," Fire Ant said to his smaller brother. Despite Fire Ant's smile, his long face was drawn and lined. Frog knew that he was saying goodbye. Frog's brothers bade him stay among the rocks while they crept down into the field.

The new sun's light was bright enough to cast deep shadows, so that he could glimpse only flashes of the hunters as they met the Mk*tk. He heard screams, and saw clouds of dust rising from the tall grass. Spears and arrows pierced the air, fell into the high grass.

In defending the rear, Frog and the youngest hunters saw little of the fight's beginning. There was thrashing, brief flashes of men clawing and slashing at one another like rabid leopards determined to consume one another in a cannibalistic frenzy. The Ibandi brothers outnumbered the larger men, were able to swarm them, but he watched their bodies tossed aside and savaged with spears, rocks, long rough arrows, with teeth and hands. The Mk*tk came straight at them, and although outnumbered were so ferocious that Ibandi arrows seemed not to slow them, and they raged on even with Ibandi spears buried in their vitals.

The Mk*tk died, yes, they died, but showed so little fear, were so terrible even in the final moments of their lives, that it was the Ibandi hunters who wavered. Even dying, Mk*tk eyes blazed with hatred.

*We want your land, your lives, your women,* those eyes seemed to say. *You are nothing. Your god is nothing. You are not even fit to be eaten.*

Frog threw his first spear, and after that, his mind seemed to break. For the rest of his life, only fragments of memory ever came to him, usually when deep in restless dream.

He remembered arrows, fired by Mk*tk archers in a rain that arched up and fell from the sky into the Ibandi, aimed poorly but still enough to scatter them, so that all their fine plans of standing together were for naught.

Frog had no time to throw a second spear before one of the giants bounded into his hiding place, swinging a great sharp spike of rock. Frog scampered back, clambering up the hill as the Mk*tk warrior came after him. Spotted Slug lunged out and stabbed the Mk*tk in the side. The giant roared and spun, starting after Frog's cousin. This was his opportunity, and Frog leapt down from his perch, driving his spear before him.

He couldn't catch his breath. *No air. No air.* The acid clutch of fear constricted his chest so that he felt as if he was wading waist-deep through mud.

The Mk*tk was wounded front and back, but a swing of a rock clutched in his hairy hand caught Spotted Slug. Blood and brains splashed Frog's face. He wiped his vision clear in time to see Scorpion lunging in, screaming, jabbing with a spear and then backing up so swiftly he almost fell. Frog seized a second spear and drove it up under the ribs. The Mk*tk screamed and turned back to Frog as Scorpion, bleeding from a wounded scalp, vaulted over the rocks and struck the Mk*tk in the back.

The stepbrothers stabbed and stabbed, and then clubbed the giant with rocks, and then finally, unbelievably, he was dead.

They leaned against each other, gasping like beached fish.

A quarter day passed as they slew Mk*tk. The very sky seemed to take on a crimson pall, as if the sun itself was a bloody eye, weeping over the field of battle.

·    ·    ·

At last the Mk*tk fled, but only after they had killed more Ibandi than the Ibandi had of them. When they abandoned the field, they slit the throats of their own wounded. More frightening still, so far as Frog could see, the wounded did not protest.

The Mk*tk howled and shook their spears at the Ibandi, bloodied knives held high as if to say: *We kill our own. Think what we will do to you.*

In the dark of night, the Ibandi held torches aloft, searching the grass for their dead.

Of the hunt chiefs, only Boar Tracks remained. All the others had perished leading their brothers onto the field. His leg bore a spear wound that needed to be wrapped with leaves and wet moss. He required the attention of a dream dancer as soon as possible.

So. They had not been total cowards, even if they had failed to climb Great Sky to learn what had happened to their brothers.

That day Frog saw many things he would never forget. He helped to bury many dead. He and Hawk Shadow found Break Spear with a broken back, mewling at the sky.

"Kill me," he begged Hawk, eyes glazed with agony.

"You were kind to me in the circle," Hawk said. "Only in respect can I do this thing," and he ended Break Spear's torment with a spear to the heart.

Frog's throat constricted when he recognized a body slumped in the grass. His sister's husband, Lion Tooth, was dead, a Mk*tk arrow in his throat.

He sank to his knees. In his mind he could clearly see Lion Tooth teasing, running, playing games . . . and fighting bravely. Lion Tooth, dead, slain in a rain of arrows.

Fire Ant and Deep Dry Hole, both covered with wounds, leaned on each other.

Frog's head spun, and for the first time he wished that his mind did not have the strangeness he had sensed within himself since childhood. He saw too many possibilities, too many ways that things might have happened, or might be in days to come. He wished he could just be with his fear and fatigue and wounds like his fellows, as they sat around the fire, frightened and exhausted.

Finally Fire Ant spoke up.

"We won!" he crowed, and they looked at him as if he was mad. "We live, and remain, and they ran."

"There were many more Ibandi than Mk*tk," Hawk said. He scratched his wounded head, looked at the blood on his fingers. He licked at the wet red stains, eyes bright with fear. Frog had never seen that expression on his brother's face. Never. "What happens next time if they bring more?"

"I say that they brought all that they have. That if they had had more, they would have sent them against us!" He had their attention now. "And further," Ant said, "I say that Father Mountain was with us. I for one felt His presence as we fought for our homes. I say that He is alive and watches over us. That the hunt chiefs were taken home because Father Mountain needed their strength, and we are more than we ever were."

Frog could see the hope in their eyes. Fire Ant may not have trained as a hunt chief, but he had something, some ability to move and sway the tribe.

And this, he thought, was a good thing. With so many hunt chiefs and fathers dead, with Hawk a shrunken shadow of his former self, new leaders had to arise. Why not Ant?

After the terrible battle, by twos and threes they returned to their bomas to lick their wounds.

Despite their momentary rousing at Fire Ant's hands, Frog had never seen the men of his clan so disheartened.

Uncle Snake called the meeting. The subject was clear: what should they do?

This was a gathering of all the tribes, all who could attend, both inner and outer bomas, Ibandi and bhan alike. Folk were still trickling to the site of the Spring Gathering even as the first speakers had their say.

Members of the men's and women's councils drew images in the dirt with sticks and fingers. The disagreement between the different genders could not have been starker. The men said that they should stay and fight. The women, wailing over the dead, insisted that they should leave.

"We fight and die," Snake said. "Or we run and die. In the beginning of the world, Father Mountain gave our ancestors this land, and now He turns His back. We water this land with our blood."

The widow Hot Tree spoke. "Our children need to live. There may be better places for us. Once, years ago, Stillshadow spoke of such things. This may be the time our dreams have spoken of."

"A woman's words!" Fire Ant mocked. "It is time to forget the words of women, time for men to be strong."

Although Hawk was stronger than Fire Ant, Frog saw that he was content to stand beside his brother and let Ant's words speak for both of them.

And just like that, as Frog watched, the power in Fire boma changed hands.


In the thick of the night, when Frog was deep in the sticky part of sleep, he was dragged from dream by violent screams and thrashing just outside his hut. His heart pounding, Frog grabbed his spear and headed out into the night, but by the time he reached the gate, the trouble was already over.

Frog had feared that the Mk*tk had already been able to regroup and mount an offensive this far north. Fortunately, it was just a small raiding party, just a few Mk*tk who fled hooting, arrows showering about their heels as soon as the Ibandi responded in force. Although the attack was intended to terrify the boma folk, it actually forced them to make a decision that had been hovering in the air from the very beginning.

"You see? You see?" said Fire Ant. His injuries during the battle had been minimal. Frog had not caught sight of him during the battle, but other hunters had said his brother had fought like a fiend and helped with the killing of three of their enemy. After the battle, Ant had carried himself more proudly than Frog could remember since his walkabout. He was known and admired, and the men seemed to listen to every word he said.

"You see? You see? We must fight or we will die. Only a fool would say differently."

"Then call me a fool," said Hot Tree, "to think that life is better than death."

"Then go!" Ant roared at the old woman. "Perhaps you are no longer Ibandi. I do not care if you are Stillshadow's sister. Go slut for the Others—we will not stop you."


When T'Cori went to Stillshadow's hut to fetch her, their teacher was unconscious. Raven and Blossom knelt over her, rubbing nut oil into her chest.

"Is she . . . ?" T'Cori started to say, and then noted the rise and fall of her teacher's chest.

"She did not awaken this morning," Raven said.

T'Cori fought panic. "The boma folk have come to see her."

Raven squared her shoulders. "I must meet with them," she said. "Blossom, come." She looked at T'Cori and bit her lip, as if the next words were like twigs in her throat. "I would have you at my side," she said.

The nameless one nodded.


"Mother is in the dream," Raven told Snake when he demanded to see her.

"She has not come back to us," Blossom said, and Frog saw that the big woman was fighting not to shiver.

It was easy to understand why. Stillshadow sick. The hunt chiefs gone. Water boma destroyed. *We are doomed.*

"What do we do?" Uncle Snake asked, his voice rough with emotion. "Please, tell us."

"We cannot decide," Scorpion said, "and thought to come to you."

"It is good." Raven and T'Cori sat side by side, addressing them. Frog thought that Raven was the stronger of the two, but that she needed T'Cori's support. "We are speaking well together."

"What shall we do?" Snake repeated.

Raven drew herself up until her spine was straight, in a single instant transmuting herself from a girl to a woman of power. "I must pull my dreams into this world. Tonight, we dance. I will speak my visions tomorrow."


That night, in the center of the encampment, for the first time Raven performed the ceremony without her mother's help, leading the dreamers and the hunters together, hands of hands of feet dancing at the fire, howling to the stars, begging their gods for wisdom. Raven and T'Cori danced at the fire's edge, at the center of the milling throng, the plant people swimming through their veins.

Until dawn the ceremony continued, Raven whirling around and around until the hunters, trying to follow her, fell. Dizziness forced Frog to stop long before Ant or Hawk or many of the other hunters, but eventually, all fell. One by one so did the dream dancers, until Raven danced alone, spinning like a feather in the wind.

Frog watched in awe as the first rays of the sun brushed her cheeks. She stopped, panting, and looked out at them all with glassy eyes.

"The dream says we must climb Great Sky," she said. "I have heard the voice of the ancestors." Raven trembled as she spoke. Clearly, she did not like what she was saying. "They say that we must go and find the hunt chiefs."

"And if they are dead?"

"Then we speak to Great Mother and Father Mountain. They will tell us how to fight the Mk*tk."

"How can this be done?" Snake asked.

"There is only one way," she replied. "We must choose heroes to climb the mountain. And there, at the top, I believe Mother and Father will speak."

"How can you say such things?" asked a man from Wind boma. "None but the hunt chiefs has ever done this."

"And where are they?" she asked. "Where?" Perhaps the others thought she was shaking with power, but Frog sensed it was fear. Raven was doing the best she could, but she was not ready for such an important role. Would any of them be?

"Where are the hunt chiefs?" Blossom asked. "Gone! They've not come to our aid, and none of you has had the courage to go and look, to see what has happened."

The men looked at one another with shame and dropped their heads.

"So we women will have to go. Someone must climb the mountain. We will need to speak with Great Mother. With Father Mountain."

"But what if they are dead?" Scorpion asked, giving voice to their thoughts.

So fierce was Raven's gaze that it was clear to all who looked, who heard, that this was Stillshadow's daughter. That she was the most powerful of all the dancers. "Then we will die!" she said. "We will die."

There, beyond the clouds, rose Great Sky, the first and greatest mountain in the world. Atop that mountain lived their god—if live He did. There was a terrible, lonely silence that seemed to last forever.

Raven stepped forward. "I will go. Mother is far too sick, but I am her daughter, and I will climb for my sisters."

Hot Tree nodded. "Yes. You are strong. But not alone. You will need companions to help you and keep you safe. Raven, which of the other women would you choose?"

Raven looked out at the others and seemed to chew over her answer. "The nameless one is strong enough," she said finally.

T'Cori would climb the mountain? Frog's mind reeled. The small, nameless one? He felt a tickle of premonition. By Father Mountain, as impossible as it seemed, he knew that his own future had just changed.

"Good. Raven and T'Cori will each need spirit twins. Who will aid your bodies, that our spirits might fly?"

The men from the other bomas clustered together. "It is death," they whispered. "Death."

Then Fire Ant stepped forward.

"Fire boma is not afraid," Ant said. "We will go."

Frog's heart swelled. His brother was indeed a leader! Hawk Shadow was a great hunter and killer of men.

Frog turned to his Uncle Snake. "You can take them," he said. "You know the way."

Snake nodded. "I know the way," he said, and then shifted his eyes away. Frog felt uneasy, wanted to question him further, but held his tongue.


In her hut's solitary darkness, T'Cori spent a quarter drawing circles in the packed earth, girding herself for the confrontation to come.

Finally Boar Tracks crawled through her doorway in response to her summons.

He stood and asked, "What do you want?" although she could see in his face that he already knew.

"For you to come with me."

Boar Tracks shook his head. "I failed my brothers," he said, then pointed to his wounded right leg, packed with herbs and moss. "I could never make the climb." He could not meet her eyes.

"If you *wanted* to climb," she said, and came close enough to smell the fear in his breath, "if you believed that your brothers, your fathers awaited you atop the mountain, could that leg stop you?"

He was shaking as she circled him. The hut's roof was low enough to make him bend over, but she stood tall, not coming within a hand of the thatch. Despite the difference in their size, he seemed to shrink back from her.

She was horrified and disgusted. "To think that you were the one that Stillshadow chose for me," she said. "To think I let you touch me."

"As you let the Mk*tk touch you!" he cried, but still could not meet her eyes. "I gave you favor. I brought you back into the tribe. How dare you speak to me in such a manner. I am a hunt chief!"

For just a moment Boar seemed to regain his strength, and she prayed that anger might empower him where courage had failed. Surely he had too much pride to let a woman, any woman, speak to him in this way!

The anger sustained him for but a few moments. Then he seemed to collapse again. "I am sorry," he said. "I cannot."

And he left her.

T'Cori sat on her hut's packed earth, listening to the wind, and thinking of what had just occurred. Had she been fair? Was his wound great enough to preclude such effort? Perhaps he was right. Certainly he knew more about it than she. Stillshadow and all of the women's circle had made pilgrimage to Great Earth's peak. T'Cori had not done so yet. But she had climbed around much of the mountain and knew that when the time was right, she would make that fiercer effort and succeed. Was Great Sky really such a farther reach?

So enmeshed in her thoughts was she that T'Cori was unprepared when Raven came to her. Never had the two of them been alone in her hut, and she was so startled to see the young woman crawling through her doorway that her mouth hung open.

Raven folded her legs to sit before T'Cori, hands resting on her knees. And then she waited, perhaps offering the nameless one the courtesy of first speech.

When T'Cori had nothing to say, Raven spoke. "We have never been friends," she said.

"Once, long ago," said T'Cori, "I hoped we would be sisters."

The older girl moved closer. "We are not friends. Or sisters. Perhaps one day one of us will kill the other. But this is not that day. Our people's future is at stake. And I would lie if I said I thought that anyone but you could make the climb."

T'Cori wagged her head. "This is so strange."

"The world is bigger than we are," Raven said, and when T'Cori looked at the girl she could see the strong lines of Stillshadow's own face. For the first time she found herself able to admit that Stillshadow had been right not to push Raven aside. This was a strong and good woman. Enmity they might feel for each other, but both loved their people.

They had to, or the Ibandi were dead.

"What do you think?" Raven said. "Who might come with us? The one named Fire Ant spoke first. He is brave and strong. I would have him as my spirit twin."

T'Cori waited, weighing her words, trying to be certain that they were correct before she spoke them. "My *num* says I will succeed if Frog comes with me."

"Frog Hopping?" Raven asked. "Of Fire boma? The boy who saved you." She nodded approval. "He is Fire Ant's younger brother."

Raven closed her eyes. T'Cori thought her smooth and placid face beautiful, and was surprised by the thought.

"I see Great Mother's hand in this," Raven said, opening her eyes. "But it is Frog Hopping's choice. He has the right to refuse."

# Chapter Fifty-two

When Frog first heard of T'Cori's choice, he simply collapsed to a seated position, squatting there in the dirt as Hot Tree explained it to him.

He was stunned, couldn't believe that he'd been correct: T'Cori and he seemed to share a destiny. The possibility of climbing Great Sky entranced him. Throughout all time, only hunt chiefs had ever braved the demons and the dead water to climb the tallest mountain in the world, there to speak with gods and ancestors. There were so many stronger and braver than Frog, but he had been chosen. His cousins congratulated him, slapped him on the back, and wished him courage. Deep Dry Hole watched him carefully, and Frog wondered at his bland, unreadable expression: would Dry Hole be happy for Frog to have a conversation with Lizard's spirit?

"Little brother, it is your time," said Fire Ant, approaching with Hawk at his side.

"What do you mean?"

Hawk sat beside him. "The nameless girl chose you as her spirit twin. She will use your strength to climb the mountain. We will climb, and be remembered in dance and song. We will see our father, Baobab, and our grandfather." His eyes were distant. "Such a day that will be!"

"The mountain," Frog said, and looked up at the misshapen peak. Gray rock glistened through the white mantle. Clouds still oozed from the cracks in the sides.

"But *can* we?" Hawk asked. Although his body was broader and harder than Fire Ant's, he seemed shrunken. "Do we merely waste our lives? How can we do this thing?"

The peak looked different to them now. The strange misting had ceased, but the very contours had altered. "The women say Father Mountain and Great Mother have taken the hunt chiefs home to Them. So many things have been said. This is our chance to learn what is true."

Fire Ant gripped his younger brother's shoulder. "We are strong. We will do this. And you will be there, if you are Baobab's son."

"I am his son!" Frog said without hesitation.

"Yes," Hawk said. "You are."

Frog smiled, a small, sad smile. "I remembered that full moon was yesterday, and that that marks my birth. I have lived ten and nine springs. I think that that must mean something."

"It means it is a fine time," Fire Ant said. "A very good day."

Every story of the climbs, every tale in memory, was danced or sung that night. The celebration continued until the old ones dropped out to chant at the fireside, until the children slept nestled in their mothers' arms, until only the hunters and the strongest of the young women remained upon their feet.

Until dawn split the darkness, they sang and danced.

The only one of them who had been all the way to the top, Uncle Snake told them everything he knew. "There are rocks that will cut through your feet, or even sandals," he told them. "You must cover them as you never have before."

"How do we do this thing?" Hawk asked.

Speaking the next words seemed to pain him. "There is a way, and the hunt chiefs knew it. I will show you. The hunt chiefs knew these secrets, and for many many lives they have defeated the mountain demons. They have tools, if we can find them." He gazed up into the heights. "And we must."

All of Fire boma, and many from the inner and outer family, had gathered to say their goodbyes. On every face Frog read an unvoiced conviction: that none of the adventurers would return. But without words, all had decided to pretend this was not the case, that they might ascend to heaven and then descend with wisdom, to be greeted as heroes.

Fire Ant stood. "Now we leave to begin this great journey."

"All of our hopes are on you," Hot Tree said. "And when you return, there will be great feasting."

"We will speak with the gods," said Hawk Shadow. "Or remain with them."

# Chapter Fifty-three

Raven and T'Cori they were, from the wise and powerful dream dancers. Frog and Fire Ant and Hawk and Uncle Snake and stepbrother Scorpion
they were, great hunters from Fire boma. For a quarter they were praised
with song and dance by well-wishers who accompanied them until the incline began to steepen. At that point the boma folk seemed to realize that they
were entering the realm of the dead. Then the well-wishers dropped back, and
the seven adventurers were alone.

Their climb began on the edge of a rain forest, walking through endless
fields of white-powdered ferns and flowers, beneath the watchful eyes of the
yellow-faced monkeys. They trekked another quarter day into a world of
tall timber, and the spot where Snake said to make the first night's camp.

"Can't we make it all the way to the . . ." T'Cori saw the expression on
Snake's face. "The camp of the hunt chiefs?"

"I do not know what we will find," Snake said. "But whatever it is, I wish
to face it in daylight."

So they made lean-tos beneath sheltering branches, completing their
work just as the clouds decided to rain. Swiftly, the thin layer of ash was
transformed into a pale mush.

The moist earth met the cool morning breezes, birthing a mat of clouds that
hovered around the travelers as they continued on. It blanketed the forest

for most of the day, muffling the very sound of their footsteps against the dank earth.

The trees were taller than any T'Cori had seen with the single exception of the Life Tree, the great baobab. Their branches interlocked to form a canopy above the forest floor. All around them, ash-covered plants of endless variety were dying. They seemed cocooned in an uncanny silence, only an occasional bird call reverberating in the branches.

And everywhere that layer of white. The forest should have been filled with blue monkeys, bushbuck, duikers, leopards and bush pigs. The few beasts they saw were smeared with ash and seemed haggard and frightened, too stunned even to flee.

"The chamber," Snake said, voice choked, standing at the mouth of a wide depression in the ground. Once, it must have been large enough for men to walk through. Now, it was clogged with mud and brush. T'Cori saw a tangle of legs and arms, as if the great hunt chiefs had been caught in the midst of some sacred ceremony. Snake wept openly.

They discovered the most terrible thing in the very middle of the clearing: Cloud Stalker himself, buried to his chin in mud. The flesh had been chewed down to the bone. His empty eye sockets stared blindly. Only his flagging, bloody braids allowed T'Cori to recognize him.

Raven turned away, gagging. She sank to her knees beside him, caressed Stalker's ravaged face, his empty eyes. "Father," she whispered.

T'Cori touched Raven's hair, and the dancer turned to look back up at her, face streaked with tears.

"He was your father?" T'Cori asked. Of course he was, but T'Cori had never really thought about it. Stillshadow was mated to Cloud Stalker, but of course had had other lovers. But shouldn't she have known that Raven had sprung from Stalker's seed?

Raven nodded. "I never really knew him," she said. "Mother told me not to talk, not to brag, that the other girls become jealous."

"I am so sorry," T'Cori said. "May I help you with the ceremony?"

Together, they prayed over Cloud Stalker, Raven dancing as T'Cori gently heaped rocks over his head. Frog and the others helped, protecting the body of their grand hunt chief from further insult.

When they were done, Raven wiped her tears away and squeezed T'Cori's hand. "Thank you," she said, and the nameless girl felt her own eyes moisten.

So much destruction. So much loss. Any small gain seemed a miracle.

"Father Mountain is gone," Fire Ant growled.

Snake dropped to his knees, digging with his hands in the white mud, and Frog and the others joined him. Beneath the surface, the soil was dark and still moist and unnaturally warm. T'Cori could barely imagine how hot it must have been when first it cascaded down the mountain, sweeping all in its way.

Snake wept uncontrollably. "I am nothing," he said to Raven. "I could not save your father." He tore at his facial scars, wailing. "And I was not fit to be here, to die with my brothers."

The others looked at one another helplessly. T'Cori watched Frog place his hand on his uncle's shoulder. "Because of your scar, you were not here," he said. "Because you live, you are leading us in our time of need."

Snake looked up at him, perhaps searching for deceit or condescension. T'Cori saw only love in Frog's face, and reckoned that Snake must have seen the same, because by the time he rose he was composed.

"There are things we will need," Snake said. He fought to keep his voice even, but it was clear that his mind had reached a brittle edge. "It is cold up there," he said. "Cold such as you have never known. The hunt chiefs knew this, and they did things. Had things to try . . . to help them . . . help *us* deal with the cold."

A crazed smile burst forth on Snake's face as he found the first of the items he sought. Hides cut with armholes. Hides cut to be strapped over the feet.

"This is good," Snake said. "There are . . . *were* caches of food and firewood up the mountain, marked with this symbol," and here his fingertip traced the sign of fire and mountain in the white mud. "Look for them. They may save our lives."

They clawed their way into the mud, and before long they had unearthed more hides, and walking sticks, and spears, and arrows. A treasure trove.

Snake showed them how to wear the furs, how to wrap their feet. The furs had already been shaped into things like sandals, only covering the ankles and even the calves. Other furs seemed much too hot and heavy to wear, but Snake assured them that in a few days they would be grateful for the warmth.

They recovered what bodies they could, and buried or burned them. Those too deep in the muck they considered buried already.

Raven and T'Cori led them in dance. There, in the muddy, ash-white clearing the Ibandi raised voices to the dead trees, black skin against white mud as they spun and called out to their ancient ancestors to receive the souls of the hunt chiefs.

Then, after prayers were danced, they walked a quarter to gain some distance from the place of so much death, and made their camp for the night.

"What do we do? If Father Mountain is dead . . . ," Frog said.

"He is not," T'Cori said to him, taking his hand.

"How can you be so certain?" he asked, looking up into the clouds.

"I know," she said.

He sighed. "There is something different in the clouds," he said. "Something strange. This was a place of power when I came for my manhood. Now it is dead ground."

Despite her faith and inner knowledge, she understood. The trees were clotted with ash. Many had been torn up by the roots and lay tumbled about like sick, broken old men.

Never had T'Cori seen or dreamt of such devastation. And she knew in her heart that it would only be worse as they continued their struggle upward.

T'Cori and Raven stood close together, almost touching, as if drawing a comfort from each other they could not consciously acknowledge.

"We must have more ceremony," T'Cori said. "To honor the great and brave men who died here."

"Who do we pray to?" Frog asked.

"Father Mountain! Great Mother!" Raven screamed. "They are not dead! They are not!"

To T'Cori's surprise, it was Frog's quiet stepbrother Scorpion who said, "Yes. They live still. We should dance."

And so that night they danced before the fire, and made shadows, and sang their love and defiance, and for a time kept the fear at bay.

# Chapter Fifty-four

In the morning they left their camp and continued onward and upward. Looking down from that height, it seemed to T'Cori that the trees and streams on the plain were impossibly tiny. Truly, Great Sky was the largest cairn of rock and dirt in all the world, even after its top had thundered into the stars.

They crossed a small valley and began their ascent.

"Look," Scorpion said, and pointed back downhill. Below them, barely within sight, padded three wolves, their white chests the color of ash. Their black tails wagged slowly as they panted, observing the humans from a safe distance. Then they disappeared into the trees. "They hunt us," Scorpion said.

"Let them come." Hawk smiled. "I've never eaten wolf."

T'Cori doubted if the muscular young hunter was truly as confident as he sounded.

These lands were littered with wild cactus plants in strange shapes. Raven touched one of them. "Groundsel," she said wistfully, as if that was a bit of knowledge from another, distant life. "Good if you shit worms."

Halfway up the trail they met a river gorge and continued to a plateau. T'Cori was beginning to have a bit of trouble breathing. Her legs felt as cold as the air around her, even with the skins that she draped around her shoulders.

"Now," Snake said, "it is time to put on the furs." They stopped for half a quarter, and he helped them tie the odd sandals around their ankles. It took some practice to get used to walking in them, and the slipping and falling was cause for general hilarity, the first laughter they had heard since the beginning of the climb.

Once they moved out of the path of the cascading mud, the seven reached a place where trees stood tall, but now there were fewer of them to stand. They were mostly broken and splintered, lay at angles, or leaned against each other, torn up by the roots.

"The trees are dying," Scorpion said, gripping his spear until his knuckles whitened.

At this elevation, there was less vegetation of *any* kind. What they did see was more like a wide, rolling meadow and the wilted ruins of small wildflowers.

Throughout the day the air warmed, but as Snake led them up the mountain the sun began to droop toward the horizon. When it did, the air cooled so quickly that it felt as if it was sucking the day's heat into the grave with it.

Snake and Scorpion circled stones as the brothers gathered firewood. When it roared, they slept close enough to it that one side of them was roasting as the other side grew numb with frost. Raven crept near T'Cori, turned her back and pressed it against T'Cori's, seeking warmth and comfort. T'Cori awakened in the morning feeling half dead, but continued on.

From time to time Raven or T'Cori called out the name of a tree or plant, entertaining themselves and the others with medicinal or ceremonial applications.

Frog stared at a spiky plant as tall as two men. "I've never seen anything like that," he said.

"Lobelia," Raven said.

As the temperatures dropped, the lobelia closed their leaves around the central core. Frog thrust his finger under a leaf and came out with a slimy thick green fluid.

He sniffed it. "Acid-sweet," he said. "I wonder how it tastes."

T'Cori's eyes widened in alarm. "Frog. Don't!"

He laughed, wiping his fingers on his thigh. "I'm not a monkey," he said, and she realized he had been teasing her.

"Yes, you are," she said, jostling him with her elbow.


T'Cori had not seen an animal all day—perhaps they were plagued by the thin air as much as the humans. But one ash-covered eland looked at them as if they were the last creatures to be found in all the world and then stumbled away, dazed.

Scorpion raised his spear to cast it, but T'Cori touched his arm. "No. We have food enough," she said softly. "Let it go."

He laughed derisively, but after one skillful feint lowered his spear. And wheezed.


For the last quarter they had glimpsed a wall of rock through the trees and rises. It grew steadily larger and more intimidating, until finally they stood awestruck in its presence. It was taller than ten tens of men, like something placed by the hand of Father Mountain, a divine boma gate protecting the afterworld.

T'Cori paused, uncertain what Snake might do next. The old man was breathing hard and seemed a bit perplexed himself.

"What do we do?" Raven asked Snake.

"We climb," he said. "The hunt chiefs cut handholds and footholds. I think . . ." He searched around the base until he found another of the hunting signs. "Yes, here. I think I can find them. Follow me." Rock ledges jutted from the splintered surface, so the climb itself was not as bad as T'Cori had feared. The furs covering her feet were the most treacherous threat, and the men seemed actually to have more trouble than either she or Raven—except Frog, who gritted his teeth and kept up. Twice Hawk Shadow slipped, and was caught once by Scorpion and once by Snake. The ground below was soft, but the higher they rose, the less that mattered. And finally the ground seemed so far below them that it was clear that any fall at all would be the end of life.

"Be careful, Ant," Frog said after a rock moved a thumb's width in his grasp. "Be careful with handholds. You are heavier than you think."

His brother laughed, but T'Cori noticed that after that warning he sought roots and rocks more carefully.

# Chapter Fifty-five

Just above Frog, Uncle Snake's old arms were unsteady as he searched for handholds. Frog paced his breathing, almost as if he was running up the vertical wall. Who had first done this thing? Who had cut the first steps in this wall? How long had they been there? Were they cut anew every year? Every generation? He was too exhausted to call out his questions to Snake, but they tumbled crazily around and around in his head like shrikes with broken wings. How many attempts had this taken? How many lives had been lost in the conquest?

T'Cori was just below Fire Ant and ahead of Scorpion. She climbed with her face aglow, all suffering and pain temporarily forgotten, suffused with an ecstasy of sheer effort. The other girl, Raven, was between Uncle Snake and Hawk Shadow, ahead of Frog. She was larger and stronger than T'Cori but climbed as if she was a lizard.

It was cold, cold of a kind he had never experienced. Frog's limbs felt as heavy as wet logs. Even considering the intensity of the effort, he was left unusually drained, as if he had made the climb carrying Wasp on his back. Frog gasped for air, and no matter how much he sucked down, it didn't seem to help.

One at a time they made it to the top. Hawk Shadow pulled Frog up. He and Snake helped Fire Ant, who in turn helped T'Cori and Scorpion and Raven. They lay panting for a time. As they waited for their hearts to stop pounding they drank a little water from their skins and ate some dried meat. As they rested, Frog studied the next territory: a plain of ice and splintered rock that opened onto a rocky flat desert like those found far to the south and west.

The skin on his face felt as if it was burning, the sun blazing bright enough to blind him. They struggled to push themselves, not knowing how long they could continue such effort, but the harder they pushed, the more strength seemed to leach from their bodies.

They tried singing songs, chanting, anything to keep the breath in their lungs, but it simply wasn't enough.

"We must go more slowly," Snake gasped. "More slowly."

"If we do, then we freeze," Hawk said, anger and fear mingled in his voice.

The air was as dry as sand, and the wind cut them like bamboo whips. There were very few plants, only lichens and small mosses. They saw no animals save a few crows. There was little to keep anything alive. They saw a mouse once, skittering between the harsh shadows. It, like the eland, stared at Frog and then disappeared.

Here on this new plateau there was something on the ground that Frog had not seen before, and he bent to touch it. It was cold, gray-black on the surface, but pale beneath. As he rubbed the stuff between his fingers, it melted away.

He sniffed. "What is this?" he asked, hands shaking.

"Dead water," Snake said. "They call it ice."

"Then, it came to life in my hands," he said.

He bent beside a tiny stream. Some kind of cold clear matter covered the water, and he cracked it with a rap of his knuckles, and then bent to sip.

Dead water? Live water? It was colder by far than anything he had ever touched, but still delicious. In one place, they were actually traversing a patch of the odd stuff, and Hawk Shadow's foot smashed through into wetness beneath. He was more startled than hurt, and they chuckled as he pulled his leg back out.

"Wet!" he said, and laughed at himself, shaking the water from his feet.

Late that day Snake saw more signs, and led them to a cave just large enough to hold both the seven Ibandi and a tiny fire. T'Cori had never been so happy for a fire in her life. The walls were close enough to concentrate the heat, keeping the brutal cold at bay as if it was a starving lion gnashing its teeth just outside the cave's mouth.

Despite the weather, T'Cori was in good spirits. As the rest of them grumbled and joked to hide their fear, she felt herself really nearing the presence of her gods for the first time. She was almost fevered with anticipation.

They all huddled together for warmth. Raven trembled, arms wrapped around herself, squeezing the skins against her body, seeking warmth. Without a word, T'Cori drew her close, and they hugged there in the cave. She let Raven cling to her, shared her heat. "Why aren't you cold?" Raven asked.

"Control your breathing, as your mother taught," T'Cori said. "Pull it down into your belly and light the fire." Raven nodded and closed her eyes. Almost immediately her shivering decreased.

The next day it took Frog almost a quarter of walking before he felt alive and loose. They wound through more of the dry, rocky plateau, littered with great startling rocks that looked as if they had never been weathered by wind and dust.

Up higher, the dead water grew thicker, and actually began to blow from the sky as flakes. The rocks were covered with the white-gray stuff. When they reached a slick, pale wall they tried to climb it. Wherever it touched their skin, it seemed to suck the life away. Fire Ant tried to climb, but his feet scrabbled without finding purchase.

"What do we do, Uncle Snake?" Frog asked. "Where do we climb?"

Snake peered up at the wall, the confusion written clearly on his face. Had things changed so much? "I . . . I don't—"

"Over here!" Scorpion cried. Off to the left, around a curve, the wall was broken into a tumble of icy boulders. The shears looked unweathered, and Frog suspected it had happened recently.

And then, without any warning, Uncle Snake began to scream.

"We can't!" he said as the dead water blew around them. "The hunt chiefs tried but never were able to go farther."

Frog stopped breathing. All the sound in the world seemed to stop as well. *What?* What had Snake just said?

"What are you saying?" Hawk said, their faces very close.

Snake could not withstand the blunt force of Hawk's wrath, and turned away. "We lied," he said. "We lied to all of you. No one has ever been to the top. Ten tens of men have died trying. It cannot be done."

Scorpion stared at his father, mouth open in disbelief.

"Did Stillshadow know?" Raven asked, eyes wide with horror and betrayal.

"Cloud Stalker never told her," he said, "But I think she suspected. Perhaps she would have warned you. I do not know."

They stood gape-mouthed and disbelieving. "We have to turn back," he said. "I'd hoped that we could make it. I'd thought that perhaps we would find the strength. I was a fool."

Frog gazed at the cleft in the great wall, the place where, perhaps only a moon before, a titanic slab of rock and dead water had burst away like the flesh of a sun-rotted melon, and a cascade of boiling mud had cleansed the mountain.

Distantly, far down the slope, wolves howled.

Frog thought of the terrible suffering they had already endured, and the brothers and cousins glanced at one another.

"Who wants to go back?"

Snake's legs seemed to melt as Fire Ant screamed, "We trusted you, and you lied." Fire Ant slapped Snake, the man who had married their mother, who had fed them, who had raised them. Again and again Fire Ant struck, until Snake's scars ran with blood. Snake took it, never struck back, did not even raise an arm to deflect the blows.

Hawk Shadow gripped at Fire Ant's arm, trying to hold his brother back as Ant vented his frustration and fear.

"No!" Hawk said. "That is *enough*."

Snake dropped his head.

"You are my father no longer," Scorpion said. "To think you tried to shame me during my manhood ceremony. To think how I sought your approval. I would have done anything for you!" he screamed. "Go, liar. Go, coward."

Snake stood, blood drooling from his lips to spatter on the ground. The spiderweb of scars covering the left side of his face had never seemed so brutal, his empty eye socket had never gaped so darkly.

Frog gripped Snake's hand. His uncle, the man who had been the only father Frog had ever known, trembled with shame and cold. Who knew what he felt, the reasons that the hunt chiefs had lied to them all?

Then Snake pulled his hand from Frog's and began his walk down the mountain.

"What does this mean?" Hawk asked, watching the old man retreat. "There is nothing up there?"

Frog was deadly calm. "That the top *cannot* be reached. That there is nothing there. That it was all a lie."

The wind howled around them, driving the cold more deeply into their bones.

"What do we do?" Raven asked. At that moment she seemed to have lost her mother's power. She was just a tired, frightened young woman.

"I don't—" Hawk Shadow began.

"We climb," T'Cori broke in, closing her eyes. "In my dreams, I have seen the top, and they are there. The spirits are there. Father Mountain is there. If we go back, our people die. We must go on."

So close. It seemed that they could almost see the summit now.

Onward they would go.


The rock-and-ice wall facing them was impossible to climb. No handholds had been cut in years past. One slip could mean a lethal fall. Their fur-wrapped feet would never find safe purchase, and their numbed fingers would fail.

So they journeyed west around the wall, until Scorpion called: "Look!"

There in the ice, a river of boiling mud had burned a tunnel as tall as a crouching man. How far had it come? How far would it reach? Was it possible that it might take them around this impossible wall?

They backtracked far enough to gather wood to fashion into torches, then climbed back to the tunnel. Hawk's hands trembled as he made the fire, but when at last it obeyed his summons they lit torches and climbed the river of mud. The walls of the tunnel were of blue ice, and sometimes jutting slabs of rock. Frog moved slowly, testing his footing, the glow of the torches reflecting back strangely, like the moon's reflection on a calm night. The tunnel rose at a shallow angle, and there were points where the ice and dried mud beneath their feet was actually warm.

Without warning, gusts of warm moist air gushed up from the tunnel floor. "It feels like a woman's breath," Frog chuckled.

"She'd have to have the biggest mouth ever," Scorpion laughed uneasily. "I feel it all over my body—"

Something in his voice, a sudden stressed rise in pitch, made Frog turn around. His brother's eyes were like twin flaming moons, impossibly wide, his mouth pursed in a surprised circle.

The ground beneath him sagged, a jagged crack running from one side of the tunnel to the other.

He tried to take a step away from the unstable area, when suddenly he dropped a handsbreadth and a scalding gout of steam swallowed him.

Oh, how Scorpion screamed! The pain and fear in that cry would echo in Frog's ears for many moons, haunting his sleep.

Frog fell backward, shocked, his brothers screaming around him. When his eyes cleared he saw Scorpion, body wedged halfway into the earth. He howled and thrashed. They clutched at his arms trying to pull him out, but then the ground cracked more and he slipped from their grasp. Another steam flower blossomed in the tunnel, and they ran, Scorpion's screams ringing in their ears.

"Demons!" Raven cried. "Fire demons!"

They fled upward, the steam billowing in pursuit. "It's alive! It's alive!" Fire Ant screamed, and clawed his way ahead of all of them. The steam caught them, and was almost but not quite hot enough to sear their skin.

They reached a point where they could see light above them in the tunnel, and climbed up the curved sides to the surface, helping one another.

T'Cori was the first, but not strong enough to help them. Hawk Shadow was next, and he and Fire Ant helped Raven up.

Frog was the last.

They stood there at the top, waiting, and then called down into the darkness. "Scorpion!" they called. "Scorpion!" but they heard nothing. Frog sagged to his knees.

His cousin. His stepbrother. Cruel, and cowardly, and loyal. For all things, good and bad, that Scorpion might have or have not been, the most important was that he was Frog's stepbrother. They had run together, eaten together, slept side by side in the hut for so long, he knew if Scorpion was there by the smell of his breath alone.

Fair and foul, Scorpion had been his brother. And now he was gone.

Raven clutched at his arm. "One who dies here, on the mountain," she said, "is already in heaven. You will see him again."

Frog was too tired to argue with her, too heartsick not to hope that she was right. He would see Scorpion again.

If an afterlife still existed.


They found themselves in a crystal valley, amid countless ice mounds sculpted by the flow of hot mud, and amid cairns taller than a hand of men. The ground beneath their feet was of frozen mud, and the ice fell from the sky upon them. Strangely, the traction was actually better here, where the mud had thickened.

Raven paused on their march. Until now, the girl had stopped frequently, seeming to grow weaker by the breath, but now she seemed inspired.

"She is here," Raven said. "I can feel Great Mother." She appeared to have regained herself. They could see Stillshadow's strength in her eyes, hear it in her voice. When she looked at T'Cori, her smile deepened. "Do you feel her?" she asked. T'Cori nodded rapidly, the ice caking her hair.

And so they went on. Raven was spitting blood, had been since awakening that morning. Her face was ice-flecked, her cheeks cracked and bleeding, but now she and T'Cori shared the same heart, filled with a single unquenchable thirst.

"We go on," Raven said. "Even if we die, we go on."

So close. So close. Their inner fire drove them on, even as their bodies began to fail.


All around them were sights no Ibandi, no two-legged had ever seen. Cracked ice towers and mountains of dead water glistened. There seemed nothing alive, save their own footsteps and voices.

Food leapt from their stomachs. Strength and enthusiasm were distant memories. In all the world the only reality was this: one foot after another, slowly, slowly, just trying to survive. The freezing thin air ate at them like a worm that devoured from within.

Frog's fingers and face were swollen and cracked, but although he could see red in the wounds, blood did not flow. He felt little save despair. He had to rest every few steps just to catch his breath.

"This is death, brother," Hawk gasped.

But Frog looked at the holy girl T'Cori and realized that there was no way that he could let her climb—that inner fire continuing to animate the ragged remnants of her body, pulling it forward into an unknown and unknowable glory—and not try to follow. Even unto death.

If he had seen no miracles, seen no spirits, demons, gods or goddesses in his life, the sight of that girl never faltering, never giving up, would have convinced him of the possibility of gods. Surely such strength was a sign that Father Mountain and Great Mother were real and lived still. Surely such strength was not entirely human.

Even when resting, his heart raced as if he had just finished a sprint. The five survivors slept no more. *Hawk is right,* Frog thought. *This is death.* They were not in mortal danger. Rather, they were already dead.

"This is afterworld," Hawk Shadow said in eerie reflection of Frog's own thoughts. "We died in the tunnel with Scorpion and now are merely climbing to heaven."

Yet if that was true, why wasn't Scorpion here with them? Then Frog remembered that it takes time for flesh to melt from the bones. Even cooked flesh. He gagged at the thought.

Perhaps they and not Scorpion had died. Perhaps *he* had turned around, descending safely with Snake, while those who went on had been frozen or burned alive.

There it was again. *Father Mountain.* How often he heard his mind crying out that name. And why not? Surely this, if no other time of his life, was the moment when he would meet Father Mountain, if such a being was there to be met. Surely, shortly, once and for all Frog's questions were about to be answered.

Surely.


Vents jetted enough foul steam to choke and cloud vision. Bubbling water boiled up through the ice. Stinking gases oozed forth from the ground, and if Frog had been able to eat that morning, he would have lost it then.

A crawl through another ice tube brought them through another wall, and onto a plain devoid of life, only tumbled rocks and fissured ice greeting them.

The sky whirled with dry, harsh, powdery dead water again, and despite their furs, their fingers and toes were stiffening, losing not just sensation but control. The nighttime fire didn't warm them, and they could not sleep, could only wait for morning's light.

"I think Hawk is right," Fire Ant said. "We are already dead."

"Then we might as well go forward," Frog said. "We have nothing left to lose."

Frog found his way to T'Cori's side. She was with Raven, who was coughing blood now, so close to the fire that her furs were singed, still shivering. He took her aside. "Are you afraid?" he asked.

"Yes," she said. "Are you?"

"No," he said.

"Do you always lie?"

"Always," Frog gasped, and despite his fatigue found the strength to join with her in laughter.

She was weaker than he, Frog was certain of that. And yet it seemed almost as if the more her flesh faded, the brighter her inner fire burned.

.    .    .

Before the sun had lent its puny warmth to the morning air or even gifted them with full light, they continued their climb. The grade now was not much less severe than the ice cliffs, but the hill was of gravelly pumice. For every three lengths they climbed, they slid back two.

"I did not think it would be so terrible to be dead," Hawk Shadow gasped, climbing past Frog. Frog just tried to concentrate on putting one hand up and then another, pushing, pulling in endless, mindless sequence. They had to keep moving. If they stopped to rest, it seemed impossible to begin moving once again.

He dared not look back. The slope was so steep that looking down triggered Frog's every primal fear. Still, there was exhilaration as well. All his life he had looked up at the clouds, and now he walked among them. Did that not make him one of the greatest Ibandi of all?

Clouds blotted out the ground, but from moment to moment, it was possible to see the savannah, impossibly far beneath them. They were above the clouds. Yes, this was heaven, or a white hell.

One step at a time, every breath an ordeal. Frog coughed, covering his mouth, and then examined his hands. Blood dappled his numbed fingers.


They settled in for sleep before the sun had gone down, so exhausted that they barely had strength to scrape the fluffy dead water from the ground before laying down their furs. A tumble of rocks to either side would protect them from wind, but only shared body heat would help them through the night. T'Cori was pressed against Frog, who groaned in her ear, "I know we still live."

"How do you know that?" T'Cori asked.

"Because I wish I was dead. And you can't wish you were dead if you're already dead, can you?"

She stared at him. "Your mind is strange," she said, and he rolled over.

Raven chattered with terror, her eyes rolling, her long lashes tinged with frost. "So cold. So cold. I cannot be warm. I will never be warm again."

"Hold on," T'Cori said. "We will make it, and we will see the new sun."

"I was wrong about you," Raven whispered through cracked lips. "Always I hated you. Because you were the one who was not afraid of me. Why were you never afraid of me?"

"I was, and then one day I was not. I saw who you were," T'Cori said to her, holding her rival's hand. "I saw that you were afraid you would never be as great as Stillshadow. And that you wanted so much to be."

"And weren't you afraid?" she asked.

"I know I cannot be Stillshadow. I can only be myself."

"I was wrong about you," Raven said again. She paused, her breath rasping in her chest. Each liquid rasp seemed weaker than the one before. "I want a favor from you," she said.

"Yes?"

"If you make it back and I do not, I want you to be a daughter to my mother."

"What are you saying?" T'Cori whispered, and the tears started from her eyes.

"You are my sister. You should always have been my sister."

T'Cori was so stunned that she could not speak.

Raven closed her eyes. "We should never have come," she whispered.

"Let her sleep," Frog said.

"She will die," T'Cori said. And wept for the sister she had always wanted, and had at last, and now would lose.


In the morning, Raven was dead.

With crooked fingers, the freezing air howling around them, they straightened her limbs and scraped some frost together to bury her, and went on. T'Cori felt the tears rising in her eyes, their heat and the chill of the wind suddenly in curious contrast.

"Was she your friend?" Frog asked.

"No," T'Cori said. "But she was my sister. Sisters fight." T'Cori wavered as if she might fall, but looked up the mountain. "Here, so close to heaven," she prayed, "I know your *num* will find the way. Lead us all, my sister," she said. "Make us proud."

"I cannot go on," Hawk Shadow said, his voice shaking. "I am not strong enough to go higher." He pulled away his furs, which had been wet and were now stiff. His feet had an odd look to them, as if burned in a cold fire. The flesh was cracked and split, and pinking beneath.

Fire Ant seemed stricken. "We cannot leave you here. There is no shelter. No wood to build fire. You'll freeze."

"Going down," Hawk Shadow panted, "is easier than going up. I can make it back to the last shelter. Can you find it?"

Fire Ant thought. "I think so, yes. Are you sure?"

"I am sure," Hawk said. "I must go back."

"I could send Frog back with you—"

"No!" Hawk said, his voice momentarily regaining its force. "Brother, remember why we are here. This is more important than my life. Than any of our lives. Go. There is food, and dead water I can melt with fire."

"It is hard to make fire in this cold," Frog said.

"Who made it last night?" Hawk asked. "Who summoned fire in the ice tunnel? I should be worrying about you!"

Fire Ant paused, weighing his choices, and finally nodded. "All right," he said.

So Hawk embraced him, and then Frog, and then the girl. "I should not touch a dream dancer so," he said, but managed to smile. "I don't know if it is right, but I think of you as a little sister."

"Thank you," she whispered, tight against his chest. "I never had a brother."

After a time he headed back down, and Frog found that there was a large part of himself that wished he could go with Hawk. That was not the surprising thing. The surprising thing was that there was a larger part of him that did not.


On and upward they pushed, picking among the rocks, climbing around ledges and up embankments, over stone and ice, leaning on their spears when their staggering legs failed them.

Late that day they finally broke through the clouds to a place of peace. The air was so shallow that Frog's chest seemed empty no matter how he heaved. Strange lights danced at the edges of his vision. He was beyond exhaustion now, pushing on by sheer will.

He clawed his way up the ash and frozen gravel of yet another slope, fearing to look down, as if the very sight of the clouds from such a height might pull him back.

The view awaiting Frog was that of a level, ice-covered plateau. The flatness was broken by a few spires, and distantly something that looked like a minor rise, but there was nowhere left to climb.

They had reached the top.

Frog gripped his spear shaft for dear life, trying not to fall. Blackness wavered around the edges of his vision. "Where . . . is . . . Father?" he asked.

"Where is Scorpion?" There was no strength left. He could feel nothing anywhere on his skin, but deep within his body, Frog ached. Never had he even imagined fatigue such as this.

He had been wrong, and could barely find the strength even to think the thought. This *was* another world. They had come where no living men should go. He heard voices in his head; lights danced in his dimming vision.

Where was Lion Tooth? Had his flesh not melted yet? Where were the others who had died?

Fire Ant leaned close to Frog. "Brother," he said, "I see nothing."

The two brothers leaned against each other as T'Cori collapsed to her knees. She seemed only a bundle of bones and fur.

Frog thought he had never seen a more frightening, wonderful thing in all his life.

What did she see? Where now did her spirit fly?

*There is a place beyond contentment, beyond thoughts of knowledge or joining or even peace. A place where the mind no longer defines itself in opposition to the outside world. T'Cori had found that place. It was a world of light, the world she had known as an infant. Her eyes were open, wide, unfocused, her tears freezing upon her cheeks. As had happened once before, long ago, she was not blind; she saw everything.*

*Father Mountain? Great Mother? Everywhere around her. Within her. She was beyond words, even words so fine and powerful.*

*"We have been fools," she whispered. "Fools to think our gods live atop the mountain. They are everywhere, or nowhere at all."*

Frog thought that perhaps they were destined to stay here, to lie on the ice and rock until the wind sucked the life from them. There was no air to breathe. Certainly they were now above the stars.

T'Cori placed her foot against the ground, pushed at her knee and managed to rise part of the way before sinking back down. Frog knew he should help her but could not move. The girl tried again, and this time rose and staggered to them, her face a death mask. "I have seen," she said. "I know. We must . . . return . . . to the living world."

They were too exhausted even to reply to her, just nodded, and staggered back to the edge, slid down the ashy slopes, climbed down far faster than they had ascended.

## Chapter Fifty-six

T'Cori's eyes were wide but sightless still. Without the help of Fire Ant and Frog she would have fallen to her death.

After a half day of walking and sliding downhill, movement as mindless as branches waving in the wind, the air thickened, and Frog found himself able to think, to speak, to understand that he had acheived something that none of his people had ever done.

Cloud Stalker had never been to the top of the mountain. Nor had Boar Tracks, or Uncle Snake, or any of the other hunt chiefs. Only the sons of Baobab, and the strange girl without a name. The reality was more wondrous than anything that had ever been sung or danced around the fires. The demons were stranger, more illusive and dangerous. They masqueraded as natural things, and slew in ways no man or dancer could defend against.

T'Cori seemed not wholly human to Frog. She was . . . something different. As Stillshadow was, as Raven had tried to be. There was no doubt in Frog's mind that this was a holy woman. From Ant's expression, Frog could see that his brother was in such supernatural awe of the girl that he barely wanted to touch her.

White flakes began falling from the sky into her blind, open, staring eyes. The powdery dead water was covering their tracks. Even Frog's numbed mind realized the dangers. "How will we find Hawk Shadow?" he asked.

Fire Ant studied the ground and then the rock formations. "I know the signs," he said.

They kept moving, not daring to stop for almost a full day, until they reached the tree line. If they stopped, they would freeze. They would die.

As creatures devoid of human thought they came gratefully to a niche in a rock wall, a notch wide enough to protect them from the weather, where shared body heat and furs might get them through the night. Even dead, the spirits of the hunt chiefs protected them—the niche was stocked with firewood.

"One more day to Hawk Shadow," Ant said. Ant labored frantically with his fire-bow there in the rock crevice, seeking to create warmth. They had nearly surrendered to despair when the first curl of smoke rose, and flame blossomed.

They groaned with pain as the flame began to drive the cold from their bones. They fed the fire until it roared, and Frog and Ant gave thanks all night long to the hunt chiefs they had cursed while climbing the ice wall.

Frog moved so close to the fire that he could smell his furs singe. *Please, Father Mountain,* he said to himself, *ancestors, whatever there is . . . let us not be too late to find Hawk. Let him be safe.*

"You are praying," T'Cori said to Frog. "I see the red in your *num*-fire."

His eyes flew open with shock. "How do you know?"

"The *num*-fire flared around your head," she said, and laughed delightedly. "It has returned!" She clapped her hands together, joyous as a child. "Great Mother, thank You, thank You! I can see again."

And although in the confined space the wash of sound seemed slightly uncanny, she could not stop laughing and giving thanks, far into the night. The two brothers looked at her askance, and huddled together for warmth, staying as far away from her as they could get without retreating into the storm.


Frog and Fire Ant awoke to see T'Cori crouched there in the cave mouth, eyes fixed on the dead white water falling from the sky, drawing symbols in the ash and ice.

She drew and then she curled into a ball and began to tremble, her eyes rolled back. There was nothing that they could do to help her, could only wait and pray that she survived.

"Soon, my brother," Fire Ant whispered. "She will come to herself, and tell us what the gods told her. We will slay the Mk*tk. I will lead our people to victory, with you and Hawk at my side. And the sons of Baobab will be the most honored of all."

There was a dreamlike quality to Ant's words, a fervent belief that surprised Frog. Perhaps Ant had had his own vision at the mountaintop, a vision neither he nor T'Cori had glimpsed.

A vision of power.

When the girl rolled up to her knees, both brothers were watching in respectful silence.

"They spoke to me," she said finally. "They told me what we must do to preserve our way."

"How do we fight the Mk*tk?" Fire Ant asked.

"Father Mountain says," T'Cori told them, "that we must find a new home in the north."

Frog could barely believe his ears. What? Leave Great Earth and Great Sky? What would they do? Who would they be?

Ant's voice was husky with shock. "What does this mean?"

T'Cori spoke as if to a frightened child. "That we must leave this land and find a new place."

"No!" he screamed. "This is wrong! It is all nonsense! Not after all we have done! I am a man! A man does not give up his dreams because a woman scribbles in dead water."

Frog tried to object. "No—"

Ant whipped his head around, pointing with his finger as if it were a spear. "Stay out of this, little brother," he said fiercely. "It is not your affair."

Unmoved by his wrath, T'Cori replied, "I say only what Father Mountain told me to say."

Ant snarled, fingering his obsidian knife, "Then perhaps I should cut out that lying tongue."

"Fire Ant, no," Frog protested. "She is a holy woman. You must not say such things."

"I speak as I will." He pounded his chest with his fist. "*I* am boma father now. Our brother did not make the climb. The hunt chiefs did not make the climb—and they are dead. *We* are the new hunt chiefs! We will make the law!"

"My brother—" Frog began.

"Be silent!" he screamed, spittle flying from his mouth. "No! We have been tricked. She was with the Mk*tk, gave her body to the Others. She is *their* woman, not ours. I say she speaks for them!"

"That is not true," Frog said.

"No?" Fire Ant snarled. "No? She says to leave without a fight. Our women are strong! They believe in their men. What filth and cowardice is this?" Ant turned back to her. "You should die for your lies," he snarled.

"Stop this," Frog pled.

T'Cori locked eyes with them, her expression bleak. "I will speak only truth, even if it costs me my life itself."

"Listen to me," Frog said, and stood between Ant and the holy girl. "I am sure you will be boma father, and one day will be the first of the new hunt chiefs. Wherever we are, whatever we do. And the tribe will follow you if you have done what must be done, seen what no one else has ever seen.

"Ant," he went on, searching his mind desperately for the right thing to say, "whether we go or stay, we need both the dream dancers and the hunt chiefs, together, or our people will die, for we will have nothing to cling to. Stillshadow may be dying. This girl is the leader now. If we must leave this place to save our people, you will be the savior, you will be the greatest leader we have ever had, and songs will be sung to you by your grandchildren's grandchildren."

"But leave here . . ." Ant seemed almost ready to cry. "This is our home. We cannot leave the mountain." He paused. "I would like songs," he said finally, voice weakening. "I just want to be a great leader. Perhaps she is right. . . ."

The girl T'Cori crouched behind Frog. "There is fear in his fire," she murmured.

For many breaths they stood staring at one another, the wind howling outside the cave. Fire Ant's tongue wetted his cracked lips. He closed his eyes and groaned. "The dream is ending," he said. "If not for that fall, I would have been a hunt chief."

Then Ant met Frog's eyes squarely, softened his voice. "Let us kill the girl, and then you will tell them that they died, they all died, on the mountain. You will tell them Father Mountain said that we are to stay, and that I am to lead. You will say these things."

Frog saw how Ant's eyes burned. He saw that Ant would not allow this girl to steal his power, and he would do anything, anything at all. Frog himself had found the title of grand hunt chief intoxicating. How much more so had Ant?

"She would betray us, brother. Betray all our people. Betray you, and me, and Hawk. We can lead, brother! Her throat is soft. Slit it, so I can see you will not betray me. Then we will find Hawk Shadow, and the sons of

Baobab will lead our people." He was almost pleading. And Frog under-stood why.

Fire Ant loved Frog and did not wish to harm him. But he would. If he must, to save his people, to secure his own destiny, yes, he would.

Fear and love and duty all warred within Frog. Where were his loyalties? To brother? Tribe? Father Mountain?

And where was a small, nameless girl in all of this?

"Kill her," Fire Ant begged.

Suddenly Frog grabbed T'Cori and pulled her frantically through the mouth of the cave. They ran, Fire Ant racing after them.

Then Frog spotted a stone just smaller than his fist. He dove, grabbed it, rolled, sighted and threw all in one motion. It soared true, striking directly between Fire Ant's eyes with a hollow *crack*. His brother roared and fell back.

"Run!" he screamed to T'Cori, and she needed no urging.

Furs flapping in the wind, they fled out into the drifting dead water, leav-ing tracks that any child could have read.

Down the mountain they tumbled. And now he was profoundly grateful that Fire Ant had lost some of his speed and that the girl was fleet of foot.

They gained some distance, enough that they were able to scramble over rocks and find a hiding place.

The snowfall covered their tracks rapidly. In most environments, Fire Ant would have found them within moments, but this was still a strange-ness.

But . . . what was this hiding place?

"Look," T'Cori said, and pointed to the wall. A few paces away a ring of stones poked through the powdered ice: another of the shelters found and marked by the hunt chiefs in their efforts to climb Great Sky. Again, even in death, the hunt chiefs protected them.

They huddled together, and distantly they heard Fire Ant's frustrated roar, his angry calls as he searched for them.

And then, silence. The great hunter Fire Ant was stalking.

"Will we die?" she asked.

"We might live," he said.

But the night passed, and the cold began to gnaw at them. They knew they could not start a fire.

She reached for him. "Once before, I offered myself to you," she said, and in the dim light he saw her lips curl in a smile. "Now I don't think you can refuse."

Fear. Awe. So much regret and confusion, all happening at the same time. He didn't know what to think or to say, but did know that he didn't have the strength to say no. Nor did he have the inclination.

T'Cori's hands flowed over Frog's furs, beneath his furs, seeking his body.

She urged him to sit upright, and she wrapped her legs around him, sitting in his lap. His root was already firm and ready for her. She took a deep breath and settled upon him, a great rush of warm air leaving her lungs as her body swallowed him.

"Don't move," she said, wrapping her arms around his chest. "We must make this last. There is a breathing way I was taught. Follow my lead," she said, and deepened her breathing.

He could feel the heat flowing through her and into him, and his shuddering ceased. He felt her breathing, long and deep. Like the hyena breath? Similar, yes, and he began his own breathing. The two melded and the heat grew stronger, so that her own eyes widened.

"How do you know this?" she asked.

"Men have their own secrets," he said, and managed a smile.

He dared not spend, for fear of freezing. Still, there on the edge of release a delicious heat cycled through him, and they remained there for quarters, until the sun rose, and they finally allowed themselves to find release. It was not a powerful orgasm, as if the night-long lovemaking had drained some of the exquisite intensity. It was more of a flowing, a gentle current sweeping them up and taking them over the edge together, into a moment of almost unendurable brightness . . . and then a comforting warmth.

Swaddled in their furs, they shared their heat.

"Where did you learn that breathing way?" he asked.

"It is a way to burn the poison from our bodies," she said.

"It is a way to run without tiring," he said.

They laughed, and held each other. With the warming air they tried to get a bit of sleep. But much to Frog's surprise, his body was swiftly ready again, and he found T'Cori an eager partner. And if the second joining was not so long as the first, it was even sweeter, and more intense by far.

# Chapter Fifty-seven

The wind was quiet in the morning, so that the first thing either of them heard clearly was Fire Ant's distant voice. "Little brother!" Fire Ant called. "Come out. You know I would not hurt you. Give me the girl, then you and I will get Hawk, and we will go back down the mountain. Hawk needs us."

So Fire Ant had stalked them part of the way but then lost the trail. Frog's brother was good. Far too good. He would pick up the scent again, and then they would die.

"Would he kill you?" T'Cori asked.

"No," Frog said. "Unless there was no other way to stop you."

She did not speak, but her breaths were a rapid panting high in her chest. He answered her unspoken question. "I will not leave you," he said.

"What will you do?"

"I will be back," he said.

"I know," she said. And he knew that she did.


As Frog crawled out of their cave, he saw that the snow was thinned in places by trickles of steam from beneath the earth, creating a dizzying mixture of heat and cold.

If he could lead Fire Ant away from her, then perhaps T'Cori might make her way back down the mountain with her message. If not . . . well, at least he had had a taste of magic, for magic she was, and he had no more doubt about it. At least he had visited the home of the gods, seen the spirits, known that the dead lived again.

"Brother!" Fire Ant cried, and Frog spun to see Ant.

Frog and Fire Ant faced each other, just the two of them braced against the wind, their life paths having brought them to an almost unimaginable moment in time. There was nowhere for him to run, and if he tried, Ant would catch him.

And kill him? Would he? Frog prayed not, but did not know. The man before him no longer seemed like his brother.

The trip up the mountain had changed them all.

Frog felt empty, not even frightened. If there was any emotion remaining to him, it was a kind of sadness.

"Where is she?" Fire Ant hissed. An enormous welt swelled above his right eye. The time for compromise had passed. Frog could not see the *num*-fire surrounding Ant, as T'Cori could, but knew she was right: Ant would kill them both.

"Here," she called, and to his despair, Frog turned to see the waifish T'Cori standing on the powdery dead water, her feet wrapped in furs, almost floating there. So beautiful. He, Frog, could run fast enough, perhaps. She could not. All was lost. Ant would kill her and dare Frog to tell a story no one would believe.

Fire Ant turned to him and smiled. "You lose, brother," he said. "We win." He stalked toward T'Cori, arms raised.

But he had taken only three steps when the surface beneath his feet cracked, and a gout of steam gushed up around his feet. He turned around and locked eyes with Frog, the anger and ambition vanished. All that remained was panic.

"Brother," he said, "help me!" He tried to take a step, but the roof of the ice tube continued to crumble.

Frog could not move, could only stare, his gaze sliding back and forth between the two of them. T'Cori's face was so cool and placid that she seemed completely above everything that was happening now, as if she was the living presence of Great Mother Herself. So small she was—small enough to stand on a thin sheet of dead water above the ice tube.

The last thing Frog saw of Ant was a flailing, and then the tube ceiling collapsed, steam gouted up around him and he fell, screaming, into the void.

Ant was gone.

Frog froze, just looking at the empty place where, moments before, his brother had promised death. Then he looked at T'Cori, who just stared. She looked at him, and despite the distance between them, he heard her voice clearly.

"He never knew his size," she said. "Never."

And then she collapsed.

# Chapter Fifty-eight

For five days Frog and T'Cori searched Great Sky's slopes for Hawk Shadow. For five days Frog thought only of Fire Ant's death, dreamed only of finding his living brother and preserving some small part of the family and life he had known. For five days they scoured the slopes until they were exhausted, until fatigue banished the guilt and pain to a dark hut in his mind, where it could scream and curse at him, but not exit to possess his mind.

Time and again he thought that he recognized some landmark—a twisted tree, a tumble of rocks—but then could not find another.

It was T'Cori who spotted the first cairn, and Frog who found the second. Half starved but spirits buoyed by hope, they followed them to the small cave and found nothing. Carefully, he traced the ragged tracks revealing how Hawk Shadow had dragged himself from the cave, trying to make his way back down the mountain.

They did find him. But the wolves had found him first.

The ground was too hard to bury Hawk, so they built a cairn of rocks to cover him. With every stone he lifted Frog shed a hand of tears and asked himself a hand of questions.

What should he have done? What *could* he have done? What was right? And with placement of the final stone, he strained, listening to the wind, hoping to hear the voice of either brother. Nothing. There would be no easy answers, nothing to ease his mind. This was one riddle he might never solve.

They continued down the mountain.

Three days later, they emerged from the forest at Great Sky's feet. Just before reaching the bottom of their trail, they found Uncle Snake. He crouched there beside a tiny fire and a poor lean-to of branches and white-flecked mud. Frog sensed that if they had never returned, Snake would have stayed there forever.

"You went all the way to the top," Snake said hoarsely, his empty left socket staring at Frog, then at the nameless girl, and back again.

T'Cori nodded.

Snake glanced behind them. "Where are the others? Where is my son?" Snake closed his eyes. "Your brothers?"

Frog had dreaded this moment. What was there to gain in telling the truth? That one brother had been torn by wolves, another swallowed by the earth? Their people's future was hard enough as it was. This, he sensed, was how legends began.

"Father Mountain was lonely," Frog said. "He asked them to stay."

Snake searched Frog's face for answers. He must have had more questions than any man could count, but merely hung his head. "What will you tell our people? What will you say about me?"

Frog thought of all the lies and pain, but also the many seasons of love, of the way Uncle Snake had taken them into his home, hunted for them, fed them, loved his mother and treated her with honor. Sadness engulfed him, but mingled with it was a great sense of compassion. Before he could voice the words in his heart, T'Cori spoke for him.

"We could not have done it without you," T'Cori said. "You were with us, do you not remember?"

Snake's lips trembled, and a single tear rolled from the corner of his good eye. Frog's uncle held his arms out to them, and the three travelers held one another.

"An old man thanks you," Snake whispered.

In the midst of the embrace, Frog opened one eye and studied T'Cori. So . . . dream dancers *could* lie? Then . . .

His head whirled. Why had he ever thought he would be clever enough to understand this world?

.    .    .

Hands of hands of their people were camped there at the bottom of Great Sky, waiting for the emergence of their heroes, drumming their feet against the ground as T'Cori, Snake and Frog arrived.

Most important, Stillshadow was there at the camp, recovered enough to walk with Blossom's help. She and the others had waited for them, and waited, and had at last been rewarded.

"Where is my daughter?" Stillshadow asked, the pain in her eyes proclaiming her foreknowledge.

"She remained at the mountaintop," T'Cori said. "She was too fine a thing for Great Mother to return."

Stillshadow's face was filled with questions, questions she would never ask T'Cori in front of the tribe. She squeezed her eyes shut, allowing herself a moment of grief, and then sighed. "And the others?"

"The mountain claimed them. They are still at the mountaintop."

"Did you see the ancestors?" Hot Tree asked.

Frog shook his head. "I did not," he said. "But *she* did. And the gods spoke to her. We are alive only because they wished this great dreamer to bring their message to the people. Listen to her, if you wish to live."


Come nightfall, the clearing was ringed with flickering torches. Before an open council, with every available adult in attendance, Frog and T'Cori told their story before the largest gathering of Ibandi ever held in the fall. She recognized elders from Fire, Wind, Earth and Water bomas. All wore their ceremonial raiment, their skins and horns and painted faces, their best braids and piercings. Every one of them understood the importance of the message to come. The hunters held their spears at the ready, believing they would be told to fight and die to protect their land. The women held their children closely, trying to strengthen their nervous hearts.

What she had to tell them was something none of them expected.

"We climbed the mountain," Frog said, taking his place at her side. "There we saw Father. He spoke to T'Cori and told her to bring her tale down to you."

"What did he say?" asked a woman from Water boma.

"We must leave Great Sky's shadow," T'Cori said. "If we do not leave, we will die."

"I do not believe!" a hunter from Earth boma said. "This girl hasn't even a name! If Father Mountain won't even give her a name, why should we give her honor?"

The sad-faced man named Water Chant stood. "I believe her," he said, gazing at her. "And I speak for my boma. I will trust the dancer's vision."

*Is this my father?* she asked the mountain silently. And she knew the answer: he was, if she wanted him.

She held his gaze for a moment, and then gave a slow nod of acknowledgment.

"I believe," said another. "But this is all I know. If the Father says leave, then we must obey, or risk His wrath."

"We have heard!" a woman cried. "We have heard, I say! We must listen to what Father Mountain has said."

"T'Cori," Stillshadow said, "you have climbed the mountain." There was something in her eyes that T'Cori could not quite grasp. Did she know about the mountain? Had Cloud Stalker told his woman the truth? Or could she have guessed? "I say that you have earned the right. Surely Great Mother will grant you a name."

"A name," the people said in chorus. Again and again they chanted. "A name. A name for the holy girl . . ."

T'Cori dared not even pray for such a boon.

Stillshadow bent her tired old legs and for the ninth time threw the bones. She peered into them, and as she did it seemed that no one breathed.

And then her wrinkled face lit in a blissful smile.

"Of course," she said, pushing her hand against her hip as she straightened. "Of course. Now I understand why the name has been withheld for so long." She laid her hands on both of T'Cori's shoulders. "Such a name cannot be given, only earned."

"What is the name?" the girl whispered.

"Great Sky Woman," Stillshadow said.

The tribe pounded the butts of their spears against the ground. Hot Tree nodded sagely.

"Sky Woman," the girl said, voice breaking. "Great Sky Woman. I have a name!" She wrapped her arms around her teacher's waist, holding on for dear life. A name! A name! After all these years, she had a name. The mightiest totem imaginable, and a name that would live for generations after her death. Her heart felt swollen with pride and gratitude.

"You have earned a great boon," Stillshadow said. "What might I do for you?"

She considered. Sky Woman knew every ear was tuned to her words. That every one of them wanted to believe life would continue on, whatever might happen to them. For that, they needed what only she could give.

"When I left to climb the mountain," she began, "there was nothing I wanted so much as to be a woman of the Ibandi. Not a medicine woman, a dream dancer. Just a woman."

The elders nodded. Frog took a step forward, reached for her hand, then let his arm drop.

"But Great Sky spoke to *me* and told *me* my people's tomorrows. And if He needs to speak to them again, He speaks through me. I must be open."

She smiled at Frog, face filled with both love and regret. "I must remain as I am."

Stillshadow nodded her admiration. "It is the only choice, Great Sky Woman."

"This is what you really want?" Frog asked her, his voice low enough that the others could not hear.

"No," she answered. "But this is what must be."

Frog closed his eyes. What was he thinking? She wanted to take him somewhere privately, to talk to him and comfort him. She wanted the touch of his body, and to share a hut with him.

Some of those things she could have, in time. She could see in his *num*-fire that Frog loved T'Cori. Could he love Great Sky Woman as well?

The tribe watched and listened to them. This was not about the two of them and what they might or might not be able to mean to each other. This was about their people's survival. And that was more important than anything else, everything else, anything else at all.

"I understand," he said, and then drew himself up. Everything in their world had changed. Perhaps in time, the rules that had governed the dream dancers and the hunt chiefs would change as well. She could hope.

"You said I would be a great hunt chief," he whispered to her. "Did you lie?"

"T'Cori thought she lied," she said, watching his face fall. "But Sky Woman says the same. And Sky Woman does not lie."

Frog searched her eyes, finally pulling back from her, wearing the first smile she had seen on his face in many days, and knew at that moment that all would be well between them. There would be danger and death and unimaginable terrors out there in the unknown savannah to the north.

But there would also be love and life.

Frog turned, and seemed at that moment to be twice his height. "Who will come with us?"

Slowly, a few of them rose to stand beside Frog. Less than a fifth of the

Ibandi gathered to hear their words. The others looked on fearfully, drawing back. Life beyond the shadow was simply too fearsome a concept.

Stillshadow rose on her rickety legs. "I know not where our path will take
us. I know only that for my whole life I have served Great Earth. And if Sky
Woman says we must go beyond the shadow to find a new beginning, then
that is what I will do."

"But you will die!" Hot Tree said, lips pressed tightly together, the grief
and fear almost beyond her ability to control.

"And you will not?" Stillshadow retorted.

# Chapter Fifty-nine

Runners had traveled to all the bomas, giving word. Those who agreed to follow the medicine woman's vision would meet up with them on the trek north.

In the morning, those members of the gathered Ibandi committed to the northern journey had lined up at the foot of Great Sky, near the path that once had led to the home of hunt chiefs and which now led to their graves.

The pilgrims had water skins and dried meat and their children by the hand or in backpacks or on sleds.

Standing at the front of the line, his mother and uncle just behind him, his brother tagging at his side, Frog held his son tightly against his chest. Hawk's widow had chosen not to make the journey, but a woman from Earth boma was still heavy with milk and would serve as wet nurse along the journey.

Stillshadow had declined to name the child, leaving that duty to the girl who had so recently earned her own title. Great Sky Woman—in his mind he still called her T'Cori—had promised to throw the bones before they began their journey.

But now she had other concerns, singing for the people, checking to make certain the herbs in their amulets were fresh, huddling with the dancers to see if their dreams had revealed new signs, new clues as to their destination.

He found her off to the right side of the line with the large girl he had come to know as Blossom. Blossom and her three daughters would accompany them on the trip, although he could tell she resented leaving Great Earth.

"Are you sure there is no other way?" Blossom was complaining as Frog approached. She trailed off, but not because of Frog. Another man was approaching the group with his head bowed.

"I would come with you if it is allowed," Water Chant said, unable to meet Sky Woman's eyes.

She stood, and it seemed to Frog that this man and Sky Woman shared some secret unknown to him.

"As Water boma's father?" she asked.

Chant rubbed his head. "It has been a long time since I was boma father. And my boma was destroyed. I would go merely as a man. A man who once, long ago, made a great mistake."

"You are Ibandi," she said, taking his hands in hers. "We need every man, every woman." She paused. "Every mother and father."

She smiled at Frog, and now he had known her long enough to understand its meaning. *Later, I will tell you. Tonight. We will talk. And other things.*

He could not wait.


Before the sun reached its height, Great Sky Woman came to him and took his boy. The infant did not scream at leaving his father, just looked up at the medicine woman and cooed. "I see his fire," she said. "There is no darkness there. Just light and love enough to share with others. This one would take the darkness and bring light. This one is a healer," she said, giving the boy back to Frog.

She bent, opening a deerskin pouch at her belt. Extracting a rattling handful, Sky Woman threw the bones and then studied them, smiling as if they merely confirmed what she already knew.

"Medicine Mouse," she said. "That is his name."

Then she gave Mouse back to Frog and walked along the line to speak to the others.

*Great Sky Woman,* he thought, watching her. *Yes, that is the name of a woman of power.*

*But tonight, in my arms, you will be T'Cori.*

*Love has no name.*

Frog pressed his son to his chest. Mouse smelled like warm dry grass, like fresh berries, like the first ray of dawn. His dark, laughing eyes held the promise Frog had left behind on the mountain. With his brothers. With his illusions. He ached, hoping that Mouse and his nameless holy woman might one day fill that emptiness.

Frog glanced at T'Cori. Was that right? *Great Sky Woman.* He did not know what she was. She might be human. She might be a child of the mountain. He did not know. He did know that she had given him hope.

For the first time *he* was the one who longed and could not fulfill that longing. He would learn to cope with it, as she had for so very long.

He could almost smile with the strangeness of it. Almost. One day, perhaps—not yet.

"Mother?" Sky Woman said, and indicated a sled constructed by Fire boma's hunters. No need to wear the old legs out. Most of the dream dancers were journeying with them, but she had agreed to allow several to remain behind, to minister to the people who would remain in the shadow.

But Stillshadow was with them, and he found that incredibly comforting.

Stillshadow settled down upon the sled with a sigh. "It is good," she said, and then glared at the two young men who had volunteered to pull. "Don't jostle me," she said, eyes narrowed. "These bones are brittle."

She closed her eyes and then nodded, raising her hand. "We begin," she said.

The line moved forward.

Frog walked on, his family and the woman he could never have at his side, strangely content. No one could know what lay ahead, but it did not matter.

Stillshadow was with them. And Sky Woman.

Even if they could not see Great Sky, the night itself was the mountain's shadow, and the stars were their ancestors' eyes.

That would have to be enough.

# Epilogue

*Atop Great Sky, the ground opened once again, and tongues of thick, sluggish lava bulged to the top. Not a liquid flow as might happen in some volcanoes, but a thick gray mass veined with fire. Slowly.*

*But in waves it came, waves that would cool. And in another day, or moon, or year, more lava would flow, so that in time, a decade, or a hundred years, or a thousand, the wound in Great Sky's peak would heal, and He would be as tall and massive as ever He had been.*

*So that those men who might look up from the plains would never see the terrible wounds. Might, in time, forget the eruptions that had occurred, the violence that had once changed a world. So that, in time, all that might remain were misty legends.*

*Ten thousand years it might take, but it would happen.*

*The mountain had time.*

# Acknowledgments

I would like to thank Betsy Mitchell for the first thought, and the resources and time necessary to complete this project to the limit of my ability. To Chagga clansman Gebra Tilda, who hosted me and my daughter for two weeks in the most beautiful locales I've ever experienced. Special thanks to one of his assistants, Justo Kimro. To Buck Tilly, Arusha station manager for Thompson Safaris, whose services I would recommend without reservation.

In Gebra's opinion, the word *Kilimanjaro* means "untravelable." Stanford graduate students and Chagga tribeswomen Aika and Naike Aswai said that the word derives from *kilima* (hill or obstacle) and *nkyaro* ("in your way"), literally, "mountain in my path." Tanzanian students are taught that it means "white mountain."

Based on my own research, I think that the truth is found in a melding of the first two opinions.

To Mushtaq Ali Shah, my very dear friend, who by bizarre coincidence came to live in the precise locale I most needed to research. One senses Father Mountain's hand in this.

To Honest, our guide on Kilimanjaro, Great Sky itself.

To Jon Wagner, Ph.D., Department of Anthropology at Knox College, and his wife, Jan Lundeen, of Sandburg University, whom I met aboard a KLM flight from Amsterdam to Arusha. Bless them for numerous supportive e-mails and a long and enlightening telephone conversation on the differences between pastoral peoples and hunter-gatherers. My Ibandi are a transitional culture, neither one nor the other. There were doubtless many such, before the pastorals won history's race. Suppositions on the relationship between storytelling and human consciousness were originally presented by the author at the Smithsonian in February 2004, bolstered by assurances from Jan that I was not, in fact, insane. Thank you so much.

Thanks go also to Professor Barbara J. King and Professor Brian Fagen, wonderful teachers of biological anthropology and the history of ancient civilizations; Dr. Jeffrey T. Freymueller, Geophysical Institute University of Alaska, Fairbanks; and Richard B. Waitt, U.S. Geological Survey, Cascades Volcano Observatory.

Although the author had the thrill and honor of personally walking much of the territory covered in this book, visual references remain as valuable as gold. I would be remiss not to mention the IMAX films *Kilimanjaro* and *Serengeti* in this regard.

There are several plants used by the indigenous population to modify consciousness in advantageous ways. One, *Hoodia gordonii*, has come to the attention of the West as an appetite suppressant, represented here by the Ibandi's "fill-cactus." Hoodia works extremely well, but there are a number of faux herbals on the market. In addition, you may believe that pharmaceutical companies are scrambling to patent it and deny the San people the benefits of their thousand-year practical research project. One brand that both contains the genuine product and respects the rights of the indigenous people can be found at the Web site www.desertburn.com.

In my opinion the human aura exists, but whether it is a phenomenon existing separate from the perceptive faculties of the observer, I cannot say. In such a case it would be referred to as an "artifact effect" or a "complex equivalency," where the mind analyzes a gigantic amount of subliminal data, then produces a simple visual or kinesthetic symbol.

On the other hand, the phenomenon may simply be the nonphysical aspect of the human experience. Whichever it is, I would like to thank Sri Chinmoy, with whom I first experienced this, and Harley Reagan, Diane Nightbird, and the teachers and students of the Deer Tribe Metis Medicine teachings, who have allowed me many times over the years to study things that, as an outsider, I had no right to expect to learn. I love you all, and thank you for being my friends, family and teachers over the years.

·    ·    ·

Any anthropological accuracies in this book are due to the help of those already mentioned, as well as more helpful folks than I have time, space or memory to thank. Inaccuracies and flights of fantasy are the author's own.

Observant anthropology buffs will quickly grasp that I have adapted many of the technological and life patterns of the !Kung and other Khoisan peoples of South Africa for my Ibandi. The sources of this information are too numerous to mention, but looming large among them are *Nisa: The Life and Words of a !Kung Woman,* by Marjorie Shostak, and *Hunter-Gatherers of the Kalahari,* edited by Richard B. Lee and Irven DeVore.

While there are many similarities between my upper-paleolithic hunter-gathers and various real-world indigenous peoples, Ibandi social customs are my own invention.

A very special thanks to my daughter, Lauren Nicole Barnes, who shared the greatest adventure of my life, researching this book in beautiful Tanzania. A doting father is inordinately grateful both for cozy nights on the freezing lip of Ngorogoro crater and for moving swiftly when a crazed Floridian tourist induced an elephant to charge.

For my wife, novelist Tananarive Due, who held down the fort, encouraged me, and in general has functioned as the finest muse a man could ever have, I love you, now and always.

Finally, to all of those who have stood beside me all these years . . .

For those who believe in the unity of man and myth worldwide . . .

This one is for you.

Covina, California,
*November 8, 2005*
www.lifewrite.com

# About the Author

STEVEN BARNES is an author, lecturer and personal consultant who has lectured on creativity and human performance technologies at locations from UCLA, USC, and the Pasadena Jet Propulsion Lab to the Smithsonian Institute.

In the field of fiction writing, Barnes has published twenty novels and more than two million words of science fiction and fantasy. He's been nominated for Hugo, Nebula and Cable Ace awards. His "A Stitch in Time" episode of *The Outer Limits* won the Emmy Award, and his alternate history novel *Lion's Blood* won the 2003 Endeavor.

In the realm of mental and physical development, Barnes holds instructor certificates in Ericksonian Hypnosis and Circular Strength Training, and created the Lifewriting seminars utilizing Joseph Campbell's model of the Hero's Journey to help individuals and organizations grasp the flow of individual and team effort enabling peak performance. Second-place winner at the 1972 National Korean Karate championships, he holds black belts in Judo and Kempo Karate, has taught Tai Chi for twenty years, and is one of only a dozen people in the country certified in Softwork, an evolution of martial arts and yoga based on a century of Soviet research.

He lives in Los Angeles with his wife, daughter Nicki and son Jason.

## About the Type

This book was set in Garamond, a typeface originally designed by the Parisian typecutter Claude Garamond (1480–1561). This version of Garamond was modeled on a 1592 specimen sheet from the Egenolff-Berner foundry, which was produced from types assumed to have been brought to Frankfurt by the punchcutter Jacques Sabon.

Claude Garamond's distinguished romans and italics first appeared in *Opera Ciceronis* in 1543–44. The Garamond types are clear, open and elegant.